# THE ISLE OF ABANDONMENT

# THE
# ISLE
## OF
# ABANDONMENT

# RYAN HOYT

Machete & Quill Press

*For those holding on to hope in the shadows
and choosing to light the way for others.*

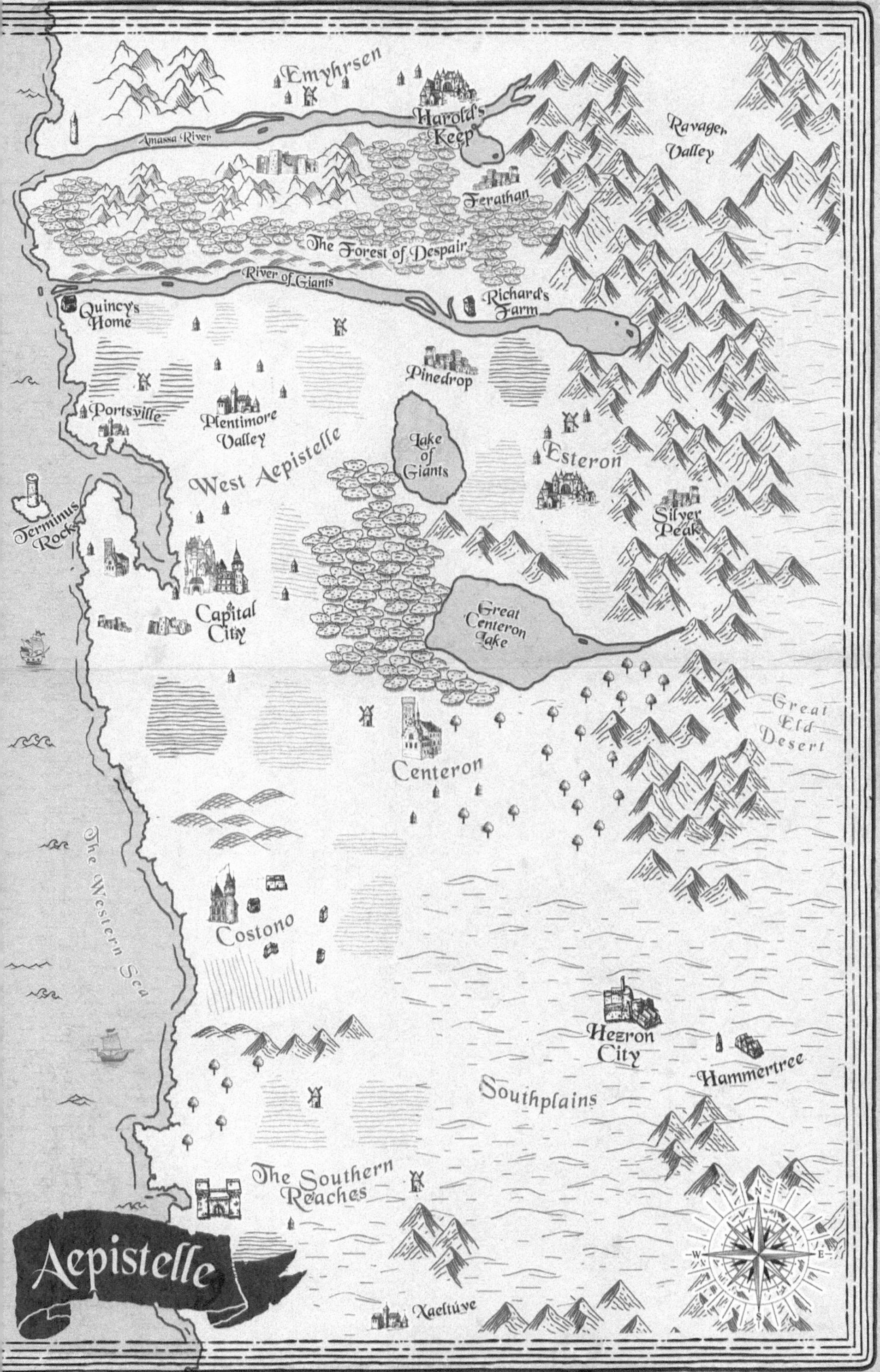

Emyhrsen
Harold's Keep
Amassa River
Ravager Valley
Ferathan
The Forest of Despair
River of Giants
Richard's Farm
Quincy's Home
Pinedrop
Portsville
Plentimore Valley
Lake of Giants
Esteron
West Aepistelle
Silver Peak
Terminus Rocks
Capital City
Great Centeron Lake
Great Eld Desert
Centeron
The Western Sea
Costono
Hezron City
Hammertree
Southplains
The Southern Reaches
Aepistelle
Xaeltúye

# Prologue
## THEN

Of all the religious orders in his father's kingdom, Davin hated the Solendaron the most.

There was an air of self-righteousness around its worshippers, and its clergy was even more sickening. The priests had their ridiculous mustaches, so carefully groomed and styled, that stuck out from the sides of their faces to represent their god's light radiating over the entire world. The priestesses wore long braids on their right sides and cropped their hair short everywhere else. The braids hung to the east when they faced north to pray each morning. They actually believed that their god, the Lord Solendaron, was the sun. Or was *of* the sun, rather. Or something like that. Davin didn't know and didn't care. He just knew that he hated them.

It wasn't just the priests' physical traits that irked the boy. The power they held over their believers bordered on treason against their true ruler, King Selvin the Third. They paid their taxes, but they also got a special exemption that predated even Davin's great-grandfather, the first King Selvin.

It was a loss to the crown that they didn't make up for in any way Davin could think of.

*When I'm king*, Davin thought, *that's all going to change. No more exemptions. No more Solendaron. No god will be worshipped more than the king. Never again in my lands.*

Of course, there was a little problem with his plan. The problem's name was Selvin the Fourth, and he was older than Davin by one year. Not wiser, mind you, or more cunning.

But that was neither here nor there, because here in the castle's banquet hall at this very moment was a gathering of the priests of Solendaron. As a money-making scheme to help line the coffers of the royal estate, Davin's father had taken to renting out parts of the castle for benefit galas, upscale weddings, and meetings between the rich and the powerful. But today, King Selvin was showing his weakness toward the priests of Solendaron by allowing them to use the space for free. The mustachioed priests and braided priestesses had traveled here from around the continent to meet, pray for divine inspiration about who their next denominational leader should be, and discuss an expansion into the unchurched villages along the Esteron Mountains, where the hills-folk still lived near enough like savages.

At all of these events in the castle, King Selvin would parade his children around, let the crowd *ooh* and *aah* over the heir, Selvin the Fourth, and flash looks of pity at the unlucky younger brother, Davin. Today, though, something was different.

While standing on the dais, as far back from his older brother as he could be without fully hiding behind a potted plant, Davin shot glances around the room. When he mistakenly made eye contact with any of the priests or priestesses, he glared or rolled his eyes, mocked their ceremonial robes inside his head, loathed their pathetic little lives. Across the room, he caught sight of his father laughing playfully, patting shoulders, smiling. King Selvin was actually enjoying the company of these pitiful losers. Davin was not a trained lip-reader like some of the spies in the royal guard, but the boy could put clues together just fine. His father and a hulking man, bald except for the signature hair above his lip, were casting glances up at the dais. To Davin's surprise, the men weren't staring at the usual center of attention, young Selvin the Fourth. Instead they were looking past the future king, directly at Davin. They were probably talking about how he'd be ten years old soon, and since he wouldn't be king, there was no use in him staying at the castle, harassing his older brother, angering his tutors, refusing to show the mannerisms fit for a prince.

"It's time for a drink, Father," Davin said quietly to himself. His brother turned to look at him, but Davin's nasty glare repelled the older boy. "It's time for a drink."

Fifty feet away, King Selvin raised a hand to catch the attention of a nearby servant, who took the king's order and walked out. A moment later, he returned and handed the king a massive mug of ale with a mountain of froth on top. Despite the quick glances of discomfort between many in the room, King Selvin chugged the beverage, much of it dribbling down his chin and all over his fine suit. A foamy mustache that rivaled the ridiculousness of the guests' own donned His Majesty's face. The king let out a massive belch. The guests pretended not to notice. Davin smiled.

"Another," Davin whispered.

"Another!" King Selvin yelled.

Two, three, four mugs later, the guests had slowly distanced themselves from King Selvin, who didn't appear to notice. Throughout his indulgences, His Majesty shot momentary pained glances across the room at his youngest son before quickly returning to his trancelike state.

"It's hot in here," Davin whispered.

"It's too bloody hot in here!" King Selvin screamed at nobody in particular. He loosened his bow tie, threw it off, removed his coat, unbuttoned his shirt, dropped it to the floor. His royal trousers followed, and that was when the priests and priestesses of Solendaron made their way out of the castle with haste, as embarrassed as their king should have been.

Davin smirked. Giggled. Cackled. Both Selvins turned to him, the elder now fully aware of what he had done. Davin heard footsteps behind him. He turned to see his flustered mother raise her hand high before bringing it down across his face. More beatings followed from both parents, but it was worth it. It was all worth it. His father meant to send Davin away with those sun-worshipping freaks, and now they wouldn't dare get near the boy again.

All in all, it was a good day for Prince Davin, first of his name, second in line for the throne.

A week later, Davin would use the same persuasive magic to force Selvin the Fourth to jump off the highest cliff near the royal family's vacation home on the coast of West Aepistelle. The ravenous waves lapped up the boy, and Selvin's body wasn't seen again in this world.

On his tenth birthday, he would officially be recognized as Prince Davin, first of his name, *first* in line for the throne.

# Chapter One

## NOW

The waves had been good to King Davin before. They would be again.

He could have ensured his freedom much earlier, but he was a man of careful planning. His contingency plans had contingency plans. He was always ready for any possible element to go wrong...at least the things he knew about. The cannons employed by those wretched women on the river in Emyhrsen had not been in the cards, quite honestly. He hadn't even known that technology had made it to Aepistelle's shores, though he'd heard rumblings of such weaponry from lands beyond the sea. Since that mistake, he'd had plenty of opportunities to turn the tables on his feckless captors, but there was still the matter of repairing his ship to make the journey home. Why not let his opponents take care of those logistics while he sat back and schemed?

"Why have we docked? This isn't Capital City," Davin called out to one of the soldiers—*his* soldier before all this began, and soon to be his again—who was descending the steps to the lower deck. Davin had only the faintest glimpse of sunlight through the one filthy porthole across the compartment, and the harbor he could barely make out was too quaint and dilapidated to be anywhere near his seat of power.

The soldier looked around nervously as he set a wooden bowl of porridge on the floor next to Davin. "We're letting off two passengers, my lord—er, sir—er, prisoner."

"Arnem Wynstone and the boy?"

"Aye. Going home, they are." The soldier picked up Davin's empty plate from the previous night. The thought of a hunger strike had briefly crossed Davin's mind—just a little something to show defiance to his captors—but he would soon have the opportunity to display his real power. Plus he was too advanced in years to skip a meal. Let younger men do such things.

"Portsville, I assume. I thought Capital Bay smelled foul, but this dump is another level of depravity."

"I'm sorry, my lord. I mean—"

"It comes naturally to you, I see. You view me as I truly am, not as some lowly criminal who belongs in captivity. You're an honorable young man, and I am indeed your king and liege. You know it to be true."

The soldier took a step back and rested a hand on his sword hilt. Conflict danced across his face. "You were my king once, aye, until I witnessed what you truly are."

"And what is that, soldier? Pray tell me."

"A traitor to your people. A scourge to your neighbors. You were in league with slavers and sorcerers. And those monstrous trees—those beasts killed my brother and several of my friends in that battle, and you were behind it all."

Davin laughed. "I only did what was necessary to protect my kingdom. Emyhrsen was a threat to me—to my people— so I set things in motion many decades ago. I am sorry that a few of your rank fell victim, but they were worthy sacrifices to Aepistelle's continued success under my rule."

"Your rule?" This time the soldier laughed. "Look at yourself—a sorry old man tied to a post on the lower deck of your own flagship. You are no longer a ruler. Soon the world will know you for the monster you truly are."

The ship rocked as it moved out of the harbor. "Headed home now, are we?" Davin asked.

"Nay. To prison you go. An island, by the sound of it."

"Terminus Rock?" Davin asked. That changed things. The craggy isle wasn't far, just a few miles from Capital Bay. His escape from Terminus wouldn't be easy. The place had been designed to interfere with abilities like those he had intended to employ to ensure his freedom. He had to act sooner.

Davin motioned for the young man to come closer.

"What is it?" The soldier rolled his eyes and bent down toward the captive king, his fingers gripping the hilt of his sword tighter.

"What is your name, good soldier?"

"Mickelson."

"Thank you, Mickelson." Davin didn't need eye contact to use his ability, but he derived immense satisfaction from watching the eyes of his targets glaze over. He whispered words in a foreign dialect he'd learned from a vizier the late King Selvin had executed when Davin was only eight years old, too late to prevent the sacred knowledge from being passed on to the then-prince.

The whispers turned to words the soldier could understand once his pupils had dilated as big as moons. "Release me from bondage, good soldier, for we have work to do together."

"Uh...I...aye," Mickelson whispered, and complied.

"Help an old man to his feet."

"Aye."

"Gather your brethren and bring them to me."

"Aye." The young man clambered up the stairs. Sunlight flashed into the dark room along with a wave of salty air.

Minutes later, a dozen soldiers of the Royal Aepistelle Army and their naval counterparts stood at attention as Davin overcame the cramps in his legs and climbed onto the deck of his ship. The soldiers reached for the hilts of their swords as Davin stepped through the door, their eyes darting from Davin to Mickelson and back.

"My good men and women of Aepistelle, thank you for assembling here. We have had a change in plans. It seems I was wrongfully locked up, a sin for which I have already forgiven you. We will now rectify that. Soldiers, about face!"

In unison, they turned on their heels to face the one other person who stood out in the crowd—a hairless man save for his ridiculous mustache, thin and middle-aged, with a confidence that now faltered. Davin winked at him through the crowd of soldiers and basked in the pain of his grimace.

A murmur swept through those assembled. Some turned back toward their former king as Davin repeated the incantation he'd used on their compatriot minutes earlier. A short man with a red beard far beyond regulation length pulled his sword from its scabbard.

"Shut your mouth, prisoner!" he shouted over Davin's voice. He lunged at Davin, but Mickelson dove between them and took the blade through his throat. Blood sprayed across Davin's face, but he remained undeterred and continued with the incantation.

Redbeard raised the sword again and screamed in frustration. Davin's eyes locked with those of another soldier, this one a burly woman with a streak of silver in her black hair. Her pupils dilated as his power took hold of her. She drove her boot into Redbeard's shin, shattering the bones. His sword came down and missed the king by two feet. The remaining soldiers turned against one another, some under Davin's enchantment, others not yet.

Davin's gaze returned to the Solendaron priest Marzele, who stood with mouth agape as the soldiers reduced their own numbers in between the two men.

"Enough!" Marzele shouted. "You are all acting like sheep. We must stand together against this tyrant!"

Davin finished reciting the incantation he'd learned as a child, and the surviving soldiers rose from the bloody mess on the deck of the ship. Two of them stepped toward Marzele, who didn't flinch, and took him by the arms. They led him down to the manacles that had held Davin minutes earlier.

King Davin hadn't used his ability in years, hadn't needed to since the other kings of the Aepistelle regions had bowed down and given him total control. Yet he had known all along that it still lived within him, that he'd recall the words to recite should he ever need them again. Power in all forms made him feel good, but there was something about seeing the despicable Marzele of Southplains falter that truly lifted his spirits.

Davin strutted to the bow of the ship and watched the vessel cut through the waves, taking command of the sea.

# Chapter Two

## MARZELE

The taste of salt on the priest's lips had already grown tiresome, as had the cold wind that carried it from the sea below. The wind never ceased to blow through the bars of the window and into his cell. His chapped lips had been bleeding for days on end, stinging anytime he turned to face the airflow. His mustache, once so finely groomed and oiled, now sagged over the stubble on his chin. He shuddered to think what his once-shiny scalp must look like.

*May the Lord Solendaron take pity on me*, Marzele of Southplains thought to himself. *May the Lord Solendaron not look upon me with disgust even in my present state.*

He lowered himself into the filthy pile of straw he called a bed and curled into a fetal position, his back to the barred window, hoping for a few minutes of relief from the biting breeze. He needed to think clearly, to find where he had strayed from the path of Solendaron, how he had stumbled upon a trail that had led him into this prison.

There had been a time when prophecies had come to

fruition, when he had witnessed the long-awaited rise of the Inquisitive One, the Protector, the Dreamer, and the Loyal One. He had been certain that his divine intuition was accurate. Gemma Calvertson, Richard the Elusive, the boy Denny, Arnem the Loyal. He had followed them in the shadows as they'd set off on their respective journeys. He'd sent word to the few fellow priests and priestesses of Solendaron who had survived King Davin's purge and scattered throughout Aepistelle, taking on odd jobs and new names while they waited for a sign. They had met right under Davin's nose in Capital City. They had convened at the castle, surrounding it, proclaiming the words of Solendaron for all bystanders to hear. And the Lord had announced His holy presence in response, knocking down the outer walls of the castle. Marzele had thought they'd failed when Davin's guards had responded, killing all of the other clergy. He alone had been spared.

He'd been taken onboard Davin's sea vessel, and they had sailed north to Emyhrsen, where a ship full of boisterous ladies had overtaken them in the midst of a battle between the four prophesied heroes and an army of monstrous trees. Lightness had prevailed. A nation had been freed from bondage, a dark power expelled by the unknowing servants of Solendaron, Marzele at their side.

Perhaps he had not praised the Lord Solendaron enough. He had not made any attempt to convince the others that their victory was His Lordship's victory, that it was for the glory of the Lord Solendaron. Perhaps, Marzele thought, he had given himself the credit that belonged to his god.

Marzele had stayed in Emyhrsen for several days while Davin's royal ships were repaired. He had helped the people of Emyhrsen ensure that the surviving Aepistelle soldiers would really help bring King Davin home, imprison him, and reveal to their people that Davin was a traitor to the kingdom. Marzele had spent those days talking with each and every soldier, gaining their trust. He'd been sure they'd understood the situation. When they had set sail for Aepistelle, everything had seemed so good. They'd brought the ship into the harbor at Portsville to drop off Arnem and Denny and then continued sailing south toward the island prison. And then things had gone wrong.

Before their arrival on Terminus Rock, the soldiers had turned against him. They'd docked on the island and placed him in the breezy cell that had been intended for the traitorous king.

Marzele wept.

All his life, he had suffered and sacrificed for the Lord Solendaron. He had given up the pursuits of love, family, and wealth in order to live a humble life of minimalism. The Lord was all he needed. He had waited through the years of darkness after most of his brethren were slain. He had studied the prophecy ceaselessly, fasted regularly, and kept a watchful eye out for signs. He had always been faithful.

And now he was here. So he cried.

"Oh, you of little faith," said a mocking voice.

For a moment, Marzele thought it was the Lord Solendaron Himself, here to punish him for his sins. He heard footsteps approaching and looked up to see King Davin in front of the bars of the cell. "Have you been burned by your god? You should have expected that, given that you believe he came from the sun."

Shame washed over Marzele, shame that his wavering faith had been witnessed by the enemy of the Solendaron. He covered his eyes with his filthy hands.

"You know, it was your faith that protected you this long," Davin went on. "Oh, I'm not saying your Solendaron is real, per se, but your conviction surely was. There is a power that comes with that kind of faith. Even my own power could not overcome it. Believe me, I've tried with your kind many times before."

"Why do you hate us so?" Marzele asked between dry coughs. He winced at the sting of his parched skin as tears dripped down his face. "We only want peace and understanding in this world."

"I hate you because my father tried so hard to make me one of you. You, who choose to be poor, who bow down to an invisible force rather than to your own king. You, who wear those ridiculous mustaches, those unsightly shaved heads. You, who reject money and belongings. I loathe you and your kind."

"Because of you, Davin, I am the *last* of my kind."

"Yes, I saw to that, no doubt. My rise to the throne meant I had to overcome your kind, but my power couldn't penetrate your faith."

"What do you mean? What power?" Marzele glared up at the freed king.

"*Visuexienes*. The power of persuasion, or whatever you want to call it. It started small when I was a child, but I didn't know quite how to wield it. A wizard in my father's court saw the potential in me and helped me understand that I had access to the *visuexienes*. I started using it on my father to get him to do what I wanted. Then I moved on to my brother, got him to do some real neat things. Jumping off a cliff to his death, for one. Father had already beheaded the wizard by then, but that didn't stop me. As I grew older, I taught myself how to reach out farther with my mind, connect with others far away. Controlling the other kings of the Aepistelle territories was simple enough, but I also reached these hateful beings across the ocean a thousand miles away. I brought down King Harold of Emyhrsen with my power. I consolidated the kingdoms of Aepistelle with it. And yet I could never directly wield that power against certain people of genuine faith, my mother included. That's what the Royal Mystic Committee was for, after I'd orchestrated the chaos in the north and gotten the people of Aepistelle to fear all religions that wielded magic and faith. Once they feared you, I didn't even need to use my special talent to bring down your kind."

Marzele turned away from King Davin, who chuckled.

"I was happy to let my power rest and coast on my skills as a leader and a schemer. Thankfully, I didn't forget how to use my ability, and it came right back to me when I needed it before we arrived at this prison. I didn't lose faith in myself all that time, unlike you."

"I have not lost my faith in the Lord Solendaron," Marzele muttered.

"I know that is not true. You once had the power to melt these bars with your hands. You could have escaped from your cell easily, but you've lost your faith, so you are stuck here to wallow in your own failure."

"You're wrong," Marzele cried with little conviction in his voice.

"Then stand," Davin commanded. Without thinking, Marzele obeyed. "Slam your head right into these bars. Do it."

Marzele complied. He couldn't stop himself. He was not in control of his own body. His head continued to pound into the steel bars until his dry skin burst open and blood flowed out. His bare hands grabbed hold of the bars, but they didn't illuminate or melt the metal.

"Okay, stop it, you're making me sick," Davin said. He turned and walked down the hall, laughing sadistically.

Marzele collapsed to the ground. His straw bed was now drenched in his blood. His eyes shifted toward the window.

The breeze had faded. The air was calm—warm, even. Marzele soaked in the sunlight. His eyes widened. He stared straight into the sun without any regard for the damage it could cause to his eyes.

*The Lord Solendaron has not forsaken me.*

*It is I who have forsaken Him.*

Marzele silently begged for forgiveness.

He received no response.

# Chapter Three

## GEMMA

The blisters on her right hand ached beyond anything she had experienced in college, back when she had drafted far more papers each week than she had in the last month. She set her quill down on the makeshift desk, knowing she would need to pick it up again momentarily to finish her letter, then to complete more pages in her manuscript about the Great Journey. Gemma stood and walked to the window. Out beyond the garden was a rocky beach that ended in the cold choppy waves of the Western Sea. She smiled as she caught a glimpse of her parents. They were laughing about something. Her mother took hold of her father's left arm and pulled him in for a kiss. It was unlike anything Gemma had seen in most of her twenty-four years, and yet it had become so common lately. She wished her brother, George, were there to see it.

The unintended adventure that had been thrust upon the entire Calvertson family had brought a spark of life back into Gemma's father, Geoffrey. The darkness that had fallen upon him twenty-five years earlier, during the war, and had consumed him ever since was now being banished by energy, awareness, even the happiness Gemma had always believed was hidden somewhere deep within her father. She feared that returning too soon to their crowded, dreary home in Capital City would suck this miracle right back out of Geoffrey and kill the newfound zeal for life that her mother now had as a result. Gemma had not yet heard any news about King Davin that assured her it was safe to return after she and her friends had aided in the mutiny against the evil monarch up in the northern kingdom of Emyhrsen. Rather than risking the loss of both her parents' happiness and all of their freedom, they had extended their journey home by dropping in on Geoffrey's old wartime colleague. Quincy lived alone in a sizable family estate by the sea in the northwesternmost portion of Aepistelle.

Someone knocked on the door behind Gemma, pulling her out of her trance. She turned to the bedroom door as it opened.

"Sorry to interrupt you, Gemma," said Quincy. The host took one step inside and peered at her. His locks of long black hair were streaked with dashes of white throughout, and he was clean-shaven. His brown skin was even more tanned from his life on the waterfront, and he looked much younger than Gemma's father, despite them being contemporaries. "I'm heading into town in a few minutes. Is the letter ready to go?"

"I'm almost done," Gemma said. "I peeked out at my parents and kind of got lost in the moment."

Quincy turned to look out the window, his boyish smile as apparent as ever.

"You know, looking at him now, I would never believe what you and your mom told me about your dad's condition over the years. He was always the toughest of our unit when we were stationed on Hallow Island, and he was the one who kept us going during the war up north. I see that same man out there despite glimpses of the trauma that seeps in when he spaces out. I see the man who loves Serena with all his heart. I think you're doing the right thing by keeping him here. All of you can stay as long as you need."

"That makes me afraid to send out this letter," Gemma said. "It's weird not to have any news about what's happened in Emyhrsen after what my friends and I did there. A couple of them should be back in Plentimore Valley. They must know what's happening. Yet a part of me feels like I'm better off here with the bliss of ignorance."

"The people you journeyed with through the Forest of Despair would be disappointed if you spent the rest of your life in hiding."

"You're right. I need to get the truth out into the world. They're all counting on me." Gemma peered over at the desk, where a stack of ink-covered papers sat next to her letter. "I'll bring the letter out in just a minute."

Gemma sat back down as Quincy went outside to prepare his horse for the short trek into town. The letter was all but signed, but she had been struggling to decide whether to add to it and risk it being intercepted or keep it as vague as she could. She found herself biting her nails as she stared blankly at the paper; that was enough to tell her that it was as good as it was going to get. She added her signature, folded the parchment, and placed it in the prepared envelope Quincy had provided. She sealed it and brought it out to Quincy to deliver to the local postal authority. She only hoped it would not be intercepted before it arrived at Wynstone and Sons Farming Supply Company in Plentimore Valley, where Arnem Wynstone and his ward, Denny, were sure to be by now.

A MONTH PASSED, AND GEMMA'S LETTER WENT unanswered. Quincy assured her that the post to Plentimore Valley took two days each way. Entertaining her paranoia, he listened around town for any talk of King Davin's Royal Mystic Committee combing the area for Gemma, which could happen if her letter had been intercepted. She knew that even if it had been delivered to Arnem, perhaps he had realized the risk of writing back and had chosen to stay quiet. Or, worse, perhaps Arnem and Denny had never made it home to Arnem's wife and daughters at all. Perhaps their entire family was locked away in a prison somewhere. It was rumored that the Royal Mystic Committee operated several shadowy prisons that held the victims of the purge of magical and religious practitioners over the past two decades. Denny's parents, who were seers just like their son, may have been imprisoned in one of those cells. The boy didn't know what had happened to them after they'd been taken from their home in Esteron City a few years ago, leaving Denny orphaned, homeless, and alone, fearing his own emerging powers. It was also possible that Gemma's friends had been executed for treason against King Davin.

"It's as if you and your father have traded places," Gemma's mother said.

Gemma shook off her thoughts and looked down at the small table between them. They were playing Stennes-et-Synes, a traditional game with colorful polished stones and a checkered board. It was one of the things that made Quincy's estate feel like home for the Calvertsons; the game had originated in their ancestral home on the Ferromin Islands, from which both Quincy's and Geoffrey's families had emigrated several decades ago.

"Are you feeling okay, Gem?"

"I can't help but feel as if I'm growing too comfortable here, like I'm hiding out when I have a job to do," Gemma said as her father reached over and patted her shoulder. "My manuscript is mostly finished, but I don't even know if I can send it to the university. We don't know what's going on back in Capital City or why Marzele never made it back with King Davin. That should have been headline news, yet all we hear is the lie that King Davin is under protection in the castle while the Solendaron 'terrorists' are being hunted down."

"The Royal Mystic Committee is doing what it always has," Geoffrey said, "telling lies to protect Davin's interests and smearing the religions of Aepistelle to maintain control. The last thing they want is for the five old kings to hear about Emyhrsen regaining freedom, lest they get ideas about their own separation from Aepistelle's rule."

Gemma hadn't considered that perspective. In Emyhrsen, it had been revealed that Davin had orchestrated the takeover by the mysterious Foreign Ones many years before. That had led not only to the slavery of the people there but also to the southern kings bowing to Davin's more powerful kingdom of West Aepistelle. Had they banded together, they would have been strong enough to defend their lands against invasion. Then, after the events of the Great Journey twenty-five years ago, Davin had cemented his power by causing mass hysteria over magic and religion. He had formed the Royal Mystic Committee to round up priests and practitioners, sack holy temples, burn ancient texts, and make the people of Aepistelle worship one entity only: King Davin himself.

Gemma was responsible for reporting what they had learned, which she could not do with Davin on the throne, as the monarch controlled the presses and publishers, including Gemma's employer, Capital University Press. But the weight of it had never quite dawned on her until now; her writing could lead to the country fracturing into separate kingdoms again or even start a civil war among the five kings who had once bowed down to Davin. Gemma's words had the potential to unite the kingdom, but they also had the power to tear it apart.

"You're right, Dad," Gemma said. "If I get the truth out there, chaos will follow."

"The people of Aepistelle lived a lie for a quarter of a century," Serena interjected. She looked over at her husband. "Maybe chaos will wake them up."

The front door opened, and any inspiration Gemma had gained from talking with her parents faded quickly when she saw the look of panic on Quincy's face. He looked at Geoffrey and Serena before his eyes met Gemma's. He lifted a newspaper.

"It's happened. King Davin escaped from his captors and returned to Capital City."

The room fell into a stunned silence.

Gemma caught sight of movement in the bright sunlight through the open doorway behind Quincy. She stood up to get a better look, and everyone followed her gaze. A man approached the front door.

"Is this the home of Quincy Harpon?" the man asked.

"Who's asking?" Quincy responded.

"I'm here to speak with Gemma Calvertson. I believe she's expecting to hear from me."

Four other people emerged from the shadows of the trees that lined the walkway. Gemma gasped.

# Chapter Four
## PALIGNON

The clouds slunk low, blocking out any illumination from the cresting moon. Lieutenant Cragen Palignon had full jurisdiction and orders straight from the top to ride in, knock doors down, and make his arrests by any means necessary, including the use of force against any who resisted. Any, that is, but one particular young target.

He liked the darkness, preferred the shadows. Sneaking around was a fun part of the job, if one could find enjoyment in their work. Palignon had a knack for the clandestine; he excelled at it, and he would take any opportunity to make himself look good right then. After all, there was an opening at the very top of his chain of command. Sir Marin Allemon had been killed in battle during a clandestine mission of his own, a fact that had come to light just days ago when King Davin had sent word of his own reemergence. For nearly two months, the key members of Davin's cabinet and their staffs had been scrambling to keep secret the enigma of His

Majesty's disappearance. Allemon's absence was not as much of a mystery; very few had even noticed that the Secretary of the Royal Mystic Committee had gone missing. Even Allemon's own wife had just assumed he was off with another woman, using the *top secret mission* as his cover for another spate of infidelity.

Palignon knew, though. It was his responsibility to know.

And now Palignon knew that this was his chance to prove himself. It was one of the most important missions he'd faced in his years of service in the Royal Mystic Committee: capturing the traitors who had tried to overthrow King Davin. The very same miscreants who had killed Sir Allemon.

Plentimore Valley was full of breathtaking landscapes, from low lush hills to fertile vineyards producing wines that were the envy of the world. The people, however, were not so attractive. *Stubby* was how Palignon thought of them. Short, chubby little fellows. Palignon had never claimed to be an expert in the sciences, and so far that hadn't curtailed his career any.

He halted his horse on the road just before a bend around an outcropping of trees and motioned for his crew to follow suit. There were three other soldiers on the strike team he'd assembled for this mission. They were damn good by all accounts, though he hadn't worked with them before. He hadn't had time to call in his usual operatives; most of his preferred folks had been called away to help with some clandestine prisoner transfer down south—a waste of talent, Palignon thought. He didn't need his normal team, though. He just needed this to go right, and he didn't expect much could fail. His targets were a little middle-aged man and his scrawny teenage companion. King Davin wanted to make an example of them, as the older of the pair had been something of a folk hero around Aepistelle. There were some other persons of interest that Palignon was to look out for, but anyone not on the list was expendable and could be executed and disposed of without regard. So he was sure three soldiers would be enough. He was almost certain the kid would wet himself and the old man would beg to be taken alive.

Palignon thrust his reins at the nearest soldier as he dismounted, ordering him to tie the horse up. The soldier complied, then tied his own to the low-slung fence nearby. The others tethered their horses as well.

"We go the rest of the way on foot so as not to announce our arrival too soon."

"Are they expected to be armed, sir?" Private Alice Taron asked. The unit's sole female soldier, she was the most hungry for one-on-one combat. She'd been undefeated in training duels during her time at Fort Braxen, but she'd seen little real action. She unsheathed her sword and rubbed a cloth along its blade.

"They may have some rusty old weapons, but nothing you lot can't handle," Palignon said. "What they do have, according to our intel, is a boy who can see the future. They may be expecting us, in which case they've either fled or are ready to defend themselves."

"If they have some freak who can divine my arrival, I'm sure they're wetting themselves. No way they'll pick up a sword and try to fight back unless they have a death wish." This from Private Markus Lang, the hothead of the group. Palignon often wanted to slap the smugness off the young man's face, but even he had to admit that Lang's confidence was a strength in a melee.

"If they've soiled themselves, you'll be the one carrying them back to base," Palignon quipped. The others laughed, but Lang just brushed it off. "Now, let us take down these traitors to the crown."

They trotted around the next bend in the road. A low gate awaited them under a wooden archway with a family crest Palignon couldn't quite make out in the darkness. He pushed at the gate, but a chain clinked. He turned and nodded at Sergeant Holman, the big brute of the group. Holman flashed a near-toothless grin, walked up, and kicked the gate. With one stomp of his unfathomably massive boot, the entire gate separated from its hinges and collapsed to the ground. A cloud of dirt wafted up around them as they stepped over the wreckage. They made their way down the driveway toward the house.

Their target's home was a two-story affair, perhaps a bit small for the region but much nicer than the crowded town houses that filled Capital City. It was as dark as the rest of the night. No smell of smoke from the chimney. No commotion inside.

"They must all be sleeping," Holman said.

"No, I think someone's still working," said Taron. She pointed across the yard toward an oversize three-story barn. Jutting off to one side was a wing that had once been horse stables but now appeared to have been converted into offices.

"Ah, good," Lang said, setting off toward the barn without waiting for the others. "I prefer to kill my targets while they're still conscious anyway. None of that sneaking around crap."

Palignon didn't bother to stop him. As he looked around the farm from just outside the house, he didn't sense any danger. He let out a sigh of relief; this would be an easy win after all, and he could get back home to his wife and daughter.

He moved to follow the others; Lang was almost to the

barn, approaching the closed door that led into the lit office wing. Holman jogged past Lang and prepared to use his brute strength to knock down the door, just as he'd done to the gate moments ago. Behind Lang, Taron readied her blade should any of the occupants attempt to flee.

Holman's boot met the wooden door, and it buckled in its frame, a few splinters flying off. One more kick and it shattered inward. Holman turned around, expecting praise from his companions, just as a large axe swung from inside and connected with his neck. For a moment, Holman stood in shock. Then he stumbled backward, and there was a sickening *slosh* as he fell away from the blade. The blood spurted out like a geyser, and he fell with a thud. Losing his usual cool, Lang stepped back in shock while Taron rushed past him, sword at the ready. She slashed at the axe, which had remained in place even after Holman had dislodged himself. It swung slightly and then settled. She somersaulted below it, leapt to her feet, and then froze.

"A trap," she called out.

Palignon made his way forward, skirting around the pile of vomit that now graced Lang's feet at the sight of his fallen comrade. He stepped over Holman's body and ducked under the axe.

"They expected us indeed," Palignon said.

"Are they watching from the house?"

"No, Private, I believe they're long gone by now."

"We won't know until we check," Taron said. "Want me to go in first this time?"

Palignon glanced over at Lang and took in the shame on the once-cocky soldier's face. "Let's send him in. Let him redeem himself." He went back outside and patted Lang on the shoulder. "Come, now, my boy; it's not as if you wanted to share the glory of this mission with Holman anyway."

"I was the one who asked him to kick the door down. I didn't even try the knob to see if it was locked. It was supposed to be me. What would my face have looked like with that axe slicing through it? I'd have been scarred had I survived it, a monster! What a life that would've been, people always looking at me like some kind of freak."

"You just faced down death and you're more worried about your dashing good looks being tainted?"

"What is the point of living if you're hideous?" Lang asked in full seriousness. He took in his lieutenant's own imperfect face and grimaced. "No offense to you, of course, sir."

Palignon turned to Taron, who stared back in disbelief.

"Well, Lang," said Palignon, "if you'd like to redeem yourself, why don't you go into the house first. We'll find a good window to send you through. I'm sure it'll be safe enough."

"But sir, I—"

"That's an order, Private. Your recklessness got your fellow soldier killed. Should you disobey me, I'll have you discharged for treason."

"Yes, sir," Lang said. He hung his head in shame, avoiding eye contact with Taron.

Lang made his way back up the path toward the house, and the others followed. By the dim light still shining from the barn's office, Palignon could make out an opening in one of the second-floor windows just above an awning on the side porch. When they reached the porch, Palignon gave the younger man a boost toward the awning. It creaked and groaned under his weight, forcing Lang to step carefully. Lang made it to the window, swung the pane open, and crawled inside.

There were no screams, no more traps. Two minutes of silence passed before Lang opened the front door.

The house had been abandoned. Arnem Wynstone, his

family, and the vagrant boy had escaped their clutches for now. The traitors to the crown were somewhere out there, on the loose, and Lieutenant Palignon vowed not to rest until he caught them.

The Royal Mystic Committee would soon be his to lead. Arnem and the boy were his ticket to the top.

# Chapter Five

## ARNEM | DENNY

"So, you must be the boy with the visions, eh?" The man blocked the doorway with his bulky frame, staring down at the newcomers.

Arnem turned to look at Denny, who cowered behind him. He met the boy's eyes, which seemed to calm him. "It's okay, Denny," he whispered. "I think this man is a friend."

A change came over Denny's face, and Arnem realized it wasn't his words that had calmed the boy. Gemma pushed past the man standing guard in the doorway and jumped off the porch toward them.

"You're alive!" she said as she threw her arms around them both at once. She held them tight for several seconds before Arnem's wife began to weep behind them. Gemma let go of the men and took a step toward her. "You must be Selah."

"Oh, Gemma," Selah managed before she began to sob uncontrollably. She ran the remaining distance to Gemma and nearly knocked the young woman over with her embrace. "It's really you! It...you...you're real! You really are!"

"Mom, let her go!"

"Yeah, you're more embarrassing than Dad!"

Arnem walked over to his two teenage daughters. They were close in age to Denny, and people had started mistaking the three teens for siblings in the weeks since Arnem and Denny had returned from their journey to Emyhrsen.

"Ladies," he said, "meet Gemma Calvertson. Gemma, these are my daughters, Rosaline Maachela and Lyria Marinah. And of course you've now met my dear wife, Selah."

Gemma managed to break the older woman's hold on her and reached out to shake the girls' hands. "It's great to meet you all. Arnem had a lot of wonderful things to say about you while we were up north. He always made it clear that everything he did was to help secure a peaceful future for you girls."

"Okay," Lyria said, "I guess Dad is actually more embarrassing than Mom."

"Sorry, Mom," Rosaline chimed in on cue.

The girls laughed and then lunged forward, grabbing Gemma's arms and talking at once.

"Is it true there were tree monsters?"

"And an insane witch who imprisoned children?"

"Tell me Dad didn't really crawl through a sewer of human waste just to get into some dusty old castle."

"And those warrior ladies—were they as gorgeous as Denny said? I think he was lying. There's no way they'd be into our dad, of all people."

"Girls!" Arnem called out. He glanced over at Selah and was pleasantly surprised to find her laughing. She had never been the type to get jealous of other women. Arnem always told her he was a one-woman kind of man. She laughed at that and said she didn't worry one bit, that Arnem was quite a homely little man but that *she* saw much more in him. He'd thought perhaps the slightest tinge of jealousy might find its way into her when he had talked about his adventures with Teyla and her Nazseke warriors, but she had laughed it off and given him a good smack on the shoulder. *My goodness, do I love that woman who married me*, he thought.

"Um, guys?" Denny said. Arnem and the ladies all turned toward him. Denny glanced nervously at the man in the doorway and then back toward them. He lowered his voice. "We better talk somewhere a little more private."

Gemma walked over to him. "Denny, there's nothing to worry about. This is Quincy. He knows all about our adventures."

"All of it?" Denny asked.

"You bet, little man! Overthrowing King Davin, the magic spell you all used to take down those slavers—all of it."

Quincy stepped off the porch and held his huge hand out to Denny. The boy's hand met it weakly. Quincy laughed loudly, which seemed to surprise Denny. "And I know all about how you came to the aid of my good friend Gemma! Stand tall. You've earned it." He approached Arnem next. "And you! It's been twenty-five years now, but you look just as I remember you. I was with Gemma's father, Geoffrey, and the rest of our unit when we met you, Maachel, Richard, and Jestan at the castle of the Ancient Ones."

"It was quite a difficult time for all of us," Arnem said as he shook Quincy's hand. "We are well met. You and the other soldiers brought us so much courage and hope with your bravery. I'm glad we can reunite after all these years."

"Come on, then," Quincy said. "Let's get you all inside!"

<hr>

"WE HADN'T SEEN THIS WHEN WE LEFT HOME YESTERDAY," Arnem said, shaking the newspaper. The newcomers were all seated in Quincy's living room, sipping tea and eating sandwiches that Geoffrey and Serena Calvertson had fixed for them. The Wynstone girls were playing the game Gemma and her mother had left on the table, ignoring the palaver the rest of the group was engaging in. "We didn't need to read the article. Denny saw it in his sleep."

"First vision I've had since Emyhrsen," Denny said. He glanced nervously at Quincy, but there was nothing threatening in the man's attentive look. If anything, Denny thought he looked protective of the Calvertson family, and that eased his fears a bit. He had learned to trust Gemma's judgment of people.

"You saw King Davin return to Capital City in your dream?" Gemma asked.

"It wasn't Davin I saw. It was the priest, Marzele. Only I don't think he'd want us to refer to him as a priest in his current state."

"Was he dead? Did they kill him?"

"No, Gemma, but he seemed to wish he were dead. He was lying on the floor of a filthy cell, and then he got up and looked out a window. It was like I could see through his eyes as he watched King Davin and most of the soldiers who threw down their swords back in Emyhrsen. They were back on Davin's side; they had helped free him. Marzele watched them sail away from there, and all hope was lost to him."

"So it was a prison on the coast, then?" Gemma asked.

"I don't know of any beachfront jails in Aepistelle," Quincy said, "but I do know of one on an island. They call it Terminus Rock. It's totally protected to keep the worst of the worst criminals at bay."

Arnem reached over and patted the boy's shoulder in a fatherly gesture. "Tell them how he was feeling, though, Denny."

Denny winced at the thought of it. "I know we weren't acquainted with Marzele for very long. He only arrived at the end of our battle, and then Arnem and I spent a few days with him on the ship back to Portsville, where we parted ways. Even so, it was clear that he was defined by his faith. He was hopeful, confident in that Solendaron god he follows. That faith had led him to some dark places in the past, but he seemed to think there was a reason for all of it. But now I think he's lost his faith entirely. When I have visions, I can usually *feel* them as much as I can see them, if not more. The vibes I got from this one really shook me."

"Did they hurt him?" Serena asked.

"Maybe," Denny said. "Physically, maybe a little. But mentally...his faith was destroyed. We all saw how he was able to use the power his faith provided him when he melted the portcullis with his bare hands. But now he can't even get out of that prison cell. He's lost everything that made him who he was."

Now it was Denny's turn to cry. These weren't tears of happiness, though, like Selah's had been upon meeting Gemma. What he was feeling was existential dread.

For years, Denny had viewed his visions as a curse. It was the same curse that had led to his parents being arrested by the Royal Mystic Committee years ago, leaving Denny alone on the streets of Esteron City. The visions had come and gone, and Denny hadn't had anyone to explain them to him, no parents to tell him what the power meant or how to control it. He had hated it. But then the visions had led him to Arnem. To Gemma and Richard. To a new home, a family. He had finally come to terms with his power over the last several weeks.

But now, as he witnessed Marzele's downfall and deeply internalized the man's loss, he dreaded what might come of his own power. The danger of having it. The danger of losing it.

"That poor man," Selah said. She walked over to Denny and rubbed his shoulders. Denny hesitated for a moment, then relaxed. He'd spent years alone, living in alleys and on rooftops without much human interaction, before he'd come across Arnem. Selah hadn't been thrilled when Arnem had brought the boy home to Plentimore Valley, but she'd understood her husband's heart. Immediately afterward, Arnem and Denny had slipped away and disappeared for weeks to journey through the Forest of Despair. When they'd returned, Selah had greeted both of them with open arms. There seemed to be no question anymore—Denny was a part of their family, and that was that. However, it was quite an adjustment for Denny to have a family again, to accept safety and comfort, care and love.

"I can't let him suffer like that," Arnem said. Denny felt Selah's hands tighten on his shoulders. "Denny is right that we don't know him well, but that didn't stop him from risking everything to come to our aid. I don't know if I can live with myself if I don't at least try to return the favor, knowing he's in pain."

"Arnem, no!" Selah shouted. "It's bad enough that you left your daughters and me with no idea of where you had gone or if you would come back to us alive. Now you want to push your luck and commit treason a second time? We've already fled our home out of fear of retribution. There will be no escape this time!"

"I think Arnem is right, Mrs. Wynstone," Denny said. He didn't quite know what to call Selah. As motherly as she was, he didn't feel right calling her Mom or Mother when he didn't know if his own mother was still out there somewhere. He also felt that calling her Selah was too casual or disrespectful.

"If there's one thing we've learned during the last couple of months, it's that these visions come to me for a reason, not so I can watch them like some stage show. There is nothing entertaining or pleasant about them."

"And I wouldn't be sitting here today if it weren't for Denny and Arnem acting on his visions," Gemma said.

"Gemma, I fear what you're going to say next," Serena said. She leaned into her daughter's shoulder and wept. "Please don't leave us again."

Geoffrey gently pulled her away from Gemma and hugged his wife. "Gemma can make things happen. Find a good group of friends to join her. Solve problems that lesser folks would shy away from."

"And she won't be alone." All heads turned to Quincy. Denny didn't know much about the man, but he wasn't afraid of him. He trusted Gemma's judgment, and she seemed as comfortable with Quincy Harpon as she did with the rest of her family and friends. "Nay, I don't think Gemma will ever be alone in her endeavors again. She inspires people. She inspired me and gave me hope with what she did on her journey. I'll join you all and help free your friend."

"That's very kind of you, Quincy," Gemma said, "but I wouldn't dream of pulling you away from your fishing business. You have a great life here. There's too much at stake."

"The business is not much more than a front, Gemma." Quincy rolled up his sleeves, flexed his arms, and flashed a proud smile around the room. "You don't think casting nets and setting sails is the reason I still look this good at my age, do you? No, ma'am. I've stayed active since my days in the military. So have some of the others from our old unit—at least the ones who didn't suffer in the same way as Geoffrey."

"So you're still part of Davin's military?" Denny felt that perhaps he *should* be fearful of the man after all.

"Certainly not, young man. Serving under that tyrant would be an affront to every man, woman, and child in these lands. I felt that way even before what I learned from Gemma. My team and I are soldiers for hire. Mercenaries, if you will. Sure, we're also the best fisherfolk on the Western Sea, but that's merely what we do when we're between assignments."

"And who do you serve?" Gemma asked. Denny was surprised that even she didn't appear to know any of this information. "You haven't mentioned any of this in the weeks we've been here."

"I didn't want to further incriminate you and your family. I hope you can understand that."

"Of course, old friend," Geoffrey said.

"My team and I mostly do humanitarian missions. Sometimes we also act as security in very special high-risk situations. We're primarily contracted by the former kings around the continent, as they don't trust King Davin and his military any more than we do. We've worked in Esteron, Centeron, Southplains, and the Reaches. We've also been dispatched to some of the island nations, where our sailing experience comes in quite handy. I can't divulge the specifics."

Silence fell over the room. Denny couldn't quite read the look on Gemma's face, so he was glad when she spoke up.

"We'd be lucky to have you, then. The prison is on an island, so your boat will come in handy for us as well."

"We'll need my team too," Quincy said. "We're going to need the numbers if we're infiltrating a prison. It's been quiet for us lately. They'll be ecstatic about this mission."

"We can't pay, though," Arnem said. "Even though Selah and the girls covered the business while I was away on our last journey, there's no way we can afford to pay what you're worth."

"Are you kidding? Serving alongside one of the heroes of the Great Journey—Arnem Wynstone himself!—is all the pay my people will require."

"Thank you, Quincy," Gemma said. "We should aim to leave the day after tomorrow, if that's enough time to gather your soldiers."

And so the preparations began.

# Chapter Six
## KING DAVIN

"Oh, fine citizens of Capital City and all who have traveled across the prosperous lands of Aepistelle to be here today, I bid you welcome. A most humble thank-you for all that you do to make Aepistelle the mightiest and most thriving kingdom in all the world."

King Davin paused and looked around the makeshift amphitheater from the dais as the crowd cheered. After half a minute, he raised his arms like a conductor, and they silenced immediately.

"You all stand here today in what was once the outer courtyard of my castle. Rubble surrounds you even now, several weeks after the cowardly Solendaron terrorists launched their failed attack on our great kingdom and assassination plot against me."

This time there was a chorus of boos and hisses at the mention of the would-be usurpers. Davin let this go on for just as long as the cheers moments earlier.

"And yet, like Aepistelle has always done, we survived. We stand here today as powerful as ever, as united as ever. A quarter of a century after the consolidation of power in these lands, when the kings of Centeron, Esteron, Southplains, the Southern Reaches, and Costono all entrusted me with the well-being of our people, we persist through strength and security.

"Twenty-five years ago, it was sorcery that nearly brought an end to this world. That was when we first saw religions for what they really were: terrorist sects and cults that wielded dangerous power. One such group in the far north attempted to expand its reign of evil into the lands of Aepistelle, but did we let that happen? Absolutely not. Brave men and women from the combined lands of Aepistelle put everything on the line and ended that threat. But here at home, these religious cults had been allowed to exist unchecked for centuries. There were no bounds to what they could get away with. My father was too soft on them, as were the generations before him and the other kings throughout Aepistelle.

"I saw the danger, though. Even before the war, I knew what perils they could bring. In fact, it was the Solendaron priests themselves who opened my eyes to their threats when I was young. They tried to convince my father to give me up to them when I was but ten years old. Had my older brother, rest his soul, not died in a freak accident, I would have been conscripted into the ranks of the Solendaron against my will. Fate had other plans, though, much to the chagrin of the Solendaron priests. They held it against me—and against this kingdom—for decades. They plotted in the shadows until they finally made their move here, and they failed.

"Aepistelle is now stronger than ever, yet there are many like the Solendaron who wish to see our great kingdom fall. What I'm about to tell you may shock you. I thought about keeping it all a secret so that I would not appear weak in your eyes, so that your sense of security and your faith in your king would not falter in the slightest. However, I have always been honest with you all, and today shall be no exception.

"Over the last few weeks, I have been subjected to another attempted coup. This one involved not only the Solendaron priests but several other individuals who conspired against the crown. This shadowy cabal tricked me into aiding our reclusive neighbors to the north, the land of Emyhrsen, and then ambushed me while I was there. It was only thanks to my own cunning and the might of our soldiers that we were able to fight back and escape to freedom with little more than our lives.

"Though they were few in number, these traitors were certainly not working alone. They were well trained, highly prepared, funded by wealthy benefactors. There are treasonous individuals hiding among us even now. They may be in any town throughout these lands. They are our coworkers, our teachers, our brothers, our sisters, even our parents. They are rotten to the core, and they spread their disease in secret."

The murmurs of shock and horror and anger rose to a roar. Davin put on a look of sadness, but on the inside, he basked in the crowd's reaction to his deception. The lies came all too easily to him, as they had for decades—no secret abilities needed to fool his own people.

"I have set several new initiatives in motion. You will see changes on all levels to root out the evil, from ridding our newspapers and books of dissent to crushing the last remnants of religious terrorism. The end is nigh for those who wish to see our kingdom fail. I am requesting that the regional governors—formerly the kings of the lands that now make up Aepistelle—recommit their loyalty to the crown. I am doubling our security forces, from Aepistelle's military to our regional constabularies, and supporting the vital work of our Royal Mystic Committee. I will ensure that those who dabble in magic, who look to gods and outdated texts instead of to their king, and who sow dissension in any way will be crushed under my boot.

"Aepistelle will prevail, and we will do it together."

# Chapter Seven
## DENNY

The fog was heavy in front of Denny's eyes, as if he were passing through a curtain of nightmarishly thick spiderwebs, sticky and damp. It disrupted his vision, but he knew by the sounds of the seagulls and the crashing of waves on the shore that they were nearing their island destination. Someone next to him on the deck murmured something, but Denny couldn't make out what it was or who had said it. He could rarely hear clearly in visions.

One of Quincy's mercenaries came close enough for Denny to see him through the haze. The man's long hair was pulled back in a tight ponytail to keep it out of the way of his bow. He nocked an arrow, pulled back the string, and released. Denny tried to follow the trajectory, but in a fraction of a second, the arrow was lost to the fog. Gemma ran up on Denny's other side and followed suit. After releasing her arrow, she turned to Denny and tried to tell him something. Again, it came out as muffled gibberish. She seemed to notice his lack of comprehension, so she pointed at something behind him, farther back on the boat. He nodded and turned.

That was when he saw the shape of another woman, fully shrouded in a wispy gray shadow. She stood directly in front of him. Her mouth opened, a bottomless black void.

"Hello, Denny," she said, and he heard it clearly. It was so unlike any other sound in these nocturnal visions. "You can see me? You can hear me?"

*That voice*, he thought. *It sounds just like... It can't be, can it?*

"Mom?"

"It's me, my little love. It's me. I'm afraid we don't have much time. I don't know how we're seeing each other right now. Oh, how I've tried to reach you. I've wanted this moment to happen for years. You've grown up so much since we were taken from you."

"Mom, how are you here? What's happening?"

"Listen, Denny. I think whatever is responsible for the gifts we share is trying to warn us that something big is coming for us. Maybe it's letting us say goodbye to each other, something we never got to do all those years ago. Denny, please know that your father and I love you. We've never stopped trying to connect with you. We've never stopped trying to escape from our captors and get back home to you."

"Where are you, Mom? How can I find you?"

"I'm right here, honey. We can't be together in person, so this is how it must be."

"I have friends who can help, Mom. Just tell me where to go, and we'll be there."

"I can't let you do that, Denny. This is the end of the line for your father and me. This is goodbye. I love you."

"No, Mom, it can't be!"

"I'm so proud of you. I can't see you clearly, but I can tell you've grown into a beautiful, strong young man. You've survived this long on your own, or with these friends of yours. Let them into your heart; they are your family now. But you must forget about me. You must forget about your father. You must never speak of your gift to anyone outside of your new family for any reason. There are not many in this world who can be trusted. Goodbye, my son."

Suddenly, through the perpetual drabness of the fog, the silhouette of his mother burst with light. It momentarily blinded Denny, then left an impression that flashed across his vision with each blink, like staring at the sun before stepping into a dark room. In those flashes, he saw a barren wasteland interrupted only by a long metal track that stretched as far as the image allowed him to see. After a moment, it was gone. Denny turned around and around, but everything on the boat seemed to fade away.

"Denny," Gemma whispered. "It's okay."

Denny sat up. He wasn't on the boat at all. He was on the floor of Quincy's dining room, wrapped in the towels he'd been given in lieu of blankets. His host hadn't been prepared for so many unexpected guests, and most of the extra blankets had gone to Arnem's wife and daughters. Denny was fine with the towels; they were far more effective than what he had used as bedding during his days living in alleyways and on rooftops.

"It was one of your visions, wasn't it?" Gemma asked him. She held a lantern that illuminated her in the darkness. A few weeks back, when they had been traveling together through Ferathan and Emyhrsen to the north, he had embarrassed himself a few times when she had noticed him blushing at the sight of her. Since then, he'd thought he had grown past that. They were friends. They had fought together on the battle-fields of Emyhrsen against an army of monstrous trees. Yet seeing her here in the dark, her eyes shining in the light of the lantern, he was sure he was blushing yet again. He only hoped she couldn't see it in the dimness.

"It was different," Denny said. "It started off like one of my normal visions. We were on a boat, presumably approaching the island with the prison. But then it was interrupted."

"Our mission will get interrupted? By a traitor in our midst?"

"No, I mean the vision was interrupted. It changed into something else entirely, something I've never experienced before."

"Could it have been just a normal dream like we all have, Denny?"

"No. Definitely not. I was having a conversation."

"A conversation? With who?"

"My mother. She was as confused as I was, but she thought it was our last chance to say goodbye." Before he could get any more words out, Denny began to weep. Gemma knelt down and hugged him.

"If that's what it was, I'm sorry. I know you haven't seen her in years. I suppose you never got a chance to say goodbye when she was first taken away. Most people probably never get that chance when their families are taken by the Royal Mystic Committee."

She was right, of course, and he knew it, but Denny didn't really feel any better. The hole his parents had left in his heart had always been deep, the scars irreparable.

"Come on," Gemma said, pulling Denny up from the floor. "I can't sleep, so I'm going out for a walk. It'll be time to leave before we know it."

Denny didn't need another invitation. He slipped on his boots and coat and followed her out to walk under the stars.

"Something's bothering you too, isn't it?" Denny asked. They were walking down the beach toward the private boathouse where Quincy and his crew were preparing two watercrafts for their mission. Gemma hadn't said a word the entire trek. She turned and met his eyes. Hers were full of tears.

"You mentioned seeing your mother in your vision. It reminded me that I'll be leaving my own parents for the second time. The first time, I didn't think there would be much danger, but we came so close to death more times than I can count. Now we're knowingly going out to face our enemies, break the laws of the kingdom, and risk everything. During the time we've been here, I've grown so close to both of my parents. My dad's progress has been incredible."

"It sounds like you're leaving them in a better place this time, Gemma."

"That's what I'm afraid of. What if I come back and my dad has reverted back to how he used to be? Back in Emyhrsen, I asked Naliah if she could put some kind of enchantment on my dad to fix his mind. She refused and told me to cherish what time I had left with him. And I have been. I just don't want it to end."

Denny didn't know what to say to that. He knew what it felt like to lose parents, but the void his had left in him was still as desolate as it had always been.

Gemma patted him on the shoulder. "It's okay, Denny. I don't expect you to fix it. I'm excited to go out there again with you and Arnem. You're my family as well."

*They are your family now.* Denny's mother's words came back to him. As comfortable as he was with the Wynstones, as much as they treated him as a member of their family, a part of him didn't want to give in to it. It felt too much like giving up on his own parents. He'd had no idea whether they were alive for so long that he'd had no real hope of ever seeing them again. Perhaps his mother was right that these people were his family now, Gemma included, but a piece of him did not want to accept it.

"You'll come back to your parents," he said. "They'll be here waiting for you, and things will be fine. I'm sure of it."

Gemma ruffled his hair and smiled at him. "Thanks, Denny. You're wise beyond your years."

They arrived at the boathouse. A member of Quincy's crew was just outside the door, smoking a pipe. Her name was Selinda—Denny and Gemma had met her over dinner a few hours earlier when Quincy had introduced them to his team.

"Cap, the little ones have arrived," Selinda yelled through the open doorway. She started to chuckle, but it turned into a coughing fit. When she regained her breath, she winked at Denny. "Smoking this stuff is a nasty habit. Don't start unless you want to end up like me."

"We couldn't sleep," Gemma said to her. "I thought we'd check in with Quincy and see how the preparations are coming along."

"Come on in," Quincy called from inside. Gemma and Denny nodded to the woman and stepped through the door. Quincy was standing at a long workbench, his back to them as he toiled away at something. "I was hoping to present this to you on the boat tomorrow, but now's as good a time as any."

Quincy turned around. The polished metal object in his hand gleamed even in the minimal light of the lanterns.

"My machete!" Gemma said. She stepped forward and accepted it from him eagerly. She turned it over in her hands and admired it. "This looks almost nothing like it. Is it really the same one?"

"I cleaned the rust off, repaired the chips in the blade, and shined it up real nice. I wrapped the hilt for a better grip in battle. I'm sure your brother could have done a cleaner job with the blade, but it's—"

"It's perfect!" Gemma held the machete off to one side and used her other arm to hug Quincy. "Thank you so much!"

Something on the blade seemed to catch her eye. Denny looked over her shoulder and spotted what looked like elaborate Ferromini script, the native language of both Quincy and Gemma's father. Several characters were engraved on the blade just above the hilt. Gemma ran her fingers over them.

A proud smile lined Quincy's face. "It says 'For hope and truth.' I thought it embodied you perfectly. Oh, and I restrung your bow, and we have plenty of arrows for you and our other archers." Quincy moved on to Denny. "And don't think I forgot about you, little man."

He turned back to his workbench and lifted a towel. Underneath it was a small sword unlike any Denny had ever seen. The blade curved one way and then another in several places, not unlike the slithering tree monsters they had faced during the battle in Emyhrsen. Even the hilt had a bend to it.

"What...what is it?" Denny asked.

Quincy waved Denny over to pick it up. He was amazed by the artisanship but also slightly scared of the weapon.

"It's called a kalis—a sword native to the Ferromin Islands, where Gemma's father and I were born. Double-edged and curved so as to not catch on the bones of its prey the way a straight blade would."

"And what's this?" Denny pointed to an engraving on the blade just above the hilt. Unlike Gemma's, it was not in the script of her ancestral lands. It was an oval with what appeared to be two eyes next to each other and a third eye centered above them.

"The mind's eye," Quincy said, "for the boy who can see

what others can't. Everyone brings something unique to a team, and each of us must proudly display our talents. I think we all know what makes you so special, my young friend."

Denny looked around. There were two women and three other men from Quincy's crew watching from around the boathouse. His mother's words came back to him: *You must never speak of your gift to anyone outside of your new family for any reason.*

*So which are these*, he wondered, *my new family or outsiders?*

"What do you think, Denny?" Gemma asked. "It's really special, right?"

"Oh, um, yes. Thank you, Quincy!" He gave the man a hug. If Gemma and her parents trusted him with their lives, perhaps there was nothing to be afraid of, though until the recent revelations, Gemma had had no knowledge of Quincy's role as a mercenary. What else could he or his crew be hiding?

Quincy patted Denny's back, then took the sword and put it in its scabbard. Denny took it from him and fitted it around his waist.

"So, did your mind's eye give you any foresight about what we're going to face out there?" Quincy asked.

Denny pushed away his mother's warning. He was deep in this already. He was about to set sail with everyone in the boathouse. There was no use in pretending he hadn't seen anything in his last vision, especially if it might be valuable for their tactical planning.

"Yes. When we arrive, it may be extremely foggy. I think we'll only know the prison island is ahead of us by the sound of the waves lapping against the rocks. But they seemed to be ready for us. I didn't see anything beyond that before I woke up."

"Approaching under the cover of fog?" Selinda asked. She had come inside while Denny and Gemma were receiving their weapons, still puffing on her pipe. "I like the sound of that!"

"Agreed," Quincy said. "We operate best under those conditions—nobody to see or hear us coming until we're right up against their walls. This may be easier than I thought."

Denny hoped so, but the ominous appearance of his mom during the vision didn't give him much optimism.

"We'll set sail for Terminus Rock at dawn." Quincy looked out the open doorway at the moon, which was on its way down toward the ocean. "Just a few short hours away, from the look of it. Go get some more rest. You're going to need it."

Denny and Gemma headed back to the house. Denny settled back under his pile of towels and wondered if sleep would bring any more visions of his mother or the impending mission.

He had barely entered a deep enough sleep before it was time to head out.

# Chapter Eight
## GEMMA

The first flaming arrow pierced the deck just three feet from Gemma. She dove to her left, away from it. Quincy reached down and pulled her to her feet while Selinda splashed a bucket of water over the small fire.

"They didn't intend to burn up the boat," Quincy whispered, "but they wanted to see if anything was approaching in this fog. They must have heard us. So much for the element of surprise."

"Nay, Captain," Selinda said. "I put out the flame before it spread. I doubt they saw the arrow hit." She turned to Gemma and pounded a fist against her shoulder. "Plus, this one didn't scream. Quick reflexes and no tears—I'd say she fits right in with our crew."

Before they could feel at ease again, two more arrows cut through the fog. One landed in almost the same place as the first while the other hit the sail, which immediately lit up.

"You were saying, Selinda?" Quincy said. He raised his voice to reach the other half of the crew on the second boat. "Take position for distance attack!"

Gemma and the other archers ran toward the front of the boats, where their bows and arrows awaited them. Gemma aimed straight ahead, but she wasn't confident she was shooting at anything, given the thick fog and the darkness. Another flaming arrow cut through the veil of night toward the ship. Without hesitating, Gemma aimed her own arrow at where it had come from. She lost sight of it after only a few feet, but she noticed several of the other archers' arrows heading in the same direction. A cry sounded in the distance, followed by the sound of a body crashing down onto rocks.

The fog cleared just enough for them to see a pair of docks twenty feet away. As the boats corrected course, a bell rang out from somewhere in the unseen prison. Selinda jumped off the starboard side and onto the dock, quickly tying the ropes while another of Quincy's crew did the same for the other boat on the parallel dock. A flock of arrows sped their way, and Selinda dove back onto the boat just in time to avoid them. The other crew member wasn't as lucky.

"Mick!" someone yelled on the other boat, and the crew began to pull the injured man back onto the deck. Arnem and Denny were near him, and they each met Gemma's eyes from a distance. She read fear in both of their stares.

"It's time," Quincy called out. "Grab your shields and watch for projectiles. Let's go!"

Quincy led the way onto Terminus Rock, followed closely by Selinda and the others. Gemma was near the rear of the procession on one dock. On the other, Arnem and Denny were in a similar position, Denny with his new kalis and Arnem with the sword he'd retrieved in Ferathan months ago. Everyone had shields of various sorts—Denny's was more of a small square board with a makeshift handle—which deflected most of the next onslaught of arrows. Quincy, Arnem, and four others broke off and went a different direction while

Gemma, Denny, and eight more mercenaries followed Selinda.

They arrived at a low wall of rocks, which provided just enough cover for Gemma and the other archers to set up their shots. As Gemma pulled back her bowstring, Selinda whistled to her.

"Use this one instead," the woman said. She held out an arrow that had a rounded bag neatly affixed to the tip. She nocked a similar arrow and winked at Gemma. "Trust me."

Gemma watched as Selinda fired it off. She wasn't expecting the explosion that followed. While it wasn't nearly as powerful as the cannons that the Tzakabya soldiers had used in Emyhrsen, it did chip away at the stone parapet where their targets were hiding to reload. Gemma smiled as she fired off her own arrow and took cover. She had a regular arrow nocked and ready when one of the guards appeared, framed by the new hole in the wall. She let loose, and her aim was true. The man took the arrow in the neck and stumbled out of sight.

After a couple more rounds of firing explosive arrows, taking cover from opposing fire, and sending regular arrows through the newly created holes, the firing ceased from the other end. Gemma caught the sound of a man groaning in pain. She aimed into one of the openings above and waited. She released the arrow at the first sight of a target, but the man was quickly yanked backward by an unseen counterpart.

"Hold your fire!" The command came from the parapet, and the archers around Gemma all lowered their weapons. She followed suit as her nearly missed target stepped back into view. It was Arnem, followed closely by Quincy, his arm around Arnem's shoulder. Quincy called down to them, "We've taken the wall. The gate is clear."

Gemma and the others rushed to the portcullis, which

was propped open enough to crouch under. One of the mercenaries was positioned there to make sure it stayed clear. Gemma strapped her bow to her back as Denny came up to her.

"Are you doing okay?" Gemma asked him. Denny nodded, but she could see that something was bothering the boy. She gestured toward the designated gatekeeper. "Why don't you stay here and watch the gate with him?"

"Sure," Denny said.

Gemma patted him on the back, unsheathed her machete, and followed the others. The gate led them under the outer portcullis, and then only forty feet of gravel stood between them and the main prison building. A few aerial walkways stretched from the parapet to the prison. Gemma looked up to see Arnem, Quincy, and the others standing thirty feet above them on the inside of the wall. She and the rest of the crew ascended a rickety set of stairs to the top, where everyone regrouped to receive their new orders.

"Other than the dozen men spaced atop the outer walls and two guards at the gate, we haven't seen any signs of life in this place. The bell they rang should have woken any reinforcements, but nobody has come through those—"

Just as Quincy pointed at a door across the nearest walkway, it opened. Quincy dropped out of sight. Gemma let go of her machete and reached for her bow. It would have been too late had the newcomer been aiming at her, but the hastily shot arrow he fired flew right over their heads. As the man reached for another arrow, Selinda took off running across the aerial walkway toward him. She gave off a wild battle cry, and the man dropped his arrow. Selinda plowed into him and disappeared through the dark doorway. The man cried out in pain for a few seconds, and then there was silence.

Gemma and the others gathered their weapons and followed Selinda into an upper floor of the prison building. Selinda was stripping the man of his weapons when they arrived. He wept on the ground, blood pouring from his smashed nose.

"Please don't kill me," he cried. "I'm just a cook. I heard screaming, so I jumped out of bed and grabbed the only weapons I could find."

Gemma noticed for the first time that the man was wearing only his yellowed one-piece undergarment, soiled with blood and fresh urine following Selinda's attack. Quincy raised a sword over the man.

"Don't do it," Arnem said, gripping Quincy's sleeve. "I believe he's telling the truth."

"We could use his knowledge of this place," Gemma said. She walked to Arnem's side. His compassion and sensibility had been welcome traits on their last adventure, and she was glad to have him by her side again.

"Very well." Quincy lowered his sword. "I apologize. This is all simpler than I expected. Perhaps a bit too simple for comfort."

"He sent most of the guards away," the cook muttered from the floor. "The guards and the prisoners."

"So nobody is here?" Gemma asked. "The prisoners were set free?"

"No, no, not free. Moved to a different location. I don't know anything else. It's not like King Davin would confide in someone like me."

"What about the Solendaron priest?" Arnem asked. "You know, bald head and big mustache?"

"Well, he ain't no priest anymore," the cook said. "Not from what I hear."

Quincy stepped on the man's left arm. "Is he here or not?

We've come a long way for him, and I don't care if he's lost his faith or not."

"Yes! He's here! He's here!"

Quincy pulled the cook up roughly and shoved him into the hall. "Take us to him, and don't even think about playing tricks on us."

The cook didn't need to be told twice. He led them down the dark twisting hallway. A torch burned on one of the walls, and Quincy picked it up. It was another twenty feet and two more twists before they passed another torch, which Arnem grabbed. The heavy, rusted doors they passed all hung open, revealing empty cells beyond. The stench of standing sewage poured out of each doorway. A rat darted across the hall and leapt over Gemma's feet. She instinctively reached for her machete but knew it was pointless.

"Just this way," the cook called a little louder than necessary. Perhaps it was out of fear. Or perhaps—

The snap of a bowstring echoed in the dark hallway in front of them. The cook hit the ground, an arrow through his gaping mouth. Footsteps rushed away from them and down an unseen staircase in the shadows beyond.

"I'll get him," Quincy said. He ran toward their attacker and disappeared into the blackness. A grunt of pain came next.

With her machete ready for action, Gemma darted forward, following the light of Quincy's torch. She saw the torch on the ground where Quincy lay prone, the flame just barely illuminating the face of his attacker. It was a woman. She held a knife, but instead of attempting to stab Quincy a second time, she dropped the weapon at the sight of Gemma.

"I...I'm sorry!" She held her hands up. Like the cook, the woman was in her bedclothes. Gemma figured she was a housekeeper or another cook. "Please don't hurt me!"

"I know," Gemma said, "you're just protecting yourself. We didn't come to hurt you. We only—"

Before Gemma could finish, splinters of wood flew from the banister next to her. The staircase the archer had fled down was just a couple of feet away. The archer didn't seem to have a clear shot from the floor below, but Gemma and the woman ducked anyway. Someone flew over Gemma's crouched figure—Selinda. The mercenary made it down two of the steps before another arrow pierced the wall. As the archer reloaded, Selinda leapt over the railing. She plummeted down through the gap between the curved stairwell toward the level below. Their attacker stood right against the edge on the other side, attempting to nock his arrow, and Selinda reached out and grabbed him with one hand and the railing with the other. She managed to hold her own weight, but the archer attempted to shake her off. He let go of the bow, grabbed Selinda by her chest armor with his left hand, and landed a punch square in her face with his right.

Another clash broke out on Gemma's level as yet another unseen attacker surprised the mercenaries. While the others dealt with him, Gemma got to her feet and sped down the stairs. Just as the man's fist struck Selinda's face again, Gemma raised her machete and swung. It connected with the man's left arm, and Gemma got to experience just how precisely Quincy had sharpened the blade. As the guard lost his grip on Selinda, she lost hers on the railing. Gemma lunged forward and reached for her, but it was too late.

"No!" Gemma screamed. Selinda fell without a word. The thud of her body against the floor at the bottom of the stairwell was all Gemma heard.

# Chapter Nine
## DENNY

The place was cursed.

Denny didn't know *how* he knew it. He just did. Perhaps it was the smell of death, stronger than the stench of washed-up seaweed or the decaying corpses of seagulls that littered the unforgiving rocky shore of the island. But mostly it was the sound.

He didn't think anyone else heard it. At least, nobody else reacted as if they did. Denny was positioned against the portcullis with one of Quincy's mercenaries, guarding against any reinforcements, though he knew it was pointless—the place was practically empty. The mercenary didn't seem to notice the sound, but it nearly drove Denny to his knees. It was a ringing that resonated in his very teeth. His sinus cavities swelled and throbbed. His eyes twitched.

"You okay, boy?" his companion asked.

Denny turned to look at him, but the motion was too much. His vision darkened as his eyes rolled back in his head. The man caught him just before his head could slam against one of the spikes at the foot of the iron gate that was propped partially open five feet above the ground.

"You're following us," a woman said. Her voice wasn't overpowered by the ringing sound, nor did it rise above it—it seemed instead to be coming *from* the tone. It was like an instrument, holding out a high note for several measures before dropping into a lower register for a few bars. Denny's eyes returned to their normal position, and he looked around. There was no woman in sight. Still the voice continued: "I told you that you needed to forget about us. And yet there you are. You must stop now. Turn back. There's only pain in that place."

"Mom?" Denny whispered.

"Well, that's certainly the first time anybody has mistaken me for their mother," the mercenary said after a roaring laugh. "I suppose I *have* let my hair grow a little too long lately."

"No, it's—you don't hear that?"

"Hear what, boy? You sure you didn't hit your head?"

Denny twisted out of the man's arms. His mother's voice was gone again, replaced by the droning high pitch. He ran toward the ground-floor entrance to the main prison building.

"Kid, wait!"

Denny ignored him and pushed open the iron doors. The stench of mold and sewage greeted him, and the ringing crescendoed as he stepped through the doorway. His legs shook, not from fear but from that sound. He felt as if his teeth would shatter or his head would explode if the tone went on any longer, yet he pushed through it. He had never been to this place, had never seen it in his night visions, but he knew the way. There were no locked doors to challenge him, no guards waiting in the darkness to attack him.

He turned down a wide torch-lined hall. The flames

emitted just enough light for him to see where the corridor led. There was a staircase at the end. A woman was sprawled out awkwardly at the bottom. As he neared her, he realized it was Selinda. She groaned, and her eyes seemed to look through Denny. Blood seeped from her mouth. But the sound was calling, so Denny stepped over her and started up the stairs.

He was halfway up the first flight when Gemma sped down toward him. She was crying and almost crashed into him as she turned the corner.

"Denny?" Gemma said as she regained her balance. "Are you okay?"

Denny didn't answer her. He continued his climb to the second-floor landing while Gemma completed her descent to aid Selinda. He thought it was pointless; she was clearly beyond saving now, her neck twisted as it was.

The sound grew louder, but Denny somehow knew he still wasn't at the heart of it. He turned toward the next set of stairs, but the sound brought him to his knees before he could reach it.

*I'm coming, Mom. I hear you, and I'm coming.*

He pulled himself up, clinging tightly to the railing. On the third floor, he was greeted by a severed arm and a pool of blood. The work of Gemma's blade, he knew. He ignored it, stepped over the crying guard who lay in a fetal position on the floor, and headed down the nearest hallway, leaving a trail of bloody boot prints behind him. The sound of combat clattered down from the floor above where Arnem, Quincy, and the others clashed with a group of guards protecting this house of death, but it barely registered in his ears.

After winding through several corridors, past some cells with bars and others with heavy doors, Denny stopped. He grabbed a torch off the wall to his left and turned to his right, where a thick iron door stood slightly ajar. His hand shook as he lifted his arm, not from fear but from pain. His legs nearly buckled, but he caught himself on the doorway. He pulled the door open and stepped inside.

The moment he passed through the doorframe, the sound stopped.

The cell was slightly larger than he had expected. There were two cots that had been pushed together; both were well worn, the middles sunken, the pillows yellowed from saliva and sweat and grease. Papers were scattered around the floor. A makeshift desk sat along one wall, covered with more papers, an inkpot, and a rotting old quill. Denny shuffled through the papers. There were words scribbled all over them, not in neat lines but at every angle, as if someone had written them with their eyes closed. He shuffled through page after page. None of it made any sense until something caught his eye.

*End of the line.*

On another page, in between a string of random words, he saw it again.

*End of the line.*

He reached for more pages, but nothing on them stood out.

He turned back around to examine the room and noticed another stack of papers jutting out from under a pillow on one of the cots. He stepped over and pulled out the pages. The words were written more neatly and in nearly straight lines. The script was much more legible, even familiar.

"Mom!" he called out in recognition.

The words on the top page were more of the same. *End of the line. End of the line. End of the line.* He tossed the page aside. The second, third, fourth, tenth pages were all the same, just that one damn phrase over and over and over again.

The ringing sound hit him again full-on, the twisted sheet music in his head calling for it be played fortissimo. He tossed the pages into the air in frustration just as a cold wind snapped through the open barred window.

The draft seemed to catch the pages and keep them afloat as Denny screamed in pain, in anger. His scream was even louder than the high-pitched tone.

Simultaneously, all of the pages caught fire. Those in the air. Those on the cots. The papers on the desk and on the floor. Even the filthy, rough blankets that dangled off the sides of the cots went up in flames.

Denny noticed what was happening, but he couldn't stop screaming. He might not have stopped even if he could; it drowned out the other noise. He stepped back, away from the cots, out the door, into the corridor. His screaming echoed down the hall in both directions; it reverberated through each of the partially open prison cells.

After a minute or two or five—Denny had no idea—his voice grew hoarse and faded out. There was silence except for the crackling of the papers and blankets burning in what he knew had once been his parents' cell. He looked around and noticed wisps of smoke protruding from all of the cells. He walked farther down the hall and peered into each room, one by one. Every blanket on every bed was burning to cinders. Shirts and undergarments that had been carelessly left behind now added to the smoke that filled the third floor of the prison. The thick cloudiness mesmerized Denny, and he followed it, not caring where it led. It took the sound of a man coughing to pull him from the spell he was under.

"Denny?" a man called between sounds of asphyxiation.

Denny swatted the smoke in front of his eyes away. There on the other side of a set of bars was a sad, broken man. His head was no longer clean-shaven; instead there were clumps of brown-and-gray hair sprouting up. His upper lip was no longer adorned with the well-groomed handlebar mustache that had once made the man so recognizable. And—perhaps most shocking to Denny—the signature look of absolute assuredness had completely vacated the man.

"Marzele!" Denny reached for the barred door of the cell and pulled, but it didn't budge. "Why are you in here? The rest of the cells are empty!"

"To die, Denny. I'm here to die. It's best you escape before the smoke overtakes your lungs. Go!"

"No, we came here for you. Let me find the key. Go to the window and breathe the fresh air. I'll be right back!"

Denny turned and took off back down the hallway. The smoke was so thick that he couldn't quite make out where he was going. He bumped into the wall and fell. As he rose back to his feet, he realized how light-headed he was.

*End of the line*, he thought.

His eyes rolled back in his head for the second time that night before he collapsed to the floor.

# Chapter Ten
## MARZELE

He could have died up there. He could have let the smoke overtake him in his cell. If not the smoke, the starvation surely would've done him in. The few members of the prison staff who were left had clearly received orders to let him die. Marzele knew it.

And then the boy had shown up. The Dreamer, as Marzele had thought of him when he had believed that Denny and Gemma and Arnem and Richard were all part of some inane prophecy. It was the same prophecy that had led to the slaughter of the few remaining old men and women who'd once called themselves clergy of Solendaron.

Marzele spat on the ground. Even thinking about that name disgusted him. It was only a matter of time before Arnem or Gemma would say the name out loud, before he'd roll his eyes at them and turn away or yell at them to never speak of that false god again.

But was that what he really believed? Marzele wanted to say an unabashed *yes, absolutely, without a doubt*, but a small piece of him knew he couldn't.

"Let's get you some food and fresh water," the big man, Quincy, said. He had helped Marzele out of the cell once the key had been located and guided him down the stairs and out the doors of the prison. Even in the courtyard, the place stank of sewage and of death. Marzele turned his eyes back toward the prison and saw smoke seeping through the barred windows on every level. He longed to be in there with it, burning, ending his time in this wretched world.

"Denny will be okay," Gemma said.

Marzele turned to see a sad, worried expression on the girl whom he had only known to be brave and cunning, or at least to be growing into those things. She looked back at him, and Marzele knew what she was looking for. It was an expression that the clergy of many faiths knew well. She was looking to him for words of comfort, for a sense of hope. Out of habit, he nearly provided her with some uplifting message, but the thought of doing so made him gag. He turned away from her and spat again.

"You'll be okay too, Marzele. I'm sorry we didn't get to you sooner. Denny saw you in his dreams and found me, and we put this crew together as quickly as we could."

"You didn't need to come," Marzele said, though his throat was so scratchy from the smoke and parched from thirst that it sounded more like a beastly growl. He swallowed what saliva he could muster, turned, and faced her. He conjured up a softer voice. "Thank you for what you've risked. I'm afraid I'm not worth the danger you and the others have put yourselves in to free me, but thank you all the same."

"Nonsense. You risked your own well-being and that of your peers back when the rest of us were in danger in Emyhrsen. You didn't shy away from helping a group of strangers then. It was never a question whether or not

Arnem, Denny, and I would help you in your time of need. We're friends. Family."

*Family*. The word stung Marzele straight in the heart. When had Marzele ever had a family? He'd been brought to the Solendaron orphanage as a baby. As far as he knew, the woman who'd birthed him had died in the process, and the man who had helped formulate him during what he'd assumed was a drunken mistake of a night hadn't wanted anything to do with him—a helpless baby, practically still covered in afterbirth, barely detached from the cord that led into the fresh corpse he'd descended from. The cold, barren old ladies from the Solendaron orphanage had become his family then and had indoctrinated him into their cult whether he liked it or not. He had never been given a choice. It was all he'd known. He'd gone straight from the orphanage to the seminary to a temple two blocks away, and he'd never had a choice about any of it. Where in that had there been room for a family?

"They broke you."

Marzele turned around to face the speaker. It was Arnem, who had carried Denny down from the third-floor hallway just ahead of Quincy and Marzele. The boy must have been okay if Arnem had left him alone for even a second; the man cared more for that kid—who was not even his own blood— than anyone had ever cared for Marzele. Arnem's chubby hand plopped onto Marzele's right shoulder. "They hurt you. Tortured you. Psychologically, if not physically. But we're here now, Marzele. We're here to bring you home with us. You're safe."

Marzele looked from Arnem to Gemma and back. And then he laughed. *Safe. Home.* Those weren't words that had defined his life at any point, even if he'd spent every minute of it pretending they did. His laugh started out cynical, then grew hysterical. Arnem stepped back, his arm dropping to his side. Gemma reached for Marzele but then pulled back in confusion. The looks of fear that formed on their faces in that moment almost made Marzele happy. It wasn't that he wanted them to fear him, but there was a power to it that made him feel something. Not something he would have admitted to liking at any other point in his life. But now?

*Yes*, he thought.

*Fear me.*

# Chapter Eleven
## PALIGNON

Palignon hadn't brought any spare body bags with him when he and his three underlings had made their journey to Arnem Wynstone's farm. It should have been a simple arrest: one middle-aged man, one teenage boy. Palignon had led dozens of raids over the course of his career, hundreds of arrests, and most had gone without incident. There had been targets who'd had the power to set him on fire with nothing more than their breath, others who'd been able to lift him into the air and hurl him out the window using only their minds. But they'd always seen that resistance was futile, and they'd always surrendered without incident. The man and the kid were the last people he'd expected to set up deadly traps.

He fetched the horses, collected Sergeant Holman's oversize bedroll—it wasn't as if the man would have any further use for it—and stuffed the hulking corpse inside. A stretch of rope secured it, and Private Alice Taron and Private Markus Lang assisted him in lifting the body up onto Holman's horse for the ride back.

The stink of Capital City met their noses almost as soon as they caught sight of it. Palignon wanted nothing more than to bypass Fort Braxen altogether and ride straight home, but he knew that a stack of paperwork and a long debriefing awaited him back at the office of the Royal Mystic Committee. Besides, Llonda and Jensa had waited this long for his return; what was one more day?

Palignon, Taron, and Lang were admitted to the fort with no issue. Their first stop was the medical center, which accepted Holman's remains. The base lacked a morgue, so Palignon assumed the staff would stash the corpse in the ice closet at the rear of the mess hall. Palignon was thankful he didn't live on base and could avoid cafeteria meals for the next couple of days while Holman rested alongside the slabs of meat that hung there.

The administrative office was in disarray without proper leadership. Under Sir Marin Allemon, the place had been spotless, and there'd been regular inspections to make sure no one was cutting corners in their duties. Now paperwork was strewn across desks, and half the admins dressed as casually as if they were lounging around their homes on a weekend. A few hadn't bothered to even show up to work. Walking among them was Lieutenant Grushka Bryne, who stopped in his tracks when he spotted Palignon. After a couple of seconds of observing Palignon's face, his usual scowl drooped into something even more indicative of disappointment. He dropped a stack of papers onto the nearest desk and motioned for Palignon to follow him.

In the office the two peers shared, Bryne collapsed into his chair while Palignon pushed aside a stack of abandoned dishes and sat on the man's desk.

"So they anticipated your arrival?"

"They were ready for us. Holman was snared in their trap. He's gone."

"No clues where they fled to?" Bryne showed no concern for their fallen comrade or the effect of the loss on Palignon.

"They didn't exactly leave a note for us. Neighbors didn't know anything, and I wasn't in the mood to torture. Any reports on the rest of their crew?"

Palignon observed Bryne's face. The man had never looked happy about anything, even in their younger days, when they'd served in Aepistelle's military together. He hadn't even looked pleased at his own wedding. How Melinda had ever fallen for the man was beyond Palignon's understanding.

"No, but rebellion is fomenting around the kingdom. What a time for Allemon to disappear. This place needs leadership. Someone with unquestionable loyalty, fearless and tough—someone to give a swift kick to half the kids we employ."

Palignon lifted his arms. "Why, thank you, old friend. I also think I would be the perfect fit to take Allemon's place."

Bryne's laughter was as ugly as his face. "You can't even keep your home in order. Why would anyone entrust the Committee to you?"

"I blame the *unquestionable loyalty* part for that. I'm too busy serving the Committee to serve as a good husband and father."

"Perhaps it's time you went home. The paperwork can wait, unless you think Allemon will rise from the grave and give you a demerit for tardiness."

Palignon agreed.

A LANTERN ILLUMINATED A WINDOW ON THE THIRD FLOOR of the townhouse that had been converted into apartments. Excitement swept over Palignon as he made his way up the stairs. Being away from home as often as he was made a fluttery feeling fill his stomach any time he returned. Each homecoming was like seeing his beautiful Llonda for the first time all over again. She was his dream woman, and that feeling never faded.

He reached the top landing, the floorboards letting out their familiar creaks as he took three steps to the door. He procured the key from his pocket, slipped it into the lock, and grunted in confusion as it scraped like a boot on gravel and halted halfway in.

"Huh?"

He jiggled the key and put a little more muscle into it. Perhaps the change in the weather had caused the lock to warp. He worked the key out, breathed his moist breath on it, and rubbed it against his shirt. His next try was just as much of a failure.

Another creak of the floorboards, this time from the other side of the door.

"Llonda, it's me," he said in a stage whisper, not wanting to wake the neighbors downstairs.

The lock clicked from the inside, the handle turned, and Palignon's face was saved only by the quick reflexes that made him duck just as a glass bottle sailed over his head. The bottle shattered against the wall. So much for not waking the neighbors.

His reflexes weren't quick enough to avoid the door, however, which Llonda tried to slam closed. Palignon's forehead blocked it from shutting all the way.

"What was that for?" he asked his wife.

Llonda rolled her eyes at him and walked away toward the kitchen. "Thought you were a burglar," she quipped coldly. "Meant to kill you."

Palignon looked back at the shards on the ground, shook his head, and followed her inside.

"You don't live here anymore, remember?" Llonda said as she resumed drying dishes and placing them back on the shelves. "Didn't you get the paperwork from my attorney?"

Palignon thought back to the office and the endless stacks of papers and piles of scrolls that graced the desks and overflowed onto the floor. "They may have gotten lost in the shuffle. Things have been a bit hectic at work."

"Things have been a bit hectic *here*, Cragen. With your family. With your *daughter*. You think you're out there saving the world? You can't even care for your own flesh and blood. We're through. Sign the papers and find your own place to sleep."

"Llonda, please don't do this. I've missed you."

"You go away for weeks or months at a time without even a letter to tell us you're alive or thinking about us. I'm here raising our daughter alone, working in the bakery, keeping house." She threw the dish towel to the floor and stomped on it.

"I'm trying to change things. Sir Allemon is gone now, and they're going to need someone to lead the Committee. If I get his position, I won't need to be on the road so much. This could be huge for us, Llonda." He bent down and reached for the towel. "We'd be able to buy a bigger house and—"

"Bigger house?" Llonda screamed, stamping her foot down on the towel before he could pick it up. "You don't even help around this one, and I don't have enough time to keep it up. How do you expect us to tend to a larger house?"

"We'll hire someone. The money we'll have, the power, the—"

The towel flew up into the air and stopped between the arguing pair. Palignon stepped back, nearly tripping over himself. A second towel rose from the counter to his right and floated toward the first one. As if someone were controlling them like puppets, the towels took the shapes of two little people, the corners protruding like arms. They came together, corners touching, and began a dance through the air between Palignon and Llonda.

"What is happening right now?" he whispered.

Llonda crossed her arms and rolled her eyes. "You weren't supposed to see this."

His attention was drawn back to the counter as the three remaining plates next to the basin launched and circled them, spinning as they went. Palignon reached out and plucked one out of the air. Suddenly the others stopped and dropped to the floor.

More shards to clean up.

"She's been doing things like this for months now, ever since she started to come of age."

"Jensa is doing this? But...why have I never seen it until now?"

"You're never here. You've abandoned your family!" Llonda yanked one of the towels from its dance and snapped it through the air, missing Palignon by an inch and cracking it against the table he'd backed into. The other towel dropped to the floor more gracefully than the plates.

A rustling in the next room was followed by the interior door opening and his daughter's bleary-eyed stare.

"Dad?"

His heart dropped. She had grown in the time he'd been

gone. Three months was more like years at her age. He'd missed so much, and whatever this was, this sorcery, must be terrifying for her.

Palignon took a step toward her, and her confusion morphed into fear. Even in the dimness of their apartment, Palignon saw tears forming in his daughter's eyes.

"Jensa? What's wrong?" he asked. He took another step, but she turned and slammed the door.

"She's scared of you, Cragen. She's scared of what you'll do now that you know."

"Know *what*?" He turned back to Llonda. "What does she think I'll do?"

"You're loyal to your Royal Mystic Committee. Every day you find others like her, lock them up, kill them, do whatever else you do that you don't like to talk about. You hate their kind. *Her* kind."

"How is this possible?" Palignon asked.

Llonda's glare bore into him. Movement caught his eye behind her as something lifted into the air.

A knife.

It wobbled two feet above the countertop. He took a deep breath and stood his ground as it launched toward him, missing his face by a fraction of an inch and lodging in the wall behind him.

"She's not alone, Cragen. I just haven't had enough time to teach her how to subdue it."

"But you—but you—"

"I'm a freak. A monster. I am what you spend your life hunting, as is your own daughter."

A long silence followed. Palignon moved his mouth, but no sound came out. Llonda shook her head at the pathetic man and turned away from him.

"Get out. Sign the papers, return them to my attorney, and never return."

He looked back at the closed bedroom door. Jensa wept loudly behind it. Again he tried to speak, to call out to her, to tell her he loved her no matter what, but he couldn't do it.

Palignon went to the front door and left without saying goodbye to his family.

# Chapter Twelve
## GEMMA

Four of Quincy's mercenaries passed through the prison doors carrying a makeshift stretcher holding Selinda. They had set her broken bones and patched her up as much as they could. Jerod, the closest thing the group had to a medic, had gone through what was left of the prison's small medical ward, but the place seemed to have been severely neglected starting long before the building had been abandoned.

"Selinda's still alive thanks to you, Gemma," Quincy said. Gemma looked at him with tears in her eyes. "If you hadn't stopped that guard when you did, it could have been a lot worse."

"It doesn't feel like I did enough, though. Look at her."

"It *never* feels like you've done enough. When your father and I were in the military and we lost nearly everyone we served with, we still had to keep going. When we struck down an enemy and shed blood, it wasn't enough. Even when we thought we'd spared Aepistelle from evil twenty-five years ago, it still was not enough. The important thing is that we keep going, keep fighting for what is good and pure in this world."

Gemma knew he was right. She had seen that same heaviness in her father for her whole life. Despite his heroics before she was born, Geoffrey Calvertson had never been at ease, never rested. His mind had deteriorated from the horrors inflicted upon him during the war. The world had moved on, and new struggles had arisen. Gemma knew that even after she was dead and buried, there would still be struggles, would still be the need for good people to rise up and take action.

"I suppose all we can do now is go home," Gemma said. "We'll get Selinda to a real doctor and then wait and see how King Davin responds to our rebellion."

Quincy chuckled. "You aren't going to get to rest that easily. Not when you have a story to tell the world." He beckoned for Gemma to follow him under the prison's portcullis and toward the boats.

They arrived at the boat Gemma and Quincy had sailed in on. Quincy disappeared into the cabin for a moment and came out with a package wrapped in a piece of hide. He handed it to Gemma.

"What is this?" she asked. She reached in and pulled out a stack of papers. "You brought this?"

"You've spent weeks working on that, revising it, perfecting it. The world is going to forget that anything ever happened if you wait until it's ancient history before you finally bring the truth to light."

"I wrote it when we still thought King Davin was imprisoned," Gemma said. "Once a new ruler was put into place, we had planned to assess the situation to see if it was safe to release. But with Davin free and back on the throne, how am I going to convince anyone to publish this?"

"Gemma, you're capable of anything. You were as effective as my highly trained fighters up in that prison. You led a scrappy team against an army of tree monsters and slavers back in Emyhrsen. Do you really think revealing the truth to the people of Aepistelle will be any harder than those things?"

Gemma thumbed through the pages of her handwriting. She had started the manuscript with her first meeting with Richard the Elusive, then had gone on to describe the eerie but seemingly lifeless Forest of Despair. Would the world believe what she'd written about the ageless town of Ferathan with its witch protector and her army of children? Or about the giant Ogressi who had been their ally in the battle against the killer trees? Gemma didn't think she would believe those things herself if she heard about them secondhand. And how about the most important part—that the king of Aepistelle was in league with the Tzakabya invaders who had enslaved the people of Emyhrsen, and that he'd been defeated by a witch and a giant and a young historian and a homeless psychic boy and a few retired heroes?

But it was true. It was all true.

And so Gemma, Denny, Arnem, and Marzele boarded one boat and aimed it toward the coast of Capital City to the east. Quincy, Selinda, and the rest of the mercenaries set off north on the other boat to return home.

*Home.* It dawned on Gemma that Capital City had been home for the Calvertson family only mere months ago. Now she'd be entering the place as a fugitive.

THE SMELLS OF THE FISH MARKET ON THE DOCKS OF Capital City had always kept Gemma away from the place in her younger years, but in the last few weeks she had gotten used to the similarly pungent equivalent up north where Quincy lived. She had taken morning walks from Quincy's home to the boardwalk where Quincy and the other fisherfolk brought up their catches, made their deals, and tendered their goods.

The scene on the Capital City piers was nearly identical, except it seemed to Gemma that there was a grungier film over everything. Soot from the nearby factories, perhaps, with their smokestacks that injected the air with gods knew what. The smells weren't just of oxidizing seafood but also of rot and filth. Of people from all walks of life crowding together, rubbing their sweaty arms against each other as they passed between stalls, in alleyways and streets.

A few months away from her hometown seemed like a lifetime to Gemma. No longer was it the place she had enjoyed exploring as a young girl with her brother, George, on her tail, threatening that their parents were going to hear about her disobedience. The restaurants she had once frequented after long days of classes at the university held no glamor for Gemma as she made her way past them now. The park in the center of the city with its grove of trees she had once pretended to get lost in like it was some expansive forest paled in comparison to the landscapes she'd visited on her journey to the northlands.

Different too was the woman herself. The Gemma of *then* would never have walked the streets with a machete hanging from her belt or a bow on her back. The company she kept was also a departure: a gangly teenage boy, a stout man her father's age, and a downtrodden priest whose eyes still couldn't quite adjust to the sunlight after he'd been locked away in a dark prison for weeks.

"I thought Esteron City was expansive," Denny said. "It's a mere village compared to this."

"Aye, Denny." Arnem patted the boy on the back. "It really makes me miss the intimate comforts of Plentimore Valley."

"I called this place home my entire life. Other than my quickly shattered dream of attending a university in the Southern Reaches, I never imagined leaving this place. Now it couldn't be more alien to me." Gemma glanced toward Marzele, and the man seemed to flinch away from her. He'd been almost entirely mute as they'd sailed away from the island from which they'd liberated him. Everyone else had stood at the bow of the boat as they'd approached the bay where Capital City polluted the waters, but Marzele had crouched in the shadows belowdecks.

It was late in the afternoon by the time the crew made it to the eastern borough. They had detoured to the south to avoid the castle district, which was sure to be crawling with guards, both uniformed and plainclothes. Gemma had no doubt that the numbers on patrol had doubled after the recent events.

Gemma's discomfort grew steadily as they approached the Calvertson family home. She was one block away when she realized it was more than that. "This isn't right," she said.

"We're walking into a trap," said Denny.

Gemma turned to face him. "Did you see it in a vision?"

"No, it's just obvious. There will be guards watching your house, waiting for you or your family to return."

"And even if there are none of Davin's guards, there will at least be some deputized neighbors of yours," Arnem said. "No doubt they've been told that the Calvertson family is naught but a band of traitors."

It made Gemma feel sick in the depths of her stomach, but she knew they were right. "Several of the families in our row worked at the castle—maids like my mother, or cooks and servers and their ilk. They'll be quite upset that their work was interrupted after the attack on the castle. I can only imagine how happily they would accept a few coins for turning me in."

"Aye, and not just you," Marzele said, his voice filled with defeat, not a trace remaining of the confident yet gentle tone he'd had when Gemma had first met him in Emyhrsen. He pointed across the street, where a large sign hung on the side of the neighborhood postal office.

WANTED FOR CRIMES AGAINST THE CROWN; REWARD FOR INFORMATION ON THE WHEREABOUTS OF THESE INDIVIDUALS, it proclaimed. There was a list of names followed by the official seals of King Davin, the Kingdom of Aepistelle, and the Royal Mystic Committee.

Gemma's heart ached more with every name she read. Her brother. Her parents. Arnem, Denny, and Marzele. Richard. Jestan. And her. There were others she didn't recognize, thrown in to fulfill some agenda or another, but Gemma kept looking back at her own name.

It stung.

Her knees buckled, but Arnem caught her. He untethered the bow from her back and guided her to sit on a nearby bench.

"It's not been lost on me that we're seen as enemies of Aepistelle," she said to her companions once she was able to catch her breath again. "But to see it in writing in my own neighborhood...it really cuts deep."

"You gave up your own comfortable life—your own future —to do what was right," Arnem said. He looked from Gemma to Denny as he spoke, addressing them both. "You put it all on the line: freed an entire nation in Emyhrsen from the bonds of slavery; slew an army of monsters; ensured that those same evils would not make their way here to Aepistelle. You don't deserve this. None of us do."

"Deserve?" Marzele scoffed. "What do any of us deserve? Who is to say what is deserved or what is right?"

"Your god, for one," Arnem replied. "Are we not serving the light with our actions? Isn't that what you risked your own safety for?"

"I did, yes. And I can see now that I was foolish. I devoted my entire life to the Lord Solendaron. I gave up my own free will to study, to preach His word, to help others in His name. And what did it get me in the end? What did it get my friends? What did it get Lord Solendaron Himself? The Light of Solendaron is still drowned in shadow. Davin is back on his throne. Everyone I knew and loved is dead because of that failed attack I helped lead. Or almost everyone."

Marzele glanced back at the sign. Gemma couldn't tell which name he was focused on, but she was certain it was one of the few that was not a member of their party. CHAUNCEY ZYTHONE. POLARIS STONEFIELD. HORACE WELLWORTH. ABERDINE ARGYLE. Not one of those names meant anything to her.

"Where are you going?" Arnem called after him as Marzele crossed the street.

The disheveled man stopped when he reached the other side. He turned and called back to them, "There's someone I must locate. Someone I trusted. Someone I believe deceived me." With that, Marzele disappeared into the crowd and, apparently, out of their lives.

# Chapter Thirteen
## GEMMA

George's shop sat in a row of flat, single-story buildings filled with tradesmen who had no need for presentable storefronts to attract window shoppers and foot traffic. It was nestled among warehouses and factories. The sun was waning. The industrial neighborhood had been steadily abandoned by its tenants as they closed up shop for the day. Gemma had avoided eye contact with any passersby who might recognize her by pretending to engage in a deep conversation with Arnem about a display of street art on an alley wall. Denny had been sent to scope out the shop while they hung back around a corner. The boy returned a minute later with a relieved look upon his face.

"There was no notice on the door," he said. He'd been the one to stroll past the Calvertson family home as well, and he'd found a red letter there with the same seals as the wanted poster, claiming the home had been seized by the crown. "It does look like the place has been ransacked, though."

Gemma and Arnem followed the boy the rest of the way once the street was clear. One of the stall doors hung crookedly off its hinges, leaving a gap large enough for the trio to enter. Gemma lit one of the oil lamps her brother had hung from the many beams and columns and took in the sight.

"All his tools are gone," she said. She checked the back room. "His inventory has been stolen as well."

"Must have been common thieves," Arnem observed. "I don't think the guards would have any use for metalworking tools and horseshoes. We should be safe here for now if Davin's men haven't bothered with this place."

"There's a couch in the stockroom. I think George liked to sleep here when he didn't have the patience to help out with my father at home. Or maybe to avoid his girlfriend, Wellyn."

"Do you think she'll come here looking for him?" Denny asked. He yawned and rubbed his eyes. "Would she turn us in if she found us?"

"I don't think she's much of a risk. She may be upset with George for leaving her without any notice, but she's always been good to our family. Denny, why don't you go get some rest on the couch. You too, Arnem."

Gemma walked over to one of the overturned tool chests and lifted it up. Underneath was a coatrack that had cracked in half under the weight of the chest. She grabbed one of her brother's oversize wool coats and a knitted cap, which she pulled low over her brow.

"Are you going somewhere?" Arnem asked.

"I came back to town for a reason." Gemma reached into her bag and pulled out a stack of papers. "I need to get this manuscript out into the world. It may put us in more danger, but it's the first step to clearing our names and correcting the course of this kingdom."

"We'll come with you," Denny said, but Gemma noticed that his voice lacked conviction.

"No, Denny. This is something I must do on my own. It's my burden. If I'm not back by sunrise, you two need to get back to Quincy's home. Arnem's family is waiting."

She didn't wait to hear their protests. She put her weapons down on a workbench, emptied her bag of everything except the manuscript, and crawled back out under the mangled shop door.

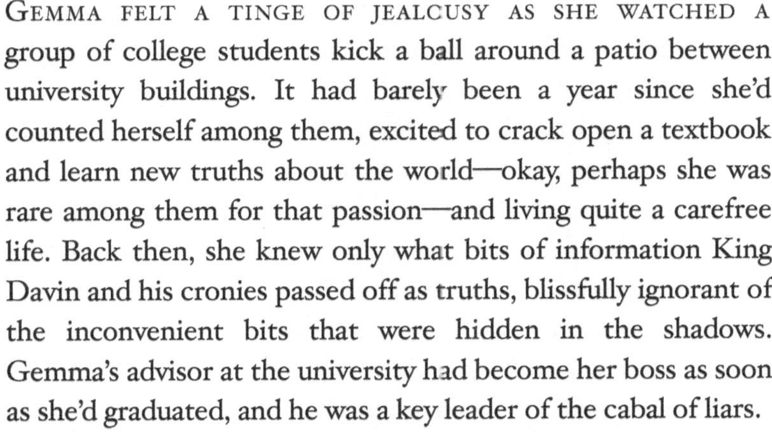

GEMMA FELT A TINGE OF JEALOUSY AS SHE WATCHED A group of college students kick a ball around a patio between university buildings. It had barely been a year since she'd counted herself among them, excited to crack open a textbook and learn new truths about the world—okay, perhaps she was rare among them for that passion—and living quite a carefree life. Back then, she knew only what bits of information King Davin and his cronies passed off as truths, blissfully ignorant of the inconvenient bits that were hidden in the shadows. Gemma's advisor at the university had become her boss as soon as she'd graduated, and he was a key leader of the cabal of liars.

*Why, then, am I going straight to him now?* Gemma wondered. Yet she couldn't stop her feet from leading her straight into the office from which he managed the University Press. As she crossed the courtyard, she looked up at the third floor, where his desk was. His flickering lanterns lit up the otherwise dark building, just as she'd expected. At the entrance, covering the sign announcing the place as the headquarters of the University Press, was another poster with the list of names that included Gemma and her family. Still she pressed on. She reached for the handle, pushed the door open, and stepped inside.

Gemma climbed the stairs in total darkness. At the third-floor landing, she saw a sliver of light escaping from under Garrod Hannon's door. She listened for a moment, heard no conversation, and opened the door.

"Not even a knock, as usual, Ms. Calvertson. It's funny how one's status as a national terrorist and fugitive doesn't change one's habits."

Hannon didn't look up from the papers he'd been combing over with his quill and the red ink he preferred for marking up his writers' drafts. He gestured with his writing hand for her to sit in the chair opposite his desk, drops of ink raining down from the tip of his quill as he did so. Gemma couldn't help but be reminded of the sprays of blood from Walker's body when he had been torn apart from the inside on the streets of Ferathan.

After a minute passed without another word, Hannon apparently decided he'd torn apart the hard work of one of his underlings as viciously as suited him. He plopped the quill into the inkpot and met Gemma's eyes. It wasn't a look of shock or terror or even pity. He looked exactly as he'd looked for years in the classroom or in this very office when he'd collected Gemma's assignments.

"Well? What have you got for me, Ms. Calvertson?" he asked as if this were any other day, any other meeting between teacher and student or manager and subordinate. Gemma was taken aback. A hundred thoughts ran through her mind, but she could not turn a single one of them into words. Hannon noticed, and the blasé look on his face turned into an amused one. "I'm only kidding. I know what you've got for me—a great reward. I need only call out my window, and within minutes, the Royal Mystic Committee will be here to take you away to the gallows. But relax, Gemma. You obviously think there's some chance I'm not as fully in King Davin's pocket as some might assume." He gestured toward a side table filled with liquor bottles and small glasses. "Can I interest you in a drink?"

"Oh, no, thank you. You go ahead."

"No, I don't really have a taste for the stuff. I take a drink with others when they want one. The alcohol puts them at ease, forms a bit of liquid camaraderie between us so I can more easily squeeze information out of them. No better way to get a source, short of blackmail and coercion. But it doesn't appear we need that. You and I have a history, Gemma, don't we?"

"We do, sir. A history in which you sent me off into a trap."

"A trap, perhaps, but was it meant to ensnare you? To ensnare Richard the Elusive? Or did it have another purpose entirely? I take it you received the scroll from my late friend, Mr. Telman Abernath of the Royal Aepistelle Library?"

"I did, but—"

"That was my idea. I wanted it to be delivered to Richard. I wanted him to have a missing piece in his puzzle about the impending apocalypse. Abernath and I worked tirelessly to acquire that lost bit of Solendaron scripture. Even the surviving priests of that order had no knowledge of its existence. That was the spark Richard needed to go off and save the world again, wasn't it?"

"It was, yes. Why would you have gone against King Davin, though? You've been part of his regime longer than I've been alive."

Hannon stood up and paced to the window. From where she sat, Gemma couldn't see the courtyard below, but the man's face didn't indicate he'd seen anything that alarmed him. He turned back toward her.

"I have a daughter around your age. Not as inquisitive. Not at all as driven. She went down to the University of the Southern Reaches, but like most of the delinquents there, she's interested only in the late-night get-togethers. The libations. Six years in, and she's not any closer to graduating with a degree or a suitable husband. She's living in ignorance of the fragile peace that exists in our world and of the lies and crimes I helped orchestrate to get us there. And then there's my role here, playing arbiter of truth—writing history as my liege wants it to be told, not as it actually is.

"I thought I was doing this so that my daughter could go off and do what she wanted without a care in the world. But blood has been spilled. Thousands have died at the hands of the Royal Mystic Committee. Friends and neighbors have turned on one another for practicing their religions or their witchcraft and sorcery. People have been dragged out into the streets and burned alive or sent off to prison camps and far-off islands to be studied like animals. Your entire generation was fed my lies from the moment you were old enough to swallow them, all so that my little Nissala could go drink her liver into an early grave in peace."

Hannon walked over to the liquor table, pulled a stopper out of a bottle, and filled two glasses. "I guess I do want one of these after all." He set one glass on the desk in front of Gemma, then clinked his own gently against hers and swallowed it in one gulp. Gemma just stared at the translucent brown contents.

"Your quest for the truth spoke to me at the right time, Gemma. You were my best student. There's a handful like you each year who stand out above the rest. Every professor on campus wanted to rope you into their program, but you chose this one. You cared so much about the world, about the war that had damaged your father. My career was built on lying about those very things, and there you were, ready to tear it all down if you could only learn what I'd been suppressing in the name of the king. Some might say it was fated, if they believe in such things. Regardless, there you were.

"Abernath and I had been friends since childhood. We rose up to our respective positions almost hand in hand. We conspired together to burn most of the books that threatened King Davin's vision for his kingdom, the fragile peace that united all the other kings and made them bow down to him and give him control of their lands. It weighed on us both, though. We never told anyone, not even each other, how much it was killing us inside. Over the years, all our internal justifications crumbled, one after another. We could see the defeat in each others' eyes. It was almost an unspoken agreement between us, sending you off to deliver that last scroll to Richard under the cover of your assignment."

"If you two never told anyone you'd given me the scroll, how did Davin know? He sent my friend Walker to follow me and arrest Richard once it was delivered. The Royal Mystic Committee was on to your plan."

Hannon dropped back into his chair. He reached across the desk, grabbed Gemma's untouched glass, and swallowed its contents down, wincing as it hit the back of his throat.

"King Davin has an army of seers. He pretends to abhor people with abilities and kills most of them for public show, but his entire rule is built upon them. He's wise enough not to trust anyone, especially those of us in his inner circle. We're his biggest threats. I'm certain he was using his seers to watch me. I didn't tell a soul about the plan, and I know

Abernath took it to his grave. Davin may be privy to this meeting right now, for all we know."

Gemma reached into her bag. She ran her fingers along the top page of her manuscript, feeling the imprints made by her pen. "You sent me out on an assignment to learn more about the Great Journey from Richard the Elusive's perspective. Obviously I learned a whole lot more than that. What you and I know about King Davin should be more than enough—"

"To get us both killed. And our families. And everyone we love. Gemma, I cannot publish what you have in that bag. It's beyond me why Davin has even let me live this long, but I've done all I'm willing to do to set events in motion." He rose and walked to the window again. "This must be our last meeting. For your own safety, I advise you to burn what's in your bag, then run away. Never look back. Take your parents and go back to Emyhrsen. Aepistelle will never be safe for you."

"But Mr. Hannon, I—"

"I know, Gemma. That's not who you are. You won't rest until the truth is out there. That's why I'm going to give you thirty minutes to get as far away from my office as you can before I flag down the Royal Mystic Committee. Escape while you can, and find a way to tell this story. I wish I could print it, but that's not going to happen. Thirty minutes, Gemma. Go."

Gemma didn't need to be told again. She stood up, slung the bag over her shoulder, and headed for the door. As she passed through the doorway, she turned her back. "I don't think Nissala is the disappointment, Mr. Hannon. It's not her at all."

She pulled the door closed and made her way down the dark hall, knowing the path to the stairway well from her own time as an underling of Garrod Hannon. She was two strides from the top step when an arm wrapped around her torso and a damp cloth was pressed against her mouth and nose.

Gemma's knees buckled as consciousness escaped her.

# Chapter Fourteen
## MARZELE

Marzele had no trouble finding Horace Wellworth's home. It was the last place he'd stayed before the failed attack on King Davin's castle. The house was nestled between many other town houses belonging to the rich and powerful of Capital City, high on Sixty-Fifth Street where the old wealth still ran rampant. Most of the families also had larger estates outside the city, either lining the coast a half day's ride south or along the Great Centeron Lake to the east.

Horace had always been a rare example of a Solendaron priest with a bottomless bank account. His mother had been devout, and his father had gone along with the faith because he'd adored everything else about his wife, so they had been among its top funders. Horace had decided at a young age that he had no mind to enter the family business, so his relationship with his father had begun to fray in his teenage years. He'd become an apprentice priest before he'd even finished his schooling, which roiled his father to no end. Horace's mother, however, had been ecstatic and hadn't let her husband deprive their son of his inheritance. There were no other children in the Wellworth family, after all. Upon King Davin's decree that religions could no longer be practiced in Aepistelle, Horace had publicly denounced the Solendaron faith and was welcomed back into the family home with open arms by his father.

It had been a ruse, of course, and Horace had remained a key part of the conspiracy to overthrow King Davin and restore religious freedom to Aepistelle. But then Marzele had seen Horace's name on the poster outside of the postal office.

That meant several things to Marzele. First, it meant that Horace Wellworth was still alive after the failed attack. Second, it could have meant that Horace had been allowed to live by King Davin, that Davin's guards had been ordered to spare him just as they'd been ordered to let Marzele live. Davin hadn't mentioned Horace on board the ship to Emyhrsen or on the way to Terminus Rock. It seemed he would have goaded Marzele about it once the tables had turned and Marzele was the one behind bars. Unless, of course, Horace had been working with King Davin and the Royal Mystic Committee all along. Marzele had blamed himself for the priests' failure at the castle walls because he'd tipped off Serena Calvertson about the attack. Perhaps the blame was not his alone.

"Lord help me understand this—" he whispered before cutting himself off. *No, Lord Solendaron is not with me. He's of no use to me anymore.*

With his disheveled appearance, Marzele normally would have attracted unwanted attention in such an upscale neighborhood. However, it was nearly dark when he arrived, and most of the well-to-do residents were inside their homes, dining on their five-course meals, being waited on by a host of servants. He stuck to the shadows, avoiding the glow of the gas lamps on the immaculate sidewalks. He saw the familiar iron gates with the gilded *W*'s. The hinges creaked loudly when he pushed open one side. He froze and looked around, but he didn't appear to have attracted any unwanted attention. Marzele turned back toward the house. No lights on inside. No sounds from Horace's stringed instrument collection.

On the porch, Marzele ran his eyes up and down the door. There wasn't a sign claiming the property had been seized by the Royal Mystic Committee, nor was there evidence that any guards had forced their way in following the massacre outside of the castle. It was the same immaculate maroon door that had always accented the place.

Marzele put his hand to the knob. Out of habit, he whispered a prayer in the tongue of the Solendaron, but no glow came to his hand. The knob didn't melt under a supernatural heat. He tried turning the knob instead, but the door was securely locked.

He made his way around the side of the building, trying each window to no avail. Marzele dropped down behind a shrub as voices rose up on the other side of the fence.

"Not on your life, Veera! Wines from the Reaches could never compete with a fine red from Plentimore Valley."

An elderly couple strolled across the neighboring property. If they had heard Marzele's footsteps shuffling through the Wellworth gardens, they apparently hadn't thought anything of it. Once they disappeared into the night, Marzele got back to his feet. He turned another corner around the back of the house and froze in his tracks.

A glass panel on the rear door had been smashed in.

Marzele crouched at the door and listened. Only silence. He wrapped his fingers around the knob and turned. He heard a click, and the door pushed inward.

He stepped inside the dark house. A smell greeted his nostrils upon his first inhale. On a small table by the door was a lantern. He lit it with the accompanying matches and looked around the room. A dining table with eleven chairs sat in the middle of the room. A twelfth chair lay on the floor at the head of the table. A serving plate holding what Marzele had no doubt had once been a fine meal crawled with insects. He walked over and pounded his fist on the table, sending flies airborne. He shined the light onto the food and watched maggots worming their way into the remains of a steak. It looked to have been a nice cut at one point. His stomach lurched.

The swinging door that led to the kitchen hung crooked. He pushed through it, and that last bit of pressure sent it crashing down onto the granite tiles. A rat leapt out of the way with only a fraction of a second to spare. It scurried between Marzele's feet and out the back door. A set of knives lay on the counter. A dark substance crusted the blade of one of them. The same color dotted the countertop, the cabinet door just below, and the tiles underneath.

Blood.

*The Royal Mystic Committee would not have used the back door. They go for a public show of authority whenever possible. I've seen enough of my friends flayed in the streets. No, this was someone else. Had to have been a group if they carried Horace into this room and held him down. He's too massive for one man alone.*

Marzele followed a trail of blood to the other side of the kitchen. It appeared that Horace had evaded his captors, made his way over here, and then, judging from the blood that had soaked into the wallpaper, had been pinned against the wall next to the cellar door. Marzele pulled the door open and thrust the lantern through the frame.

*I've been down there before*, he thought. He took the steps carefully. There was no more blood here, no more signs of struggle. Horace must not have made it through the door before his assailants had grabbed him and removed him from his house.

Marzele reached the bottom. The cellar was just as he remembered. It was full of excess: excess jars of food lined one shelf; excess bottles of wine filled every nook and cranny; excess furniture was stored carefully under large sheets, ready to be brought upstairs for the next gala. Marzele knew there would be nothing worth finding here, though his stomach growled at the sight of the preserved foods after eating nothing but mysterious gruel at the prison for the past few weeks.

Marzele walked between the lounge chairs and dining tables to the other side of the basement. He opened a door. It led to another chamber and another door into what looked like a mere closet. Marzele stepped through and pulled open a hidden panel, revealing a latch. He undid the latch, and the wall opened up on unseen hinges. Another staircase led deeper below the ground. There, an elaborately carved wooden idol of the Ever-Giving Sun hung from a wall. Below it, several robes of the Solendaron priesthood hung on hooks. Many other hooks remained unused.

There were seventeen priests and priestesses who had set out on the march against King Davin. If Marzele had counted the empty hooks, though, he'd have found that only sixteen were empty. He didn't need to count—Horace's robe was big as a tent and easy to spot. It hung there, as spotless as the day the man had taken his vows, not a speck of blood or dirt to be seen.

Marzele turned around, about to make his way back up the stairs when he noticed the desk. It was a rolltop, and it was locked. Marzele checked the drawers, but they were filled only with spare quills, pots of ink, and blank rolls of parchment. He glanced around the room. A bookshelf held mostly texts from their order. He ran his thumb across the spines. In between a book on prayers for the dead and another on officiating wedding ceremonies, there was a book Marzele didn't recognize from his own collection, which he had burned years ago when the texts had become illegal. He pulled it out, and something fell from within and clanked to the ground.

The key.

He picked it up, unlocked the desk, and rolled the top up. There were clippings from the *Capital City Courier* strewn about, each of them describing an unsolved homicide in the city. Several pieces of paper were covered in Horace's neat, prep school–trained handwriting. In the middle sat a map of Capital City. In the southern ward, there were several stars drawn in thick ink. Around that section, Horace had drawn a circle. Marzele swept up the newspaper articles and gave them a closer look. Every act of violence described had taken place in the locations Horace had marked on the map.

Marzele stacked the clippings and Horace's notes, folded them roughly into the map, and stuffed the bundle into his pocket. There was a crumpled pile of cash in one corner of the desk, which Marzele helped himself to as well. He turned to leave, but the idol of the sun drew his eyes again. He stared at it transfixed, remembering his youth in the care of the priestesses, his training for the priesthood, the years of darkness after Davin had banned religion, the deaths of his friends in front of the castle. And Horace, who had apparently set them all up to die and then come home and hung his robe neatly back on its hook.

Marzele lobbed the lantern at the robe. The glass shattered, and the robe took only seconds to go up in flames. The fire spread to the other robes and lapped up everything around it that would burn.

As Marzele ascended the stairs from the cellar, the idol of the Ever-Giving Sun caught fire. The flames rose, spreading to the first floor and the support beams. By the middle of that night, the Wellworth family home had collapsed in on itself, turning the last remnants of the Solendaron faith into a charred mess buried several feet below the ground.

# Chapter Fifteen

DENNY | ARNEM

Denny's eyes opened just before his head slammed into the bottom of the table as he sat up. He peeked across the room at the couch. Arnem turned onto his side, but the pattern of his slumbering breaths did not change. Gemma had suggested that Denny take the couch in the back room of her brother's shop because the boy had looked so exhausted, but Denny still hadn't gotten used to the comforts of a cushioned bed. His spine had apparently developed in its own unique way during his years of living on the streets, and the only place he could sleep deeply was on a hard flat floor. He had settled under the table, where the floor of the shop seemed slightly less dusty, and gladly allowed Arnem to take the couch.

Denny walked to the window, peeled back one corner of the curtain, and took in the night sky. He hated this polluted city. Even Esteron City had a better view of the stars, though the last couple of months had revealed that the eternal canopy of the sky held thousands more bright lights than he'd ever seen from his rooftop abode. Whether it was from a clearing in the Forest of Despair or the Wynstone family home in Plentimore Valley, Denny had taken to enjoying the sights overhead when the night was clear enough. Here, though, between the exhaust from smokestacks, the fog from the bay, and the light of the countless lanterns around the city, Denny could hardly make out a single familiar cluster in the sky.

He let the curtain drop back into place. As he turned around, Denny's elbow bumped a tool off of a shelf. The metallic clank accomplished what the sound of Denny's head against the table had not. Arnem bolted upright and glanced around the room with groggy eyes.

"It's just me," Denny said.

"It's still night, isn't it?" Arnem asked. "Is something wrong? Was it another vision?"

"I think that's the problem." Denny pulled a chair over and sat across from Arnem. "I haven't had a vision since the one of my mother. There was a sound that called me into the prison, and I thought her voice was mixed into it. It led me right to her cell. I need to connect with her again, to find out where she is."

Arnem ruffled his own graying hair, then flattened it down on the sides. "Denny, I want you to know that you have a family in me and my wife and daughters. You don't need to keep running. Your mother doesn't want you to come after her—you said so yourself. Let's help Gemma complete her quest, and then we'll travel far away from Aepistelle, just you and me and the ladies."

Denny shot to his feet, the chair falling over behind him. "I know you mean well, Arnem. I love your family, but you aren't my father. He's out there somewhere. Selah has been so good to me, but she's not my mother. My mother is out there too, and I've seen her with my own eyes. Or with my mind—

I'm not sure. I know she's still alive, and until I'm with my parents again, I can't just relax."

Denny reached under the table and picked up the coat he'd used as a blanket. He put his arms through the sleeves and made his way to the front room. The midnight wind whipped through the gap in the vandalized door. It wasn't welcoming, didn't feel like an inviting start to a new journey. Denny didn't care. He got to his knees and crawled through the opening.

A hand grabbed his foot before it left the protection of the shop's interior.

"Denny, hold on a minute, will you?"

Denny wriggled free, turned around, and faced a crouching Arnem.

"I just need to leave a note for Gemma so she knows we weren't captured by Davin's guards. I also saw some full jars on the shelf in the stockroom. We may as well take a few rations with us; it's not like George is coming back anytime soon from his overseas jaunt with Jestan."

Denny crawled back inside and stood up. "Listen, I can't ask you to leave your family again. Your girls are waiting for you to return home."

"No, Denny. They're waiting for *us* to return home. You're a part of the clan now. And if the delay is because you were reuniting with your parents, they'll completely understand."

Denny threw his arms around the man. Arnem returned the embrace. During his years on the streets, Denny's memories of familial love had all but faded. He'd had to relearn the meaning of *family* and the strange concepts of *security* and *home* with the Wynstones.

*Would I feel the same with my parents if we were reunited?* he wondered. *After all they've been subjected to, would they even be as I remember them?*

The thought scared him, but it didn't discourage him. He followed Arnem around the shop, gathering any supplies that might help them endure another journey into the unknown.

A BENEFIT, PERHAPS, OF BEING IN CAPITAL CITY WAS THAT the taverns were open all through the night. Unlike most other parts of Aepistelle, here there was no curfew for establishments to stop serving alcoholic beverages. Industry was on the rise, and shifts ended at all sorts of hours, so barkeeps were ready for the masses at any time of day or night. The Iron Bar was one such establishment, and it primarily catered to the guards of the local detention center.

Arnem did not fit in at all with the burly folks who were tough enough to put up with hundreds of locked-up convicts in the penitentiary, even if he privately prided himself on how toned his recent endeavors had made him. Denny hadn't put up any argument about hiding outside. Arnem had watched the boy climb up on a rubbish bin behind the building to get to the roof. Perhaps it reminded him of his home atop the train station of Esteron.

The stench of a full day of work made its way to Arnem's nose quicker than the boisterous calls for "the usual" hit his ears as dozens of patrons filed in. The man slinging glasses and bottles behind the bar looked like he could have been one of them; perhaps he'd been the only one smart enough to quit and go into business for himself after realizing just how much cash his peers shelled out after every shift. He'd made no attempt to converse with Arnem when it had been just the two of them in there. He'd merely pushed Arnem's chosen ale across the counter and hadn't even bothered wiping up the mess he'd made when the foam sloshed over. Now that the regular clientele had arrived, however, the man's demeanor had shifted to a rough but jovial mood.

Arnem could feel the eyes of off-duty prison guards on him, and he spotted a couple of shrugs and eye rolls from the bartender that he knew must have been about him. Arnem paid them no mind and continued to sip a little of his drink at a time. Once the first round of drinks had been distributed and everyone had congregated into their chosen groups— Arnem seemed to serve as a rock on the shore, splitting an incoming wave—the conversation flowed.

He picked up bits and pieces of shop talk where he could. *The warden's been showing up to work already sauced. Prisoner so-and-so is moving drugs with the help of a recently terminated cook.* Arnem was on his third drink when he finally caught something interesting.

"As long as I don't get shipped off to Terminus Rock again, I'll put up with anything the warden wants. I'd rather spit shine his boots with my hair than work a rotation on that island."

Arnem turned his head just enough to catch a glimpse of the man. He stood a full head taller than Arnem. His black-and-gray-streaked hair hung in long, greasy curls. His beard was crusted with bits of that night's dinner, and the tip was moistened by the compilation of liquors that had spilled onto the portion of the bar he was hunched over.

"Not that I have to worry about that now. Just got word that they closed it for good," the man said. "They had one last inconvenience to deal with, and now the rest of the crew is coming home."

"What about the prisoners, Venko? I didn't see an increase in our ward," the man's companion inquired.

Venko set his mug down and looked around nervously. He met Arnem's eyes, held his gaze for a moment, and then turned back to his friend. "Can't talk about that. Wouldn't tell you even if I knew. Committee business. You know how it is."

"As if the Royal Mystic Committee would have entrusted *you* of all people with their secrets," Venko's friend said.

Venko apparently didn't like that. He jumped to his feet, sending his barstool flying to the side and into Arnem's knee. Venko grabbed the other man by the collar and pushed his face into the pool of ale on the bar. Everyone hushed for a moment. Then the bartender whistled between his teeth, which was enough to get Venko to step away. Instead of throwing him out, the bartender slid another frothy mug Venko's way. Venko downed most of it in quick gulps. Whatever didn't fit in his mouth soaked into his beard.

Venko slammed the glass down, belched loudly, and looked around. Everyone seemed to take a step back in unison. One woman coughed, and then the conversations all resumed.

"Gonna take me a piss out back," Venko said, as if to let the bartender know he wasn't dashing out without paying his tab. He slammed his shoulder into a couple engaging in a sloppy kiss as he stumbled toward the door on unsteady feet.

Arnem reached into his jacket and pulled out a few bills, more than enough to cover the three rounds he'd nursed over the last couple of hours. He hurried past the unfazed lovers and out the door behind Venko.

"Excuse me, sir! Excuse me!"

Venko had already unfastened the front of his trousers. He turned to look at his pursuer, scowled, and then made his way around the side of the building. Arnem tailed him into the alley. He had only just turned the corner when he nearly stepped into the man's high-pressure stream.

"You're new here, ain't ya?" Venko slurred. "Was this your

first day on the third shift? I ain't seen you around these parts."

Arnem tried to avoid looking at the hosing job the man was giving the wall of the Iron Bar. "Well, you see, I...um, yes. Yes! First day. Not sure I'm in the right line of work, but—"

"Right line of work?" Venko finished draining his stores and fastened his pants. He turned toward Arnem and sized him up. "What do you mean, *right* line of work? A wee little man like you is too good for it?"

"Oh, no, not at all," Arnem said as he backed up against a bin full of empty bottles. "I think it's great work, very important."

"Cut the act, shorty. I saw you in there, spying on my conversation." He grabbed Arnem by the collar, apparently his signature move. "You from the Committee, then? They want to make sure I keep my mouth shut?"

"Shut about what?" a smaller voice asked.

Venko started to turn before he felt the steel against his back. He smiled, then released Arnem's shirt and smoothed it. Arnem wished he hadn't, not after he'd just seen the man use those hands to do his business against the wall. Venko raised the same hands and turned slowly to face Denny, who was gripping his curved sword.

"What are you two on about, then?" Venko asked. Arnem stepped around him and took his own blade from Denny's other hand. Venko took a closer look at what Denny held. "And where did you come across a kalis like that? You'd have to be blind not to see that you pale boys aren't from the Ferromin Islands."

"It was made for me by a friend," Denny said. His hand trembled a bit, but he kept the sword aimed at the man.

"Well, that's a friend I'd like to meet. Perhaps I already

have. Not too many in Aepistelle would know how to make a blade like that. He serve in the military, by chance?"

"Forty-third regiment, I believe it was," Arnem responded.

Denny gave him a confused look, as if to ask why Arnem was divulging that information. Even Arnem wasn't quite certain, but he lowered his own sword and nodded to Denny to do the same.

"Well, I'll be a dragon's liver. I wouldn't have taken you lot as part of Quincy's crew. Nobody else could have made that there blade, though."

"Listen, Mr. Venko, I'm sorry to have approached you under the guise of a lie, but we could really use your help," Arnem said. "It's about that prison on Terminus Rock."

Venko looked up and down the alley, then back at the newly crafted sword now in its sheath at Denny's side. "This *feels* like a setup, but it don't *look* like one. Quincy wouldn't be working with the Committee, at any rate. Not after all they've done to try and erase our history."

"So you knew Geoffrey Calvertson as well?" Denny asked.

"He'll always be *Lieutenant* Calvertson to me, but yes. Quincy and I served under him."

"Then we served together too, in a way," Arnem said. "I'm Arnem Wynstone. My friends Maachel, Richard, Jestan, and I were there at the castle of the Vheisenia in the north."

Venko took a step back and reassessed Arnem. His brow furrowed as he looked the man up and down, and then his face relaxed. He lunged forward and embraced Arnem. "Arnem the Loyal! It's no wonder I didn't recognize you— we've both put on the years and the pounds since those days. Ha! And to imagine I thought you might be part of the Royal Mystic Committee just now. So tell me, are Quincy and Geoffrey together again? Those two were a wild pair in the taverns wherever we went. At least they were before the war. I know Geoffrey hasn't been well since."

"We've been traveling with Geoffrey's daughter, Gemma," Denny said. "Quincy was with us for a short time as well. He helped us save a friend, but we parted ways. Now it's you we need help from."

Venko punched Arnem in the arm playfully. "A real serious one this kid is, eh, Arnem? I'll do what I can to help friends of my old compatriots—just tell me what you need. What were you on about with that prison?"

"My parents were there," Denny said. "They've been in captivity for years. My mother got a message out to me recently, and I need to help her. I need to find her."

"Can you tell us where the prisoners were relocated?" Arnem asked. "The boy has been without his mother and father for most of his life."

"Now, Arnem, I know I said I want to help you two out, but you have to understand that I'm a man of the law." Venko tapped the badge on his breast that indicated his status as a deputy warden. "If they're locked up, it's because they violated the laws of our fine kingdom."

Arnem caught Denny reaching for the hilt of his sword and put his hand on the boy's arm to calm him. "Their only crime was being born with abilities. Not dangerous ones, either. They can see visions of the future. They are not violent criminals."

"But a law's a law, Arnem."

"You know as well as I do that Davin only created those laws to bolster his own power. Denny's parents did nothing wrong. They need our help now, and we're going to provide it. Now, I respect you for ensuring that violent criminals remain locked away for the acts they've committed. But these two are *not* those kinds of criminals. They are good people. You and I did not fight that war so that our kingdom could live in this kind of darkness. We did it to bring light to our people and our future generations. For safety, for security, for righteousness."

Venko didn't speak. He looked down at the ground. Arnem wondered if it was shame in the man's eyes. Denny seemed to be growing impatient. As Venko turned his back on the pair, Denny took a step away from Arnem and drew his blade.

"Denny!" Arnem shouted.

"If this man has no honor left in him, if he's not going to help us, then he's a liability. We've told him too much!"

Venko turned back around, but instead of confusion or fear or anger on his face, Arnem saw a toothy grin. "The boy is right! Working for the crown, even in as lowly a role as mine, has made me less honorable." He reached a hand toward Denny. "I am sorry, truly I am. I don't know where your parents are exactly—I'm not high enough up the ladder to have that information, nor is the senior warden at my prison. Those who were locked away on Terminus Rock were moved somewhere even more secure than that island. I have no idea what is more secluded than that place, but wherever it is, it'll take a lot more than the two of you to break in and get your parents out alive."

"We'll take care of that part on our own," Denny said. "We've gotten quite good at that sort of thing. We just need to know where to go."

"There was a special train sent to the docks one night months ago. It was heavily armored. I'd never seen anything like it. The trains that go on that route usually just pick up imports from the ships or deliver exports to them for the trade circuits. We'd never done a prisoner exchange with Terminus, but even if we had, it never would've necessitated something so large. I had to send a few of my men out to assist with the transfer from the Terminus ships to those train cars. Some of the men never came back. I wasn't allowed to ask questions. I wasn't told where the trains were going, but no prison in our system completed any intake for those prisoners. The main administrative building is here in Capital City, and I would have heard something about it. I'd say they were taken somewhere far, far away from civilization, but the rail lines in Aepistelle only go so far."

"End of the line," Denny muttered.

"What was that?" Arnem asked.

The boy looked to Arnem with tears in his eyes. "End of the line. My mom said it in the vision and wrote it all over her cell on Terminus Rock. I don't think she meant that she's at the end of the rail line, but it stuck with me. I've been hearing it over and over in my head ever since."

"Well, we know the tracks go northeast and end in Esteron," Arnem said. "There's no way a prison would be there."

"Nay, too populated up there," Venko agreed.

"South, then," Denny said. "It must be south."

# Chapter Sixteen
## GEMMA

Gemma's consciousness returned with a cold slap of wind. She sat up under the polluted sky of Capital City and looked around. She was on a flat rooftop. Several chimneys blew their exhaust around her. She coughed and rubbed her eyes. She felt around on her head, but there was no bump, no blood.

"I'm sorry I had to do that," a man said, stepping partially out of the shadow of a smokestack. "The Royal Mystic Committee was on their way."

"Hannon said he was going to give me a head start. He couldn't have contacted them before you attacked me."

"Attacked you?" Gemma heard offense in the man's voice, but she couldn't see his face in the shadow cast by the chimney. "Please believe that I never would have attacked you. I couldn't let you scream or even speak and let Hannon know I was there. He'd have come after you himself and turned you in to preserve his reputation. I couldn't risk that."

"And who are you to be so concerned with my safety?" Gemma asked.

The man took a few steps toward her. She got a better look at him when a cloud moved away from the moon, but she still couldn't see his face.

"This mask is for my safety." He rubbed the side of the knitted fabric that obscured his facial features. "And yours."

Gemma jumped to her feet and lunged for the mask. In his shock, her captor froze. Gemma pulled the mask off, revealing the face of a man not much older than her. His blond hair was voluminous even though it had been smashed under the mask. His nose was slightly bulbous. He opened his mouth in surprise, revealing finely maintained teeth that were straight and white as bone. He had an air of wealth about him.

"You're new at this kind of thing, aren't you?" she asked with a cautious smile.

Gemma expected anger, but he shocked her by bursting into laughter. "I am, yes. Well, now that you've seen me, I suppose I can introduce myself. My name is Kosar." His lips trembled, and Gemma wondered if he hadn't intended to divulge his identity. Perhaps she had some charm in her that worked to her advantage.

"I'd ask what you're doing so far from the mansions of Western Heights, but I detect a slight accent in your voice."

Again he looked insecure. Her experience with Walker and other boys of his privileged ilk had shown her that they could unravel quickly when things didn't go according to their plans.

"You're good, Gemma. I see why Davin and the others aren't quick to underestimate you."

"If you know what I've experienced the last few months, which it seems you do, then you must know they absolutely did underestimate me."

"Nonsense. You gave them what they wanted. Your little

stunts up north and the actions of your shiny-headed priest friend here in Capital City gave Davin the clout he needed to take his power one step further. He feeds on chaos."

Gemma felt the heat rise in her as her heart pounded. She had never been quick to anger, but hearing this stranger tell her that everything she'd gone through had only served to empower her enemy was too much for her.

"How dare you say that? Maybe my friends and I should have been more careful in how we took care of King Davin, but I never asked to be put into that situation. The events I witnessed and the things I did and the people who died—"

"Hush!" Kosar whispered. Fear swept over his face. He put his hand over Gemma's mouth again and pulled her behind a chimney just as a door opened on the other side of the roof. Kosar put a finger to his pursed lips. Gemma nodded, and Kosar removed his other hand from her face. She peeked around the brick chimney and spotted a man in the red-and-gold uniform of the City Guard. He had a short sword sheathed at his waist, and one hand rested on the hilt.

"Oh no," Kosar whispered. Gemma noticed it at the same time as the guard—Kosar's mask lay on the ground where Gemma had dropped it. The guard pulled the sword halfway out before something bounced his way, exhaling smoke. Kosar had thrown it. He ran toward the newcomer and pulled a knife from his belt before disappearing from view behind the growing cloud of smoke.

Metal blades clanked against each other. Gemma could make out only the occasional outlines of the two men as they tussled. She reached for her own blade, but it wasn't there. She'd left it at George's shop because she hadn't wanted to draw attention to herself by carrying it through the university campus.

Kosar stumbled out of the haze and fell on his back. The

knife flew out of his hand and slid a few feet before coming to a halt. The guard stood over him, sword lifted high. In a fluid motion, Gemma ran out of hiding and ducked down to grab the knife. She meant to pick it up by the handle, but she overshot and grabbed the blade instead. She flung it up at the man, who hesitated to bring his sword down on Kosar as he watched Gemma in action.

It flew through in the air only briefly, but Gemma was sure she could see each rotation of the knife. The handle hit the guard between the eyes.

It clanked to the ground between his feet as Gemma came to a halt to the man's left. He looked at her in astonishment for a moment before his lips curled into a mocking smile. Before Gemma could move, he shot out his left leg and drove his boot into Gemma's face. Her nose made a crunching sound, and the blood didn't hesitate to flow. Kosar spun around on the ground and wrapped his fingers around the knife, but the guard brought his boot down onto the young man's wrist. Kosar dropped the knife and groaned in pain as the guard pressed his weight down.

Gemma felt around. Her fingers brushed against something—a brick. She picked it up and lobbed it up at the man standing over her. It bounced off the thick shoulder pad of his uniform and fell right back to the ground, hitting Gemma's hip, but it was enough to make the guard step off of Kosar's wrist. Kosar lunged forward again, ignoring the knife, and bit the guard's ankle. Gemma rolled away from the pair, grabbed the brick again as she turned, and shot back to her feet. She dove at the distracted guard and drove the brick into his face.

*A nose for a nose*, she thought.

Kosar used the opportunity to grab his knife. He stabbed it into the guard's calf. The man screamed. Gemma found another brick and smashed it into his hairless skull. He fell beside Kosar, unconscious.

"Are you okay?" Gemma asked, though it sounded odd given the state of her nose. Kosar rose up and put a hand on Gemma to steady himself.

"Let's fix that," he said. Gemma looked at him with confusion. "Your nose."

He reached for her face, put his palm on her nose, and pushed. It cracked and ached as much as the first time.

"Sorry, Gemma. I should have protected you better than that. You really can hold your own in a fight."

"Yeah," Gemma said, leaning over with her hands on her knees. The blood dripped between her feet. "Talk about underestimating me."

THE HOTEL SUITE KOSAR BROUGHT HER TO WAS ENORMOUS.

"This place is nearly the size of my family's home," Gemma said. "If I didn't know any better, I'd think you were trying to impress me."

"Is it working?" Kosar walked over to a wet bar in the sitting room while Gemma dropped down onto a plush sofa.

"Not really. I've dated a rich guy before. Learned my lesson."

"What happened to him?" Kosar asked. He poured two glasses of wine and handed one to Gemma.

"He's dead," she replied as Kosar took a sip.

He spat out the wine in shock, spraying Gemma's shirt. "Um, sorry about that."

Gemma brushed the fresh stains on her top for a moment and then gave up. "It'll blend in with the blood from my nose. No big deal. Thanks for setting it back into place."

"I've got an older brother. We had our fair share of accidents while roughhousing. Had to learn to do that before my parents saw my nose twisting completely off to the side."

Gemma downed the contents of her glass. She'd never been much of a drinker, but walking around her hometown as an outlaw and knowing she'd never be able to go back to the house she'd grown up in had really taken a toll on her. Not to mention George's ransacked shop, the previous day's jailbreak, and that night's rooftop combat session. A drink sounded like just the right medicine in that moment.

"Now, are you going to tell me why you came for me in Hannon's office?" she asked. "How do you know about me? Or maybe first you can tell me who you really are."

Kosar dropped into an accent chair that faced Gemma's sofa. He polished off his own wine and set the glass on the floor. "I'm a journalist."

"A journalist? In a mask?"

"It's a recent development. You see, King Davin returned from his weeks-long absence with fire in his veins. His first order was for the Committee to burn down the remaining Solendaron temples. There weren't too many still standing, really, just the ones in Briarpatch, Esteron, and Pinedrop. Those had all been abandoned and boarded up for two decades, but it made for a good show of power.

"His next order of business was to clamp down on the press. Now the printers of any newspapers, books, or pamphlets must have the Royal Mystic Committee's sign-off on everything they print. King Davin sent teams of agents to every known printing press. Journalists have all been catalogued, briefed on the new limitations, and made to sign new contracts that make them fully liable for any harm committed in response to their work. Punishments for journalists and publishers who violate the new speech laws include public execution and forfeiting all property to the crown."

"What about the mask?" Gemma asked.

"Well, most of the smaller papers outside of Capital City have closed down. There is too much at risk for reporters and staff, and the Royal Mystic Committee is too unpredictable right now. Those of us who wish to continue to dig for the truth and bring it to light are now doing so independently. We must work from the shadows. Hence the mask." He pulled the mask out of his coat pocket and tossed it to Gemma.

"And how can you get your stories out if the printing presses are being guarded?" Gemma asked. She turned the mask over in her hands, stuck her fingers through the slits cut out for Kosar's eyes, and then set it on her lap.

"I said every *known* printing press is being watched. There are a few others out there for underground and independent publishers. Some of them have been around for years, printing banned religious materials, criticism of Davin and his regime, and other contraband. Now they're working overtime as the only sources of truth around Aepistelle."

"Is Hannon a part of it?"

"In a way. He's a benefactor for some of the printing houses. The supply chain is being guarded almost as closely as the printers themselves, so the free press syndicates have to figure out work-arounds. Hannon sends supplies in tiny increments in order to avoid the suspicion of the Committee."

Gemma stood up, grabbed the open bottle of wine, and refilled both glasses. She gestured around the hotel suite and furrowed her brow at Kosar. "And tell me about this place. I didn't think a journalist could afford a place like this."

"Journalists now aren't who they used to be. The experienced reporters out there are all being watched too closely. I'm not a journalist by trade—I just took up the calling. What you're getting at is that I'm too wealthy, too privileged to do this job. You're right, of course. I come from a family of high pedigree, if you will."

"And who is your family? Have I heard of them? What great house do you come from?"

"I'll let you know when we get there, but we must leave tonight."

Gemma nearly choked on her wine, but she avoided spitting it out the way Kosar had done a few minutes earlier. "Leave with you? Tonight?"

"Yes, Gemma. If you want to get that manuscript published, it's not going to happen here in Capital City. It won't be Hannon who helps you get it out there. You must come to the Southern Reaches with me. Davin and the Committee already suspect that you're back in town. Since we let that guard live, he's going to tell them who he saw once he wakes up from his little head injury. We should already be far away from here."

"But my friends are here. They're in as much danger as we are."

"They will be safer without you, and more so if they don't know where you're going or who you're with. There are a lot of important stories being printed by these underground presses, Gemma, but yours is the most important of them all. The kingdom needs to hear it. It's the only way we can all rise up together against King Davin and end his rule."

"But—"

"You are our only hope, Gemma. It's time to tell your story to the masses. We need to get to the docks. I have a boat to take us south. The rails are too well guarded these days."

A patterned knock at the door—two, a pause, then three more—sent Gemma back to her feet. "Who could that be?"

she whispered. She noted a look of calm on Kosar's face, but it didn't make her feel any better.

"That'll be Syntha. You don't need to worry." Kosar rose and trotted across the room. The door flew open as soon as he unlatched the bolt. A young woman just a bit taller than Gemma stepped inside with a wrapped bundle in her arms, which she swiftly unrolled on the coffee table between the sofa and chairs. Gemma's machete, bow, and quiver of arrows clanked onto the table.

"Is this all you need?" Syntha asked. Without waiting for an answer, she reached into her coat, pulled out a folded piece of parchment, and thrust it toward Gemma. "I believe this was intended for you as well."

Gemma hesitated for a moment and then took it from the woman. She opened it up and read Arnem's note.

"Your friends were going to leave you behind," Syntha said. "It's good we found you tonight, yes?"

Gemma looked past Syntha to Kosar, who flashed his perfect pearly whites at her.

"I hope so," Gemma said, but deep down, she wasn't so certain.

# Chapter Seventeen
## MARZELE

Marzele had visited Capital City several times, but he'd never had reason to visit the seedy neighborhoods in the southeastern quadrant. It had taken a couple of hours to get there on foot from the affluent district uptown. He'd nearly been approached by some rough-looking gentlemen about two blocks back, but they'd taken one look at the former priest and thought better of unleashing the rage within him.

Marzele leaned against a pole, using the light of the gas lamp atop it to get a better look at the map he'd taken from his pocket. Horace had circled this area. Marzele looked around, uncertain what his former brother of the cloth had been searching for. Horace had never been interested in crime and was certainly no secret vigilante. Had the man grown so bored over the last several years since their order had been abolished that he'd taken up sleuthing? Marzele didn't think it likely.

Rowdy laughter broke the silence. Startled, Marzele shoved the map back in his pocket. Two men stumbled out

the front door of what seemed to be the only business operating in the middle of the night. They took no notice of
Marzele. The burlier of the two men took three steps down
the sidewalk and collapsed. In a fit of laughter, the other man
dropped down to the curb and then vomited at his feet.

*The drinks must be strong, then*, Marzele thought. He crossed
the street and entered the establishment.

While alcohol had not been expressly forbidden for clergy,
Marzele had never really had a taste for it. He'd occasionally
had a glass of wine in social settings but couldn't tell the
difference between a fine vintage from Plentimore Valley and
a less-regarded bottle from the Centeron or Costono region.
He had never dared touch spirits, and the heaviness of ales
disgusted him. Even at his lowest points during his two
decades in hiding, Marzele had not been tempted in the
slightest by the escape others found in a bottle. He had
instead relied on his faith to get him through the storms. The
Lord Solendaron had provided.

Or so he'd always thought, foolish as he was. Not
anymore.

Marzele walked up to the bar and stood between two men
passed out on their stools. The bartender, an ancient-looking
man with eyes that appeared to have seen everything, gave
Marzele a distrustful look. Marzele ignored it.

"I'll take something strong. Don't care what."

The bartender took in Marzele for another few seconds,
grunted, and turned away. He returned a moment later with a
small glass, poured some kind of amber liquid into it, and slid
it across the ale-stained surface to Marzele.

Instead of picking up the glass, Marzele just stared at it as
if insulted.

"Something the matter?" the old man growled.

"Is this a joke? I'm not a child. Give me more than that!"

An unexpected smile broke out on the bartender's face, revealing several missing teeth. He picked up the glass, downed its contents, and then pushed the bottle toward Marzele. The former priest pulled out a few of the bills he'd nabbed from Horace's desk and paid for the liquor. He turned away from the bartender and took in the room. A group of men sat around a large table on one side, several of them glancing over at Marzele and murmuring softly to each other. On the other side, a fire burned strong in the hearth. There was an unoccupied table and chair near it with enough light from the fire to read. Marzele crossed the room and settled into the chair.

After the shock of the first couple of swigs, Marzele decided that he didn't mind the taste of the liquor so much. It warmed his throat, even burned his nostrils a little. He reached into his pocket and pulled out the handwritten notes he'd taken from Horace's desk, but as he stared at the top page, the letters seemed to dance off of the paper. He swallowed another mouthful and began to feel uncomfortably hot so close to the fireplace. He'd grown up learning to love heat in all its forms; it was all a blessing of the Ever-Giving Sun, of the Lord Solendaron. In his adolescence, he'd trained for years to absorb power from the sun, to store its energy within him, to wield it like a weapon. He'd melted metal with his hands. He'd willed fires into existence. It was all of the Lord, and it was good.

Now, however, he felt no such connection with the heat of the fire. He had no fondness for the light, no faith in the god he'd revered for more than fifty years, the god who'd abandoned him, who'd let all the most loyal servants of Solendaron suffer brutal deaths at the hands of the enemy. No, he *abhorred* the light.

It was fitting, then, that a shadow fell over him just as his eyes started to close. The bottle fell to the floor, its contents forming a puddle under the chair, but Marzele was in no frame of mind to notice.

MUCH LIKE THE MAN HE HAD PASSED ON THE WAY INTO THE bar earlier that night, Marzele bent forward and unleashed the contents of his stomach between his feet. His vision swirled. His head pounded. Sweat streamed down his face, yet his body shivered. He felt undeniably hungry yet repulsed by the thought of consuming any food or drink ever again. Like anyone in his position—though the first time the thought crossed the average person's mind, they were usually three decades younger than Marzele—he swore to himself that he'd never drink again. He closed his eyes and immediately felt worse. His body miraculously managed to find something remaining in his stomach and send it back up out of his mouth.

It was then that he realized there was no fireplace in front of him. He'd been moved.

Marzele jumped to his feet, ignoring the increased velocity of the spinning in his head, and looked around. His first worry was that the bartender had called for the local police to lock him up in a cell to sleep off his drunkenness. But as his eyes adjusted, he realized he'd been on a bed, much nicer than the pathetic excuse for a cot he'd slept on in the prison on Terminus Rock. This was certainly no jail cell. He turned away from the bed, but it was too dark in the room to see more than a couple of feet away.

The sweat dripping down his forehead intensified. *Breathe*, he told himself, *just breathe*. He bowed his head and began to whisper a prayer, then abruptly halted the habitual act. *No, Solendaron will not save me now.*

Marzele took a step into the darkness, then another. He heard a clinking sound on the floor but ignored it. Each movement increased the spinning of his head, but he tried to press on. He picked up speed and took another step, and something pulled taut at his ankle. He collapsed to the floor with a thud and blacked out once again.

He wasn't sure how long he slept the second time, just awoke knowing he'd been snoring. He was still on the floor, a putrid ring of bile caked around his face. He sat up too quickly, and again the world spun around him. He looked over at his right ankle, which was bound by a manacle and a thick chain. He tried to focus his eyes and let his equilibrium settle. Slowly the room came into focus. The ceiling was quite high with a narrow window at the top of the wall behind the bed. Most of the glass pane had boards sloppily nailed over it, but some light managed to squeeze through the top few inches.

Marzele wrapped his fingers around the chain. He instinctively whispered a familiar incantation in the tongue of the Solendaron, but nothing happened.

"It seems the Lord has abandoned you, old friend," came a voice from behind Marzele. "Or perhaps you have abandoned Him."

He didn't need to turn to know who was speaking. "It was you who abandoned the Lord and your own brethren," Marzele said.

Horace walked over and plopped down onto Marzele's bed. He clicked his tongue and looked down at Marzele. "You shouldn't have come looking for me. I should have known you would, though, if you were still alive after everything. Ever the hero."

"Hero? I didn't come to save you, Horace. I came to kill

you for what you did. You turned us in. Got everyone killed. Shenesa. Gregory." Marzele's lip quivered as he thought about his own mentor, the closest thing he'd ever had to a father, but he said the name anyway: "Bertram."

That last name was too much. Marzele leapt to his feet, lunged at Horace, and punched the man in the face. The dizziness returned more intensely than ever from the sudden movement. Marzele's vision blurred, and he fell back to the floor.

"I did what I had to do," Horace said, standing over Marzele as blood rained from his nose. "Davin's spies were all over our plans. They'd been watching each of us for years. It was quite obvious when we all converged in Capital City. I still thought we'd be able to accomplish our goal, though. Then there was your little stunt the morning before our attack on the castle—you tipped off the girl's mother. There was too much of a risk that she would report it to the king, so I slipped a note to my manservant before we marched on the castle and sent him out ahead of us. Davin spared me for it, and our entire order did not die out in one swoop after all...at least not right away."

"What do you mean, right away? We're both still alive."

"Yes, Marzele, we are both still here, but which of us is still in the Lord's favor? I think we've both seen the truth and moved on. Solendaron is as dead to me as He is to you."

Marzele lay there in shock, not even bothering to move away from Horace's dripping blood. He'd given up his faith in Solendaron, it was true, but it stung to hear it said so bluntly by a man who had once practiced it with him.

"So, that's it, then?" Marzele asked. "Our entire lives were a lie?"

"Solendaron is not a lie. I've no doubt about that, and I don't think you do either. We both saw miracles firsthand, even performed them ourselves. But he has abandoned us. He has abandoned humankind at large."

"Left us to rot," Marzele added.

"But while the Lord has turned his back on us, there is another who will greet us with open arms. One of power. Of vengeance. Of darkness."

Marzele pushed away from Horace and sat up slowly. "You don't mean—"

"He Who Dwells in the Shadows. Yes, Marzele, that's exactly who I mean."

"The Cult of Arun? They're responsible for those murders you were collecting news clippings about? You've *joined* them?"

Horace took a few steps away. When he turned back to face Marzele, his features were in shadow. "That's precisely it. I've been tracking them for many years, even before their arrival in Capital City. They aren't so different from us, you know."

"They're murderers, Horace!"

"They murder those who are tainted by evil. They are *of* Solendaron, even if their methods are nothing like the Order of Priests."

"But they worship the darkness!"

"The shadow. There's a difference. Darkness is the complete absence of light, but shadow is created by light. Think of them as a clandestine branch of the Solendaron faith, if you will."

"I will not. They represent nothing Solendaron was about. Their founder was a maniac who bastardized the powers afforded to him by the Lord. He slaughtered entire villages in his mad quest across the north to hunt down some harmless witch."

"Priest Arun was a crusader. He brought the Lord's judgment, as was his divinely appointed task. His methods were different from ours, I'll give you that, but they led him to discover the shadow—the *Tïhn*—and all of the powers it afforded. Times have changed, Marzele. This world has moved forward. Why should our understanding of the divine remain static? We see where our traditions have led us. We see how our dedication to the light has been rewarded. Maybe the Lord Solendaron hasn't abandoned us after all. Maybe He has led us to this moment. To this understanding. To the way of the Tïhn."

Horace took a step forward so that the beam of light from the window illuminated his face. Marzele rose to his feet, using the wall for support. He stared at his former colleague, and the man's honest conviction was apparent. Horace had completely bought into this murderous cult. Marzele couldn't blame him for abandoning the old faith, as he'd done it himself over the past several weeks. But could he justify the terrible things the Cult of Arun had done during the last several decades?

"We will overthrow this bloody regime, Marzele. The Tïhn will see to it that King Davin's rule is in its final days. We will succeed where the Order of Solendaron failed. Where you and I failed. I'll have my redemption, old friend. Will you?"

Marzele thought about the women who had raised him in the orphanage. He thought of Bertram, who had walked with him through the hardest of times. He thought he felt shame but then realized it was entirely in his own mind. They were dead, all of them. He'd been the man they had raised him to be, and it had led him nowhere. What was there to lose?

"I won't murder innocent people," Marzele said.

"I'm not asking you to do anything I wouldn't do myself."

"I'm not convinced this is the right way, but I also have

nowhere else to go. I don't think I can ever trust you, Horace, but I do believe I was led here, the same as you."

"Then come, my friend," Horace said. He pulled out a key, unshackled Marzele's ankle, and walked across the room to a second door Marzele hadn't noticed. "Let us walk in the shadow together."

Marzele limped toward him. Horace flipped through his ring of keys, unlocked the door, and pulled it open. Dank air greeted Marzele like a slap in the face. Marzele peered in but could see nothing in the darkness beyond the frame.

He turned to Horace. "What is this?"

Horace placed a hand on Marzele's back. "Your future."

The large man shoved Marzele. As he tumbled down the steps into the damp maw, the door slammed shut. Marzele was alone in the pitch-black room.

# Chapter Eighteen
## ARNEM

Arnem wasn't sure if it was the fates or the gods or just random chaos that made the world spin in the direction it did. Plentimore Valley wasn't known for the serious worship of any deities, though further back in its history, the local farmers had utilized their own rituals to ask for rain and plentiful crops. Though, as the name of the region implied, it wasn't really needed; Plentimore Valley had always been lush and fertile during Arnem's lifetime and his father's before him. The lack of dependence on a higher power meant the lack of worship of any particular god.

So Arnem wasn't sure who to blame for the way things had gone for him and his friends. They should have been heroes, lauded by the kingdom, showered with riches. In some ways, they were; Jestan had written a book about their adventures during the war two decades earlier, which had spread their names around to the common folk of Aepistelle. However, King Davin and his Royal Mystic Committee had made sure the book was watered down, its accuracy questioned, and any bits of mysticism and magic were removed from later editions.

Then it had happened again with his most recent venture through the Forest of Despair. He and his friends had freed a town full of children from a witch's ancient curse. They had fought off an army of tree monsters and driven slavers out of Emyhrsen. Yet the group had returned home as wanted criminals. It seemed there would be no word at all of their heroics this time, no book bragging about their adventures.

His status certainly didn't afford him a pass to the front of the line at the ticket booth of the central rail station in Capital City.

"We're going to miss the train," Denny complained. "Isn't there something you can do?"

No, there wasn't anything Arnem could do. The portly middle-aged farm supplies salesman had to endure the wait with everyone else, listening as the southbound train blew its whistle to warn of its impending departure.

"Ah, here we are, Denny," Arnem said as ticket vendors appeared behind some of the other windows in time for the morning shift change.

The tired old man who had been working the one open stall during the night shift leaned out and yelled, "Break it up into four lines, you animals!" And with that, he flipped the sign on his own window to CLOSED and walked away, ignoring the elderly woman who was standing right in front of him, cash in hand. Arnem and Denny rushed to the left-most window and made it just in time. A woman perhaps ten years Arnem's senior was behind the glass, setting up her station. She straightened up a stack of papers, arranged some flowers in a vase she'd brought with her, and looked at her reflection in the glass as she patted down her poof of hair.

Arnem cleared his throat and tapped on the glass. She

put up her pointer finger to indicate that she needed another moment. She bent down, dug through an unseen compartment below the counter, and came back with her final bit of flair: a fabric name placard in a wooden frame with AGATHA embroidered across it. She opened the window at last.

"Good morning, Agatha," Arnem said, trying his hardest to swallow down his frustration. "How do you do?"

"Hello, my dear. Well, if you must know, I'm excited for what is sure to be a lovely day. In fact, when the sun comes up just a little higher, it really warms up the booth, and I—" She paused, finally taking in the sight of Arnem.

*Perhaps my wish for recognition was a bit misguided*, Arnem thought as Agatha turned to glance at the wall of her stall. Denny grabbed Arnem's sleeve in fear. Arnem shifted to get a better look, and then he saw it.

Hanging next to Agatha was a poster with an artist's rendition of the entire group that had ventured from Aepistelle to Emyhrsen. An uncannily accurate drawing of Arnem sat in the top right corner, and a thinner, more sickly version of Denny's face was drawn just below it.

Without hesitation, Agatha reached for a bell and rang it incessantly.

"Run," Denny said. He pulled on Arnem's coat, but Arnem just stood there in shock. He felt the eyes of everyone waiting in line around him piercing through the back of his head.

"Wait, is that who I think it is?" one patron asked.

"Maachel?" another responded.

"No, it's Arnem!"

"From the Great Journey?"

"He's a wanted man! Haven't you seen the newspapers?"

"Stay right where you are!" It was Agatha this time, glaring at him from behind the glass. "Security is on its way. We don't need a big scene here, though I know I can't expect honor from a traitor to the crown."

Arnem felt Denny's tug once again. He didn't need another prompt. He took off running alongside the boy.

A door opened behind him. Arnem peered over his shoulder to see Agatha leaping out of the ticket booth. She was moving uncannily fast.

"To the left!" Denny shouted. They jumped just in front of a fast-moving horse. Its rider pulled on the reins, and the horse reared. One of the hooves connected with Agatha, who collapsed to the pavement.

"Sorry!" Arnem called back, but he knew he couldn't help the poor woman.

"She's trying to get us killed, Arnem!" Denny said.

"She's only doing what she thinks is right. I'm sure Agatha is a fine woman. Now, where do we go?"

Denny led Arnem behind a station office just before the doors opened and security guards flowed out. It seemed that they too were in the midst of a shift change, and the new arrivals hadn't yet begun to patrol the station. Denny turned a corner, and Arnem followed him to a set of rubbish bins. Without hesitation, the boy jumped onto one of the bins, then leapt up and grabbed hold of the eave of the office rooftop. He pulled himself up and glanced down at Arnem. "Come on! We can hide up here!"

Arnem had never been agile like the boy was, even in his youth. But he heard Agatha screaming at the guards that they'd run behind the office—there was no more time to waste. Arnem lifted a leg and lunged up onto the bin. He weighed a lot more than Denny, though, and the bin began to tip backward. Before it angled too far off, he hopped up, grabbed hold of the roof, and found himself dangling. His legs windmilled as he struggled to pull himself up. Denny lent a hand, and together they managed it. He rolled away from the edge just as the guards entered the alley. The rubbish bin was on its side, which would give them away. Denny motioned for Arnem to follow him quietly across the roof. Arnem nodded and began to crawl behind the boy but accidentally kicked a loose shingle. It crashed down next to one of the guards.

"Up there!" the guard shouted.

Arnem and Denny got to their feet and ran across the rooftop. On the other side, they looked down and spotted a wagon full of imported produce that had been unloaded from a train. It was just exiting the station. Arnem locked eyes with the boy and nodded, and they jumped in unison.

"What do you think you're doing?" the stunned driver asked them as they landed with a splat in crates of berries that now looked more like spilled jam.

"Sorry, sir," Arnem offered. He and Denny jumped down and continued their flight away from the station. He turned a corner, dove behind a stack of wooden crates, and waved for Denny to follow.

"The train is off limits," Denny said as they crouched behind the pile. Tears dotted his cheeks, mixed with sweat from the pursuit. "I'll never find my parents if we can't get on that train."

Arnem pulled the boy in for a hug and held on tight while Denny let out a cry he'd been holding in for days. "I may have another way, Denny. It won't be on the train, but I think I can get us close enough."

THEY ARRIVED AT THE PRISON EARLY ENOUGH TO CATCH the first shift of guards passing through the high walls. A few guards who recognized Arnem and Denny from the previous night cast them sideways glances; many more were hungover, eyes nearly closed, swaying as they walked, clearly lacking in energy. Venko, however, walked with authority. His smile was warm as he joked with his men, though his expression quickly morphed into a wary frown at the sight of the two unexpected visitors.

He stepped out of line just outside the guard booth and motioned for Arnem and the boy to follow him. He led them across the street to a park and sat on a bench. Arnem and Denny settled onto a neighboring bench.

"I thought you guys were hightailing it out of town today. Did something happen?"

"They recognized us at the station," Denny said. Venko glanced around to make sure they weren't being watched. Arnem did the same, but the only people he saw in the park were a mother and her twin toddlers, who were chasing pigeons in the grass. "We can't leave this place."

"Not by rail, anyway," Arnem added. He turned fully toward Venko, not seeing the need to play clandestine games. "I thought you might be willing to help us find another way out of here."

Venko turned his gaze to the gravel at his feet and grunted. The man's eyes narrowed, and he sat perfectly still as if deep in thought for nearly a minute. Then a few pigeons flew just over their heads, and the flutter of their wings snapped Venko out of his daze.

"I think I've got a way," he said, "but you may not like it."

Denny spoke up. "If we stay here, we'll be caught within a day. They'll lock us up in your prison over there, and by sunset tomorrow, they'll execute us in front of the whole city. I don't think any idea could be worse than that."

"That's exactly it—the part about getting locked up." Venko laughed at his own idea. Arnem and Denny exchanged nervous glances. "The prison doesn't pay much, not enough for me to take good care of my wife and kids and put a decent roof over their heads. My boys are in a good school; there's no way I'm going to let them follow in my footsteps and work in such a miserable place. But I can only work so many extra hours a week before I drop dead from exhaustion. So I may have a little side business to help supplement."

"Side business?" Arnem asked. "I'm thinking the less we know the better."

"Exactly. Let's just say I have a little import/export network going on. With a few exceptions, every cargo vessel entering or leaving Capital City is checked by the city guard. Prison transports are one of those exceptions. The guards look at the transfer papers, but anything else on board can fly under the radar."

"Has it failed yet?" Denny asked.

"Not with, um, *goods*, no."

"So what's the problem?" Arnem asked.

"I haven't moved *people* before. I mean, there are always prisoners on the wagons, but they're *supposed* to be there." He looked at Arnem and Denny and chuckled. "Let's see how the two of you look in striped jumpsuits!"

# Chapter Nineteen

## GEMMA

Aepistelle looked peaceful from the sea. Beautiful, even. There were no visual clues on the distant shore that the land was ruled by a psychotic despot who used his secret abilities to repress, imprison, and execute people for having their own abilities. And Gemma's current situation was quite a bit more comfortable than her previous trip on Quincy's small boat under the cover of night. She was almost able to forget that she was a fugitive on the run from that very same despot.

Perhaps it was the distraction of her present company that allowed her to feel as comfortable as she did.

"When I was in school, I traveled abroad for a semester," Kosar said. "My father insisted that I study diplomacy and political science. He had quite high hopes that I'd join King Davin's cabinet one day. So I interned with Aepistelle's ambassador to the Rethan Islands for three months."

"A semester in an actual tropical paradise? Sounds rough."

Kosar rolled up his sleeves and held his arms out to

Gemma. "As you can see, any tan I may have gotten while lounging on those beaches has faded."

"You're as pasty as the moon," Gemma quipped.

"We can't all be so lucky as to be from the Ferromin Islands," Kosar said with a laugh. Gemma glanced at her own skin, which was not quite as dark as her father's. She'd stood out among her peers in school and even among her relatives on her mother's side of the family, but she was proud of her complexion.

"My father was born there, but he came over as a child. His parents were so intent on him assimilating here in Aepistelle that they forbade him from speaking Ferromini. It wasn't until he joined the Aepistelle military that he even spent time with anyone from his birth country. They were lumped together in a single unit and pretty much kept separate from everyone else."

"To their benefit in the end, wasn't it?" Kosar asked. "They were the only survivors of the Forest of Despair during the war."

Gemma's thoughts turned to her parents. Each mile she sailed south, she traveled that much farther away from them. It had taken twenty-four years for her to feel like she really knew her father, and after just a couple of short months, she'd left him again for whatever this mission was.

Kosar put a hand on Gemma's shoulder. "Should I not have brought him up? I'm sorry. It must be difficult to have to flee without sending word to your parents. That was insensitive of me."

"No, no, it's okay," Gemma said. His touch was warm, welcoming. She felt a sudden urge to lean into him, let his arm wrap around her shoulders. She noticed her heart rate increasing and turned away. The ocean breeze kept her face cool, and she hoped she was not blushing as she peered out over the railing of the ship toward the coastline.

"Well, your father was a brave man in his younger years, and he surely passed that trait on to you. You must be fearless, given what you've done over the last few months."

"I'm not fearless," Gemma said. She turned to face him again and nearly melted when she met his eyes. They were a brilliant green, brighter than the emerald on her mother's wedding ring. They almost glittered in the light of the sun over the sea. With some effort, she caught her breath.

"What are you afraid of? If your story is true, you braved a hallucination-inducing cave, a haunted forest, and a soul-sucking witch, *and* you tamed a giant. And that was before you went to war against an army of foreign invaders. I can't believe you have any fears at all, Gemma."

"Superficial fears, like the creepy-crawly type?" she asked. "Or, like, the deep, existential, mess-with-my-head type?"

"Well, I'm fascinated to hear if there are any creepy-crawly types that would stop you in your tracks when a giant or a tree monster didn't. Do tell me."

"I guess you're right—that kind of thing doesn't scare me so much. Well, except one thing, but it's stupid."

"Can't be worse than mine," Kosar said. "If you must know, I'm terrified of chitter-wenches."

"Chitta-what?"

"That's right, you haven't spent much time in the Southern Reaches. Chitter-wenches are these disgusting little guys. They're arachnids—huge, poisonous ones—and they make a chittering sound. They can call to each other for help catching prey or defending themselves."

"That sounds disgusting! Well, mine may not be so bad, then. I'm afraid of fire."

Kosar cracked a smile. "I suppose we shouldn't sit in front of the fireplace when we get back to my family's home, then."

"No, that's a nice contained fire. It's more the fire of a match that I don't like. You know, inches from my fingers, ready to eat up that short span of the wood before the flame nips at my skin. It—"

"Kosar!" The voice came from across the deck of the ship, and Gemma and Kosar turned. Syntha stood at the helm with two of the ship's crew, concern on her face. "There's a ship that might be on a path to intercept us. Still too far off to make out any insignia on the sail."

"Probably a fishing vessel," Kosar called back. "Frankly, I'm surprised we haven't seen more out here this morning. Stay on course and update me if anything changes." He motioned to Gemma. "Come with me."

Kosar led Gemma down to the lower deck. He opened the door to his cabin, which was more spacious than Gemma's bedroom back at her family's former home in Capital City. He opened a rolltop desk filled with books and scrolls and scraps of parchment. He fumbled through discarded quills and other miscellanea before pulling out what he was looking for. He held it out to her.

"A match?" Gemma asked.

"If this is truly all you fear, let us conquer it together." He pulled out a second match and struck it on a rough wooden column. Gemma gazed at the little flame before catching his eyes behind it. "Nothing to worry about. See? My fingers are just fine."

Gemma swallowed down her embarrassment, knowing it was a silly thing to be afraid of. She struck her match on the same beam. It ignited. She brought it close to her face, hand trembling slightly, but she held her breath rather than blowing it out. Kosar was right. There was nothing to fear. No risk of serious harm, unlike the tentacles of those trees that had animated and tried to strangle the life from her back in the Forest of Despair. This was nothing.

She felt warmth on her face, but it wasn't from the match. Kosar had leaned in close. Without overthinking it, she closed the rest of the distance between them, and their lips met.

"Ouch," she uttered a few seconds later as she pushed away from Kosar and dropped the match. The flame had nipped her fingertips after all. She smothered it under her boot and turned back to Kosar, hoping the moment wasn't ruined. He reached for her hand and brought it to his lips. He gave her fingertips gentle kisses before Gemma pulled her hand away and pushed herself against him.

Her lips parted as her eyes closed. It had been too long since her last real kiss—she'd ended her relationship with Walker more than a year ago. They had come close to rekindling things a few times, but he hadn't been trustworthy. He had valued power and status more than Gemma was comfortable with. And yet she'd still held on to her feelings for him. As they had trekked through the last stretch of the Forest of Despair together more than two months ago, she had felt their spark rekindle. That had been cut short, though, when he'd been brutally killed only hours later in the town of Ferathan.

She pulled back from Kosar.

"Now you look scared of something else," he said. "Tell me what's troubling you."

She didn't want to bring up Walker and ruin whatever was developing between her and Kosar. "I was just thinking about your question."

"I've already forgotten. The matches?"

"The fears. The matches were the superficial part of my

answer. What I really fear deep down is that I could inherit my father's afflictions. He came back from the war damaged, and it continued to get worse over the years. His mind...for most of my life, he didn't seem to know who I was. Who he was, even. I don't want to lose my grip on what is real, on what matters. The people I love. The things I've accomplished."

Kosar took Gemma's hands. "You will never forget all that you've done to make this world a better place, Gemma. The people of Aepistelle will not forget, either. I'll make sure of it. Your story will resound through the lands. It will change the very structure of power in this kingdom. It will make Jestan the Just's book about the Great Journey look like a children's story."

Gemma kissed him on the cheek. "Your turn, then. What's your existential fear, or are chitter-wenches the only bane of your existence?"

"Perhaps it's not too different from yours. I'm afraid of losing the agency to do what I want. Some men live their lives trapped under the boot of another, ready to be squashed like a cockroach. Constantly told what to do, forced to live in a way prescribed by someone else. I want none of it."

His grip tightened on Gemma's hands, his face anxious. She leaned in to plant another kiss on his cheek, hoping to calm him. "I understand," she whispered in his ear. She leaned into him, and they stumbled back against the rolltop desk.

"They've caught up to us, sir! They'll initiate boarding protocols within minutes."

Gemma hadn't heard the door open behind her. She and Kosar pulled away from each other and turned to face Syntha.

"It's the Coastal Patrol," Syntha said. Her eyes locked with Gemma's. There was something behind those eyes that Gemma didn't know how to interpret. It was more than alarm over the situation. Was it jealousy? "We need to hide you immediately."

Kosar walked over to a slim door, opened it to reveal a closet, then decided against it. He glanced around the room.

"How about the desk?" Gemma asked.

"Can you fit?"

Gemma pushed the papers and other items out of the way and boosted herself up. She curled into a fetal position, as small as she could make herself. "Pull it down," she said.

Kosar walked over, kissed her exposed ear, and then rolled the top down. It snapped into place. Splinters of light pierced through the cracks between the wooden slats of the lid and the decorative carvings on the sides. There would be enough air, but Gemma silently prayed that the openings weren't large enough for the soldiers to see through.

The lock clicked. "I'll keep the key with me, Gemma. You'll be safe."

She heard Kosar and Syntha walk out of the room and close the door behind them.

The ship shuddered as it came into contact with their pursuers' vessel. Boots stomped on the deck above. The voices that carried through the porthole were distant and muffled, but Gemma could hear tension in them. Kosar's slick voice stood out among the others, and she was sure he was deescalating the situation, whatever it might be.

The footsteps resumed. The newcomers were searching the deck.

Minutes passed. Gemma half expected to hear the clashing of swords, the screams of Kosar's crew as they were ambushed by the soldiers, but it didn't happen. Any dialogue that made its way to her ears sounded neutral. Jovial, even.

A single set of footsteps descended the stairs to the lower deck. Crates were shuffled, and a knob turned. The soldier entered Kosar's cabin. The light that seeped into the rolltop was cut off abruptly as the newcomer stood just in front of the desk. Gemma silently took in a breath, which smelled like a salty mix of the sea and the soldier's sweat, and held it.

"Find what you're looking for?"

It was a woman's voice—Syntha. The man turned, and Gemma felt a bump as he backed into the desk. "It looks clear to me. I'm just following orders. Want no trouble."

"Nor do we, sir. As we told you, Kosar Herron was on a diplomatic mission for his father. He came to Capital City to welcome King Davin back on behalf of the governorship of the Southern Reaches."

"I understand completely," the man said. "I know that dear Governor Herron's health requires him to stay home in his beautiful southern palace. He has raised a responsible son in Master Kosar."

*Governor?* Gemma thought. She slowly let out her breath as the soldier stepped away from the desk.

"I'm from the Reaches myself," the man said. His voice faded as he walked out of the cabin and closed the door behind him. "Got my start in the governor's royal guard before the Aepistelle Consolidation. I may serve King Davin these days, but Herron will always be the ruler of my youth."

Another jolt rocked the ship minutes later as the Coastal Patrol vessel undocked. Gemma heard Kosar call a pleasant farewell to the soldiers. He rushed down the stairs and through the door and unlocked the desk. As the top rolled up, Gemma looked him over.

She could see it now. Kosar wasn't just the spoiled rich boy she'd expected him to be.

He was royalty.

# Chapter Twenty
## GEMMA

"Not quite royalty, actually," Kosar said. "King Davin has always made it clear that we're not to think of ourselves as such. *Family of the regional governorship* doesn't have quite the same ring to it, though."

The castle loomed above them. From Gemma's current vantage point, it appeared to be superior to the palace in Capital City in every way, including its size. The design was striking. Instead of the cold gray stones of Davin's gothic monstrosity, which was surrounded by a sprawling and filthy metropolis, Herron Castle was constructed of a light tan material, possibly sandstone. It stood on a tree-covered hill overlooking the bay. A pretty little village spread out along the coast at the foot of the hill, but there was plenty of open space between clusters of houses and shops. In the port, sailors on smaller fishing or cargo vessels waved with a genuine politeness that Gemma had never witnessed in her hometown.

As the ship docked, Kosar continued, "When my father

and the other one-time kings gave up their lands to Davin, that was the end of any talk of royalty amongst us. I'm actually surprised Davin didn't force our families to raze our castles. Our quality of life isn't anything to complain about, though. We may have to send the bulk of our tax revenue to Capital City, but we get to keep enough to invest in our communities and still live well."

A team of port attendants wheeled a covered gangplank down the dock and secured it against the port side of the ship. Gemma chuckled at the sight of a red carpet that spanned the length of the ramp and met up with another that ran from the dock to an awaiting carriage. "These still look like the trappings of royalty to me," she said.

Kosar took her hand and guided her down the ramp and into the carriage. Gemma settled into her seat and glanced through the open door. Syntha was a few strides away when Kosar reached out and pulled the door shut. Syntha stopped in her tracks but did not say a word. Kosar gave a slight wave and then tapped the side of the carriage. The driver spurred the horses into motion.

Gemma didn't know what that was about, but she quickly turned away from Syntha's gaze in embarrassment.

"I'm sorry I didn't tell you who I really am sooner," Kosar said. "It wasn't a secret that I was in Capital City, but my official itinerary didn't quite line up with all my actual activities there. I didn't want to put either of us at risk more than we already were."

"What was your official reason for being there?" Gemma asked.

"King Davin was gone for two months. His people had various explanations for where he was, but anyone with half a brain knew those were lies. My father sent me to express his relief that Davin had returned home safe. I was there for his little victory speech, sitting up on a balcony with the other representatives from the Aepistelle regions."

"Why didn't your father go himself? Can't he stand to face his master in person?"

"My father lost his left leg to a blood clot eight years ago. He has been confined to a wheelchair—and to the Southern Reaches—ever since. He could still make the trip, but he chooses not to. Davin hasn't shown any animosity toward him all this time, and my father is not the only governor who keeps his distance from the capital. Most of them send representatives whenever possible."

"So he sent his son, the prince, in his place," Gemma said.

Kosar laughed. "I'm not a prince! Even if my father had maintained his title of king of the Southern Reaches, my older brother, Ysidro, would've been heir to the crown. Alas, I'm but a lowly second-born son of a regional governor. Certainly not a prince."

"Why didn't Ysidro go instead if he's the older brother?" Gemma asked. Of course, she knew that siblings varied quite a bit in their aspirations and skills. She couldn't have been any more different from her own brother, George, if they'd been born in separate parts of the kingdom to different parents.

A scowl crossed Kosar's face. "Ysidro is a drunk. He would tell you that he stays home to assist our father in his regional leadership role. In reality, he spends much more time hiding out in our wine cellar with a growing collection of empty bottles than he spends at our father's side. He's a lost cause."

"And what of Syntha? Is she your sister?"

"Goodness, no! She is my dear cousin, though you may not think it from the looks she gives me. Officially, she's my aide when we travel to Capital City. An attaché, if you will."

"And unofficially?"

"Syntha is a highly skilled fighter. She's my guard, though the two of us grew up training together and I can beat her in a sparring contest." Gemma raised an eyebrow at him, and Kosar shrugged. "Sometimes. Okay, maybe just one time, and it was my birthday, so I think she was going easy on me."

Gemma laughed. Without thinking, she set her hand on his left thigh. She realized what she was doing almost immediately and pulled back. Had he noticed? Gemma didn't try to find out; she turned to her left and glanced out the window. The carriage had made it to the final stretch of the climb, and the castle towered over them. A group of women passed by, smiles on their faces, waving to the occupants of the carriage. Gemma waved back, thinking about her mother.

"Your father must treat his staff well," Gemma said, hoping Kosar would forget about her misplaced touch. "My mother was a maid for King Davin, but she and her peers never left the castle looking half as happy as those ladies."

"Father can be a bit demanding at times, but he pays them fair wages, provides meals, and greets them all by name. It's not a bad gig at all. If you decide to stay a while, we could send for your parents. I'll ensure that your mother has a position on the staff here, if it's to her liking. I guarantee she'll be happier here than she ever was at Davin's castle."

Gemma wanted to lean in and kiss him again, but the carriage came to a halt. An attendant pulled the door open and assisted her outside.

"Welcome to my humble home," Kosar said as he climbed down and stood beside her. He gestured toward a thick pair of open doors that led into a courtyard. The entryway was flanked by the castle staff on each side. Four footmen broke off and hurried to another approaching cart piled with Kosar's luggage. Syntha sat amidst the load, embarrassment clear on her face.

Kosar gestured for Gemma to follow him. He led her past the staff, greeting many of them warmly. Gemma returned the smiles and welcomes she received as she tried to keep up. At the sound of footsteps behind her, she turned and saw Syntha's towering figure approaching. She opened her mouth to say hello, but Syntha avoided eye contact and brushed past. On the other side of the walls, she made an immediate turn and went through a narrow door that Gemma assumed was for the staff. Kosar made no sign that he'd seen his cousin as he led Gemma straight ahead through the main doors and into the castle.

Where Davin's castle was cold and unwelcoming and Harold's in Emyhrsen was in severe disrepair, Governor Herron's palace was bright and lively. Windows lined the outer walls, and murals depicting scenic locales from the province adorned the inner walls. The furniture looked comfortable and inviting instead of stiff and formal. There were plants everywhere, watered and immaculately maintained. The place was teeming with life. Aides and footmen greeted them with genuine smiles as they passed. Nobody looked as if they would rather be somewhere else.

Gemma thought about Kosar's offer to bring her parents here. Her mother would love the environment. Serena Calvertson had always felt like she was walking on eggshells under Davin's staff manager. One mistake and she'd be screamed at; she had feared she'd be flogged in the palace courtyard after two. Here, though, it was clear she'd be treated with the dignity she deserved. Then again, could the happiness last? Surely there was at least one loyalist to Aepistelle's leader here who would leak news of the Calvertson family's whereabouts. If that happened, Gemma had no doubt that Davin would send the entirety of his army to destroy not only Gemma and her parents but also Governor Herron's castle and all of its inhabitants for harboring fugitives.

She felt a squeeze on her hand and turned to Kosar. "Gemma, I must meet with my father in private." He gestured to the elderly butler who walked alongside them. "Carsten here will take you to your quarters. Take some time to freshen up from the journey if you need, and I'll send for you when lunch is served."

Gemma leaned in. "Will your father be upset that you brought me here?" she asked in a low voice. "I don't want to cause any trouble for your family or for the Southern Reaches."

"I know the risks, and I'm perfectly willing to take them. My father will feel the same." With that, Kosar nodded to her and turned down a hall.

"This way, madame," Carsten said.

The butler guided Gemma to a wide staircase lined with plush burgundy carpet. Up two flights of stairs, the air was warmer, but open windows along the corridors ushered in a pleasant breeze. Even with the scent of the seawater just down the hill, the air had a freshness that reminded her of the safety she'd felt with her parents at Quincy's house on the north coast. Carsten led her through a dizzying series of turns on the third level before stopping at a green door. The wood was elaborately carved with branches and leaves. Even the knob was in the shape of a leaf. Carsten grabbed it and turned.

"I hope you will find this suite comfortable, my lady," he said. He stepped aside to let Gemma enter.

She gasped as she took in the room. It stretched the depth of her entire childhood home before ending in an open set of doors that led out to a veranda. Even from the doorway, Gemma could make out the endless stretch of the sea beyond. Far to her right, a bed with four posts and an elaborate canopy looked nearly as big as her bedroom back home, yet the behemoth took up only a fraction of the suite. In the center was a table with a pitcher of water, bottles of white and red wine, an assortment of glasses, and a platter of fresh fruit. On the left was a sitting area with two well-stuffed chairs facing a fireplace. Floor-to-ceiling shelves filled with books lined one interior wall. Gemma walked over to them and chuckled with delight as she ran her fingers along the spines of the leather-bound volumes. Wherever there was empty space between the windows and the furniture, exotic plants grew from painted clay pots. Gemma glanced through an opening and into an adjoining powder room with a washbasin, a counter with neatly arranged perfumes and powders, and a mirror.

Gemma remembered that she was not alone. She turned back toward the gentleman at the door and made her best effort to compose herself. "Yes, thank you, Carsten. I'll be very comfortable here." It felt disingenuous, however, and she cracked an embarrassed smile. "Are you sure this is the right room? I'm fairly certain this was intended for visiting royalty."

Carsten chuckled at this, but Gemma didn't think he meant it in a mocking way. "I assure you, any guest of the Herron family is treated as royalty. It is the way of the Southern Reaches." He pointed toward a tasseled cord that hung from the wall next to the gargantuan bed. "Please do not hesitate to ring for us should you need anything—tea and cakes, some more books, anything at all." With that, he exited and pulled the door closed behind him.

As Carsten's footsteps faded down the hall, Gemma took in her surroundings and laughed. "Oh, Mother, I wish you could see this." She thumbed through the books, considered a volume on the relationship between the Southern Reaches and the neighboring nation of Xaeltúve to the south, then grabbed a collection of fairy tales instead. She took the book out to the veranda, settled into a lounge chair, and fell asleep in the warm breeze within minutes.

# Chapter Twenty-One
## DENNY

Capital City was miles behind them, but still their faux jailers refused to free them. Denny and Arnem exchanged looks, but not a word passed between them; it didn't need to. Arnem crawled toward the front and called up through the iron bars, "What do you say we pull off the road and remove the lock?"

One of their two captors turned back, his auburn bush of a beard flicking sweat onto Arnem's face. It was the closest thing either passenger had received to a drink since they had boarded back at the prison.

"This look like a luxury cruise to you, wee man?" he growled. His companion roared with laughter and pounded a fist on the joker's knee.

"It's just that we must be fifty miles outside of Capital City by now, and Denny and I have been quite patient."

"Patient? You want a prize for that? You're bloody prisoners. Do we look like chauffeurs to you? Should I get me a little fancy hat and a pressed suit and take you to a luxurious dining establishment?"

His companion doubled over laughing and nearly toppled off the side of the platform before the bearded one reached over to steady him. The companion pulled on the reins, and the horses halted. He turned to face Arnem for the first time.

"Perhaps it would be a good time to pop a squat. Don't want you or the boy to soil your britches back there." He turned to his friend. "Come on, Grez. When you're this cranky, I know you need to let one loose."

Grez picked something out of his beard, considered it for a moment, and popped it into his mouth. After swallowing it, he patted his companion's hand. "Aw, Petey, you know me too well."

Grez and Petey hopped down from the wagon. Petey walked to the other side of the road, loosening the rope around his waist that served as a belt. The back of his slacks immediately slipped down, revealing an ample bottom.

"Well, at least I'm not hungry anymore," Denny quipped.

Grez chuckled at that. "The kid's got some humor in him after all," he said to Arnem. He pulled a key from the depths of his coat and unlocked the door, which groaned on its hinges as it swung open. Denny climbed down first, and Arnem made to exit behind him, but Grez pushed him onto his back.

"One at a time, wee man," Grez said. He slammed the door and locked it again. "Don't need the two of you rushing me at once and escaping."

"We're not your prisoners," Denny said. "Venko paid you to get us out of the city and transport us south."

Grez pushed Denny into the brush on the side of the road. The boy wanted to turn around and hit back, but his hands were bound, and he knew he'd be no match for the brute.

"I know what I was paid for. Don't make any difference.

Transporting prisoners is what I do. Anyone comes by and sees you two free like you're hitching a ride, how's that going to reflect on ol' Grez and Petey? We got us a business to run, all respectable-like." He cleared his throat and spit a wad of phlegm at Denny's feet. "Now, get going, baby bird. I know you little ones have frequent accidents and all that."

"I'm fifteen years old. I don't have accidents." Denny narrowed his eyes at Grez. "Do you mind giving me a little privacy at least? I don't like being gawked at by dirty old creeps while I'm trying to go."

"He's a feisty little guy," Grez called back to Arnem. "Where'd you find this one?"

"He's my son," Arnem shot back. "Just let him be. He won't run off without me."

That seemed to be enough for Grez, as he waved Denny off. Denny walked into a grove of trees and relieved himself. He and Arnem hadn't been there when Venko had made the arrangements, but he couldn't believe the man would have agreed to this kind of treatment. He had told them that he trusted these transporters to smuggle them out and get them where they needed to go, but he hadn't indicated that they'd have to play the roles of prisoners the entire ride. Since they weren't able to make the journey by rail, it would take a few extra days to get to the Southern Reaches, where the track terminated. *End of the line*, Denny recited to himself.

The sound of three sets of hooves shook Denny from his thoughts. He pulled up his pants and started making his way back to the road when a hand slammed into his chest and pushed him to the ground.

Grez stood over him, one finger to his lips. "King's men," he said. "Bullocks." Grez bent down, grabbed a handful of mud, and picked Denny up by the collar with his other hand. He smeared the mud onto Denny's face. "Don't say a word."

Through the muck, Denny glanced toward the prison transport wagon. Arnem appeared to understand the danger they were in, as he lay facedown in the filthy straw that littered the floor as if the enclosure were a rodent cage.

"Good afternoon, fine gents," Petey called, diverting their attention to his side of the road. He emerged from the weeds that grew along the edge, tying the rope around his waist as he approached the riders.

"It appeared you left this prisoner on his own," said the head rider, gesturing at Arnem. "Is he even alive in there?"

"Got a bit of a whack on the old noggin, that one," Petey said. "Wouldn't stop singing a rather randy song. Couldn't have him doing that if any little ladies came riding past while I was doing my business."

"Aye," Grez called, causing the riders to turn and look toward him. He thrust Denny forward. "This little delinquent's been corrupted enough by that one. Couple of dangerous ones, even if they look soft."

"Present their papers at once," the lead rider demanded.

"Right away," Petey responded. He jogged to the front of the wagon and pulled a sack out from under the driver's bench. He shuffled through the contents and pulled out a scroll. The rider snatched it, unrolled the paper, and scanned the words.

"Signed by Deputy Warden Venko Garrick himself," Grez called out as he unlocked the wagon door and shoved Denny back inside. "Couple of serial burglars, these ones. Warden said they were caught in the girls' dormitory at the university. Not the first time, either. Get their kicks from that sort of thing, apparently. Crime spree spreading all the way from the Southern Reaches to Capital City. Warrant's been out on them for months, but the good old City Guard finally caught them in the act."

The rider crumpled the paper into a ball and tossed it toward Petey. "I've half a mind to kill them right here in the road and save you cretins a trip to that hellhole of a territory."

"Same here, but we get paid on delivery," Grez said. Denny knew the man was lying—Venko had paid them in advance because they'd been hesitant to smuggle humans. They'd bragged about it their entire trip.

"Go on, then. Get out of our jurisdiction," the rider said. "If I see either of those two on the side of the road again, I might just caught off their bits and feed them to our horses."

All the men laughed, and then the riders continued on their way down the road.

"I'll be sure to bill Venko for any more trouble we come across along the way," Petey said, the jovial look now fully absent from his face. "Any trouble from either of you and I'll do what the soldier wanted, only I'll mail your little parts back to Venko instead."

Grez and Petey mounted the front of the wagon and resumed their journey.

# Chapter Twenty-Two
## GEMMA

The slightest scraping of metal woke Gemma from her nap on the balcony. Even before her eyes opened, her hands flew to either side of her waist, searching for something that was not there.

"Is this what you're looking for?"

Syntha stood over her, wisps of brown hair blowing in the warm breeze. The sun glinted off the blade of the machete Quincy had reworked for Gemma only days before. The woman turned it over in her hands, admiring the craftsmanship. Then she gripped it in her right hand and tested it out with several swings through the air.

"It's quite a nimble weapon," she said as she flipped it with ease and held the hilt out to Gemma. As soon as Gemma grasped the machete, Syntha pulled her own sword from her belt. The sound of its unsheathing was far less quiet than the whisper of the machete. "Let's see how you handle it."

Gemma hesitated. She glanced behind Syntha and into the room, curious if Kosar had put her up to this for his own enjoyment, but the man was nowhere to be seen. Had

Syntha's jealousy over Kosar's attention on Gemma led to this moment? Gemma knew she was no match for this woman, whom Kosar had described as a skilled fighter.

Still, Gemma had no intention of just sitting there and taking it. Whether or not Kosar was watching, she had no doubt word of this would get back to him. A part of her really wanted to impress him. She pushed the book off her lap and leapt to her feet.

"It's been through a couple fights of before, but—"

"I've no doubt that little blade can slice a man," Syntha interrupted, "but I'm more skeptical about its wielder. Come, Gemma Calvertson, and show me what you've got."

Gemma lunged forward and thrust the machete at her. Syntha whipped her sword in a circular motion, and the machete flew out of Gemma's hand.

"It's a slicing weapon, Gemma, not a piercing one." She gave it a gentle kick across the ground toward Gemma. "I won't fault you for the odd choice of a blade, but you may as well use it properly. Pick it up."

Gemma did. This time, she made a swiping motion toward Syntha's sword hand. Syntha moved the hand out of the way in time, moved it in a circle, and used the back of her fist to hit Gemma's hand. The machete dropped to the ground again.

"Better, but your grip is weak. You don't want to over-tighten, either. Loose enough to be fluid." Syntha spun her own hilt in her hand and moved the blade in a figure-eight pattern three times. It came close enough to Gemma that she wondered if Syntha hadn't snipped a few loose hairs that hung from her bangs. "Once more."

Gemma reclaimed her machete, took a deep breath, then repeated her previous move, this time bringing her body toward Syntha's, leaving her opponent unable to swing her own sword. Gemma's shoulder slammed into Syntha, who took three quick steps back and brought her sword down. Gemma blocked the blow just above her left shoulder with the machete and used what little strength she had after her nap to push the blade away. Again she closed in the distance between them. Syntha took two more steps back before hitting the railing of the balcony. She pushed off and lunged at Gemma, who stumbled backward in surprise. Syntha whipped her sword in a circular motion once more. Gemma lost her grip as she tumbled onto her bottom on the balcony floor. She watched as the machete flew through the air and clanked against the railing. Syntha effortlessly darted forward and caught the machete by the hilt before it could plummet three levels to the ground below.

"Let's work on that some more," Syntha said. Her smile took Gemma by surprise. It seemed genuine, like she'd greatly enjoyed their quick melee. Gemma took a deep breath of relief as she realized Syntha wasn't trying to intimidate her.

"I'd like that," Gemma said.

Syntha returned her sword to its scabbard and then reached over to help Gemma up. "Truly, the metalwork on this is outstanding." She swung the machete at a small potted tree behind the chair Gemma had fallen asleep on. The figs that grew from the tree plopped down on the ground. "You can surely do some damage with it, but surviving a skilled opponent is another matter entirely."

"It sure helped with fighting off the trees during the battle at Emyhrsen," Gemma said, then felt foolish. Nobody except those who had been there had even heard of the events. That was the entire point of her manuscript, which Kosar had brought her there to publish. "Sorry, that—"

"It's your story to tell. Kosar believes it's one worth risking everything for. He's been convincing his father of that all afternoon." Syntha handed the machete back to Gemma. "Oh, yes, I came to tell you that dinner is nearly ready. Kosar and his father should be in the dining hall shortly. Let us join them."

"Dinner?" Gemma turned and noted that the sun was no longer directly overhead but on its way down, as if it meant to crash into the Western Sea. "I must have slept straight through lunch."

Syntha gestured for Gemma to follow her inside. An assortment of covered trays had been left on the table. Under one of them was a note. Gemma skimmed the apology from Kosar, which explained that he was occupied and would not see her until dinner.

"The servants didn't wish to wake you for lunch, it seems," Syntha said.

A dress had been laid out on the bed for Gemma to wear. Its warm colors and elaborate patterns put anything Gemma had worn back home in Capital City to shame. She brought the dress into the powder room, changed into it, and quickly cleaned herself up before Syntha led her through a maze of hallways and down a narrower staircase than the one Carsten had guided her up earlier that afternoon.

THE DINING HALL WAS EASILY AS GRAND AS THE ONE IN King Davin's castle—Gemma had been there with her mother for the staff luncheons Davin's advisors held—though only one table was laid in the center of the room. The others were curtained off on either side of the room, spares for banquets and gatherings. As Gemma stepped into the hall, she noticed that Syntha was no longer at her side. Gemma turned back to her. "Aren't you coming?" she asked.

In a hushed voice, Syntha said, "I mostly eat in the staff dining room unless my presence is requested here." She looked past Gemma at the occupants of the table and then smiled. "I'll leave you to get acquainted with the family. Enjoy your meal." With that, she closed the doors.

There were only three people at the table. Kosar was the first to rise. He flashed his charming grin at Gemma. A man who must've been Ysidro noticed a second later that the family had company, and he too rose to his feet and nodded. He didn't sway drunkenly or look like the deadbeat Kosar had described. He had darker hair and skin than Kosar, different shades of brown from Gemma's, and his features were much more similar to those of the Xaeltúve people in the south. He was shorter than his brother and void of his cockiness yet equally handsome in his own unique way.

Gemma turned her gaze toward the head of table. She knew not to expect the young men's father to rise, as he'd lost a leg a few years back, but Governor Herron had indeed hobbled up onto his one remaining foot and leaned awkwardly yet respectfully against his end of the table. He matched Ysidro's appearance in nearly every way, though a large streak of white shot straight through the center of his full head of brown hair. Like Ysidro, he looked almost nothing like Kosar.

Gemma suddenly realized that she didn't know how to greet a regional governor properly. She settled for an awkward half bow that she imagined looked like someone bending down to fix their boot and then thinking better of it. Kosar laughed.

"No need to bow to my old man," he said, reading her intentions clearly. "That's yet another thing King Davin would probably have our heads over."

"Don't be so crass, Kosar," his father said before turning

to address Gemma. "Welcome to the Southern Reaches, Miss Calvertson. Please, come join us on this end of the table."

The men remained standing as Gemma walked down the length of the table, which appeared to be built for thirty guests or more. The extra place setting was next to Ysidro. Kosar was positioned across from them. She sat and pulled in her chair, and the others followed suit. A server came by and filled up her glass with a deep burgundy wine. She looked around and found that the same liquid filled the glasses in front of Kosar and his father, but Ysidro's glass held only water.

"Thank you for dining with us, Miss Calvertson," the governor said. "It's not often that Kosar brings us guests to entertain."

"The gratitude is all mine, Governor Herron. And please, call me Gemma."

"And you may call me Joseph. I have gotten used to the title of governor, but I still think my own father must turn in his grave each time it is used to address me."

"Careful now, Father," Ysidro said. "It is an honor to retain any title under our gracious king."

"No need to be formal here, Ro." Kosar said. He winked at Gemma. "Our special guest is not going to report any of us to Davin's people."

"You are right, of course, Ysidro. I am grateful to still be able to govern the people of these lands and continue in the footsteps of our forebears, even if in a lesser capacity. May King Davin rule long and prosper." Joseph lifted his glass in a toast and then sipped his wine. Gemma thought she detected a tinge of sarcasm in his voice and a subtle eye roll. He set the glass down. "So, Gemma, Kosar tells us you are a fugitive. You and some of your friends have made it onto the Royal Mystic Committee's most-wanted list."

Gemma nearly choked on her wine. Ysidro shifted uncomfortably in his chair next to her while Kosar's grin returned. Something about his mischievous looks made her blush.

"Yes, that seems to be the case. I—"

She stopped when she felt Kosar's foot rub hers under the table. He winked at her. "Father is only toying with you, Gemma. I've explained everything, so there's no need to elaborate. Besides, look how uncomfortable it makes my brother."

Gemma didn't feel right about glancing at Ysidro. She continued, "I'm very grateful that Kosar found me and pulled me out of Capital City. I do hope I haven't caused you any trouble by coming to the Southern Reaches."

"I give it a few days before word gets to Davin's people and they send someone to investigate," Joseph said. "Happens quite frequently. They're always on edge about one thing or another. I swear, for a king, Davin is quite insecure about himself and his legitimacy. At least as far as I know, he's not a bastard son like Kosar here."

This time it was Kosar's turn to choke on his wine and shift uncomfortably. "Well, you just came out and said it, didn't you, Father? Yes, Mother was unfaithful for a short spell, but I'm as much a part of this family as anyone."

That explained it, then. Kosar's fairer skin and light hair made him stand out next to his father and brother, but in every other way, their dynamics were as familial and congenially dysfunctional as any Gemma had come across in her lifetime, including her own.

"Aye, that you are, and I miss your mother dearly," Joseph said. He put one hand on each of his sons' hands and patted them gently. "Let that be a lesson to you boys. Never take your partner for granted. Family is more important than anything, even kingship."

"Governorship," Ysidro corrected without warmth in his

voice. He pulled his hand out from under his father's and gulped down his water. Gemma was sure she'd been to more awkward dinners, but at the moment she couldn't actually recall any. She smirked across the table at Kosar, hoping it matched the cockiness of his own expression.

Just then, a line of servants entered the dining hall, each bearing a different bowl or platter. All the courses were served at once, the juices and sauces of each item mixing on the large plate in front of Gemma. She felt relieved that the meal was as informal as any she would have had with her parents and George back when they'd had a home together in Capital City.

Small talk filled the air between bites, and the Herron family threw considerably fewer barbs at one another. Ysidro and Kosar even seemed to get along for a few minutes, joking about their father and reminiscing over inconsequential events from their childhood. There was no further mention of Gemma's predicament or the potential trouble her presence might cause, though she did suspect it remained on Ysidro's mind. He was cordial enough to Gemma, but she could tell it was weighing on him.

When their plates held only crumbs and puddles of grease, the servers returned to clear the table. Ysidro rose and declared that it was time to bring Joseph back to his quarters for the night. He wheeled his father the length of the dining hall before turning back. "Good night to you, Gemma. Please, be careful of my brother. He may be charming, but he plays by his own rules with little regard for others."

With that, the doors were opened by the footmen, and he pushed his father's wheelchair out of sight.

When they were alone, Kosar scooted down one chair to place himself directly across from Gemma. "Well, can't say I didn't expect that to be awkward, but they went straight for it."

"They're sweet," Gemma said. "You told me Ysidro was a drunk, but he stuck with water the entire meal. Is he recovering?"

Kosar flashed a rare look of guilt like a child caught in a lie, but he quickly put a smile back on his face, showing his pearly teeth. "He's showing off for the guest, I think. As soon as he's handed our father off to the valet, he'll slink to his rooms and get back in his cups."

"Your father seemed quite open to talking about your mother."

"Yes, he blames himself for driving her to infidelity. He's always been a warm presence, at least when he *is* present. Unfortunately, that wasn't often the case early in their marriage. It was just after Davin had consolidated the lands of Aepistelle. Father took it a lot harder than he lets on. He wanted to prove he still held power and show that he still cared for these lands. He traveled all over the Southern Reaches, striving to be visible to the people who had once called him king. Mother grew lonely. The depression after Ysidro's birth didn't help. She took to drinking in Father's absence. Perhaps that's where Ysidro gets it from."

Gemma wasn't sure if he would answer her next question, but she asked anyway. "How did she meet your father? Um, I mean, your..." She didn't know what to call it.

"The man who intruded on their marriage?" Kosar laughed, but Gemma sensed he was more uncomfortable than he let on. "Mother visited Capital City for a retreat hosted by Queen Elise, along with the other former queens from the regions of Aepistelle. She was gone for a couple of months, and less than a year later, I was born. I'm not even sure if my father—Joseph—knows the real story there, but he's never treated me as anything but his own son."

"He's a good man," Gemma said.

Kosar pushed his chair back and jumped to his feet. His overly joyous expression made it clear that he was ready to drop the subject.

"Come, let us enjoy this warm evening."

He led Gemma out a back door, down a narrow hall, and out into a lush garden. The stars were out in full effect. Unseen katydids and crickets and frogs harmonized in a screechy yet lovely song. Kosar pulled her through an arched trellis covered in morning glories to what felt like a remote section of the courtyard. They sat on a bench, no words passing between them. Gemma wondered if Kosar was thinking of his mother; perhaps the topic wasn't as open as Governor Joseph had made it seem. Gemma reached over and put her hand on his cheek, feeling a line of tears that had fallen. She pulled him closer and met his lips with her own.

# Chapter Twenty-Three
## GEMMA

For the second time in as many days, Gemma woke with a blade aimed at her. Once again, Syntha was its bearer. The young woman wasn't merely standing at the side of the bed; she was on top of the mattress, feet on either side of Gemma, her sword pointed inches from Gemma's face. She was partially hunched to fit under the bed's canopy.

"Got you again, Calvertson," Syntha roared as if it were the funniest moment of her week, and perhaps it truly was. "All too easy. If you're going to survive this whole fugitive life thing, you need to be aware of your surroundings at all times."

She bent a little lower and leapt off of the bed, careful to avoid the lining of the canopy that hung over the side. She used the sword to pick up a pile of folded clothes, then flung them at Gemma before returning her sword to its scabbard.

"Why are you here?" Gemma asked. With the heavy curtains over the windows, she had no idea what time it was. The only light in the room came from the lanterns Syntha had lit before waking her. "Did I sleep late again?"

"It's an hour past sunrise. Time to ride."

Syntha didn't bother leaving the room so that Gemma could get dressed in privacy. Instead, she pulled open the curtains and then poked at the books, thumbing through them but not appearing to read any of the words. Gemma pulled on the undergarments, slacks, and shirt Syntha had provided. They were all slightly too large for her, and she assumed they belonged to Syntha. They were quite a bit less formal than the dress from the evening before, but they were much more her style. She moved into the powder room, used the commode, and tied her hair back into a ponytail.

"Where are we going?" Gemma asked as she picked at a tray of fruit that had been delivered at some point during her slumber.

Syntha pulled a long knife from its sheath on her belt and stabbed a quartered nectarine. "Somewhere not to be spoken of here," she said through her chewing. She reached for a satchel and thrust it at Gemma, who had to drop the grapes she was about to consume in order to catch it. "Your manuscript is in there. Protect it well."

Gemma followed Syntha down the narrow service stairwell to the lowest floor of the castle. They cut through a pantry and the servants' dining room—everyone around the table rose to attention as she passed by, and she flashed an embarrassed but warm smile at them—and out a back door. The yard was full of crates and barrels that had been delivered that morning for the day's meals. Chickens ran free and pecked at grain sacks. Gemma wanted to stop and enjoy the setting, but Syntha moved determinedly toward the horse stable, where two mares were saddled up and waiting for them.

Gemma was a city girl and had ridden horses only a few times. Syntha jumped on without a problem, but Gemma had trouble boosting herself up in the stirrup. "These are well-trained gals," Syntha said, realizing Gemma's inexperience, "and as long as you treat them kindly, they won't throw you off." Gemma made it into the saddle and breathed a sigh of relief. Syntha spurred her mount into motion and clicked for Gemma's to follow.

The horses broke into a full gallop once they reached the winding street. Gemma gripped the reins hard as they made their way down the hill from the castle. She wasn't even sure if she was remembering to breathe. Syntha looked back a few times and laughed and whooped, her hair flying back wildly. Gemma idolized her freedom in that moment, her ability to cast off the weight of the world and just enjoy what was around her. Gemma let herself smile, and she too bellowed an excited whoop as they sped away from Kosar's palace.

They rushed past the village at the bottom of the hill and turned down an uneven road barely wide enough for carts. "There may be some dips in the road, but the horses are quite agile," Syntha said as she slowed to a trot alongside Gemma. "They've been down this way many times before and know the potholes well."

"And where does this road lead to?" Gemma asked. They were now surrounded by fields of crops and could see barns off in the distance on either side of the road. Field hands tended to the berries and tomatoes and lettuce that grew around them. "If it's safe to talk about that now, I mean."

"We have a team that Kosar assembled months ago—those who wish to reveal the truth about Aepistelle. Other guerrilla reporters like Kosar fancies himself."

"You don't sound enthused about it," Gemma observed.

"I mostly run security for them. I have a few friends who take shifts, make sure nobody comes poking around. Davin's spies could be anywhere." Syntha looked around distrustfully at the workers toiling in the fields. "Anyone can whisper. So, was dinner last night awkward?"

Gemma chuckled at the bluntness of the question. "A little bit, yes. The governor and Ysidro were quite sweet, though. Why didn't you eat with us? I thought you were family as well."

The smile faded from Syntha's face. "Uncle Joseph is a kind and generous man, but I come from his late wife's family."

"He seems to be fond of his wife, though, even after her transgressions."

"Ah, he mentioned that? I bet Kosar turned red as a strawberry. No, you're right. He was still as in love with her on her deathbed as he must have been in their marriage bed. That's just it, really. I remind him of her. I can tell. Grief washes over him anytime he sees me. He says I laugh exactly like her and that I look as if I'm a sculpture of her carved by the most skilled artisan in the land. My mother was her twin sister; Kosar and I were born within months of each other. Then consumption took them both not long after our births."

"I'm very sorry to hear that," Gemma said. They'd ridden some distance since the last active farm, but she spotted another barn on the horizon.

"He would treat me like his own daughter if I let him, and he did for many years. I learned from the same tutors as Ysidro and Kosar. I sat at the table with them for meals. Once I was old enough to develop skills with a blade, however, I wanted a different path. Politics don't appeal to me the way they do Kosar. I support the ways he strives for truth and justice, but I prefer different tactics. I excelled at our physical training and put Kosar to shame during our swordsmanship lessons. That was for me. That was my truth, not negotiations and treaties." She patted the hilt of the sword at her side.

"I understand completely. My brother, George, and I couldn't be any more different from each other. School was always where I excelled, but he left early to apprentice as a blacksmith. He found his calling in the forge."

They closed in on the barn Gemma had been eying. Just inside the gates, a man in a wide-brimmed hat poked at a bale of hay with a pitchfork. He looked Gemma over suspiciously but nodded to Syntha in recognition. Gemma smiled at him, but he looked away and continued his charade of working the farm. "One of my team," Syntha said to her.

They dismounted and tied their horses up. Syntha led Gemma around the corner and pulled open one of the barn doors. Inside, three women and four men were huddled around a makeshift table littered with parchment, inkpots, and pens. Kosar rose to his feet at their arrival. He jogged over to the entrance, took Gemma's hands, and kissed her on the cheek.

"I'm so glad you made it," he said quietly before turning back toward the onlookers. "Crew, this is Gemma Calvertson."

To her surprise, all six people around the table stood and clapped. Gemma didn't know how to respond, but she felt herself blushing. A hand hit her hard on the back, and she turned around to see Syntha grinning, reveling in Gemma's embarrassment.

"As I told you all this morning," Kosar continued, "Gemma has been on a truth-seeking mission for several months now, using her position at the Capital University Press to gain access to Richard the Elusive. She traveled with him through the wastelands of the north to the kingdom of Emyhrsen and saw everything we've all dreamed of teaching our countrymen with her very eyes."

The people at the table murmured amongst themselves in

awe. It was so surreal to Gemma to be thought of as some kind of advocate for truth. She'd just been doing her job before fate had brought her on her journey with Richard, and after that she was only trying to survive. Yet what Kosar said was true: the places she had traveled and the things she had experienced had been nothing short of illegal under the laws of King Davin. Many enlightened folks across Aepistelle, like those gathered in that barn, could only dream of experiencing even half of what Gemma had done in a few brief months.

"Thanks for the welcome," Gemma said. Kosar took her by the hand and led her to the table. She turned back to see that Syntha had once again walked off as if she didn't belong with Kosar and his ilk. "What are you all working on?"

One of the women stood up. "I'm Alyssa. I cover international relations, previously of the *Esteron Daily Courier*. I fled down here after I ruffled some feathers with my story about Hinterland migrants being turned away by the crown because of their alleged history of elemental magic. The Royal Mystic Committee ransacked my parents' home but stopped short of imprisoning them. I arrived here with nothing but the clothes on my back last spring, and the crew welcomed me in. Right now I'm looking into the relationship between Davin's regime and the Xaeltúve government. There's a new rail line that was built over the summer that runs through the border and into—"

"Don't overwhelm Gemma with all that just yet, Lyss," Kosar interrupted. His tone was harsher than Gemma expected.

"My name is Clarnen," said a man who looked to be about twenty years older than Gemma and the others. "I'm working on a series on possible secession attempts by the regional governors."

"Just leave my father out of that one, please," Kosar said.

"Byrna," said the woman directly to Gemma's right. "I've been investigating a string of killings in Capital City that may be related to additional murders around Aepistelle. Most of the victims are former officers of the Royal Mystic Committee."

The others went on about their work, all presenting stories that would get them arrested or even executed by Davin's regime. Some focused on misdeeds of the king himself while others hinted at the continued use of magic in parts of the kingdom or spoke of foreign relations that were not public knowledge.

"Wow, you're all heroes in your own ways for what you're doing," Gemma said. "This is all so important. This is what the people of Aepistelle need to hear, and it's the reason I set out on my own assignment earlier this year, even if there was little chance of getting the truth printed by my employer. Even if I can't tell my story to the world, I'm so proud of the efforts you've made and risks you all are taking."

"Nonsense," Kosar said. "Your story *will* be told." He reached across the table for Gemma's satchel and pulled out the stack of papers. "Everyone, this is Gemma's record of her time with Richard the Elusive. It contains firsthand accounts of King Davin and his soldiers defending the slavers that held Emyhrsen in bondage. It tells of a giant and a witch and a forest of tree monsters."

"Sounds like a fairy tale to me." This came from a grumpy-looking bespectacled man with red hair who had introduced himself as Henry.

"You question the veracity of Gemma's claims?" Kosar asked. The others were silent in shock.

"I don't mean that," Henry said. "But I'm not so sure it fits in with the issues we're reporting about what's happening in this kingdom right now, things that directly affect the daily lives of the people of Aepistelle. Besides, we already have enough trouble printing the stories by the seven of us and all our companions in the field. How are we supposed to expand our production to this degree, even if we serialize that monstrosity?" He pointed at Gemma's hundreds of hand-written pages.

"Ah, that brings us to the important topic of the output of our little paper," Kosar said. "Alyssa was just telling us this morning that we can't keep up with demand. Our two little hand-cranked presses print off only enough papers per day to supply a couple of local villages."

Alyssa nodded and took over. "Most people in the Southern Reaches are still in the dark, and word is that Davin's troops ransacked the office of the Reaches' only official paper, *Our Daily Freedom*, just yesterday. It's not as if they were reporting any of the same revelations we've been printing, but they printed an editorial column questioning elements of Davin's recent grand return speech. Now the entire staff of that paper is hanging from the trees outside their office."

"That's horrible," Gemma said. She felt sick to her stomach.

"Isn't it?" Henry said absently. "To make matters worse, their printing press, which is the most advanced in the entire kingdom, is being dismantled as we speak and loaded onto a train bound for Capital City."

"Steam-powered," Clarnen said.

"Double-barreled," Zinnie offered.

Henry regained control of the conversation. "They can print two sides at a time, more than a thousand copies per hour. The distribution opportunities with that kind of output are unfathomable."

"With that kind of machine, we could get Gemma's story

out into the world and still have plenty of production space for our weekly edition," Byrna said.

"So what's the plan?" Kosar asked.

Everyone turned to Gemma in unison.

"Um...what?" she asked, though she was certain she knew what they were thinking.

"We hear you have experience breaking into places," Lorne said. "We've all gotten pretty good at putting on our masks and sneaking around, talking to sources from the shadows, making drops of our newspaper in secret. But none of that compares with what we're looking to do."

"If Gemma goes, I'll be right there with her." Gemma turned to find Syntha standing at the door, patting the hilt of her sword. "You all may be good at sneaking around, but for this, you'll need protection."

# Chapter Twenty-Four

## MARZELE

Every droplet of water that fell from some unseen crack was like an explosion, every creak from the floorboards far above his head a roar of thunder. Marzele had expected his eyes to adjust to the darkness after what felt like a week in this makeshift dungeon, yet he could still see nothing, not even light around the edges of the locked door at the top of the narrow staircase down which he'd been pushed. Without the sight that he now realized he'd always taken for granted, his ears were more sensitive than ever before. There was a light scratching of claws, the pitter-patter of a mouse's feet somewhere in the room. There were the infrequent coughs, scraping of chairs, and shuffling of his captors somewhere in the building above him.

He wasn't sure if his sense of smell had increased as well, but regardless his eyes watered from the stench of the place. He didn't doubt that the dripping liquid he could hear had been excreted by a human or an animal. He could even taste it with every breath he took through his mouth. Foul. Filthy.

And then there was the feel of the place, the grime and dampness everywhere he attempted to sit or lay his head. Unseen crawling things used his face as a roadway as he tried to sleep.

In addition, his sense of time had completely disappeared. With no light, no clock, and no discernible pattern to the noises his captors made upstairs, Marzele had lost track of how many hours or days he'd been locked up. He'd felt his way around the room in his inaugural hours and had found a chest containing jugs of water, jars of dried meats and fruits, and a loaf of stale bread. He hadn't found a chamber pot, so he'd combined the contents of some of the jars and had been doing his best to contain his waste to those he'd emptied.

Why had Horace locked him in this place? The man had seemingly invited Marzele to join him in the Cult of Arun just before tricking him into walking right into this prison. Had that been a lie?

Perhaps this was all some sick hazing activity. If it was a test of whether he still resented Solendaron, it confirmed that he did. Had Marzele's passion for the Lord reignited, he also should have regained the powers the Lord had once provided. He'd tested it. He had prayed, just like he had in the prison on Terminus Rock, and again he'd been met with silence from his god. He had no power to melt the metal bolts that kept him trapped in here.

Perhaps, then, he was expected to gain something from this experience. He was in the dark, away from the sun, buried in shadow. Was he supposed to connect with the Tïhn, find some new power in the antithesis of Solendaron and use it to escape? There *was* something poetic about leaving the light of Solendaron and entering a land of shadows, emerging as a carrier of darkness. But he hadn't studied the Tïhn before, wasn't versed in their prayers. Marzele knew they spoke the same tongue as the followers of the Solendaron faith, but the incantations were unknown to him. He tried to meditate, to absorb the shadows, become one with the unseen. And still nothing happened.

"Horace, you monster!" Marzele screamed at the ceiling, hoping his words carried to the room above. "Why have you locked me down here? I told you I would join you. What did I do to deserve your scorn? Let me out of here at once!"

He knew it wouldn't work. He'd called out to Horace and to any other ears that may hear him dozens of times, and his captors had made no indication that they'd heard a word of it.

"Please!" he yelled, then broke into a coughing fit. His lungs had felt as if they were deteriorating in the damp cellar for what felt like two or three days now. Marzele stumbled over to the chest, unlatched it, and opened the lid. He felt for the last jug that held any water. Even that one contained only a couple of sips, but he needed those sips now. He drained the liquid into his mouth, and still he felt unsatisfied.

Was there any place in this world he belonged? He'd been abandoned by the Lord of the Light, Solendaron, to whom he'd dedicated his entire life. He had led his fellow priests into a trap that had resulted in their deaths. He'd abandoned his new friends, Gemma, Arnem, and Denny, to seek revenge after they'd risked their own lives to free him from bondage on Terminus Rock. And now this. He'd never quite considered Horace a friend; even though they'd been equals in the faith, Horace had always looked down on his fellow priests. Horace, with his inherited wealth and status, his fancy family house in Capital City, his position in society that had been restored even after the criminalization of religion in Aepistelle meant they could no longer practice their faith. But during that brief moment upstairs, he'd trusted Horace. He'd had no other choice. And now he'd been left to die in this wretched place.

His cry was as full of sorrow as it was of anger.

MORE TIME PASSED. WITH NO FOOD OR WATER LEFT, Marzele had no energy. He slept. Felt sorry for himself. Slept some more. Crouched at the door whispering, pleading with what strength he could muster. And still no man or god took pity on him. He stood and began to make his way back down the steps when he lost his footing, cracked his head open on a step, and landed sprawled at the bottom.

"Darkness take me," he murmured. "Bring me home to Your realm of shadows. Take me from this land of light."

And that's when the door opened.

The newcomer held a single candle, but after the days of darkness, it may as well have been a torch. It burned his eyes, and he covered them. He took in the scent that wafted in— stale leftovers of food cooked days ago, but it could have been the smell of a gourmet meal prepared for royalty by the way it made Marzele's stomach growl.

"Food...water...please," Marzele croaked from his parched throat. He listened to the footsteps descending the stairs— heavy steps from a heavy man. "Horace, please."

"Hello again, old friend. You've survived this ordeal despite your stubbornness. I thought you'd go back to your first love, Solendaron. You called on him—I heard it—but your heart was not truly in it, even at death's door. However, neither did you pass this test. Survival wasn't what we sought from you. I told them you'd succeed, but you've made a fool out of me."

Horace kicked him in the ribs, but Marzele had no

strength to cry out. Even the grunt of pain that escaped him only begot more pain.

"You were the most powerful in the Order of Solendaron, the ideal practitioner we all aspired to be like. Maybe we never told you that; your humbleness was probably what made you so special, so we didn't want it to go to your head. Knowing that, I truly thought you'd emerge from this place on your own, channeling the power of the Tihn and bringing down the door or the ceiling with strength provided to you by the Shadow."

Horace trotted across the basement and kicked the chest onto its side. The empty jugs and excrement-filled jars rolled out. He picked up one of the jars and lobbed it toward Marzele. It shattered three feet from his sprawled-out body, the contents splashing Marzele's face.

"You made me look like a fool. I overestimated you. Over-promised. If it were up to me, I'd leave you here to die. However, it seems you are in His Darkness's favor. The others have insisted that your survival this long is proof enough that you're ready to ride with us."

Marzele took a deep breath, mustered his strength, and rolled away from the shards of glass and the splattered waste. He sat up, leaning against a damp mossy wall.

"Ride?" he whispered. "A horse can hold your weight?"

He braced for another jar to come sailing through the air at him, but instead Horace broke into a hearty laugh.

"Well, perhaps your spirit is not as broken as I thought. Not yet, anyway." Horace walked over and offered his hand. Marzele took it and allowed Horace to pull him to his feet. The world spun, but the man held him up. "Yes, the Cult has been holed up in the capital for too long now. It's time to demonstrate our full potential, to show King Davin and his regime that their time is done. They may have the political power, but we have *true* power, divinely appointed."

"Time to come out of the shadows?" Marzele asked.

"No. We will cast the shadows over them, over all of Aepistelle. It is time for a new era, and we will lead it. Even you, Marzele, if you are up for it."

# Chapter Twenty-Five
## GEMMA

The last time she'd been on a train, Gemma had unexpectedly been given a room in the first-class car, the ticket paid for in secret by the Royal Mystic Committee. She hadn't been dispatched directly by the Committee to interview Richard the Elusive but rather by her boss at Capital University Press, yet she had been unknowingly acting as an agent for the mysterious organization.

This time, her ticket was paid for by Kosar, and she was on a mission to steal from that same clandestine committee.

She was crammed into a private room with Lorne. The pair was posing as husband and wife embarking on a trip to Centeron from their home in the town of Castillo in the Southern Reaches. Gemma wasn't into the idea, but Alyssa had planned this escapade, and Gemma quite liked the younger woman and wanted to support her. Lorne didn't seem to have a problem with the cover story; he leaned his head on Gemma's shoulder when he heard porters or fellow passengers approaching the windows of their chamber. His unkempt beard was scratchy against Gemma's neck, and she wanted to swat him away, but she kept up the act for the sake of the mission.

"A glass of white for the lady and red for the gentleman," their server said as he brought them the complimentary beverages they'd ordered. Actually, Lorne had ordered for her, assuming she'd prefer white wine, which really got on Gemma's nerves. "Please let me know if I can do anything else to make your journey with us more pleasurable." With that, he left, and Gemma scooted away from Lorne. He slurped his drink like a child.

"I sure could get used to this," he said. "I didn't get as lucky as Kosar when it comes to the parental lottery. My mother tutored Kosar and Ysidro, and my father was a knight who served their father back when he was a king."

"And what about you?" Gemma asked. She was a bit repulsed by her companion but was trying her best to be amiable.

"Oh, I don't have the brawn of my father or the brains of my mother. Officially I'm an accountant, but I've been working with Kosar and the group for the last several months. I do economic analysis for our little paper. You'd be surprised how much the crown lies to the people about the kingdom's financial situation. Did you know that King Davin's minister of finance has borrowed millions from nations overseas in order to keep things running smoothly?"

He droned on about economics, and Gemma did her best to stay interested, but she just didn't have the heart—or the stomach—for it. She rose to her feet and slid open the door to the hall.

"I need to stretch my legs," she said. She closed the door before she could hear her faux mate object and headed down the hall. At the end, she pulled open the door and made her way into the next car.

The dining car was quite crowded even though meals weren't yet being served. Windows stretched across it, allowing for breathtaking views of the scenery. The train was speeding north through rocky canyons and climbing the hills that stretched into the Costonoan border. Gemma glanced around the car, pausing briefly on three soldiers who were enjoying the sights on a break from their duties. Her eyes stopped on a couple who stood at the bar at the far end of the dining car. Alyssa had paired herself up with Kosar, and they held hands as they waited in line to order drinks. Even though Gemma knew they were just acting, Alyssa was doing too good a job of it. The young woman's free hand stroked Kosar's arm as she laughed at some joke he must have told. She leaned her head against his shoulder, then raised her face to meet Kosar's and kissed him on the cheek.

To his credit, Kosar looked as uncomfortable as Gemma felt. The patrons in front of them received their drinks and moved to a table, so Kosar stepped forward, shaking off Alyssa. Henry stood on the other side of the bar, dressed smartly in a white server's jacket and bow tie. Zinnie's father was an executive of the Southern Aepistelle Rail Company and was sympathetic to their cause. He'd gotten them onboard easily and had planted Henry as a bartender with few questions asked. Henry leaned over the bar and whispered something to Kosar, who turned around and briefly glanced at Gemma. Alyssa followed his gaze and shot Gemma a wink before she wrapped her arms around Kosar.

Gemma found a vacant table next to the window and sat. She found it a bit dizzying to watch the landscape speeding past, but it was quite a way to take in part of the country she'd never seen before. She got lost in the sights, enjoying her moment of solitude, until someone dropped into the seat next to her.

"Ah, there you are, my love," Lorne said. He placed a hand on Gemma's, but she quickly pulled hers back and dropped it into her lap. Lorne leaned closer and whispered, "Sorry, was that too much?"

"Just a little." Gemma resumed watching the trees and hillsides flash by out the window. Footsteps approached, and she looked up to see Kosar and Alyssa walking their way, hand in hand. Kosar smiled at Gemma and Lorne.

"Good afternoon," he said casually, then guided Alyssa to the table directly behind Gemma. He spoke to Alyssa just loud enough to be audible to Lorne and Gemma. "Well, it seems we're just about ten minutes from entering quite a long tunnel. The bartender said it's a good idea to sit tight, as it's about to get quite dark onboard."

Ten minutes before they would act. Gemma hoped she could put up with Lorne for even that much longer. She sat with him for another five minutes, barely even pretending to listen to whatever he was babbling on about. She winced when he touched her arm and did her best to ignore the enjoyment that Kosar and Alyssa seemed to be taking in each other behind her.

After five minutes had passed, Gemma proceeded with the next stage of their plan. She rose and approached Henry at the bar. "Hello, sir," she said. "I'd like to order a bottle of Plentimore Falls Red for my husband and me."

"Now, that's quite a pick," Henry said. "You must be celebrating."

"Yes, it's our anniversary."

Henry turned and pretended to search the shelves for a bottle that the train's otherwise well-stocked bar didn't actually carry. "I don't seem to have one here—I'll need to check our storage in the luggage car," he said. He waved down one of the servers, who came over in a hurry. "Rigby, will you please watch the bar for a few minutes? I need to go fetch a bottle."

"May I come with you?" Gemma asked as planned. "I'd like to pick the right vintage."

"Very well," Henry responded. He motioned for Gemma to follow him and led her through two crowded coach cars before they arrived at the luggage car.

They were relieved to find no attendants present. Normally the car was off-limits to passengers, but first-class patrons could sometimes throw their privilege around, as long as they were assisted by a porter. There was also the risk of soldiers patrolling, as they were on board to protect the printing press in the boxcar behind the luggage car. Most were stationed in the caboose just behind the boxcar, but the three presently lounging in the dining car were likely supposed to be keeping an eye out from this end.

"I gave the soldiers complimentary beverages," Henry said. "May have slipped sedatives into their drinks. They were getting quite comfortable in their seats. We should be fine in here as long as Lorne is keeping an eye on them as intended."

"He was a bit into his own drink," Gemma said. "Hopefully it won't interfere with his reflexes should the soldiers decide to return to their post."

"Kosar and Lyss will keep him on track. By the way, did I sense a bit of jealousy back there, or was I imagining it?"

That caught Gemma off guard, but she saw no reason to lie. "I'm not usually the jealous type. I guess it's just been a while since I've been in a relationship, and Kosar's been really kind to me. I've known him only a few days, but things have been really nice between us amidst all the craziness happening in our lives."

"You've got nothing to worry about with Lyss. She's a phenomenal actress, that's all. It's clear that Kosar is into you. She knows it too."

Gemma felt enough relief to put it all behind her for now. She needed a clear head to finish off their mission. She searched the shelves of luggage until she spotted what she was looking for—an oblong canvas bag just big enough to hold her machete and her companions' swords.

"Here it comes," Henry said.

Gemma followed his gaze out the window. A second pair of tracks now ran alongside theirs, as it would for the duration of the tunnel that had been dug through the mountain decades earlier as part of a mining operation. That operation was still active and necessitated its own small stretch of rail to carry wares to processing plants on either side of the tunnel. The shadow of the mountain loomed ahead.

A whistle echoed through the tunnel and was answered by a second one from the train they were on. The others would be approaching now. Gemma pulled the bag from its place on the shelf and set it down with a loud clang. She opened it up and threw the first mask she found to Henry, who caught it and rolled it over the crown of his head. The knitted cap stretched over his face to his chin, and he aligned the holes to reveal his green eyes.

Gemma reached in for a second mask, but it was caught in a tangle of blades. "Hurry," Henry said as he unlatched the sliding door on the side of the train that faced the second set of tracks. The wind blew in when he pulled it open. Gemma wrestled the mask free, but it had torn straight down the side.

"I'll have to go without it," Gemma said as she tossed the mask aside.

Henry shook his head. "That's not the plan."

"Sometimes things don't go according to plan. We'll just

have to improvise. That printing press is important to you—to us. We have to do this."

"Fine," Henry said. He shuffled through the bag and retrieved his sword in its scabbard, then adjusted his belt to accommodate the weapon. Gemma did the same with her machete. She rubbed her hand along the hilt, still impressed with the work Quincy had done on its grip. She hoped she wouldn't have to use it in combat, but she was glad to have it at her side.

Henry motioned for her to follow as he strode to the other end of the luggage car. He pulled the door open, and the next car came into view. It was a boxcar meant for cargo trains, one that wouldn't normally be attached to a passenger liner like this, but its presence on this run had been ordered by the crown. Its contents were quite precious to those who understood their power.

The boxcar was not intended for foot traffic in the way the passenger cars were. No door existed on the front of the car that Gemma and Henry could step through. Henry pointed at the ladder to their right. Gemma nodded, climbed out of the luggage car and onto the narrow ledge, and leapt across the small gap between the cars. She gripped the ladder on the boxcar, but her feet slipped. Henry reached across with one hand while the other held on to a handle behind him. He helped steady Gemma until she could bring her feet up onto the ladder. She had made it.

Gemma looked back and nodded to Henry. Even with his mask on, she could tell he was smiling with relief by the creases around his eyes. She hadn't thought of him as a very nice or warm person when she'd first met him in the barn, but she realized now that she had misunderstood him. He was highly passionate about the causes he cared about, and he would do anything to help them succeed.

Gemma stepped aside onto the rear ledge next to the ladder, making room for Henry to jump over. He leapt, and like Gemma, his hands connected with the ladder, but his right ankle rolled at an awkward angle and he nearly slipped off. Gemma returned the favor and supported him until he found his balance. He groaned in pain.

"Are you okay?" Gemma asked.

"My ankle," Henry said. "I broke it when I was much younger. It's been quite fragile since then. I think I'll still be able to climb. Let's go."

He made his way up a few rungs and stopped just before his head crowned over the top. He looked down at Gemma and nodded, then slowly lifted his head enough to peer over the roof.

"It's clear," he called down. He clambered onto the roof and crawled out of sight. Gemma reached for the ladder and made her way up but nearly lost her footing when she heard someone yelling. She regained her composure, then climbed the last two rungs so she could see over the top. Henry crouched a few feet away. On the far end of the boxcar, a soldier had just ascended and spotted him.

Henry rose to his feet, hunched forward to keep his balance, and pulled out his sword. He charged at the soldier, who scrambled to get to his feet, still shocked to see another person there. Gemma finished her climb to the top just as the shadow of the mountain fell over her. Rather than slash at the soldier, Henry tackled him, and both fell over the back side of car and plummeted down beyond Gemma's field of vision. Gemma turned just in time to see the low clearance of the tunnel's entrance approaching her only fifteen feet away. She dropped onto her side with mere seconds to spare before her head was lopped off by the rocky ceiling.

Her eyes adjusted to the darkness while her ears rang with

the endless reverberation of the train in the cavernous surroundings. Gemma looked up to find that the ceiling was high enough for her to crawl toward the other end of the car where Henry and the soldier had disappeared. She was nearing the halfway point when she again heard the whistle of the second train, which was traveling in the opposite direction. The noise became unbearable, and Gemma dropped back to her stomach and covered her ears as she watched it speed past. She turned her head to look behind her and spotted several shadowy figures from the other train jumping into the side door Henry had slid open a few minutes earlier in the luggage car.

As the other train sped out of view, Gemma resumed her crawl through the dark. She was nearing the other end of the boxcar's roof when the sound of clashing steel rang out. She peered over the edge to see Henry. He was sprawled on his back on the open front platform of the caboose, where the rest of the soldiers were stationed to protect the printing press stowed in the boxcar. Henry was surrounded by four soldiers, and a fifth—the one Henry had brought down with him—lay three feet away. Henry was using his sword to block the blows from the soldiers, and they were all too distracted to notice Gemma.

When she arrived at the edge, she turned and reached a foot down until she felt a rung of the ladder. She lowered herself down halfway, then pushed off and leapt across the gap between the boxcar and the platform of the caboose. As she was in the air, one of the soldiers noticed her hurtling toward him. He didn't have enough time to swing at her, and her body collided with his and brought him to the ground. She reached for her machete just as another guard turned away from Henry and swung his sword at Gemma. She stepped back and stumbled over the first fallen soldier, nearly tumbling off the edge of the platform before regaining her balance. She felt the rush of air as the blade missed her by mere inches. Henry kicked the swordsman, who turned his attention back to Henry as Gemma pulled out her machete.

She didn't want to fight. She and Henry were only supposed to sneak back and unlatch the coupler to the caboose to separate it from the rest of the train once they reached the tunnel. They hadn't expected a patrolman to climb the boxcar and spot them seconds before they entered the darkness.

Yet here she was, and her new friend was about to be killed. She had no other choice.

"Hey!" Gemma yelled just as the swordsman in front of her made to skewer Henry. He turned back to Gemma and blocked the blow from her machete just in time. Henry kicked out and connected with the back of the soldier's knee while simultaneously blocking the blows from the other two soldiers. One soldier stumbled right into the tip of Gemma's blade, but as Syntha had pointed out back at Kosar's palace, the machete was only a slashing weapon—the soldier was possibly nicked or bruised, but not impaled. He made to step back and lifted his sword, then caught the wayward blade of another soldier who was in the midst of swinging his own sword down on Henry.

The soldier screamed in pain, and his sword dropped to the platform at Henry's side. A portion of his arm had been sliced open. Gemma used the advantage to lunge forward and slam into him, knocking him to the ground. The soldier who had accidentally injured him came to his defense, then froze, apparently shocked at the sight of a woman. Gemma swung her blade and sliced open his right cheek, then kicked him while he was stunned. He tripped over his fallen friend and fell over the edge of the landing.

One soldier still tussled with Henry. His blows were fast and fierce to keep Henry from getting back to his feet. All Henry could do was block the onslaught. Gemma was raising her machete to strike when the last soldier noticed her. He blocked her, and Henry used that distraction to his advantage. He swung at the man, slicing his belly. Gemma tried to block a blow from the soldier at the same time, but the cut threw off his trajectory, and Gemma's machete missed his sword entirely. It made its way down unopposed.

Its tip sliced through Henry's throat.

"No!" Gemma screamed.

The soldier bent down in pain, grasping his belly. Gemma threw a punch, which connected with the soldier's nose. He stumbled back and over the front of the platform. His head hit the boxcar's narrow rear ledge, and he dropped down into the gap between the two cars. The soldier's mass was just enough to be felt as it was crushed under the train's speeding wheels.

Gemma knelt at Henry's side. He sputtered, unable to get air into his lungs. Blood gushed from the wound on his neck.

"You must finish this," he choked out before the life left his eyes.

Gemma sensed movement behind her. The soldier she'd knocked down when she had jumped onto this car had regained his feet, but his sword had gone over the edge when he'd tumbled. He kicked Gemma before she could stand fully, and she fell, landing on her hand that held the machete. She felt the edge of the blade cut into her outer right thigh and winced in pain. The soldier kicked again. His foot connected with the back of her left thigh.

He took another step toward her, and his next kick landed on her back. Then he dropped into a crouch behind her and threw a fist into her left cheek, knocking her head against the platform. His next blow caught her ear. She spat out blood and tried to turn, to block the blows, to fight back, but the man was angry and determined.

Suddenly, light washed over them as the train exited the tunnel. The soldier reached down and grabbed Henry's sword. Gemma brought a hand over her face, as if it would protect her from what was to come, but then a shadow fell over her.

Gemma and the soldier both looked up to see the towering form of Syntha standing on the roof of the boxcar. Her right arm darted forward, and something flew through the air. Blood splattered down on Gemma as her attacker stumbled backward against the door to the caboose. The door opened inward, and he fell just inside its entrance with a dagger protruding from his left eye.

Syntha leapt from the roof, over the gap, and down onto the platform.

"Look out!" Gemma cried as the soldier whose arm had been sliced open jumped up and rushed at Syntha. Gemma rolled onto her injured left side, which freed up her right arm and her machete. Her blade connected with the man's leg just between his boot and his knee, not enough to sever anything but with enough force to trip him. Syntha pulled out her own sword, and the soldier fell into it. Syntha pushed him to the side, where he collapsed on top of his friend in the doorway.

"Thanks for leaving the door open in the luggage car," Syntha said. "The others are securing the passenger cars now. I thought you and Henry might need some help. Looks like I was right." She helped Gemma to her feet, then stepped over the two bodies and yanked her dagger out of the soldier's eye.

Gemma knelt over Henry and wept for him.

Syntha gave Gemma a few minutes to mourn Henry and reel from her injuries, and then the train came to a halt. The others had apparently worked their way to the front of the train and forced the engineer to terminate the journey. Gemma hobbled off the platform of the caboose and looked toward the front of the train to see the three members of Syntha's security team who had jumped on board with her forcing the train's staff off the locomotive. They were followed by the passengers from the middle cars, who were led out by Kosar, Alyssa, and Lorne.

A few minutes later, three covered wagons arrived, driven by Zinnie, Clarnen, and Byrna. They pulled up in front of the boxcar, which Syntha forced open. Together they unloaded the pieces of the massive printing press, which had been disassembled for its journey, and transferred them into the three wagons. The passengers and crew were then led back onboard the train and allowed to continue on their journey as Gemma and her team sped off with their precious cargo. Henry's spot remained empty.

# Chapter Twenty-Six
## DENNY

Denny tried both the bench and the floor, but he couldn't get comfortable. It wasn't that the ground was hard—he actually preferred that to a fluffy mattress or a couch after his years living in alleyways and rooftops—but the fleas and straw made him itch anytime he came close to falling asleep. The problem had only gotten worse each night. Arnem, on the other hand, didn't seem to mind either of those hardships. His snores were evidence of that.

What Denny wanted even more than a restful few hours was to enter a state of dreaming. Whether it was a vision that hinted at what was to come or another chance at communicating with his mother, Denny just wanted *something*, some kind of escape from his present situation. Even when he had managed small stretches of sleep the previous few nights, they had been dreamless. There had been years when he would have given his right hand for dreamless sleep, but over the last few months, dreams had brought him Arnem.

Gemma. The Wynstone clan. The rescue of Marzele. Visions of his mother.

And to make matters worse, it was raining.

Grez and Petey had left them parked outside of an inn. On previous nights, the men had set up a tent on the side of the road. They'd even hunted and shared their charred meat with Arnem and Denny one night. Tonight, however, the smugglers had arrived at a favorite inn, gone in for ale and supper, and paid for rooms. They hadn't even brought out meals for Denny and Arnem or let them out to relieve themselves. Fortunately the innkeeper's grandson had smuggled out two loaves of stale bread and two apples that were more wrinkled than the Witch of Ferathan in her true form.

Denny didn't have so much as a blanket to block the rain out.

"At least it'll wash the stench off of us," Arnem said when he woke from his slumber. "Have you been up this whole time?"

"I can't keep doing this, Arnem. We're like rats trapped in here."

"Well, no. Rats would be able to escape. I don't think you can fit through these bars, even as thin as you are." Arnem smiled, but Denny didn't return the gesture.

"I might be able to tolerate it a little longer if I could at least escape in unconsciousness, but the dreams won't come. What if my mother is trying to reach out to me? I can't communicate with her when I'm not asleep."

"Denny, I've wondered if perhaps you could learn to control your abilities with some practice."

"How am I supposed to do that?"

"Well, I don't know. Perhaps if you...um...*think* really hard?"

Denny looked at him with disbelief. Arnem's chin quivered.

"Okay, stupid idea," he said. "I'm sorry, Denny. It's just that there are so many folks—*were* so many folks—who had all kinds of abilities and powers they could use on demand. Marzele and his superheated hands, for instance. I know it takes years of training to develop that kind of control. But perhaps if you could get a better feel for what triggers your powers or precisely how you feel when you have visions, you could figure out how to control them."

Denny was silent.

"I don't know, Denny. Never mind. It was stupid." Arnem lay back down, but the makeshift bed he'd assembled out of loose straw was now a soggy mess from the rain.

Denny lay back on the bench and closed his eyes. He thought about what Arnem had said. Perhaps there was something to it. If his mom was able to reach out to him in a new way, she must have been honing her abilities and reshaping how they worked for her. If she could do it, Denny thought he should be able to as well.

As he pondered, his eyelids closed, and the sleep he longed for finally overtook him.

It didn't last.

Within seconds, three riders galloped down the muddy road toward the inn. Arnem shook Denny awake. "It's them," he said. "The same riders from the other day."

The three soldiers rode past the entrance to the inn. They came around the side, where the wagon was parked.

"Hello, boys," the lead rider said. He jumped down from his horse and dug through his saddlebag. "We meet again."

He pulled out a large piece of paper and unfolded it, and the contents became clear to Denny.

The wanted poster.

The sketches of their faces.

They'd been caught.

"Well, well, what do you guys think?" the leader asked his men. They dismounted their own horses and crowded around the poster.

"That's them, all right," one of them said.

"Our lucky day," said the other.

Denny looked around, but he already knew there was nowhere to hide. No way to run.

---

THE THREE SOLDIERS LEFT THEM ALONE FOR THE MOMENT. There was nowhere for Denny and Arnem to go, after all, and there were bound to be no riders in the middle of the night who would stumble upon the pair and recognize them as wanted fugitives.

Denny watched the soldiers make their way around the corner of the inn, pulling out their swords as they strutted toward the entrance.

"If only you'd had one of your dreams," Arnem said. "Maybe we would have seen this coming and could have warned our traveling companions."

"I guess they'll get what's coming to them," Denny said.

It took only seconds before they heard signs of a scuffle. There was the breaking of glass—perhaps mugs of ale had shattered when a table was toppled. There were screams as a woman and four men ran out the door and headed for the nearby woods. A chair flew through a window and landed ten feet from the wagon. The sounds expanded to the second floor. More screams. More furniture smashing into walls and glass shattering.

And then came the body. Someone was thrown through an upstairs window and landed inches from the wagon.

"It's not Grez or Petey," Denny said as he squinted through the iron bars. "It's one of the soldiers." Another soldier ran out of the bar, yelling in agony. He illuminated the night, as his hair was engulfed in flames. He ran to a horse trough and dove in, but he never reemerged.

There was more commotion inside, then silence.

The rain stopped shortly after, and the night was still. Arnem and Denny looked at each other, shrugged, and settled in to sleep when nobody else emerged from the inn.

THE NEXT MORNING, A JOYOUS TUNE WOKE DENNY FROM A sleep he hadn't realized he'd entered. Grez emerged from around the corner, whistling. Denny squinted to make out what the man was carrying.

A sack?

No. A head.

Grez approached and tossed the head on top of the bars of the wagon. Denny looked up and found himself face-to-face with the lead soldier.

"You think that's bad, look at this," Grez said. Denny turned to see him pulling at a section of his beard. "The guy nicked some of my beard off! I was going to chalk it all up to a misunderstanding, but then he had to go swinging that sword of his as if I had done something to offend him. Wasn't until I'd made his neck a few pounds lighter that I saw what he had in his other hand." At this, Grez reached into his coat and pulled out the poster. "Seems you two are worth quite a bit more coin than Venko paid us."

"I take it we aren't going to the Southern Reaches anymore," Arnem said.

"Oh, no, Petey and I never go back on our word. We'll finish the job. Venko never said what should happen to you once we get there, though. The prison down there is just as much a crown facility as anywhere else. We'll turn you in there and get our reward. Yes, boys, things are starting to look up for Petey and me!"

A drop landed in Denny's hair and made its way down his forehead. He wiped it away and looked up. It was blood. The severed head was already covered in flies.

Grez laughed. "Well, boys, a couple more days and your heads will look just like that one—detached and covered in flies."

Denny began to shake uncontrollably. Arnem reached over and put a hand on his shoulder.

"Breathe, Denny. Just breathe."

# Chapter Twenty-Seven
## MARZELE

Silver Peak loomed over Esteron. Unlike the filthy towns over which it cast its shadow during the morning hours, the mountainous enclave Silver Peak gleamed in splendor. Every shop catered to the wealthy clientele who visited or owned vacation homes in the region. A single course at any one of the restaurants on the main strip cost more than many Esteroni families' entire monthly grocery bill, and yet the reservation list for each stretched into the next year. Half a dozen shops carried the finest diamond rings, rare gem pendants, and tiaras that would put any royal crown in Aepistelle's history to shame. Tailors imported the finest fabrics from across the seas and frequently sold out of their custom wares within days during the high season, allowing them to live comfortably for the rest of the year while they waited for more materials to arrive. And the less said about the various ways in which the community catered to the more carnal desires of its affluent visitors, the better.

It was precisely the kind of place Horace Wellworth and

his obscenely wealthy ilk would have spent their summers. The kind of place Marzele would have prayed against—a den of depravity where money that could have been used to alleviate poverty and suffering throughout the kingdom was instead squandered on fleeting pleasures.

Marzele itched in his tight-fitting suit. He unclasped the top button. Horace, sitting opposite him in the carriage, shook his head and tutted. "You must keep yourself presentable, old friend. The last thing you want is to stand out in this crowd. They'll already question your presence in town as it is."

"Why is it that you want me here with you?" Marzele asked. "I should have gone ahead with the others. I fit in better with them."

"They don't trust you yet."

"Locking me away for days in their basement and nearly starving me to death wasn't enough for them?"

"Marzele, you were baptized by shadow, and you emerged victorious. Must you continue to dwell on it? We are being called to do dark deeds. If we make any mistakes, we'll be caught and executed, and our failure means the injustices of this kingdom will continue. The Cult of Arun has been preparing for the reaping for some time now. You should consider yourself blessed that they've even allowed you to be a part of this. I put my reputation on the line for you."

"Yes, you are so generous," Marzele spat. "The sacrifices you've made...Bertram, Shenesa. All their lives lost so you could wear your suits that cost more money than they could ever have dreamed of holding."

Horace slammed his fist against the wall of the carriage. "Damn it, Marzele! I did what I had to in order to survive another day. My mission has not changed. My aim is still to see that Davin's rule ends, that his regime falls, that the people of these lands once again have the freedom to practice their religions without fear of imprisonment or execution. Only my methods have changed."

"And when Davin's reign of terror ends and we've purged Aepistelle of the Royal Mystic Committee, what then? Should there be any followers of Solendaron left alive, who will lead them? We were the last, and we've turned our backs on the Lord."

Horace looked at his feet in shame, his anger subsiding. "Perhaps then the Ever-Giving Sun will reemerge and overtake the Shadow." He lifted his head and met Marzele's eyes. "Perhaps He will forgive us and radiate His loving light upon us once more."

The two men sat in silence as the carriage completed the journey up the mountain road and halted at the gates that blocked their path. A town guard requested identification, and the chauffeur presented the papers Horace had provided.

"It's going to work just fine," Horace whispered. "As long as Davin has not seized all my assets in the last few weeks, my family still owns a sizable vacation home here."

A knock came at the door, and the chauffeur pulled it open.

"Pardon me, sir, but before we can enter the city, your identification must be verified." The man stepped aside as the guard approached and peered into the carriage.

"Good afternoon," Horace said in a snootier tone than Marzele was accustomed to hearing. "What is the holdup here? It's been a long journey, and I'd like to get to my family's home and freshen up."

"Yes, sir," the guard said. He was calm and clearly used to being talked down to by the elite men and women of Aepistelle who journeyed there for vacations. "I just had to make sure it was truly you. I hope you and your companion have a wonderful time."

He closed the door and gestured for the gates to be opened, then waved them on their way.

THE FIRST COURSE SERVED TO THEM INCLUDED A BED OF crisp green leaves, a pungent cheese made from the milk of a particular breed of goat that lived only in the Esteron mountains, candied meat of those same goats, and a vinaigrette infused with a tart purple berry that grew on the slopes around them. Marzele shuddered to think that each leaf he consumed probably cost as much as an hour's wage for those who had picked them. Still, he was delighted by the tastes that converged in his mouth.

"You may be disgusted by this lifestyle, but you cannot hide the exquisite enjoyment you are experiencing right now," Horace said. The larger man had polished off his salad in seconds, ravenous after their journey.

A server returned to their table with two glasses and a bottle of wine. He poured a small amount into one glass and passed it to Horace. Marzele watched as Horace swirled the red liquid, sniffed it, and took a small sip. He nodded in approval, and the server filled both glasses. Once they were alone again, Horace lifted his glass and nodded at Marzele.

"To our fallen friends; may we honor their legacy with our actions and rebuild the world as they would have wanted," Horace said. Marzele didn't reach for the second glass. Horace rolled his eyes. "This is where you lift yours in agreement and drink with me."

"In all my years, I never had a liking for the stuff until I lost my faith."

"No, I can't imagine you did. Do you know how much this bottle costs? It sure isn't the cheap drab you'd get from the Plentimore Valley vineyards. This is imported."

"That's not what I mean, Horace. I've kept a clear mind for my entire life. That night I stumbled upon the Cult, I had my first drink in some time. Even during the two decades I was in hiding from the Royal Mystic Committee, I wanted to honor Solendaron. I wanted to be alert in case they came looking for me or in case I was needed somewhere."

"Solendaron never forbade us from partaking in drink, Marzele. The Illuminarion includes many examples of wine and even ale being consumed by the priests and prophets."

"Yes, I am aware, but I still did not want to give up control of myself. I was afraid of what I might become. The priestesses who raised me after I was abandoned often told me that my father was probably a deadbeat drunk, my mother likely a back-alley whore addicted to Lord knows what. I wanted nothing to do with that."

"And that isn't who you became, Marzele. A little drink here and there would not have changed that."

"No, perhaps it wouldn't have." Marzele picked up his glass and downed its contents, not bothering to be pretentious about it, sniffing it and savoring it. He slammed the glass down on the table. "No, perhaps things would have gone quite differently for me had I not held myself back."

The waiter noticed the empty glass and returned with the bottle to refill it. Again Marzele poured the contents down his throat in a single gulp. He felt a warmth in his innards that excited him. The sudden dizziness was less welcome, but it didn't stop him from downing a third glass. Horace looked on in fascination. He motioned for the waiter to split the remaining contents of the bottle between their two glasses.

"Perhaps we should slow down," Horace said. "We don't want to alter our plans now."

Marzele held the glass to his lips but had not yet begun to drink his fourth serving. He set it down on the table. "I suppose you're right," he said with reluctance.

Their salad plates were cleared and replaced with the second course. Marzele's stomach lurched at the sight of it. His plate was oblong and placed horizontally in front of him. Stretched across the dish was an entire fish. Its fins and gills and scales and eyes were all intact. It had a metallic look to it, the candlelight reflecting off each scale. What stood out most to Marzele was the razor-sharp teeth protruding from the creature's gaping mouth. He would have expected such a thing on a shark, but not on a river dweller such as this.

"The *iimrav jianti*," Horace said with a faux accent. "The indigenous Treskar people in this region used to feed their prisoners of war to these little beasts in the rivers atop the peak. Dangerous creatures."

Marzele pushed his plate away. "I don't have much of an appetite right now."

"You're missing out on the true delicacy. It's not the fish itself." Marzele thought he saw the fish move but decided it must have been the effect of the wine on his mind. Then Horace used the tip of his knife to slice open the belly of the iimrav jianti, and suddenly the fish came to life.

No, not the fish.

As the opening expanded with Horace's delicate slicing, dozens of thick, bloodred worms emerged from its innards. Horace set down his fork and reached for one of the wriggling worms with his bare fingers. He brought it to his lips and slurped it in like a noodle. After swallowing it, he smiled at Marzele, a trail of bloody red residue stretching from his chin to his lips to his front teeth.

"The iimrav jianti may have a lethal bite, but it is not the biggest threat in the river." Horace picked up another live worm and let it dangle from his fingers. "These little guys start off smaller than grains of rice. The jianti swallow them in between meatier meals. Then, these worms slowly feed off of their innards, lay eggs, and grow in the beasts' bellies until they finally consume their most vital organs from the inside." Horace thrust a second worm toward his mouth and bit off the tip. "Sometimes the most effective fighter is unseen. Belittled. Hiding right in front of their enemy's eyes, ready to strike when least expected."

Horace pushed his chair back from the table. He raised his worm-stained hands to shoulder height and faced his palms toward the ceiling. With his eyes closed, he began a low chant in the tongue of the Solendaron. Marzele recognized the words, though not this particular prayer. It was not from the Illuminarion; this was a twisted, bastardized version.

"May the shadow of the Tihn fall upon us in the name of Arun. Your servant calls upon your mighty power. Fill me with the darkness so I may spread it to the enemies that surround us. As Solendaron forbade the leaders in Lantyss to harm their subjects, so You have forbidden the same aggressions toward the powerless in Aepistelle. Like Arun, may we rise up now against our oppressors. May we take control of the Shadow and suppress the false light in this place."

Horace's voice grew louder with each word. The patrons of the restaurant stared at him with as much astonishment as Marzele, though Marzele at least spoke the language; unless any of the men and women around them were former priests or priestesses, it was unlikely they understood what Horace was saying.

And then the candles extinguished at every table.

The torches followed suit.

Windows lined the restaurant, but the early evening was suddenly as black as night. Marzele thought he could make out dark storm clouds blocking any remnants of the sun.

Horace rose from his seat and walked across the room to another table.

"Grigor Pontessa, former unit commander of the Royal Mystic Committee in Esteron, you have committed grievous acts of violence against men, women, and children under orders from King Davin," Horace said in the common tongue. "Their crimes? Loving their gods. Reading holy books. Praising their maker. You tortured them, burned their houses down, confiscated their inheritances. Killed them in cold blood."

"I...no, I was just doing my job. They were breaking the law," Grigor said. Marzele couldn't see him clearly from across the room, but he could just make out his shadow as he rose to his feet.

Horace's large shape moved closer to Grigor. "You blindly followed orders from a mere man and ignored the sanctity of life, which is given to us by a higher power. You took for your own gain, and now you must pay the price."

Horace broke into another language entirely, one Marzele didn't recognize. There were few words in common with either the standard dialect or the Solendaron. Suddenly Horace's silhouette seemed to shift. No, something seemed to emerge from him. At first it seemed to be a dark cloud in a shape similar to Horace's own, but then it morphed into something shapeless. Grigor screamed as he was consumed by this new entity.

Horace turned to the man seated in the next chair over. "Alfie Poulter, you were second-in-command to Grigor Pontessa. He gave the orders, but you and your soldiers laid your hands on those poor children. You relished the screams of the women. You mocked the men as they took their final breaths at the end of the noose. For that you will pay."

The formless cloud moved to the second man and consumed him, his screams cutting off abruptly.

After the initial shock, the other patrons ran to the doors and found them locked. Some tried to push through the swinging doors into the kitchen, but those too seemed to be held in place by an unseen force.

The carnage continued: a former mayor of Esteron City who had allowed his city guard to be conscripted by the Royal Mystic Committee; estate owners who had turned in their own servants for practicing their religions; a woman who had reported her own father-in-law because he had powers of premonition and she stood to gain his wealth after the arrest. It went on for nearly an hour. Marzele sat glued to his seat, frozen with fear. The screams caused his ears to ring. Tables were overturned as people attempted to flee from the consuming shadows, but everyone avoided Marzele, as he was the companion of this mad sorcerer who was bent on ending their lives.

When it was all over, the silhouetted Horace made his way back toward Marzele. He plopped down into his chair at the only table left standing. A breeze blew through the room. The candles and torches reignited. Marzele watched as Horace reached into the fish on his plate and pulled out a fistful of worms. He stuffed them into his mouth and groaned in ecstasy at their taste.

Marzele turned and vomited.

# Chapter Twenty-Eight
## GEMMA

It took a few days for Gemma and her new friends to bring the wagons back to the farm and figure out how to assemble the printing press. The loss of Henry weighed heavily on everyone. At night, when Gemma, Syntha, and Kosar returned to the castle to sleep, Gemma tossed between her sheets, unable to stay asleep for long before she was awoken by bad dreams of Henry with his throat slit open and of the soldiers she had fought and killed while defending herself and her companion. Every morning, she found herself pacing the balcony before the sun rose from behind the castle, then rushing to get dressed and return to the farm.

During the day, the work on the printing press held most of their attention, and nobody spoke of the loss or trauma of their escapade on the train, but Gemma knew they all felt it. On the fifth day, they finally got the press up and running. The type for their articles was prepared, the drums were readied, and the stream behind the barn was diverted to create the steam required to run the machine. The first copy needed only minimal adjustments. By the afternoon, they'd pumped out the first three hundred copies of their latest edition. Alyssa uncorked bottles of wine while Clarnen passed out glasses to everyone.

Just as Gemma and the others raised their glasses in a toast, the sound of a wagon approaching interrupted their celebration. Gemma followed Zinnie to the door and peered out. The covered wagon was pulled by two mules. Byrna rode up front with another member of their network whose name Gemma didn't know. As they passed Syntha and another guard and came through the gates, Byrna jumped down and ran toward the group.

"Were you able to get the paper stock?" Kosar asked.

Byrna bent down with her hands on her knees, panting. Once she caught her breath, she nodded. "Yes, the deal went smoothly. We have enough paper to finish off this week's run."

"Why are you so worked up, then?" Clarnen asked.

"I was about to get to that, you dolt," Byrna teased. "When I was in Sunfyre to meet our supplier, I had a quick meal with one of my top sources. She told me she's been getting word from her connections around the kingdom that the regional governors have been sending representatives to private meetings in Centeron to work out treaties in case of secession."

All eyes turned to Kosar. There was shock on his normally cool face, but he tried to brush it off. "I know nothing of this. Perhaps I should pay my father and brother a visit this evening and press them for details."

Clarnen, Zinnie, and Alyssa went out to unload the fresh supplies. Byrna and Lorne rushed over to the large table, rapidly throwing out ideas for how to frame the story for the next edition. Gemma hooked her arm through Kosar's and led him behind the new printing press, which took up most of the center of the barn.

"Why would your family keep that from you?" Gemma asked. "We've had dinner with them every night this week, and they haven't let on that anything is happening."

"I suppose it's because of exactly this—they don't want it to leak out, and they know I'm not one to keep our countrymen in the dark. Smart of them, I'll admit."

Gemma didn't like the look of hurt on his face, so she pulled his head toward hers and leaned in for a kiss.

"Get a private room, you two," Alyssa joked as she carried in a case of paper and dropped it along the wall behind them. Gemma pulled her lips away from Kosar's and rolled her eyes playfully. Despite the jealousy Gemma had felt toward Alyssa on the train, she'd become good friends with the girl two years her junior. Alyssa's unceasing optimism had kept them all going in the dark days since Henry's death, and Gemma hadn't seen any further flirtation between Alyssa and Kosar.

She turned back to Kosar to find him deep in thought, troubled. She leaned in again, but he stepped back. "Sorry," he said. "I think I just need to go out for a walk."

GEMMA RODE HER HORSE ALONGSIDE KOSAR THAT EVENING on their return to the castle. He was silent for most of the trip, only emitting little grunts in response to Gemma. When they arrived, he walked away without a word as she handed off her mare to the stable master. She went through the back door and up the servant stairs Syntha had shown her. She washed up in her room, and when she was informed that it was time to dine, she changed into one of the nicer dresses that had been left for her and made her way downstairs for supper.

As had been the case since she'd arrived, only Gemma and the immediate family sat around the table. They rose when she entered and sat once she had settled into her chair next to Ysidro. As usual, Ysidro's glass held only water while the others drank wine. Joseph kept the conversation going with Ysidro and Gemma, but Kosar was silent.

When dessert was served, a flaky cinnamon dough fried to a crisp in butter and topped with fresh cream, Gemma finally addressed him. "Kosar, is there something on your mind that you'd like to discuss?"

Kosar had dipped a spoon into the bowl of extra cream. He pulled it out and held it over his dessert. The spoon shook in his hand, causing the cream to slide off and plop onto the table. He threw the spoon down, and it clattered against his plate. His eyes moved between his brother and father.

"Whatever you two are hiding from me, I wish you would just come out and say it. Are you working to commit treason against the king?"

Joseph seemed taken aback. He gasped and glanced around the room, then calmed slightly when he noted that the servants had left them for the moment. "Keep your voice down about these matters, son. This is no place to talk about such a thing. And no, we aren't doing anything that could be construed as treason."

Kosar's phrasing shocked Gemma as much as it had Joseph. It sounded as if Kosar were on Davin's side.

"And how about you, Brother?" Kosar's last word had venom behind it. "Are you doing anything that will put this territory at risk?"

"Why would you even ask that, Kosar? You know I'd do anything to protect our people."

"I know you keep secrets just to spite me. Perhaps you should take up drinking again. We've got a nice bottle open right here." Kosar grabbed it and shoved it toward Ysidro, causing some of the red wine to spray across the table. Some drops landed on Gemma, who pushed her chair back in shock.

Ysidro slammed his glass of water against the table, and it shattered. "Dammit, Kosar! You know I do not touch that stuff anymore. I don't need you rubbing it my face or splashing it on me during meals. Perhaps my first order of business as governor when my time comes will be to send you away as a diplomat to the farthest outpost from the Southern Reaches."

Kosar jumped to his feet and threw his napkin down onto his plate, his chair falling backward and clattering onto the tile floor. "It's no wonder Mother wanted better than this terrible family," he said as he stormed out of the dining hall like a child.

As soon as Kosar disappeared, a server entered through the service door. "Is there anything else I can get for you all?" the server asked.

Joseph cleared his throat and pushed back from the table in his wheelchair. "Perhaps you can bring me back to my rooms," he said. The server promptly wheeled him out of the dining hall, leaving only Ysidro and Gemma.

"I'm very sorry you had to witness that," Ysidro said. He didn't turn to look at her; his eyes were locked on the wine bottle that remained within reach next to Kosar's plate.

"I have a brother as well," Gemma said, not sure what else to do. "We fought just like that for years."

"Oh, really?" One corner of Ysidro's lips raised in a slight smile. "Which one of you was the struggling alcoholic trying to do the right thing and which was the cocky know-it-all little brother?"

Gemma laughed. "Okay, maybe our dynamics were slightly different from yours. George and I have a father with disabilities, and most of our fights were about who would take care of him while our mother worked so the other could go out and live life."

Ysidro pushed his chair back from the table. "Let's get some air," he said.

He led Gemma out through the glass doors and into the courtyard. "My brother and I love each other, but our differences go beyond having different fathers. Perhaps it all started there, though. Kosar has always felt threatened by his parentage, as if my father would withhold his inheritance and leave everything to me. Or, if something were to happen to me, that Father would publicly declare Kosar a bastard and find someone else to take his title."

"I think I can understand that," Gemma said as they strolled along the garden path under the moonlight.

"The thing is, Father absolutely sees Kosar as his legitimate son. He's never treated Kosar any differently; it's possible he spoiled him even more than me. You'll hear no jealousy from me about it, though. He's my brother, and that's all there is to it. No other qualifier needed."

"What do you think his feelings are toward King Davin?"

Ysidro slowed to a halt. "What do you mean?"

"Well, the way he talked about treason at dinner—he thinks you two are meeting with the other governors about seceding from Aepistelle and returning to individual rule. I thought he would be all for that, but now I'm not so certain."

Ysidro looked around just as his father had done in the dining hall to make sure they weren't being spied on. He responded in a hushed tone. "We cannot speak of this. I know anything I say around Kosar, and maybe even around you, will be reported in your newspaper. I support the work you're doing, even if Kosar doesn't want me to be a part of it. That's all I can say on the matter. I hope you understand."

"I do," Gemma said.

They continued on the trail around the garden, discussing lighter subjects until they arrived back at the dining hall. The table had been cleared by the time they returned.

"Well, I should go check on my father, make sure his feelings weren't too hurt," Ysidro said. "Good night, Miss Calvertson."

"Good night."

Gemma trekked up the stairs to the third floor. She felt better about the evening after spending time with Ysidro. He was much better company than she'd expected and a more genuine person than Kosar had let on. Perhaps jealousy over Ysidro's parentage was the reason for Kosar's attitude toward his brother, but perhaps there was something deeper going on.

KOSAR'S HORSE WAS ALREADY GONE BY THE TIME GEMMA arrived at the stable the next morning. Syntha had work to do at the castle and needed to hang back, but both Gemma and her horse had traveled to the farm enough times to know the way without guidance.

The press had broken down, and Kosar and Zinnie were hard at work repairing it. Kosar didn't greet her when she arrived, but she did hear a plethora of swearing from his place underneath the section of the press he was toiling on. The others were gathered around the table, writing up their stories or tinkering with the printing drums to get their words ready to transfer when the press was up and running again.

Gemma sat near the doorway, watching Syntha's security team pretending to work the field in their big hats. Dust kicked up in the distance, and then the sound of a galloping horse reached Gemma's ears. She got up and ran out to greet Syntha but was taken aback by the look on her face.

"Kosar!" Gemma yelled into the barn. "You better come out here right away."

She met Syntha a dozen paces outside the barn as the woman jumped off her horse, and Kosar arrived moments later. "What is it?" he asked, sounding annoyed at the interruption. "Syntha? What's going on?"

"They've come for you," Syntha said, her eyes boring into Kosar's. "They're at the castle now."

"Who's at the castle?" Gemma asked.

Syntha turned to Gemma. "King Davin's attaché, along with a cache of soldiers."

"Did they find out about the printing press?" Gemma asked. She looked at Kosar and was shocked to see that his demeanor had calmed.

"No, it's not that," Syntha said. "They are demanding that Ysidro and Kosar travel to Capital City and meet with King Davin. All of the first- and second-born children of the regional governors have been summoned."

A smirk formed on Kosar's face just before he turned to grab his horse. He mounted it and rode off without a goodbye.

Gemma and Syntha looked at each other, confused.

# Chapter Twenty-Nine
## MARZELE

Hammertree may as well have been an invisible village. It didn't appear on any maps; the cartographers had likely mistaken it for some inbred homestead compound or oversize ranch. The kings of Southplains had never been quite as organized as those of the other territories that would later make up Aepistelle, and they hadn't established an accurate count of their citizens and the towns in which they resided. Southplains stretched along the southeast end of Aepistelle, Centeron and Esteron to the north, Costono and the Southern Reaches to the west. The southern border bumped up against the country of Xaeltúve, and the eastern border was where the Esteron Mountains petered out and formless desert began, stretching as far as the eye could see. Southplains itself primarily comprised of dried-up weeds and dust storms with only a handful of fertile areas, along which most of the towns were clustered.

It seemed forgivable that Hammertree had mostly been forgotten except for two things. For one, the southeastern stretch of the Aepistelle Railroad terminated at the village; that was probably an oversight on the part of the builders, likely a contractor who had continued to lay down track and bill the crown until they had been found out. There was no other conceivable explanation. The train came that way only once every fortnight, rarely with passengers onboard. Small amounts of goods were imported and exported, but that didn't seem to justify the cost of running the locomotive so far outside the civilized world.

The other footnote in the village's otherwise colorless history was the Hammertree Massacre fifty-three years prior. This was the reason Marzele had arrived there on horseback with the Cult of Arun on this otherwise unremarkable day.

"I grew up not fifty miles from here but never knew of this town's existence," Marzele called from his saddle.

Horace, who rode a few feet ahead on a particularly strong horse, looked back in shock. "You're speaking to me? That's something. It seems you're starting to trust me now." He gestured toward the other riders. "Starting to trust *us* now."

Marzele hadn't given the subject much thought in the last few days. The fear that had filled him in Silver Peak and in the other towns they'd visited along their bloody trail had not subsided. The things he'd seen—the powers Horace and the others had gained in their darkness and hatred—overwhelmed him. Riding so close to his childhood home, however, brought out a sadness in him, one tinged with nostalgia. It was powerful enough to override his pure terror of his new companions.

"I don't approve of these methods, Horace. I understand the why but cannot condone the how. I want to see our fallen brethren avenged as much as you, but there are other ways."

"There is no better way than to return the pure brutality

and hatred the Royal Mystic Committee and others have inflicted upon our kind." Horace nodded toward the unremarkable cluster of shacks down the road. "It goes back farther than the Committee, though. That's why we're here. I'm quite shocked you weren't taught about the Hammertree Massacre in your childhood. It must have happened around the time of your birth. I suppose the priestesses who raised you were trying to protect your fragile young mind."

"What massacre?" Marzele asked. He thought back to the lessons he'd sat through at the Solendaron orphanage but could not recall learning about any such thing.

"The Cult of Arun was not the only sect to branch off from traditional Solendaron teachings of the Illuminarion. There was a group that called themselves the Shining Truth who believed that the priests at the Hezron City temple here in Southplains were not preaching the word literally, as it had been written. They believed that the lands the Illuminarion spoke of were not across the seas at all but were actually right here in what is now Aepistelle and its neighboring countries. It's not hard to mistake the ancient Qolamity Desert for our own Great Eld Desert just beyond the eastern border.

"The Shining Truth headed toward the desert, convinced that the Later Prophecies would play out here with the Lord Solendaron Himself riding over the Great Eld on His winged horse. They tried to establish their own village out in the Eld, but it wasn't long before their sources of food and water were depleted and they had to move on to the nearest semblance of civilization—Hammertree.

"The people of Hammertree didn't welcome them with open arms. They weren't tolerant of organized religion. They were downright hostile, in fact."

They were a bit closer to the town now, and Marzele cut

in as he took in the sight of it. "It looks like they could have used all the population growth they could get. I've seen farms larger than this place."

"That's what a handful of the townsfolk argued as well. Visitors meant additional revenue outside of the trade-and-barter system they usually resorted to with such a limited economy. So the folks in Hammertree relented and opened up their barns to the newcomers. There were no hotels, so haylofts were the best accommodations that could be expected. Still the case to this day, I hear."

"It seems we'll find out soon enough," Marzele said. He scratched his scalp, where dried skin had flaked off from the days of exposure to the sun. He felt a speck of relief that his hair had grown out since his captivity on Terminus Rock—otherwise the sunburn would have been far worse.

Horace ignored the comment, seemingly lost in what he knew about Hammertree's history. "As smoldering as it is right now, it's hard to imagine that it actually does rain out here. This packed earth doesn't absorb it easily, so water sits and creates floods. The buildings are lifted off the ground several feet to account for this. Well, after the Shining Truth rode in, the members spent their days kneeling at the edge of town, facing the desert and praying for Solendaron to make his grand return. The people of Hammertree laughed and mocked them but otherwise felt that the group was harmless and peaceful.

"And then the clouds came in.

"It wasn't the rainy season, as brief as that is out here. So imagine the shock of the townsfolk when water began falling from the sky in droves. Legend has it the rain came down as if an entire lake had been lifted, held overhead, and dropped at once. Even the stilts that held up the buildings were not enough. Dwellings filled with water. Animals drowned. Practically the only dry places were the haylofts of the barns that had faultless roofs, the very haylofts where the sect slept at night. Any crops the farmers of Hammertree had been fortunate enough to grow were destroyed immediately."

"They must have starved so far away from the rest of the world," Marzele said.

"They came near enough to it, but no. That's when the massacre began. Fifty-seven members of the Shining Truth had trekked into town that year. None ever left it."

"Were they drowned by the townspeople?"

"No, Marzele. As I said, the people of Hammertree did not starve, for they killed and ate all fifty-seven of the strangers they blamed for the flood. It wasn't until the next year, when the rains came just as hard even though there were no cultists left, that some of the folks realized maybe it had just been nature's own unpredictability. One family left, headed west into civilized society, and told the story of the massacre."

Marzele found that his knuckles were white; he'd been gripping the reins of his horse too tightly during the story. He took a deep breath and loosened his fingers.

"Fifty-seven wayward brothers and sisters," Marzele said, "eaten by these savages."

"Indeed. They were never made to pay, as this town was too far out to be of any concern. But now we will bring them to justice. They may not be the Royal Mystic Committee, but they are just as evil. We will crush them."

They rode on toward the village. For the first time, Marzele felt in sync with his companions.

"*In a land where sin and injustice are the rule,*" he recited from the Illuminarion, "*there I will rain fire upon My enemies and bring righteousness.*"

Marzele looked around. He and Horace were twenty feet

ahead of the others. Behind them rode Malia, Allicent, and Mick. "Where is Pector?" he asked.

He didn't like the grin Horace flashed him. "He stayed back in Hezron City to send the message," Horace said.

"Message? To whom?"

"All things in due time, my friend. Just be calm and courteous as we ride into Hammertree. We'll get the lay of the land, make them feel uncomfortable for a time, and then we'll strike."

Marzele didn't like this either. There was obviously something sinister—more sinister than the last few days had been, even—behind whatever the plan was. But it wasn't as if there were any turning back after the things they'd done. Marzele had sold his soul to the darkness.

*No,* he thought, *the Lord Solendaron Himself banished me into the shadows. If not for this, than why?*

THE FIRST VILLAGER THEY CAME ACROSS WAS ON HIS KNEES, pulling root vegetables out of the ground. The man didn't look up as they approached but instead kept at his work. He wore a bandana around his face like a bandit, and Marzele soon understood why. As he pulled up another root, dust from the scorched earth rose up in a brown cloud. More dust puffed up as he dropped the crop into the large basket at his side.

Marzele had moved ahead of Horace and the others as they closed in, and he was the first one to set his boots down at the perimeter of Hammertree. It wasn't until he knelt down to the man's eye level that the man looked at him.

"Smelled you lot on the wind," the man said. Marzele noticed a deep drawl in his voice. Though he didn't understand why, Marzele's heart skipped a beat. The voice was almost familiar, though there was no way he could have met this man before. They locked eyes as the man continued, "Afraid you're going to have to pay a pretty penny to water them there horses. Well's drying up. We're generous people, but desperate times these are."

"Have we met before, sir?" Marzele asked. He couldn't shake the feeling.

"Not 'less you somehow escaped from this here place. I can count on one hand how many folks I know of who ever found their way out, and they sure as hell never came back for a visit."

"I suppose you're right." Marzele turned back to see Horace, Mick, Allicent, and Malia dismounting. "Could you point us to a place where we may rest? An inn, perhaps, sir?"

"Name's Kenneth," the man said, but didn't offer a hand. He nodded toward a low cluster of structures a few hundred yards away. "Ain't gonna find some fancy hotel here. Even a spare room in someone's abode is too much to hope for. That said, a few coins will go a long way toward some hospitality."

Kenneth looked expectantly at Marzele, who reached into his trouser pocket and came up with three coins. They were warm and damp from his sweaty legs, but Kenneth didn't seem to mind. Marzele expected him to stand and guide the newcomers into the village, but instead the man hunched back over and continued his work.

The cultists pulled their horses by the reins, guiding them past Kenneth. Mick stopped over the basket holding Kenneth's harvest and pulled out one of the vegetables. He brought it to his mouth, took a loud bite, attempted to chew the chunk, then spat it out and dropped what was left back into the basket. Marzele shook his head and dropped another soiled coin near Kenneth as an apology.

Marzele followed his companions between two shacks and onto what amounted to Hammertree's main street—its only street, really. To his right, seven children who looked to range between four and twelve years old huddled in a half circle below a porch. Weeds grew rampant under the lifted building and its staircase. Three of the children held long dry sticks from one of the few scraggly trees. Marzele stepped closer to see what they were doing.

"Pin its head," the oldest girl ordered. She didn't have a stick, but she seemed to be calling the shots with these youngsters. "Ain't gonna carry you babies to the healer if you get bit."

"I'm trying to get its head," one of the younger boys cried, "but he's just too quick!"

"Move over," said a girl who could have been the little boy's twin sister. She forced the stick from his hands and bumped her hip against him. The boy fell over under the porch stairs, one hand stretched in front of him.

The snake saw its opportunity. It briefly coiled back with a hiss, bared its needle-sharp fangs, and lunged at the boy's fingers. It was two inches away when the little girl jabbed at it. The forked tips of the stick were spaced perfectly to fit over the top of the snake's head.

Unfortunately, the bone-dry stick splintered from the force.

Marzele jumped toward the boy and lifted him off the ground as the snake made another attempt at an attack. Its fangs locked onto Marzele's right hand instead. Marzele stood up, swung to his left to set the boy down safely, then used his left hand to grasp the snake's neck as it dangled from his right. He grunted in pain and squeezed the reptile, forcing it to open its jaws and release his flesh.

He heard a quick unsheathing of a blade, felt a sudden

rush of air as someone swung a long knife toward him. Blood splattered his forearm as the tip of the snake's head was lopped off just millimeters from his fingers. The snake went limp. Marzele did too as a fogginess overtook him in seconds and he collapsed to the ground.

# Chapter Thirty
## MARZELE

Her voice was soft, even melodious. Though he didn't recognize this, there was a clear sadness in it that she tried to cover for his sake. He wailed the way babies do when they want something but don't know quite *what* they want or how to ask for it. And yet she never lost patience with him, never complained about him weighing her down.

Marzele was two years old at most. He was nestled in a long cloth that had been wrapped securely around his mother's shoulders and torso. She kept one arm in front of her to hold him in—he was getting too large to be carried this way—and her other arm carried the oblong wicker basket he used as a bed. It was filled with his spare clothes, blankets, and cloth diapers.

"Hush, little one," she said to him, tilting her head down to kiss the top of his nearly hairless scalp. She had an accent. The word *little* sounded more like *lee-uhl*. She sounded much like Kenneth.

Young Marzele tilted his head back from his mother's

breast and took in the view around them. The moon was nearly full, the sky cloudless, displaying a full array of stars. He was in the desert on the same trail he had ridden with Horace and the others, but moving in the opposite direction. Sleepiness washed over him as his mother sang him a song. He leaned back into her chest and fell asleep.

He awoke to his mother kissing him on the forehead, but now he was not strapped to her body. He looked around him to see the shallow confines of the basket.

"I'm sorry, my love," she said through sobs. "They won't let you stay any longer. This is for the best. You'll be with your people, back where you belong."

Two women in gold frocks approached and stopped on either side of her. One pulled her into a hug while the other turned to look down at Marzele. He saw annoyance on her face as she calculated the extra work another baby would cause for the temple. She made a tutting sound and reached for the basket. The jolt from the rough way she picked it up made Marzele cry again. The other priestess tightened her arms around his mother to keep her from chasing after him, though he could see her struggling.

It was the last time he ever saw his mother before she returned to her village. Before she returned to Hammertree.

***

"Marzele?"

Horace's flapping jowls were not his preferred sight when he awoke from his slumber. Marzele felt itchy and reached for his face. It was covered in sticky sweat. Heat radiated from him.

"You're feverish," Horace said. "They gave us one

scrubbed-out trough to share with the horses, and I've used a quarter of it to keep you hydrated."

"Water, please." Marzele's whisper came out as a strained growl. His throat felt full of gravel. Horace picked up a battered tin cup.

"I pray you don't throw up again. Your body has rejected every drop I've attempted to give you." He used one hand to lift Marzele's head at an angle and tilted the cup to his lips. "Easy now," he said as Marzele chugged the contents.

The effects were almost immediate. The pain in his throat faded away. He sat up and felt a rush of dizziness. Sweat dripped down his back like a waterfall. Horace propped him up against a wall.

"How long was I out?"

"A full night and most of the day. It's nearly suppertime, though I'm not sure you're going to enjoy this meal. Do you think you can stand?" Horace got to his feet and reached a hand down for Marzele. He took it and rose but felt too wobbly. Horace wrapped an arm around his shoulders and guided him slowly forward.

Marzele took in his surroundings for the first time. There were wooden crates full of goods, sacks of flour, and pristine shovels, pickaxes, and other tools.

"The back room of the general store," Horace said. "Beats the barn where the others are holed up, and I have you to thank for it."

Horace guided him through a door into the front half of the shop. The proprietor at the counter turned and flashed a smile. "There's the hero now," the man said. Marzele heard his mother's accent once again.

"Thank you for your hospitality. I apologize that I've been unwell," Marzele said weakly, though he already felt a touch better now that he was up and moving.

"Nonsense. It's you who deserves the gratitude. My name is Greg Chilsen. You saved my son yesterday from a daggerblood snake. It's one of the most poisonous breeds in these parts. Its bite could kill a child easily, and those it doesn't take to the grave have some nasty chills and hallucinations while the poison works its way through the body."

"That explains a lot, then," Marzele said, thinking of his mother's face. Had that really been what she'd looked like? He'd never had a vivid memory of her like that. Marzele hadn't thought he'd remembered a single feature about her, not even the sound of her voice. "I'm glad the boy is safe."

"Safe, maybe, but still stupid. All of them, but it's not like there's much the kids can do here besides get into trouble." Greg motioned for them to follow him.

Horace assisted Marzele across the room and through another door. As they neared it, the smell of a freshly cooked meal wafted through. Marzele's stomach growled, eliciting a chuckle from Horace. "Like I said, you may not enjoy this meal."

The door led into the attached one-room apartment where the proprietor and his family dwelled. Narrow cots lined the wall nearest the door. Across the room were a cookstove, a counter with a washbasin, and a few cabinets. A table stood in the center of the room with four matching chairs and two overturned crates that Marzele assumed had been brought in for Horace and him.

Sprawled across two long sheet pans on the table was a snake. At first Marzele couldn't make out which side was the tail and which was the head, but then he realized it was because there was no head. His stomach lurched.

"Easy there," Horace said between laughs. "You helped catch tonight's meal—you should be proud!"

Another door opened, and a warm breeze entered the

room along with a woman, a young boy, and a nearly identical girl. The boy ran up and threw his arms around Marzele's legs, bowling him over. Marzele barely avoided slamming his head against the wall, but he couldn't be angry. Everyone laughed warmly.

"It's him, Mama!" the boy called.

The woman set a pitcher of water on the table and approached Marzele as he struggled to rise. As he lay on the floor, the image of his mother flashed back into his head, looking down at him in his basket for the last time.

"Are you sure you're okay, sir?" she asked. "Why don't you lie down on one of the cots and rest a little more?"

"Nonsense, Kiersy," Greg said. He poured water from the pitcher into tin cups that matched the one Horace had given Marzele in the stockroom. "He's the guest of honor, and the serpent is crisped just right. I'm glad we got that spiced oil in on the last train. You'll see when you taste it. Just melts in your mouth!"

Marzele made for one of the crates, but Kiersy gently guided him toward a chair. "The children can sit on those. You need a back behind you or you'll fall right down in your state." Marzele complied and settled in. Everyone else followed suit.

Greg used a large fork to shovel a piece of the snake onto a plate, then scooped up what appeared to be a mashed root vegetable from a pot. He plopped some next to the meat and passed the plate to Marzele. He repeated the process for the other four and then himself. "Dig in!" he said, and everyone complied except Marzele.

He wanted food, and he did not want to offend his hosts, but Marzele didn't know if he could eat *this*. The very creature that had nearly ended his life sat in pieces in front of him. It *did* smell quite delicious, though Marzele thought the spiced oil probably accounted for that.

"Are you sure it's safe?" Marzele asked. He picked up his fork and poked at the meat.

"If you don't eat it, I just might have your portion," Horace said through a full mouth. The scaly skin flaked off at Marzele's prodding like the outer layers of a puff pastry.

"You can eat the scales," Kiersy said. "Tastiest part, and not as chewy as the meat."

"Not chewy when I marinate it overnight," Greg said proudly. "My best yet, I think."

Marzele was ravenous. He decided he could wait no longer. He dug in and devoured the meat. He reached for a second portion with his fork, then hesitated, but Greg gave an encouraging nod, so he went for it. Even the vegetables were enjoyable. The food seemed so comforting to Marzele, like something his body had needed for years, though he'd never realized it.

The company was wonderful as well. Greg told stories about other visitors they'd had over the years. He told them how the train brought curious travelers every once in a while, how the townsfolk needed some time to get used to being a new travel destination thanks to the rail line.

When the conversation slowed, the twins, Jack and Cressia, broke into a silly song about bodily functions. Horace roared with laughter.

"Enough of that, you two!" Kiersy yelled. "Not in front of the guests. Sing something nice with those voices of yours."

Jack made an obscene sound effect and crossed his arms in protest, but Cressia began a new song. The melody was very pretty and a bit familiar. Was it one of the lullabies Marzele knew from his childhood in the Solendaron orphanage?

*No*, he thought, *I heard it somewhere else.*

The vision of his mother flashed through his mind again. She had carried him through the desert and into the next town, singing to him the whole time, on that final night they'd been a family. This was the song she'd sung.

"Marzele, are you okay?" Horace asked. Marzele glanced at him through his tears and nodded. Horace turned to Greg. "Are you sure the snake isn't still poisonous?"

"It's very safe," Greg said. "Daggerblood snakes have a single dose of poison in them, and they release it all at once. Your friend already absorbed it so that we could have this wonderful feast together." He smiled, lifted his cup, and took a sip.

"That song," Marzele said. "My mother sang it to me when I was a baby."

"Surely you can't recall that," Horace said. "Weren't you orphaned at a very young age?"

"You said the poison from daggerbloods can cause hallucinations, right?" Marzele asked Greg, who nodded.

"Yes, though some say they can remember things when they're under its effect. Memories they'd suppressed years before. Traumas they'd tried to forget."

"That's it, then." Marzele gestured at the remains of the meal. "This beast has brought something back to me, a memory I did not know I had." He smiled at the others around the table.

The fever and dizziness were gone. He still felt a warmth, but it was different. Familial. Loving.

For the first time he could remember, Marzele truly felt at home.

"You're getting soft for these people," Horace said from his makeshift bed in the stockroom. It was the middle of the night, but the heat had not yet subsided. The chirping and buzzing of insects both outside and indoors was unrelenting. Coyotes howled from somewhere nearby. And Marzele welcomed it all.

Horace sat up in frustration. "I can see it in you. This is the family you always wished you had."

Marzele considered this. "You're right, of course. During our exile these last couple of decades, I've been more alone than ever, lost without a purpose once our faith and profession was outlawed by Davin. I suppose I never knew what family truly was until I lost my only support system—our brothers and sisters in Solendaron. I wish I had taken the path our dear former colleague Bertram did during those dark times. When last I spent time with him, he told me how he'd met the Brevor family. They needed a farmhand in Centeron, and Bertram needed an occupation and a place to live. Lindon Brevor had inherited a farm from his father and left his job as an accountant in Capital City to operate the place, but he didn't know enough about farming. He brought his wife and children along, who despised life outside of the city at first.

"Bert convinced them that he could help them, and they gave him a chance and a nice little shack. It was humble but he had all that he needed to be comfortable while he tried to etch out his place in this new world. As Lindon came to trust Bert more, Lindon invited him into his dining room nightly for supper with the family. Bert became like a grandfather to those children. He told me he loved them almost as his own, yet something inside him kept him from being fully satisfied. His life had been upended so suddenly by Davin's ruling against religions. His accounts were unsettled, so he was not fully able to be there for that family. Still, it was more than

I've ever had. My life, especially in those years of exile, has been nothing but lonely. But the people here remind me so much of my mother. I feel a deeper connection with them than I've ever felt."

"Don't forget who these people are, Marzele."

"Nay, I have not let the dark history of this town escape my memory, though I do not know that it's fair to hold it against all those who live here now. Greg and Kiersy Chilsen were not even alive when the massacre happened, nor their children. Must they all perish?"

Horace pounded a fist into his bedding with a muffled thump. "If we want the attention of Davin and the Royal Mystic Committee, we must be willing to make bold moves. Executing a handful of the old-timers here is not going to accomplish that. Besides, the sins of their forefathers have been passed down to them. They would not think twice about committing murder against us if they found out we were once priests of Solendaron. They hate our kind; don't you forget that."

"I need to know who my mother was, Horace. If she was one of them, then I suppose *my* blood is tainted by this town's past as well. Now, let us sleep, and perhaps tomorrow the truth will emerge from the shadows."

# Chapter Thirty-One
## DENNY

The treatment Denny and Arnem received from their captors actually improved once Grez and Petey found out about the reward. If the smugglers wanted to get paid, they had to deliver the prisoners alive. Meals became more regular and wholesome. The pair was allowed to relieve themselves at reasonable intervals. At night, Grez and Petey didn't dare leave them unguarded, lest some other enterprising individuals stumble upon them. It would have been like leaving a pile of gold out for anyone to snatch.

And yet everything seemed much more sinister than before. Denny felt like a pig that was being fattened up in preparation for the Settler's Day feast. Even Arnem's usual optimism had all but melted away.

Arnem sat on the bench across from Denny, looking in Denny's general direction but not directly at him.

"You'll see them again," Denny said. "Your girls. Selah. They're going to be so ecstatic to see you when you arrive back at Quincy's house and bring them home to Plentimore Valley."

Arnem still avoided Denny's eyes. He looked down at the waterskin that Grez had given them the previous day. They hadn't been sure if Grez would continue his generosity, so Denny and Arnem had rationed what was left, taking only the smallest sips when their throats felt parched.

"You haven't dreamed, Denny," Arnem said. His voice was more hopeless than the boy had ever heard him sound. "You can't possibly know how this is going to end."

"You're right, I haven't dreamed this whole time. But that only means I haven't seen anything bad that may happen to us. That's a better sign than dreaming something terrible."

Arnem's eyes finally met Denny's, and they were full of tears. "I have found myself in so many precarious and terrible situations over the last thirty years. Every time, though, I've had my friends there to bail me out. Maachel. Richard. Jestan. Teyla. But this time it was *my* job to be the protector. To take care of you. I've failed, though. I've let you down."

"I was fine taking care of myself on the streets of Esteron City, Arnem. If I had never been given those visions of Richard, if fate or some god or whatever hadn't led me to you, I would have continued to care for myself. Sleeping on rooftops, finding meals in rubbish bins. But since we met, we've taken care of each other. This isn't just on you. If anything, *I* failed us."

"You're just a boy, Denny."

"So were you when you set off to fight evil in Ravager Valley. When you and your friends avoided the destruction of the Forest of Despair. When you led an army to vanquish evil. Just because I'm young doesn't mean I shouldn't try to be useful. I have nothing to lose. You still have a family who depends on you. I'm sorry I wasn't able to tap into my visions before all this happened."

A wad of phlegm hit Denny in the cheek. From the front of the wagon, Petey roared with laughter. "Bet you didn't see that coming either, did you, boy?" He knocked fists with Grez and then turned back to his reins. Arnem gathered a handful of straw from the floor of the wagon and wiped the spit off Denny's face.

"I'm sorry, Denny. You're right. We're a team. We're equals. After everything we've been through, this can't be the end for us."

Denny smiled, but he wasn't so sure. His mother had warned him not to come for her, that the end was upon her. Perhaps he should have heeded her warning. Perhaps by attempting to go to her, he had locked his fate and Arnem's into step with hers. Perhaps he had doomed them both.

DENNY AND ARNEM CONTINUED TO TRADE OFF BETWEEN optimism and despair. It became more difficult to keep their spirits up as the landscape around them dried up, the lush valleys of Costono giving way to the barren deserts of the Southern Reaches. Denny had never experienced the sheer amount of dust that now blew all around them, and his sneezing fits evidenced that he might be allergic to it.

"We'll make it there by nightfall, little one," Grez called over to him as he packed up his tent. "You can sneeze your brains out after we've claimed our prize for you, but don't even think about croaking on us now."

Arnem appeared from behind a leafless, dried-up husk of a tree after relieving himself. Petey was behind him with a large knife in case the man suddenly decided to make a run for it, but they all knew there was no possibility he would leave without Denny.

"Your turn, child," Petey said when Arnem had climbed back into the wagon. "This might be your last piss as a free man. Or, you know, a not-so-free boy."

"I'm fine," Denny said, though he knew he'd regret it later. "Let's just get this over with."

"Your choice, but I plan to make good time today," Grez said. "No stops unless we really need to."

With each mile they covered, the anxiety grew in the core of Denny's soul. He'd talked up Arnem's past to encourage the man, to give him hope, and yet Denny knew his own story was one of seemingly endless trials. The disappearance of his parents. Life on the streets. The journey to save Richard the Elusive and free the people of Emyhrsen. Now what mattered most to him was to save his parents, possibly the most important mission he'd ever have.

Grez and Petey exchanged verses of a lewd song in the front of the wagon. Arnem rolled his eyes at the most crass lines, likely imagining what his wife and daughters would think were they there to hear the lyrics. Arnem was a man who cared. When Denny had met him, he'd already had a family of his own, a safe and comfortable life. He'd risked everything for a homeless boy with what must have sounded like insane hallucinations. He'd fought admirably. When it was all over, he'd accepted Denny as part of his family. And even after all that, he'd left everything behind once again to rescue Marzele, to bring Gemma to Capital City, and now to venture into the unknown to help reunite Denny with his parents. If that wasn't a shining example of family, then what was?

If they escaped their captors, made it all the way to Denny's parents, and freed them from bondage, would that mean saying goodbye to Arnem? And should they fail, what would happen to Selah and the girls? They'd be left without a husband and father, no better off than Denny had been when his parents were ripped away from him at a young age. Should they manage to get free, would it be best for Denny to turn around and bring Arnem home? Forget about his parents and leave them to fend for themselves?

Denny wrestled with these conflicting thoughts as the sun bore down through the bars of his traveling cage. He turned to Arnem, who felt his gaze and met his eyes.

"What is it?" Arnem asked. His eyes narrowed nervously.

"Where they're taking us, your story doesn't end there. Your family doesn't end there." Denny looked up front, where Grez and Petey continued their obnoxious tune, but their voices had quieted a bit as if they were listening in. Grez's head cocked slightly, his left ear aimed toward Denny. The boy didn't care. He looked beyond his captors at the road, which was ascending into the hills. Just off the road was a pond struggling to retain even the slightest bit of moisture in the unceasing sun. Flying insects swarmed around it. The trees at the bottom of the hill were scraggly and dry, but with every few feet of incline, the vegetation grew greener and healthier. Denny knew they'd have shade in just a few more minutes.

"Neither does yours," Arnem replied. "We're in this together, little friend."

"No. I've asked too much of you already. You've sacrificed your time and safety, and Selah and your daughters are the ones suffering for it. I will not let them be abandoned any longer. You'll go back to them, live out your days as the world-class father and husband you are. The fates have given me my abilities. They've put me into this position. They've set up whatever has happened to my family."

"And they've put me in this position as well, Denny. You are my family too now, blood be damned. Like you, it seems I was made for crazy adventures. Don't let my short stature and overgrown paunch fool you."

Arnem laughed, but Denny wasn't affected by the humor. This was his burden alone. He knew it to be true. The Wynstone family would not be dragged down on his account.

"Don't give up on us now, blokes," Petey called to the horses. Denny looked around and noticed that they'd slowed considerably on the climb up the hill.

"Might need you two to get out and push from behind," Grez quipped to Arnem and Denny. "Then again, if these horses croak, the whole wagon will roll backward and crush you, and there'll be no reward for us."

"That little one would be pretty as a splatter of roadkill though, wouldn't he?" Petey glanced back at Denny through his tears of laughter. "Don't you have a sense of humor? May as well make the most of your final hours. Once we get through these hills and into the valley, the prison ain't much farther."

When neither Arnem nor Denny replied, their captors shrugged at each other and continued to steer the horses up the road.

Denny turned back to Arnem. "I'm serious. This is the end for us. I appreciate all you've done, but I'm not willing to put your life at risk any longer. I don't want your children to be orphaned like I was. End of the line."

"I won't turn back, Denny." Arnem's face had a hard resolve to it. He was truly willing to sacrifice his family's future for Denny's sake. Denny knew he should feel moved, but anger surged through him instead.

"No. No!" Denny started to shake with rage. He picked up handfuls of straw and threw them at Arnem. It was a childish act, a tantrum, but he didn't care. "I don't want you with me, don't you understand? You're not my father. I'm not your responsibility. All you do is slow me down. You're too recognizable. You put us at risk. It's your fault we were noticed! You think anybody ever noticed me when I was a street rat? You think anyone gave a second thought about me? You're putting my mission at risk!"

He didn't mean any of what he said; he just wanted it to hurt. And still Arnem looked at him with fatherly concern.

"Pipe down back there!" Grez yelled, his frustration growing. "Your fates are locked together now, stupid child. There's no escape for either of you."

Denny considered throwing another handful of straw at them, but it would accomplish nothing.

Petey turned back and mocked him. "Is the baby going to cry? Look, Grez—he really *is* going to cry. Maybe we really should reunite him with his jailbird mommy so she can wipe his little snotty nose."

Grez twisted his face into a look of mock agony. "Oh, Mommy, Mommy, please," he said in a high-pitched impression of a crying child. "Please make me feel all better! I miss you, Mommy! I miss you so much!"

"Wipe my tears, Mommy," Petey said in a similar tone. "Wipe my arse while you're at it!"

The men burst into laughter. They both leaned into the middle of their shared bench so they didn't fall off the side due to their gut-busting giggles.

Denny felt his pulse speed up. His breaths were rapid. A slight groan escaped him—a growl.

"Denny, calm yourself," Arnem said with care, patting Denny's knee. "Don't let them get to you."

The noise coming from deep within the boy grew. It was animalistic. Feral. He screamed.

"Nooooooo!"

Their captors sat up and looked back at him in surprise. Denny got to his feet and stomped toward them, screaming with each step.

"I'LL KILL YOU BOTH! I'LL MAKE YOU PAY!"

He wasn't sure which man caught fire first. Grez rose to his feet, nearly toppling off the wagon as he pulled at his shirt. Smoke rose from the collar.

"What...what is this?!"

Petey pulled off his hat, and the smell of burning hair wafted back to Denny. His scream had spooked the horses, who took off at a pace that seemed impossible after their long haul through the desert and up into the hills. Grez toppled backward and slammed his head into the bars behind his bench. All of his clothing burst into flame.

"What's happening?!" Petey reached over to try and help his companion pull off the burning fabric when his own slacks lit up and immediately spread the fire to his shirt.

"Denny, control yourself!" Arnem yelled. Denny turned back to him, and whatever Arnem saw on his face clearly terrified him. "This isn't who you are. You can stop this!"

The horses continued their panicked run. Denny faced the front and saw the road curve ahead. The horses were going too fast. They turned left with the road, but the wagon tipped.

"Aaaah—" Grez's pained scream was cut short by the sound of his bones crunching under the wagon as it toppled onto its side. Denny and Arnem were thrown into the bars around them as the wagon somersaulted down a steep slope. The wagon tongue snapped, releasing the horses. Somehow Petey managed to grab hold of the reins as they slipped away, but the force yanked him off the wayward wagon. The horses dragged him several yards, still engulfed in flames. He was a speeding fireball behind the animals, causing them to panic further. The wagon was completely upside down now as it fell down the hill. It slammed into a tall tree, which stopped its descent. Denny looked across to Arnem, who was bloodied but seemed to be in one piece.

The trunk of the tree groaned. There was a snap, and the entire thing toppled over. The wagon resumed its slide down the hill, though it no longer rolled like a wayward ball.

"The lake!" Arnem called through his pain. Denny looked in the direction they were heading. There was a small drop-off above a body of water.

Denny scrambled to his feet and walked along the bars that now made up the floor of the overturned wagon. He helped Arnem up, knowing there wasn't time to point out the large knob protruding from his friend's forehead or the blood that hemorrhaged from his nose. Together they attempted to drag their feet to stop the slow slide of the wagon toward the drop-off and into the water, but it was no use. The wagon must have weighed a thousand pounds with its iron bars and solid oak base. There was no way they'd be able to interfere with its inertia.

Denny looked ahead, ready to face the end he'd brought upon himself. Arnem squeezed his hand. They both took deep breaths and held them as the wagon met the lip of the drop and fell ten feet into the water.

This was it. They would drown in a place nobody would ever find them. Denny braced himself for the water to cover him, for the wagon to sink to the bottom of the lake. Water splashed his legs. The wagon sank a few inches into mud, which made its way into Denny's boots. He closed his eyes to let death take him.

Arnem laughed. "It's shallow! It's bloody shallow!"

Denny let out a chuckle, which morphed into a cry. Tears

mingled with the muddy water that had splashed him. "We...
we didn't drown," Denny said. "But we're still trapped here,
aren't we?"

"Maybe, maybe not." Arnem trudged toward the front of
the wagon and reached through the bars. "Looks like good old
Grez left his coat behind."

Of course Grez had removed his coat. It had been unbear-
ably hot under the desert sun that morning. Denny didn't
know how his burgeoning powers worked, but clearly only the
clothing the captors had been wearing had gone up in flames.
The coat had merely picked up some dirt on the way down
the slope. Part of it dangled into the water now, caught in a
cranny of the wooden bench and hanging within reach.
Arnem grabbed it and pulled it into the cage. He searched the
left pocket, then the right, but there were only scraps of food,
a handkerchief, and various other little bits.

"He always pulled the keys out of the inner pocket,"
Denny reminded him.

Arnem nodded and opened the coat. There in the left
inner breast pocket was a metal ring with four keys. They
sloshed across to the back of the cart, and Arnem tried two
keys before succeeding with the third.

They were free.

Up the hill, they found the baggage that had been tossed
on the tumble down. Grez and Petey had kept the bags
stuffed under their bench in the front. Denny tore one open
and pulled out the curved sword that Quincy had gifted him.
As he stared at its glinting blade, he heard a whimper farther
up the hill. Without waiting for Arnem, he made his way up,
stepping over the fallen branches and trunks they'd left in
their wake. At the top lay Grez, his beard dark with blood. In
concert with the man's cries, a raspy sound escaped as he
exhaled.

Denny pointed the sword at him and pushed the beard aside, revealing a gash in Grez's throat from the wagon wheel that had crushed him.

"Puh...puh...please," Grez croaked out.

"Please help you?" Denny asked, his voice calm. "I'll do that for you. I'll help you."

Without remorse, Denny split the man's neck the rest of the way open with his blade, and Grez's final breath escaped.

# Chapter Thirty-Two
## MARZELE

A knock pulled Marzele out of sleep the next morning. Sweat dripped off his forehead and splattered on his bare legs as he sat up. He grabbed his sheet from the floor, covered his legs, and called out, "Enter!"

"Good afternoon, Marzele," Greg Chilsen said as he stepped into the storeroom.

"Is it afternoon already? I apologize for taking up your space for so much of the day. With the windows covered, I suppose my body doesn't know to rise with the sun."

"Nonsense. It's the poison still working its way through your blood. It takes several days. I think some fresh air would do you good." Greg walked toward the back of the room and unlatched an oversize door. He pushed it open, and Marzele flinched as the sun penetrated the dark space. Greg chuckled. "Sorry, my friend. I must load sacks of feed into my cart and make a delivery. I could use your help if you're up for it."

Marzele wanted to say yes, but he knew Horace would balk at the choice. He glanced over at Horace's empty cot—his companion had probably been gone for hours already.

"Yes, I think it would be wise to seek a change of scenery and repay the debt I owe you for this shelter."

"Like I told you before, you saved my child's life. Giving you a place to sleep here costs me nothing." Greg grunted as he lifted a sack of feed. "That said, I would very much enjoy your company. It's a bit of a trek to Franklin Dorich's farm, and the coyotes sometimes give me trouble when I'm alone."

Marzele pulled his slacks on, buttoned his shirt, and slipped into his boots. He walked over to the pile of grain sacks, bent down, and grabbed one. His knees buckled as he tried to lift it.

"Easy there," Greg said, catching Marzele and taking the sack from him. "Just go on and sit in the wagon. The horses are hitched up already. You're still too weak from the poison to carry fifty-pound sacks. Your company is all I ask for today."

Marzele felt incredibly useless, but he knew Greg was right. He made his way into the wagon without a word. Greg had already loaded in several other things from the front of his shop for the delivery.

"That basket behind you has our lunch in it. Kiersy fixed a little extra for you. Feel free to grab a bite while I lock up." Greg dropped the last sack onto the wagon. He went back into the storeroom and pulled the door closed behind him, then came around the perimeter of the shop a minute later. "All set!"

The sun burned bright, and Marzele was again grateful to have hair on the top of his head. He'd seen no point in shaving it off the way he had for decades before ending up on Terminus Rock. Many customs from his life as a priest of Solendaron had stuck long after Davin had outlawed the religion, but letting his hair grow out was one he didn't mind letting go of. It almost tickled now as the warm breeze blew his burgeoning curls. And Greg was right—fresh air was just what he needed to feel like himself again.

Thirty minutes into the journey, Greg turned to Marzele. "You look like you have something you want to say."

"I suppose you're right. A memory from my childhood repeated several times in my dreams after the snakebite. I'm trying to process what I saw."

"Yes, daggerblood snake venom will do that do you," Greg said. "The Juerticán folk who once resided in these parts used to have a way to extract the venom and consume it as part of a ritual to connect with their past and recall repressed memories. Is there something you wanted to forget that has come back to haunt you?"

"I'm not so certain it's haunting me. It's a memory of a traumatic event, but seeing visions of my mother warms my heart. I had no recollection of what she even looked like until now. She gave me up when I was little more than a toddler. A part of me always thought I must have been unloved, even hated. Now I know that is not true. If these truly are memories, then my mother did not despise me. She was driven by fear to bring me to a safer place. What I'd really like to know is why this specific memory has come back to me."

"Normally there is a trigger for a specific memory to appear after infection. Did you have a conversation about your parentage with Horace and the others before the bite?"

"No," Marzele said. At the mention of his name, though, thoughts of what Horace would say about this moment crept into his mind. Horace had discouraged him from getting too close to the people of Hammertree; they were in town to enact revenge on the locals, after all. Still, Marzele felt that Greg was a kindred spirit. "When we rode into town, we came across one of your fellow villagers. There was something in his accent that immediately felt familiar to me. Even though I grew up in the orphanage only three hours west of Hammertree, I don't recall ever having visited the town before. Yet there is a very specific way you all speak out here that is nothing like the rest of Southplains. It can't be a coincidence."

"Your mother has the same accent in your dreams?" Greg asked.

"Indeed."

A suspicious look came over Greg's face. "You mentioned an orphanage. Which one was it?"

"It was sponsored by the regional governorship in Hezron City," Marzele lied. It was the first time he had sensed danger in Hammertree. He suddenly understood why Horace had warned him against getting too friendly with the locals. Marzele stared ahead, but he could feel Greg glancing at him, perhaps studying his face for signs of dishonesty.

"Well, that was good of them to take you in. As much as my parents and the generations before them wanted to be free of King Tyran Lam and his predecessors, I must admit that Tyran was an effective leader before the consolidation of power. His wings were clipped once he gave up his title and Southplains's independence to King Davin. I can't see the current regional government funding an orphanage. They'd sooner let children starve to death in the streets. Not here in Hammertree, though. We take care of our own."

They spent the remainder of the ride mostly in silence with only occasional small talk about the local flora and fauna to interrupt the awkwardness. Eventually the barren landscape gave way to a field of green. Marzele thought it was a mirage at first, the change in color on the horizon was so jarring.

"The spring in the middle of Franklin's property feeds his

fields. Attracts a lot of wildlife as well. He keeps his livestock plump, but then the wolves and coyotes come after them."

"You mentioned the coyotes earlier. Do they really give you trouble?"

"Normally they're scared of us. Give them space, and they'll return the favor. You never know, though. Nature has ways of surprising you. Mags Sanderson was mauled by three of them right out in her field at high noon a month back. Her farmhand, Karn, can't really be called that anymore seeing as he lost both hands trying to save her. There have been a couple of other brushes with them in the last few weeks. No idea what's gotten into the little beasts."

As they got closer, a fence came into view. Perched atop a long stretch were dozens of vultures. The massive birds of prey didn't show any fear of the intruders. Their calmness brought back memories of one of Marzele's abilities that the Lord Solendaron had blessed him with: his connection to pigeons. He'd heard of other priests who could control more majestic birds, like falcons and eagles. He wondered if any priests had found success with vultures.

After they drove past the outer rows of corn, they came upon beds of lettuce, vines of tomatoes, and even some fruit trees. They rolled up to a barn at the center of the property. Franklin pumped away at a handle, filling a bucket with water from his well. The man looked like an apple that had been left out in the sun for too long, his skin shriveled and baked brown. He was ancient yet fit and agile from tending the farm. He flashed a smile at the newcomers, revealing a sparse assortment of teeth that had apparently never been cleaned.

"I was about to come out lookin' for ya, Chilsen," Franklin said. "One more day and my chickens were gonna starve without them there grains. Figured you might have been mauled by them coyotes"—he pronounced it *kai-oats*—"which would be a damn shame, seein' as they'd also eat up all the goods you brung."

"Maybe you should hitch up your horses and ride into town more often," Greg responded. "It can't be too healthy having only your livestock as company for months at a time, old man."

"I'd get bored talkin' to ya anyway," Franklin said. He blocked one nostril and blew out a thick brown stream from the other. Then he met Marzele's eyes for the first time. "Seems ya got a newcomer. Even I know that don't happen more than once a decade or so in Hammertree."

"I rode in with a group of friends a few days ago," Marzele said. "Wanted to see the town. The factory we all worked for closed down a few weeks back, so we figured we'd use our free time to see the country."

"Picked a horrendous vacation spot, ya did." Franklin said. Greg laughed along with him.

"The farther we can get from King Davin, the better," Marzele said.

Franklin waved his hands in the air and called out to his animals, "Careful, boys, we seem to have an outlaw here today!"

He motioned for the men to follow as he turned and headed for his house. It was a small structure that appeared to lean into the robust barn. Marzele thought the shadow of the larger building must keep the house quite cool. Inside, Franklin poured some juice from an ancient-looking pitcher and pushed cups across the table to Marzele and Greg. "Fresh squeezed right here. Got a basket full of fruit for you to take back and sell, Chilsen."

The glass felt crusty, and Marzele saw the remains of old liquids caked all over it, but he sipped the juice anyway. His face lit up when it touched his tongue. "Not sure I've ever tasted something so fresh before! This is incredible."

Franklin's laugh sounded like the braying of a donkey. "Well, you can bring this fella back anytime, Chilsen!"

"I'm Marzele, by the way."

"Marzele? Marzele..." Franklin's eyes rolled back into his head. Marzele worried for a moment that the man was having some kind of seizure, but it turned out he was just plumbing the depths of his memory. "I've met one other Marzele in my time. Can't forget a name as dumb as that. No offense." He reached across the table and slapped Marzele's shoulder. Marzele laughed, though the man had used more strength than he may have intended.

"It's an uncommon name, I'll admit," Marzele said.

"Chilsen, I'm sure you are too young to remember that Marzele. It was back when them folk came to town. The..." Franklin trailed off as he looked at Greg questioningly. At the same time, Greg's eyes bored into Marzele as if searching for a reaction.

"The Solendaron folks," Greg finished for Franklin.

Marzele struggled to turn his eyes toward Greg. Only hours ago, the man had seemed like he could be long-lost family. Marzele had felt more at ease with him than he had with anyone in months, even years. Since the mention of the orphanage, though, the man had grown suspicious of Marzele. Distrustful.

And he was right to feel that way, Marzele reminded himself.

"Do you know that story, Marzele?" Greg asked.

Marzele started to answer, but Franklin didn't wait. "He was one of them baldies, sure enough. No, sir, can't forget a name like that. He was a married man, come into town with his woman and the rest of the group, but he fell for one of ours. Harry Grausen's girl. Beautiful thing she was before he went and sullied her. Damn shame what happened to her." Franklin reached across the table and ruffled Marzele's patchy hair. "Can't hate a man over his name, though. I'm sure *this* Marzele ain't that kind of person."

"No, sir," Marzele managed to say. "Thanks to King Davin, the Solendaron are all gone anyway."

"Praise Davin," Greg said with a bit of distrust in his voice. His eyes bored into Marzele.

The fever rushed over Marzele all at once. Suddenly the day's journey no longer seemed like a good idea.

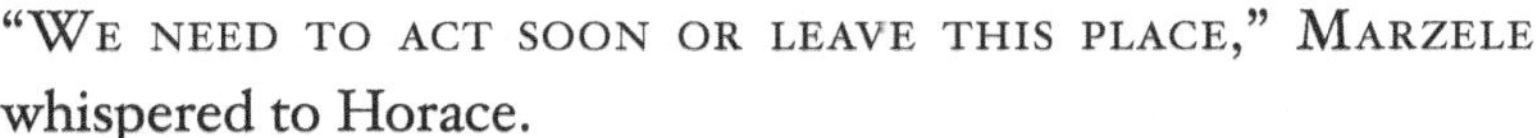

"WE NEED TO ACT SOON OR LEAVE THIS PLACE," MARZELE whispered to Horace.

"Why the sudden change of heart?" Horace asked from his cot. "Yesterday I was certain you wanted to take up permanent residence with this family. Now you're ready to burn the town into oblivion?"

"Greg knows."

"Knows what?" Horace asked.

"He knows I'm of the Solendaron. As soon as I mentioned being from a nearby orphanage, he seemed to suspect it. The Solendaron orphanage must be the only one around here. Then the farmer Greg took me to visit told us about a Solendaron priest with my name who visited this town years ago. It must have been my father. He must have been one of the victims. The guy seemed to know of my mother as well."

"Damn it, Marzele. I warned you not to get close to these people. Now you have compromised us." Horace rose from his cot and paced around the room in the dark. "You're right, then. The time to act is now. These people seem nice on the surface, but they are savages."

"I think they killed my mother for falling in love with my father. They truly did hate our kind here."

"They're animals, Marzele. We'll slaughter them like animals. Now, you're a lot less formidable than me"—Horace slapped his bare belly—"so it should be you who sneaks out to the barn to warn the others. Fortunately everyone in this town turns in early. We can strike easily while they sleep. Allicent will send her carrier pigeon to Hezron City with a message to Pector."

"You still haven't told me what Pector is doing," Marzele said. "We could use his help here."

"We certainly could use extra help. Perhaps this time you'll actually get involved. The others are starting to wonder if you have it in you, if you really care about avenging our fallen brothers and sisters."

Marzele didn't know how to respond. He rose from his cot and dressed into the same outfit he'd worn that day. "You're right that I don't want to harm anyone. I do believe that things must be made right, but I question whether this is the way. But I'm here with you all anyway, and I will not stop you from doing what you wish. Now, let me rouse the others."

With that, Marzele carefully opened the back door and snuck out into the night.

# Chapter Thirty-Three
## MARZELE

There was no tavern in Hammertree where people congregated once the sun went down, no nightlife whatsoever. The villagers worked hard and rested hard, but they seemed to do very little else. Perhaps that was what it took to survive the harsh conditions they lived in, hours from the nearest real city. In order to beat the intense heat, most of the citizens woke before sunrise and started their days. Marzele and his companions stood out like Ogressi in Plentimore Valley with their sleeping patterns. Tonight Marzele didn't see a single soul out and about on the streets, and nary a lantern burned in any window he passed.

The first sign of life he came across was at his destination, where Malia, Allicent, and Mick sat around a fire pit outside the barn they'd called home for the last couple of days, whispering to each other so as not to wake the neighbors. Marzele purposely dragged his feet in the gravel of the road as he approached to get their attention.

Their distrust of him still showed clearly on their faces. Horace was the only one who had made him feel like part of the group. He wasn't even sure how Horace had inserted himself among them, though Marzele assumed it had something to do with Horace's wealth. It seemed the man single-handedly bankrolled their entire operation, whereas Marzele offered them nothing. Up until now, he had tagged along but not partaken in any of their avenging. In Hammertree, though, the way he'd saved the Chilsen child had given them some clout. They'd had very little hope of being welcomed into the town had it not been for Marzele's actions. A few days later, they had not yet been driven out. Marzele was the distraction—the bait, as it were—and now it was time to go in for the kill.

"Did Horace send you?" Mick asked. He spat toward Marzele, the splatter landing inches from Marzele's boots. "Or have you grown tired of the comfort of that little family you've been staying with?"

"That shopkeeper is a real looker," Allicent said, elbowing Malia. "Care to introduce us to him?"

"I think old Horace is keeping that one for himself, ain't he?" Malia quipped to a burst of laughter.

Marzele put a pointer finger to his lips. They quieted, but they looked annoyed. "It is time. Tonight we strike." A chorus of howls sang out in the night, as if the beasts could smell the blood that was to be shed.

"Why the change of heart?" Malia asked. "Oh, stars, did Horace actually go for the shopkeeper?"

"It's nothing like that," Marzele said. "It seems Greg and another man may be suspicious of us. I don't think we have much more time before our identities are brought to light. If we want to get a jump on things, this is our last chance."

"Too bad, I was really enjoying my slumber in that drafty old hayloft," Mick joked. "Who knew the desert practically froze over at night?" He rose to his feet and kicked dirt on the fire. The others coughed at the dust cloud he created.

Allicent was the next to stand. She gestured for Marzele to follow her. She led him into the barn and up a set of creaking stairs. Marzele looked around the loft and saw the makeshift beds the three had made. He was grateful he'd not had to sleep up there with them. Perhaps the snakebite had been a blessing after all, if he still believed in such a thing.

Allicent walked over to one of the blankets and swiped it, sending dust and loose hay flying. Marzele sneezed. After wiping his eyes, he saw the scroll that had been hidden under the blanket. Allicent unrolled it.

"We've been mapping out the town. There are five of us, but as you see, we've only quartered the area." Allicent looked at Marzele with ridicule. "Would be a bit easier with your help, but Malia and Mick are convinced you're still not ready. Why Horace still carts you around with us, I've no idea."

Marzele wanted to be useful, wanted to say he was ready to participate in their slaughter, but he knew better. He hadn't the heart or the stomach for it. He believed in their cause and wanted all those who had harmed his kind to pay, but he also didn't feel like the darkness had fully taken him over the way it had Horace.

"I'll do what I can," was all he could promise.

Allicent rolled her eyes at him. She rustled through a burlap sack that reminded Marzele of the ones he'd delivered to Franklin's farm with Greg that afternoon, though this one let out a metallic clinking sound.

"We have three or four hours before people start waking up around town. Should be enough time to install these." She pulled out rectangular iron plates with holes drilled for bolts. Some were flat while others were bent at ninety-degree angles. "For their doors. Angled ones for inset doors, flat for flush. Once these are installed on every residence, we'll light this place up."

"Why fire? Why not attack with the shadows of the Tïhn?"

A grin twisted across Allicent's face. "They cooked the priests and priestesses of the Shining Truth to a crisp back in the day before consuming them. We're merely returning the favor."

"I can help with the doors," Marzele offered. "Horace moves slowly, so I'll start by helping him with his quadrant. Please leave Chilsen to me, though. I need to speak with him before we proceed."

Allicent's eyes narrowed, but she seemed satisfied enough. "Fine," she said. "Take care of whatever kink you need. Just don't jeopardize us any more than you already have." She moved toward another blanket and whisked it away to reveal her birdcage. Her carrier pigeon cooed at the sight of the lantern.

"Hello, little friend. Ready to fly?" She unlatched the cage, held her hand close to the opening, and clicked her tongue. The pigeon jumped onto her hand. She uttered a phrase in the Solendaron dialect, one Marzele knew quite well. The bird cooed back as if it understood her words. She switched back to the common tongue as she spoke softly to it. "The attack starts now. Complete your mission. We'll be ready."

She walked toward the window of the loft and flicked her arm. The pigeon jumped off and took flight.

"You can still control them?" Marzele asked. He felt an unexpected jealousy. "You didn't lose it when you turned from Solendaron?"

She looked at him with ridicule. "Of course not. Nor have you. The Shadow works through us just as much as Solendaron. You just need to stop cowering at the darkness within if you want to find what you once had." She picked up the sack and the scroll and made her way back down the stairs, then stopped at the bottom and turned up to Marzele. The disdain in her eyes made him flinch. "You're a pathetic broken man. I don't know what Horace sees in you, but he is putting all of us at risk by bringing you into this."

With that, she continued outside to meet the others. Another chorus of cries from the coyotes rang out. They were nearer than before.

It was easy to fix the metal plates to the dried-out wooden doors of the houses around town. Marzele and the others made quick work of it until there was but one abode remaining.

Marzele stepped quietly through the shop. He made his way behind the counter to the door that led to the one-room apartment. Greg Chilsen rose at the sound of the door opening.

"Something wrong, Marzele?" Greg asked as he wiped the sleep from his eyes.

"Follow me into the store. Don't want to wake your family." Marzele fought the urge to look at the children sleeping peacefully; he didn't need to make the situation more difficult for himself. He stepped back through the doorway and set his lantern on the countertop next to Greg's cashbox.

Greg took a moment to adjust his eyes to the light, then looked warily at Marzele. "Well? What's this all about? What's the story?"

"I'm here to ask you that. What's the true story about this place? About my mother?"

A mocking half smile formed on Greg's face. "Should have

known." Greg pulled a stool from under the counter and sat on it. "This was before my time, you understand, but everyone in town knows the stories. Hammertree never used to get visitors before the train ran out this way, so it was always memorable when someone stumbled upon it in those days. In a small town like this, there are no secrets, and nothing lives in the past."

"No, I can't imagine the murder of dozens of guests could remain a secret of the past," Marzele said with contempt.

"Murder? Try self-defense. You're talking about those Solendaron freaks, no doubt. They're a dangerous bunch, yourself included."

Marzele sighed. "How did you know?"

"The only orphanage in Hezron City was that sun god freak show. Once they got you in their clutches, you were brainwashed for life."

"I will not deny that I was a priest of Solendaron for most of my life," Marzele admitted, "but that changed not long ago."

"So you came here for revenge because you heard what happened back in my father's generation? Even though you claim you no longer believe in that filth?"

"All I want to know is what happened to my parents. What did they do to deserve the scorn of Hammertree? You all seem like lovely people. I enjoyed my short time here with you."

"Like I said, it was self-defense. We had to defend our way of life. It wasn't all that common to be independent of religion, but that's all the folks of Hammertree ever wanted. We'd been hospitable to some of your kind before when one or two stumbled upon us at a time, but these ones were different. They had some new philosophy, I don't even know what, and they were intent on spreading it. They came to our town to try and seduce some of our people."

Marzele walked around the counter and leaned against it across from Greg. "If the people of this town prided themselves on being free thinkers, shouldn't some of them also have been free to choose the ways of Solendaron if that was what they wanted?"

"Let's just skip to your mother. That's what you want to know about, isn't it? Mariza Grausen was betrothed to none other than Franklin Dorich. He may have seemed light-hearted about it earlier, but I assure you, in those days he led the mob to lynch her. Your mother didn't even have a bump in her belly until a couple of months after the slaughter of the outsiders. Your father, the first Marzele, must have spoiled her up in the hayloft, probably the same one your friends are sleeping in now."

Marzele gripped the edge of the counter. "Why did they allow her to give birth?"

"Our people aren't savages. They weren't about to kill a girl with a baby inside of her. In case you didn't notice, there isn't a very large population around here. Every person has value, and every new generation deserves a chance to live in the footsteps of their forefathers."

"Then what became of my mother?"

Greg let out a nervous chuckle. "She gave birth to a baby —to you, as it turns out—and raised you for a time. Franklin had no interest in marrying Mariza, as she was spoiled goods at that point, but he collected his dowry from old Harry Grausen regardless. It was everything Harry had, and he had to pay it. The farm Franklin runs to this day belonged to your granddad. Harry and his daughter and his little bastard grandchild moved into a shack just a couple of doors down from here. His status was as ruined as your mother's.

"One day he came home from his new job as a laborer in the Garza fields to find your mother with a book, reciting some chant in a language she didn't even understand. He knew what it was, though. The book had belonged to the freaks who were long gone by that point. He'd already lost enough and wasn't going to have any of it. He told his daughter to leave, and that's just what she did—took you away from this place, left you in the orphanage, then came back with nothing but that book. She walked into the center of town screaming in that ridiculous tongue of your people. My own pappy, just around her same age at the time, stabbed a pitchfork right into her throat in front of everyone. He was lauded as a hero." Greg laughed with pride.

Marzele reached across the counter and grabbed him by the neck. Marzele's entire body shook. He emitted a pained groan, unable to find any words. It turned into a scream, and yet Greg continued to laugh in his face.

No heat formed in Marzele's hand. Just months ago, he'd been able to melt iron with his bare flesh and the power granted to him by the Lord Solendaron.

Now...

Now the power was no more, gone along with his faith.

He pulled, slamming Greg's face into the counter. It was all he could do to stop the laughter.

When he released the man, Greg stood up, blood pouring from his nose. And still he laughed.

Marzele let out another scream, more animalistic than before. He reached for the nearest object, a jar of dried meat, and smashed it into Greg's head. It shattered, leaving a gash across Greg's brow. Marzele leapt over the counter and knocked his opponent to the ground. Greg kicked at Marzele, but it was no use. Visions of his mother flashed in Marzele's mind as he beat the life out of Greg Chilsen.

It took the creak of a door just a few feet behind him to pull him out of his act of rage. He turned to see the young boy he'd saved from the snake. At the sight of the carnage, the boy gasped and slammed the door.

Marzele looked back at the body beneath him and wept at what he'd become. The coyotes howled, even closer now, but Marzele's own cries and those of the family on the other side of the door were all that he heard.

The smell of smoke snapped him out of it. The others had begun. Marzele pulled out the last metal plate in his pocket and fixed it to the Chilsens' door. The tremble of his hands slowed him down. He dropped the bolts twice but eventually finished the job.

Outside, he joined Horace and the others. Allicent handed him a bottle stuffed with a cloth that had been soaked in a putrid liquid. She brought the flame of her torch to it and nodded at Marzele, though her look was nearly as mocking as the one Greg's face had worn before Marzele's attack. Once Marzele lobbed the flaming bottle through the Chilsen family's window, however, Allicent patted him on the back with approval.

The cries of the coyotes were drowned out by the screams of Greg's wife and children.

Marzele turned and walked straight out of the town and toward the animals. At that point, he felt he was nothing more than one of them. If the coyotes wanted blood, so be it. He was ready for them to take him.

THE COYOTES NEVER CAME.

Marzele sat on a low hill that crested just above the eastern edge of Hammertree. The sun rose behind him, giving off a new flavor of light distinct from that of the flames he'd watched consume the entirety of the town. The dry wood had made for quick work, and the last of the desperate screams had faded away thirty minutes earlier.

After their previous attacks, the Cult of Arun had skipped town immediately, not wanting to risk confrontations with anyone arriving to defend the victims. From his perch above the town, however, Marzele noted that his companions were in no rush to flee today. They sat around their fire pit, charring meat and laughing about the carnage. Marzele wasn't in the mood to join them; the disgust he felt over what he'd done had already made him vomit a few feet away from where he sat. The early morning breeze brought wafts of smoke scented not just by his companions' cooking meat but also by the burnt flesh of the people of Hammertree.

The patter of small feet caused Marzele to turn. He expected to see the drab colors of the dried weeds and sunbaked dirt that defined the region and perhaps a groundhog skittering around behind him. What he took in was a sea of blacks and browns with sprinkles of red. Ruffled feathers. Beaks that curved into sharp points.

The field behind him was covered in vultures—hundreds of them. He felt as if the birds were staring right at him. Perhaps a thousand eyes, dark and gleaming in the fresh light of dawn, boring straight into him.

Marzele felt deep in his heart that they could sense the rot inside of him. They could smell the decay of his soul that had begun back on that isle of abandonment when his world had been turned upside down—not for the first time, but in a way he'd never seen coming. When his faith had been rocked and his freedom and powers had been stolen from him, leaving him an empty shell of a man. The vultures were here to do what they had been created for: to consume the rotting flesh of the lifeless. He was certain that they were here for him.

"Come, then," he said in a voice that grated like the scraping of stones in his parched throat. "Take me. I am ready."

As if on cue, the entire flock ruffled their feathers, stretched their wings, and took to the air. Marzele closed his eyes and listened to the whoosh of a thousand wings around him. A sudden breeze swept over him. He braced for the pierce of their sharp talons, the gnash of their needle-sharp beaks. He was the prey, left for dead, and they were the shadows of death come to collect their dues.

And yet, nothing happened. He opened one eye and then the other. They were gone. He turned back toward the town and found the vultures swooping into what was left of Hammertree's structures. With the roofs burned out or caved in, the birds easily disappeared inside the barely standing walls. They found what flesh remained on the men, women, and children of the town and had the feast of a lifetime.

Marzele wept.

He'd wanted revenge for his mother's death, but he'd been decades too late. Greg Chilsen wasn't responsible for the injustices of his parents' generation. Most of the people in town hadn't even been alive when she'd been killed; few survived more than fifty or sixty years in the harsh climate of the desert, and those who had been around when the tragedies had occurred had been mere children. This hadn't been like the other attacks the Cult of Arun had perpetrated. These people weren't former commanders of the Royal Mystic Committee who'd once blindly followed King Davin's orders to purge the land of the religious and the gifted for no reason other than the consolidation of power. Marzele hadn't had the stomach to participate in those killings, but he had at least understood why Horace and the others had targeted those former inquisitors. The previous residents of Hammertree had been a superstitious lot who had thought they were protecting their way of life. They'd committed horrendous crimes against a group of outsiders they'd thought were there to convert or attack them. But that had been a generation ago. Their descendants did not necessarily carry the sins of their fathers.

This slaughter had been pure malice, and Marzele had participated in it. He had hoped it would bring him some comfort, cure the deep loss caused by the recent dreams of his mother.

But as he sat on the hill overlooking the carnage, he felt no comfort. No peace. The remains of innocent children were being torn to shreds by the savage vultures, and Marzele was to blame. Those children had done no harm to Marzele's mother nor to his father's group of refugees. Perhaps if Horace and the others had targeted only the elder folks, those who likely *had* committed the brutal murders of old, this would have felt more like a victory. Folks like...

Another sound caused Marzele to turn toward the desert wastelands once more. He expected another flock of vultures arriving for the fresh meal, or perhaps the coyotes had come for him after all. That wasn't what he saw, however.

Franklin Dorich rushed toward the town on horseback. His farm was one of the few that sat a good distance from the town, and Horace and the others hadn't bothered to attack those that resided outside of Hammertree. Those loose ends had never crossed their minds.

Franklin Dorich, the man who had been betrothed to Marzele's mother until he'd found out about her pregnancy. The man who had abandoned Mariza Grausen and yet had still taken her father's farm. He was one of the few who was still alive from the days of old. He was one of the few whom Marzele would have felt justified in attacking, one of the few who actually deserved death.

Marzele emitted a guttural scream as he got to his feet and stalked down the hill toward the rider. Franklin pulled back on the reins and brought his horse to a halt.

"Whoa," the old man said, patting his horse. "Well, well. I reckon I knew you was trouble, Marzele." He spat after saying the name, as if it disgusted him. "You really are one of them Solendaron freaks, ain't ya? Should have known."

"I was once," Marzele said, though it came out as more of a growl. He slowed his approach and stopped thirty feet from the man. "I can no longer call myself a true follower, however. Not after what I've done."

"Yessir, smells like you've gone and burned the town down." Franklin reached for a rusted sword at his side and unsheathed it. "Maybe we done your kind wrong in the past. Maybe I done your mama wrong. I could have been your pappy, I think, if it really is you. You do got her eyes. She was a whore, though. Your daddy was a married man and a foreigner, and she laid with him anyway. Broke our betrothal and all."

The old man kicked his horse into a trot and closed in on Marzele, sword at the ready. Marzele realized then that he was unarmed save for his own rage. Again he screamed, sounding entirely inhuman, animalistic.

The horse reared up in response. Franklin tumbled off and hit the ground hard, missing his own blade by mere inches. To Marzele's surprise, he rose to his feet and collected the sword. He took one step toward Marzele, who flinched and threw his arms up in a defensive position rather than rushing the man.

*Coward*, Marzele thought. *All I've ever been is a coward.*

Marzele took a deep breath, ready for his miserable life to

be ended there at the edge of the desert by his would-be step-
father, when the cries of a dozen coyotes rang out from just
beyond the brush. Franklin barely had time to lower his sword
and look around before the pack rushed at him, some
snarling, others licking their chops.

Franklin screamed, but his throat was torn out within
seconds. Marzele stood and watched. The animals paid him
no mind as they devoured their bloody breakfast in front of
him. When they'd eaten all they could, the coyotes licked the
blood from their paws and ran back toward the brush. One
stopped just at the edge and turned back to look at Marzele.
He locked eyes with the creature for a moment before it
resumed its course.

"Marzele?"

He took a deep breath before turning toward the hill.
Horace looked like a hill himself as he crested the low peak.

"What is it?" Marzele managed to say. To his surprise, his
voice was back to its usual smoothness.

"It is time."

"We're leaving?" Marzele asked.

Horace let out a booming peal of laughter. "No, old friend.
This is where we make our stand."

"What more can be done here? We have already
murdered dozens in the name of the Shadow. What revenge
is left? What other act of depravity can we possibly
commit?"

"We came here to make an example of this town, but it is
too far from society for people to realize what we've done.
The reason we left Pector behind in Hezron City was so he
could alert the Royal Mystic Committee of our actions once
he received our carrier pigeon."

"The Committee? But why?"

"Infamy, my dear boy. The word will get out not just to

King Davin but to all the people of Aepistelle who wish to see the faiths return to these deprived lands."

"And what if they send an army? There are only five of us here."

"That's entirely the point." Horace held up a cupped palm, which glowed as bright as the early morning sun. "It is beyond time you fully embraced the Shadow. Your powers are still within you; you need only conjure them. The Shadow consumes us, fills us, waits for us to reciprocate. We've been patient with you all this time, but now you must step up."

Marzele felt a rumble beneath his feet. He looked around, confused, and then he heard it.

A train approached.

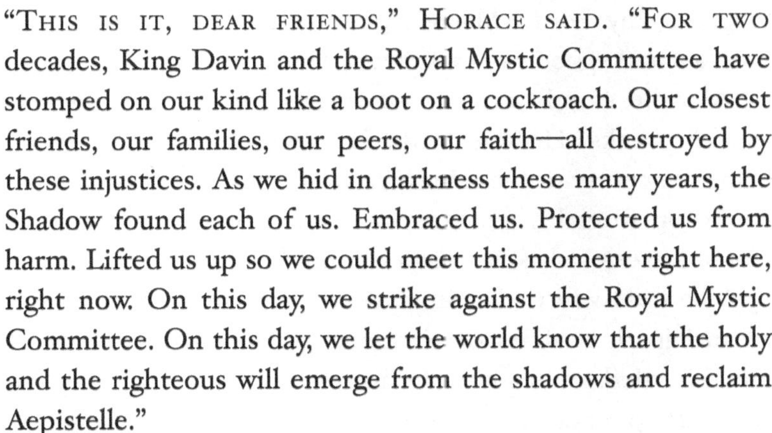

"THIS IS IT, DEAR FRIENDS," HORACE SAID. "FOR TWO decades, King Davin and the Royal Mystic Committee have stomped on our kind like a boot on a cockroach. Our closest friends, our families, our peers, our faith—all destroyed by these injustices. As we hid in darkness these many years, the Shadow found each of us. Embraced us. Protected us from harm. Lifted us up so we could meet this moment right here, right now. On this day, we strike against the Royal Mystic Committee. On this day, we let the world know that the holy and the righteous will emerge from the shadows and reclaim Aepistelle."

Allicent, Malia, and Mick roared at the sorry little pep talk. Marzele looked on in disbelief.

He knew better.

This would be the day that they died.

And yet a slight feeling of doubt crept over him. In spite of the wretched things he and his companions had done, he'd achieved one thing: he'd gotten revenge on one of his mother's killers. One week ago, he hadn't even known what his mother had looked or sounded like, who she was, where she came from. He'd been given all of that along with the chance to avenge her.

Solendaron *had* provided after all, hadn't He?

Or had it been the Shadow?

Marzele pushed his confusion aside as smoke rose on the horizon from the train's engine. He bowed his head and prayed, not knowing exactly which deity—or which side of his deity, if the Shadow truly was of Solendaron—he was addressing.

In that odd tongue, he offered praise and gratitude for the knowledge and dreams he'd been given, for the fact that Franklin's life had been taken in his presence. He prayed for strength and protection during what was to come.

"Return to my hands the powers I was blessed with so long ago, my Lord," Marzele prayed, "and may these hands once again do good works in Your holy name."

Marzele stood tall. He felt wholly himself for the first time in weeks. He was ready. He walked toward the train along the center of the railroad tracks, ignoring the sounds of confusion from his peers as they stood on the platform of Hammertree's sad excuse for a station.

The train whistled as it came into view. Even as it slowed in anticipation of its destination, thousands of pounds of metal hurtled toward him. In his frail state—all one hundred and thirty pounds of former priest—Marzele walked toward it as if he were a god.

He could now smell the black smoke rising from the engine's smokestacks. He saw the engineer's head emerge from a side window. The whistle blew frantically.

Marzele knelt in the middle of the track. He put one hand

on each rail. The vibrations from the impending train were fierce, but his grip was strong. He bowed his head and spoke another prayer. Despite not knowing exactly who he was praying to, he spoke with full confidence and faith.

Heat shot down his arms. It felt as if flames filled each of his fingers. He opened one eye to take in the glow coming from his hands. He opened the other eye, continuing his prayer as he watched the rails. The dark metal was heating before his eyes. It was now a fiery orange and red. Steam rose off of it. The bright colors shot toward the approaching train as both rails melted away.

The train screeched loudly. From his position in front of the engine, Marzele watched the train buckle. It wobbled as if it were nearly weightless, not a massive hunk of metal. He saw why—the heat had transferred from the rails to the train's wheels. A set of axles flew off one side of the engine. The entire bogie collapsed under the front of the car, melting like a candle. That corner of the train nosedived.

The screech of metal on metal was now deafening. Gravel shot out from under the flailing train. Another wheel became disfigured from the heat, melted off its axle, and flew up into the air. It launched toward Marzele and landed just three feet to his right, but he did not flinch. It bounced and rolled toward the station behind him.

The engine car rolled and slid on its side, still moving forward from momentum and the force of the cars behind it. The hopper car was next, piled high with coal, and it too lost its wheels and derailed. Behind that, a passenger car's windows revealed the shocked faces of the soldiers within. Marzele watched as they were tossed to and fro as that car too derailed and was crushed by yet another passenger car behind it.

The enormous pile of steel and bodies rushed toward Marzele.

Five hundred feet away. Rocks and debris flew at him, yet he did not budge.

Three hundred feet. The ground quaked like nothing he'd ever felt, and yet his balance remained steady.

One hundred feet. His peers hollered from behind him in shock and fear and wonder.

Fifty feet. Marzele lifted his glowing hands and held them out in front of him.

Five feet. Marzele took a deep breath.

The bulk of the train hammered into him, and yet he stayed put exactly where he was. Anything that came in contact with Marzele melted in an instant. The wreckage consumed him, passed around him, forming a tunnel. The pile of debris, the train cars, even the occupants had been split by the power of Marzele's hands. The entire mass was now behind him. He let out his breath and looked himself over.

He was unfazed. Unharmed.

The Lord had protected him.

Silence washed over Marzele for a full minute. Then he turned and took in the scene. The entirety of the mangled train had come to a halt just inches from the platform where Horace, Mick, Malia, and Allicent stood in shock.

A door opened upward from one of the overturned passenger cars. A soldier clambered out, crawled to the edge, and fell over the side. Glass shards crunched under the hands and knees of others who crawled out the broken windows. Marzele and his companions watched as the stunned soldiers gathered in a group. Marzele counted twenty-four bruised and bloodied men. The newcomers took in their surroundings, spotted Marzele and the others, and pulled out their swords. One of them took command.

"Men, attack these monsters!" the soldier yelled.

Those who had swords unsheathed them. Others found debris to use as makeshift weapons. Six men approached Marzele while the others climbed through the wreckage toward Horace and the rest.

Marzele unleashed a bellow of laughter, shocking not only himself but those who approached him. They stopped for a moment and looked at each other before resuming their charge.

At the approach of his would-be killers, a memory came to Marzele, as is said to happen often in the final moments of one's life. He remembered his connection with the pigeons. It had started in his youth, when he'd snuck away from the priestesses and climbed the steep spiral staircase up to the bell tower of the Solendaron temple in Hezron City. He'd spent all evening among the pigeons, looking out over the city from that great height, dreaming of having the freedom to explore the world, wishing he could just fly away like those birds. In his early teens, the priestess Petricia had caught him up there, and rather than scolding him, she'd taught him the Solendaron prayers to enhance connection with the pigeons and even commune with them. It had taken another two years of practice, but he'd eventually become one with the creatures, even feeling sometimes as if he was meant to *be* a pigeon but had mistakenly been given a lowly human's body instead.

And now, as the soldiers approached him, Marzele called out the prayers he'd learned all those years ago. He hadn't seen any pigeons in the desert around Hammertree, but there were other birds.

The great mass of black-and-brown feathers and red-dotted foreheads and sharp beaks flew over the smoking horizon from Hammertree and shadowed the sky.

The soldiers stopped and looked up. The vultures swooped down on them and pecked out their eyes in seconds.

Marzele couldn't see the carnage through the bulk of the vultures, but the cries of pain told him all he needed to know. He uttered another prayer, and the creatures flew off as quickly as they'd arrived.

Once the birds cleared out, Marzele approached a trembling man on the ground. He knelt down and turned the man onto his back, only to find that the man was not shaking in fear or crying but laughing hysterically.

"What do you have to be happy about?" Marzele asked him.

The soldier spat out a mouthful of blood as he tried to control his laughter. "You may have won the battle, but this war is far from over. You freaks don't know what's in store for you, do you?"

Marzele furrowed his brow. "What do you mean?"

"King Davin is preparing a new army."

"And who would fight for him and support his unjust inquisition against people of faith? Who in Aepistelle would want to join his tired mission to stamp us out?"

"An army of freaks just like you. People with powers. He's been collecting them for years. Experimenting on them. Gaining control over them in his prisons. He's moved them all into one camp now. He's readying them."

Marzele thought back to Terminus Rock, how all the cells had been empty as if the place had been vacated just days before his arrival. Denny's parents had been among the former prisoners, and there'd been something about that place that had tempered his and Denny's control of their unique powers. Those prisoners must be among the ones the soldier was referring to.

"Who is he expecting to use this army against?" Marzele asked.

"Anyone who stands against him. Even before you creeps attacked his castle, he knew it was only a matter of time before people started to resist his rule. The former kings of the other lands in Aepistelle have all been ready to try to reclaim their independence for some time now. Nobody would be stupid enough to stand against an army like this, though."

Marzele reached down and grabbed the soldier by his collar. He yanked the younger man up and thrust him into a chunk of mangled steel. The soldier grunted in pain, but his mocking laughter quickly resumed.

"And where are they now?" asked Marzele. "Where is this army being trained?"

The laughter continued. Marzele slapped the soldier across the face—once, twice—but it was no use.

"South," another soldier said in a strained voice, so low and scratchy that Marzele wasn't sure he'd actually heard it. He turned to find a man whose legs had been crushed under a section of one of the cars. Marzele let go of the soldier he'd been talking to and crouched next to the crushed man.

"What did you say?"

"Sss...south," the man muttered. "Xaeltúve. Middle of a forest. Secret camp..."

The soldier trailed off as his last breath escaped. Marzele ran his fingers over the man's face, closing his eyes, and patted his cheek.

"Thank you," Marzele whispered. "May you find peace in the realms beyond."

Marzele stepped around the debris and the dying soldiers. He made his way back through the smoking remnants of the town toward the barn that held their horses. His companions struggled to keep up.

"What do you think you're doing?" Mick asked as Marzele hopped onto his steed.

Marzele clicked his tongue, and the horse stepped through the open barn doors.

"Riding south." Marzele looked at the others with authority. He saw a proud smile on Horace's face. "This isn't over yet. Things are about to get much harder for us if we do not act. Davin is building an army of the gifted."

"And you want to recruit them?" Malia asked.

"On the contrary. They'll only be used against us. We must wipe them out before they can do more damage to what remains of our kind."

Marzele sped off. There were plenty of miles ahead for his companions to catch up. As he left the smoldering town and the wreckage of the train behind him, Marzele heard the pack coyotes howl one final time. He looked up to see the vultures circling overhead. He thought again of the pigeons and the tower he'd spent so much time in as a child.

For the first time, he felt truly free.

# Chapter Thirty-Four
## KING DAVIN

"Fine citizens of this most powerful and prosperous kingdom, I am most grateful for your presence today. The support of every man, woman, and child is what makes Aepistelle a truly special place. It shows the world that our leadership is acting in the interest of the people in all we do, attempting to maintain security and safety."

King Davin paused and allowed that to sink in. Even though he knew a large percentage of the crowd had been forced to be there, ushered in by his army from the streets of Capital City, he still reveled in the presence of an audience.

"As some of you may have heard rumblings about—though I know not one of you here today is among them—there are despicable lowlife rebels acting throughout the lands that make up this fine country. Some are challenging our control of the newspapers and our attempts to ensure that only honest and true news makes it out to you. These terrible people are operating their own pirate newspapers, printing every fiction they can think of and passing them off as truth.

"Their goal is to undermine my rule and cast doubt on the legitimacy of my cabinet secretaries and the efficacy of our infallible policies. As you all know, Aepistelle is safer now than it has ever been. We've removed people with unchecked powers from the streets. We've clamped down on dissenters, such as the Solendaron priests who attempted to destroy the castle and every hardworking man and woman in it. Their attempt to take my life and that of your fair queen Elise was cut short thanks to my fine intelligence service.

"Even now as we gather here, our security forces are engaging in operations throughout the kingdom to curtail planned acts of terrorism against our fine nation."

Davin turned to his left, where a door of the castle opened. Ten men and women were led out onto the dais and guided toward seats on Davin's right.

"That brings me to the purpose of gathering today. It seems that many of these rebel groups have received funding, shelter, and protection from the most unexpected of places. It hurts my heart even to say it, just as I know it will hurt yours to hear it. There are five pairs of guests joining us right now—the first- and second-born children of the regional governors from Centeron, Esteron, Costono, Southplains, and the Southern Reaches. Only the family of Assistant Governor Santis, my appointed watcher here in West Aepistelle, has been spared this exercise. These other families, however, are outside my regular purview, and it seems they have taken full advantage of the distance between Capital City and their own regional capitals.

"Despite their pledges of loyalty when they surrendered independence more than two decades ago, these regional leaders and their households are now actively undermining our longstanding agreements, undermining my sovereignty.

"I have let this go on long enough. You are all here to

serve an important role in this historic moment. Before your eyes, I, your fair king, will administer punishment within the confines of our system of justice. It pains me, but it is my duty.

"For the crimes of treason committed by their fathers, by them, and by their households, I hereby sentence to death the first-born children of Governor Stanton of Esteron, Governor Pyke of Centeron, Governor Lam of Southplains, Governor Lockland of Costono, and Governor Herron of the Southern Reaches."

The crowd gasped, but it was the commotion to his right that drew Davin's attention. The governors' children jumped out of their seats in shock. Kelvin Lockland of Costono darted toward the front of the dais and jumped off into the crowd, but four burly and brave citizens tackled him and dragged him back. Davin's guards took control of the others.

A large curtain was removed from behind Davin, revealing a long wooden gallows. The four men and one woman were led into place, and their siblings and the citizens of Capital City witnessed their final pained breaths at the ends of the ropes.

The crowd cheered as King Davin waved and walked back into the safety of his castle.

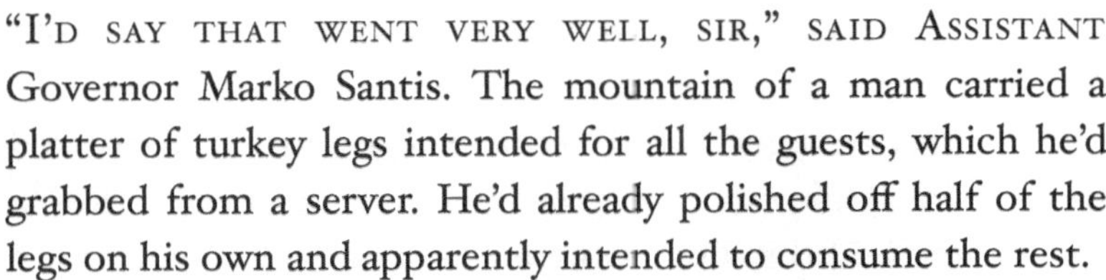

"I'D SAY THAT WENT VERY WELL, SIR," SAID ASSISTANT Governor Marko Santis. The mountain of a man carried a platter of turkey legs intended for all the guests, which he'd grabbed from a server. He'd already polished off half of the legs on his own and apparently intended to consume the rest.

"Don't think you're completely in the clear, Marko," Davin said.

The man's jowls shook as he nodded frantically. "Of course not, Your Majesty. I would never presume."

"As you should not. I'm watching every move your family makes. Your daughter Krysta has been quite friendly with a young man named Morris Malen, from what I hear. His grandfather was one of the priests of Solendaron who attacked this very castle earlier this year. It would be wise to see that relationship terminated."

Santis choked on his food. The platter tipped, and one of the last remaining turkey legs rolled off and down his paunch before splatting to the floor. It left a trail of sauce on the belly of his white shirt. Davin turned and strolled away as he heard the man cursing himself and his daughter.

"Excuse me, Your Majesty," Davin's assistant, Nadia, said. "Your requested guest is waiting in your study now."

A smile formed on Davin's face. "Thank you, Nadia."

"Clear the way," Nadia called out to the guests, and the guards stepped in to create a path to the door for their king.

Davin strutted down the hall to his study. It was a two-level library filled with centuries of texts documenting the dynasties that had ruled the lands of Aepistelle. Upstairs, he had holy books from many of the religions of the land. These same books were outlawed elsewhere in the kingdom, but Davin didn't care. What was the point of power if he couldn't abuse it for his own gain?

The young man at the desk in the center of the room stood at his arrival and bowed his head. "Good evening, Your Majesty."

"At ease, young Kosar. I see your eyes are clear, not red from crying. Did you not care for your own brother, Ysidro?"

He watched the discomfort on Kosar's face as he tried to come up with a proper response. "Ysidro was a good man, but he was lazy and a drunkard. He didn't take his responsibilities seriously and was no help to my father in overseeing the Southern Reaches. He did not appreciate his station or your graciousness in allowing our father to continue to serve as governor."

"*Our* father, you say?" Davin asked. "Tell me, has Governor Herron treated you as a true second-born heir throughout your life? Do you feel at home with him there?"

Embarrassment made the young man's face flush. "Ah, I see you know about my questionable heritage. I am sorry if my presence here as a bastard brings shame to you, Your Majesty."

"I'm not looking for an apology, young Kosar. Please answer my question."

"My father—Governor Herron, I mean—has always treated me as fairly as he did his own flesh and blood. It was Ysidro who cast me as an outsider and never let me feel like a real part of the family, if I'm honest."

"I hope you will be honest with me always. Now that your station has risen, bastard or not, there is a lot I will ask of you. Well, for however long I have left, anyway. I am quite an old man."

"May you live and rule forever, Your Majesty," Kosar said.

Davin laughed at this. "If only that were possible. But even with the best care, access to foreign remedies, enchantments from some of the practitioners at my disposal"—Kosar started at this revelation—"my eighty-five years have led me close to the my end."

"Eighty-five years, sir? But that isn't possible. You don't look older than sixty, maybe sixty-five."

Davin slapped Kosar's shoulder as he roared at the comment. "My good man, thank you for saying that, though perhaps I should be insulted. Most sixty-five-year-olds are hunched and missing half their teeth and smell like death."

"Oh, Your Majesty, please, I didn't mean that in a bad way."

"I'm teasing you, son. I—"

He had said it. *Son.* He hadn't meant it that way, and yet...

"Kosar, what has Governor Herron told you about your parentage?"

Kosar shifted uncomfortably. "Only that my mother spent a lot of time here with Queen Elise. Once she was here for several months without my father or brother. She hadn't been getting along with the governor for a while, and they needed the time apart. When she finally came home, she was pregnant. That's all I know."

"Well, you should also know that Queen Elise and I tried to have children for many years. I have no heir to show for it —no legitimate son or daughter, anyway. These days, all my cabinet members and advisors talk about is who I will choose to rule Aepistelle when I'm gone. The time is approaching for me to announce to the world who will succeed me. While I have no children with the queen, she was not my only love."

"What are you saying?" Kosar asked.

"You masterminded this entire event during your last visit to Capital City. It was your idea to make a show of power over the regional governors by executing their first-born children. Your scheming, your intelligence, and your natural aptitude for ruling and demanding respect—those all come from your true father."

"You? It's you?" Tears formed in the corners of the young man's eyes, but in his shock, he didn't move to wipe them away.

"I loved your mother, and she loved me. Queen Elise approved of the relationship. The reason your mother didn't get along with Joseph Herron was that her heart had always been mine. He knew it too. He knows that I am your true father, but he's kept it from you for your entire life. I wanted to tell you sooner, but out of respect for him, I've held off, though it was against my better judgment."

"Why tell me now?" Kosar asked.

Davin stood, walked around his desk, and pulled Kosar to his feet. He wrapped his arms around his son in an awkward embrace the young man did not return.

"Because I am so proud of you. You've ensured that our rule over all of Aepistelle will continue. I couldn't let this event end without telling you that." Davin stepped back and leaned against his desk while Kosar dropped back into his chair and buried his face into his hands. "I will not publicly declare you my heir at this time. I need today's events to strike fear into the hearts of each of the governors and the rebels they allow to prosper in their lands. In the days to come, we will target the rats that undermine my rule."

Kosar stood and faced his true father. "And what can I do to help?"

"You can keep your distance from your little barn."

Kosar took a step back and nearly tripped on the chair behind him. "You know about that?"

"I know everything, my son. Word of your involvement will not leave this room, but unfortunately, your friends and cousin will not be so fortunate."

# Chapter Thirty-Five
## DENNY | ARNEM

The nights came and went, but dreams continued to elude Denny. It was cruelty, plain and simple. Denny didn't know if he believed in any of the gods of Aepistelle, even having seen what Marzele could do, but they did exist, Denny felt that they had played a devastating trick on him. His mother was there, visible to him for the first time in years, and then she was gone. Even the unwanted visions that had plagued him his entire life had suddenly disappeared just when they would've been more useful than ever. He needed a sign that he was headed in the right direction. He needed a dream to tell him what dangers awaited him and Arnem.

On the bed across the room, Arnem snored. *Dreaming of his healthy wife and children, not a care in the world,* he thought, then scolded himself. *No. He's not carefree. Their safety became just as imperiled as my own when Arnem took me in from the streets of Esteron.*

Denny knew that Selah and the girls had come to accept him as family. They'd fled their own home only days ago, losing everything they owned to the Royal Mystic Committee. It was Denny the agents of the Committee had been after. Denny was the reason Arnem had journeyed north through the Forest of Despair and fought against the corrupt Aepistelle army and against King Davin himself. Perhaps now was the time to slip out while Arnem slumbered. He could leave a note apologizing for everything, promising to make it right. Family was everything, and yet Arnem had potentially sacrificed his own family for Denny's sake. It was too much to bear.

Denny rose to his feet and stood over Arnem. By the light of the last dying embers in the fireplace, he took in the man's peaceful, loving face. In a more just world, perhaps Denny would have been born into this man's family. Where were the gods who could make such things happen? A snap of their fingers could change the course of Denny's life. And yet here they were. The damage was done. Denny could leave Arnem under the cover of the night, but it would change nothing. Selah and the girls would still be in hiding. The Wynstone farm and their business would still be seized. Arnem's status as a hero and a legend would still be as tarnished as it was now. And so Denny decided he would stay with the man who was more of a father to him than his own father had ever been, as far as he could remember.

Sleep would not come for Denny that night, so he slipped on his coat and boots. He grabbed his small sword but then thought better of it and returned it to its place before he quietly slipped out the door and down to the bustling dining hall.

Despite the late hour, the Flaming Horse Inn was busier than it had been when Denny and Arnem had checked in that afternoon. The town of Canton didn't have much else going for it—they'd walked around, hoping to find food other than the goat stew the inn served, though they'd failed to find any cuisine worth risking their stomachs for—so perhaps that was why the inn was so full of locals and travelers alike. Denny managed to find a sticky table when the barkeep kicked out its previous occupants, who'd started fighting just as Denny had descended the stairs.

The barkeep turned toward Denny and scowled. A minute later, the old grouch slammed a mug of cloudy water in front of him.

"That's all I've got for you. We ain't in the business of watching out for children. Do I look like a governess to you?" He turned back toward the counter without waiting for Denny to utter a word of gratitude.

Denny reluctantly sipped at the water, which tasted more like the ale that had clearly graced the mug earlier that evening. Perhaps a rinse was too much to ask for. He looked around the room, but nobody seemed to be paying him any mind. His gaze stopped on a woman in the far right corner. He looked away, then back at her. She was beautiful. She appeared to be around Gemma's age and height, perhaps a bit more muscular, and she had a fairer complexion and light brown hair tied securely behind her head. She wore a wool poncho, which was the garment of choice for many of the riders Denny and Arnem had passed on their way through the Southern Reaches. Most noticeable of all was that she returned his stare. A smile broke out on her face, causing Denny to drop his head and gaze into his cup.

Only five seconds passed before a shadow fell over Denny.

The woman scooted into his booth, stopping mere inches from him.

"Aren't you a little young to be in a place like this so late?" she asked.

Denny noticed that her scent wasn't as appealing as her looks. She'd clearly ridden a long way on her horse, perhaps for several days. Denny thought she probably smelled just like he did—he'd merely become accustomed to his own stench during his trek.

"I'm not alone," Denny said. "My, um, father is upstairs. He should be down any minute."

"Is that so?" The woman glanced toward the stairs. "Well, looks like I only have you for a short time, then." She dropped a hand onto Denny's, pinning it to the table, and gave it a squeeze. "My name is Alice."

Denny felt his hand shake in her grasp. He didn't meet her eyes, so she brought her other hand to his chin and turned his face in her direction.

"This is when you tell me your name, silly." Her smile seemed warm enough. Denny relaxed a bit.

"I'm De—Daniel," he said. "My father and I are just passing through on our way south. Selling farm supplies."

"Sounds like a lucrative enterprise," she returned, forcing herself to sound so interested that it came off as completely disingenuous. She let go of his face and gestured to his mug. "How about I order you a real drink?"

Denny swallowed hard and looked at the barkeep across the room. "Um, I don't think it's allowed here."

"Oh, don't worry about old Marlin over there. His bark is worse than his bite. You're in the Southern Reaches now. They don't care how old you are. I'm sure Marlin just isn't convinced you can handle your drink yet, but he won't give me any trouble."

Without waiting for an answer, Alice got to her feet and walked to the bar. While most of the other patrons ignored the situation, Denny briefly met the stare of a man sitting in the corner Alice had come from. The man turned away quickly, but a chill tingled down Denny's spine. He wore a poncho similar to Alice's. He had a mug in front of him, though the liquid in it seemed to be as clear as Denny's. Next to the man's mug was a small wooden chest just larger than a loaf of bread. It appeared to be clasped shut.

Alice's body blocked Denny's view as she set two mugs on the table. "I told you it would not be an issue." She slid one across to him, causing some of the froth to spill over and contribute to the table's stickiness. Alice settled back into the booth next to Denny, then held up her mug and nodded for him to do the same. Denny lifted his, and she clanked the two together. "To new friendships," she said before chugging half her mug's contents.

Denny took a sip and gagged, but he didn't want to embarrass himself further. He forced himself to take a mouthful of the stuff and swallow, then turned to Alice with a strained smile. "Thank you," he said as his stomach lurched.

Alice broke into laughter. She reached over and used her sleeve to wipe a layer of foam from Denny's upper lip. "And here I didn't think you were old enough for a mustache," she teased. "Is this your first ale, then?"

"I suppose there's no use trying to hide it," Denny managed. He took another sip, this time enjoying the warmth as it traveled down into his belly. "Better than I expected." He began gulping it down before his companion reached over and eased it away from his lips.

"Easy, now. If there's one way to make old Marlin livid, it's to throw up all over his tavern."

Denny recalled something just as his head began to spin.

"When we checked in this afternoon, he introduced himself as Gus."

Alice laughed. "Gus, Marlin, what's the difference? I'm not actually from here either, just wanted to appear confident. Never know what kind of people you'll meet when you're away from home—even a young man like you."

Denny understood that. He had spent half of his short life on the street and had misplaced his trust more times than he could count. He nodded and then finished his drink. The room spun around him. He hoped Alice wouldn't notice his current state, but her laughter said otherwise.

"I'd offer another round, but I think that was enough for you," Alice said.

Denny didn't know what to say next. If he asked her where she'd come from or where she was traveling to, he'd have to divulge the same information about himself. He could have lied about it under normal circumstances, but the buzz he felt was strong, and even though this was his first time in such a state, he knew his mind wasn't sharp enough to come up with a cohesive story. They sat in awkward silence for a few moments.

And then a shadow fell over him again. Denny turned to find the man from the other end of the room now standing behind his booth. The man opened the chest, and a high-pitched squeal erupted from it.

"Ah!" Denny cried out as he covered his ears. The pain was excruciating; he hadn't felt this way since the island. He clapped his hands over his ears, but Alice pulled them away. The man reached into the open chest and took out what appeared to be a hood encrusted with gemstones that glinted in the lantern light. He brought it toward Denny, and the sound intensified, though no one else in the tavern seemed to be reacting. It was as if Denny was the only one who could hear the sound. Denny tried to lift his hands and swat the hood away, but Alice's grip tightened. The man slipped the hood over Denny's head, and all went dark.

Arnem was awakened by the creaking of the floorboards. The last embers of the fire had burned out, and only the dimmest moonlight made it beyond the room's curtains. It was just enough for him to make out a shadow across the room, one with too much bulk to be Denny.

Without giving away that he was awake, Arnem slowly slipped a hand down the side of his bed, but he felt nothing.

"You won't find your sword there, old man." The shadowy figure lifted the weapon. "Had to protect myself, you see. Can't go dying when I have a kid at home waiting for my return."

"As do I," Arnem said as he sat up in bed. "Two of them." He thought of Denny. "No, three, actually."

"How cute," the man said. "You're counting the boy. Unfortunately, he's not going back home. Nor are you, though I suppose one of Aepistelle's illustrious penitentiaries will be your home once a judge decides exactly where to send you. That is, if execution isn't in the cards."

"And what of the boy?" Arnem asked.

"He's going to a different destination. In fact, you did half the work for me, bringing him this far. We'll take him the rest of the way, though."

Arnem got to his feet, not caring that he wore nothing but his underpants. "Do you intend to take him to where his parents are being held?"

"Indeed, Mr. Wynstone."

"You can't do that. Something will happen there. Denny's

mother sent a message to him. She foresaw her own end. Please, Mr.—"

"Palignon. Lieutenant Palignon of the Royal Mystic Committee."

"Please, Lieutenant Palignon, don't send him there. Don't do this." Arnem walked slowly across the room toward the intruder, holding up his hands to show he was not a threat. "You're a father—you said so yourself. Imagine if your own child had been born with an affliction beyond his control. This kingdom has done nothing but vilify Denny his entire life. Took his parents away. Left him alone in the streets to fend for himself, no one to watch his back. Imagine if that was your child—alone, scared, hated for something they never chose."

"I..." Palignon began.

*Could it be? Did I strike a nerve in him?* Arnem wondered.

"You do know what it's like, don't you?" Arnem asked.

Palignon unsheathed Arnem's sword and threw aside the scabbard. He aimed the weapon at Arnem to stop his approach, held it inches from Arnem's bare belly. "Take another step and I'll gut you, and I'll be sure to let the boy see your corpse before we take him south to Xaeltúve."

"You won't, though," Arnem said, understanding all he was risking. "You see yourself in this situation, don't you? Father to father, Mr. Palignon, you understand exactly how this must feel. Your child has abilities as well?"

The point of the sword dropped to the ground as emotion seemed to wash over Palignon. Arnem reached his right hand out and placed it on the man's shoulder.

With his left hand, Palignon reached for Arnem's wrist and snapped it. The bones broke, and Arnem screamed.

"Do not presume to know my situation. That boy is not

your son, and my daughter does not have abilities. She..." Palignon's voice faltered, and he began to weep.

Arnem stumbled back and sat on the foot of the bed, cradling his broken wrist. It was a sorry sight, had anyone been there to see it: two grown men in a dark room, one nearly naked, both weeping over children not yet lost to them.

"We can change things," Arnem managed between sobs. "We can make a better world for them. You do not have to follow your orders any longer. Join my friends and me. Please, for the sake of your child and mine."

"It's too late," Palignon said. "Your Denny is in the hands of my agents. There is no escape now." He wiped away his tears and stood up straight. His soft voice mutated into a growl as he kicked a pile of clothes toward Arnem. "Get dressed immediately, and let us leave here without further quarrel. The boy is valuable to the Committee, but you are disposable. Do not make me show you how unimportant you are."

With that, Arnem put on his clothes that reeked of horses and sweat while Palignon gathered up the belongings scattered around the room. Once Arnem's arms were bound, Palignon led him out of the room. In the light of the lanterns in the inn's hallway, Arnem could see no sign of the grieving father from minutes ago. Palignon was nothing but a hardened commanding officer of the Royal Mystic Committee, one who would gladly tear families apart, execute religious men and women in the streets, and imprison harmless children. Yet Arnem knew that deep under the surface was a man who could be reached. A man who could be turned. An ally to be made.

# Chapter Thirty-Six
## PALIGNON | ARNEM

"Everything okay, Lieutenant?" Taron asked. "We nabbed our targets, even if it took a few extra days and a few hundred additional miles. Thought you'd be happier."

"Been pouting ever since we stopped at home," Lang added from his horse a few feet ahead of Palignon. He held one end of the rope that was tied around both Arnem and Denny, who shared a horse the crew had obtained from the stable outside the inn.

"Trouble with the missus, boss?" Taron asked. "You might find this hard to believe, but as a woman myself, I could help you out with any problems you may be having in that department."

Lang laughed at this until Palignon turned his glare on the man.

"It's none of your damn business," Palignon said at last.

It had been a full day since they'd crossed the border from the Southern Reaches into Xaeltúve, following the track that the Royal Mystic Committee had laid in secret over the last two years. He knew they were approaching their destination, as he could see the track disappearing into the forest on the horizon, but it couldn't come fast enough.

"Ask him about his child," said Arnem.

"You speak when we tell you to," Lang growled. He yanked the rope. Arnem and Denny lost their collective balance and toppled off the horse.

"Lang, what the hell are you doing?" Palignon yelled as he halted his own horse and dismounted.

"The hood!" Taron shouted. She jumped from her horse and beat Palignon to the boy.

Before she could reposition the gem-crusted fabric over his head, Denny looked around at his captors. Palignon met his eyes, and his heart leapt. Denny was young, innocent, much like his own daughter back home in Capital City. His look was one of desperation. Denny's eyes widened as if he were pleading with Palignon to help him.

It was more than that, though. The boy could clearly see through Palignon's mission-focused exterior. He could read Palignon's secrets.

Palignon pulled his gaze away. "Damn it all, Lang. Get them back on their horse, and do not pull something like that again!"

"Sorry, sir," Lang said. He jumped down to assist Taron. "It's just that I—"

Lang was cut off by a rumble in the ground. They all felt it and turned around, looking back at the rail in the direction they'd come from. Black smoke rose on the horizon.

"Maybe they'll give us a ride the rest of the way," Taron said.

Palignon felt deep in his gut that this wouldn't happen. He didn't know the Committee's schedule for transferring prisoners or replacing guards, but somehow he knew that something was wrong.

"Let's move away from the tracks," he called. He helped Arnem and Denny back onto their mount, as awkward as it was with them tied together. Arnem cried out as he was lobbed up unceremoniously. The man didn't deserve the broken wrist, and Palignon felt bad about having caused it, but he wasn't about to show the prisoner mercy. "Keep quiet or I'll break the other one too," he said instead.

Once the prisoners were secured, they all rode into a cluster of shrubs just before the train came into view.

THEIR CAPTORS HAD WRAPPED ARNEM'S BROKEN WRIST, BUT it didn't matter, what with the way they'd tightened the rope around him and Denny, smashing his arm against the boy to keep the two of them from escaping. The journey south from the inn had been supremely uncomfortable, not only because he was tied to Denny but also because Denny had been silent the entire time.

"Denny, we'll get out of this somehow," Arnem whispered as they hid from the approaching train.

To his surprise, the boy spoke. "They're taking us right to my parents." His voice was scratchy. For the past two days, Denny had rejected the water from the canteen their captors had offered, along with all food. Arnem knew he had gone days without proper meals back in his time on the streets of Esteron, but the boy couldn't go much longer without drinking.

"If that's the case, then you need to take care of yourself. We'll need to fight them off before we get there, or we'll be brought in as prisoners and be no better off than your mom and dad."

At last Denny nodded, resigned. Arnem requested water for him. Lang scoffed, but Palignon ordered him to comply.

As Lang lifted the hood and held the canteen to Denny's lips, the train came into view.

"That's it?" Taron asked. "Two cars?"

"Probably just the dregs from the remaining prisons," Palignon said. Arnem stared hard at the man, wondering if he was imagining his own daughter as one of those prisoners, removed from society because of the powers she'd never asked for and would never use to intentionally harm anyone in Aepistelle. Arnem wanted to speak up, to reassure Palignon that his daughter was safe at home, but he knew that wouldn't end well. It was clear to him that Palignon had not told his subordinates about his daughter's situation. Arnem could only assume that Lang and Taron would put duty above their loyalty to their commanding officer.

"Get them down," Palignon ordered.

Lang capped the canteen, then worked with Taron to guide Arnem and Denny off the horse. Four of them watched the train while Denny listened from behind his hood.

The train was fifty feet away, chugging slowly along its route. It was slow enough for Arnem to get a look at its occupants when it passed. He gasped.

Denny turned toward him. "What is it?" the boy whispered.

"I think I recognized one of the riders on that train," he answered.

"Who was it?"

"This sounds impossible, but I'm quite sure it was Marzele."

# Chapter Thirty-Seven
## DENNY | MARZELE

The ringing in his head hadn't ceased, but in some sick way, Denny had learned to lean into the pain it caused. It was like when his lips were chapped and he couldn't resist the urge to bite them, cracking them back open until they bled. Denny took in the sound the minerals in the hood made, embracing the migraine-like pain. He learned to hear beyond it, to listen to his captors mocking him, to lull himself into a light sleep to the clopping of his horse's hooves and Arnem's reassuring whispers informing him about their rapidly changing surroundings.

At night, though, he was unable to block it out and drift into a deep sleep. All he wanted was to connect with his mother again, reach his father for the first time, or catch a glimpse of what was going to happen. Yet all he could hear tonight was Arnem's snoring, Palignon's heavy breaths of slumber, and fragments of two voices whispering to each other.

"...the boss...soft on them..." This was from the man, Lang.

"I've noticed, too," Taron whispered back. "...should leave him behind...the prisoners ourselves...reward between two instead of three...bigger cut."

Denny tugged at the ropes around his wrists. The only times his captors allowed him to be separated from Arnem was when one of them needed to relieve himself and when they were sleeping. At night, he and Arnem were each tied to a tree by their wrists, though this caused Arnem to whimper in pain. By morning, Denny always lost feeling from his shoulders to his fingertips from stretching his arms above his head all night.

Tonight, however, Denny realized the ropes were looser than usual. He thought back a couple of hours to when they had made camp at the edge of the forest. Palignon had tasked Lang with building the fire and Taron with tracking down game they could cook for dinner. Palignon was much gentler with him and Arnem than Taron or Lang had been on previous nights. It was the first time on their ride south that Palignon had handled them himself; otherwise he had kept his distance whenever possible. Arnem had whispered to Denny that he thought the man would help them in the end, though Denny didn't understand why Arnem had come to that conclusion.

Denny wriggled his hands and prayed that his whispering captors weren't watching. Perhaps if they were staring into the light of the fire, their eyes wouldn't be able to make out Denny's hands slipping out of the rope should they glance back at him.

Once he was free, he flexed his fingers to regain feeling. He reached for the hood and slipped it up over his mouth, took a breath of unfiltered fresh air, and then pushed it up above his eyes. He turned toward Arnem to find the man still deep in sleep. A few feet past him was Lieutenant Palignon, also sprawled out in slumber.

Denny reached over to Arnem but stopped himself inches from the sleeping man's shoulders. He knew Arnem would make noise if Denny attempted to shake him out of sleep, and then they were sure to be caught, beaten, and tied up tighter than ever before.

Denny peered through the trees, seeing only blackness. Somewhere beyond his sight, perhaps only a mile or two away, his parents waited for him. He had to get to them tonight, with or without Arnem at his side. The man would understand.

Denny peeked over at Taron and Lang. They sat shoulder to shoulder, their backs to Denny, as they planned their mutiny and how they would collect their reward. He got to his feet, then disappeared beyond the tree line.

A few feet away, Denny found another clearing. The horses were tied to trees, and propped up alongside one of them were two travel sacks with Arnem's and Denny's belongings. Denny's curved sword, the kalis Quincy had crafted for him, protruded from one bag. He crept toward it, careful not to startle the horses, and pulled the sword out. He secured its scabbard to his belt and walked past the horses and into the cover of the trees.

Five steps in, he heard a commotion near the campfire.

"The kid's gone," Lang said.

"What do you—oh no," Taron responded. "Lieutenant, wake up! We have a problem."

Shuffling. Murmuring. Then, "Run, Denny!" This from Arnem.

Denny didn't wait. He darted through the forest, ignoring his exhaustion. In the darkness, he collided with wayward branches, tripped over roots, flailed through thick spiderwebs, but he sped on. He heard the others pursuing him. He veered to his right, where the trees had been cut back, and made his way into the rail corridor, not caring that Lang and Taron might see him more easily there. The track led to his parents, and so he followed it.

That is, until his ankle gave way and he slipped down a ravine on the other side of the track. The hill was steeper than he expected, and he found himself rolling down, unable to catch hold of any roots or stumps. His head slammed hard into a large rock and everything went dark.

Darkness.

Darkness.

And then light.

It was fire. Not the fire from that night's camp. Perhaps this one had started as a small campfire, but it had spread, finding its way to the cabins around it. Its greedy flames stretched out and licked at the walls, consumed them. People screamed. Steel clashed against steel.

A guard with the seal of Aepistelle came into view, only to be struck down by a blade. He fell back into a wall and was engulfed in flames.

Two women in tattered clothes ran past, screaming. Someone lunged at them and cut them both down in one fell swoop.

The view shifted, and Denny realized he was not in control. He was seeing this scene through someone else's eyes.

The person dove down to the ground and crawled under a cabin, past the stilts it stood on, through thick webs and sprouting weeds. Smoke filled the space, and the person coughed miserably, but they made it to the other side and back to their feet. Across the camp, they spotted a man crouched alongside a barrel, hiding from the attackers. One arm ended at the elbow, the stub wrapped in a rotting bandage. The other arm was in motion, waving over the person whose eyes Denny looked through. The man's hair was long and shaggy, barely revealing his eyes. It was light brown with patches of gray, and through it, Denny could make out the man's face.

"Dad!" he called out, or at least he thought he did.

The person through whose eyes he was watching the scene rose to their feet and took a few steps toward Denny's father, then stopped suddenly, turned around to see nobody behind them, then spun back to his father.

Denny realized who it must be.

"Mom?" he asked. The word reverberated. It hadn't been spoken at all, and yet he knew she had heard it.

"Denny!" He could tell she was speaking out loud. "Stay safe, my love. If you're able to reach me right now, it seems you're getting more powerful than I ever could have imagined."

Ahead, Denny's father waved more frantically. "Hurry!" he screamed. "It's clear!"

At the same moment, Denny and his mother both witnessed a figure coming around the cabin behind his father.

"Look out!" they yelled in unison.

Denny's father spun around. He was unarmed, but the newcomer was not. Denny's mother broke into a run, but the attacker brought down his axe before she could reach him. She turned away to spare Denny the sight, but he still heard the thunk of the axe as it sliced into his father's skull.

Tears filled his eyes—his mother's eyes—as his mother turned and ran for the gates of the prison village that had been left open by the attackers.

Their weeping merged together, and his mother whispered through her sobs, "I'm sorry, Denny. You shouldn't have had to see that. I'm sorry."

"Mom, I'm coming for you. Find a place to hide. I'll be there soon. I just need to wake up."

She made it past a guard, who was too busy tussling with one of the intruders to notice her. She darted across a small clearing toward the tracks, where she spotted the train that had passed Denny and Arnem earlier that day. She rolled under the second car and lay still below its undercarriage.

"Denny, wake yourself up from this, but do not come for me. It's too late. There's nothing here for you. King Davin's soldiers want to weaponize us, and these intruders seem to want us dead. They'll kill you, too. You must run away from here and never look back. I love you."

"No, Mom, I won't abandon you. I won't go back—"

Denny broke off as he heard footsteps approaching his mother. A hand shot out and grabbed her by the ankle. She was pulled back out into the open, where she stared up at a man with thin hair and an unkempt mustache.

Denny recognized him.

The man lifted his axe over his head, Denny's father's blood still dripping from it. His mother brought her hands up to shield her face.

"I love you, Denny. Goodbye, son," she said aloud.

The man's eyebrows furrowed.

He hesitated.

"Did you say Denny?" he asked.

"Mom, I know him. His name is Marzele. Tell him who you are and he'll—"

Out of the corner of his mother's vision, another figure emerged. Marzele turned to the newcomer. "Wait," Marzele said, but the person shook his head.

"Using the shadow of the Tíhn is much simpler than this

but not nearly as much fun," the large man said with a demented smile. "They may be able to block our powers here, but they sure can't stop me from doing this."

His sword came down, and everything went black.

IT WAS ALL WRONG. MARZELE HAD NEVER INTENDED FOR things to go this far off the rails. This was not who he was. This was not the will of Solendaron; he doubted it was even the will of the Shadow, unless the Shadow of the Tïhn had nothing to do with Solendaron after all.

No, this was pure evil. Marzele himself was pure evil.

He looked at Horace through the blood splattered on his face. The larger man looked gleeful as he hacked at the unarmed woman on the ground.

"Enough!" Marzele called.

Horace stopped. He bent down and grabbed the woman by her shirt. He hoisted her lifeless body up and thrusted her toward Marzele.

"Come on, old friend. This is exactly what we came here for. These people were being made into weapons to destroy us, to give our kind a bad name. If we hadn't—"

"We deserve a bad name after this," Marzele said, "after everything you and the Cult of Arun have done these past few weeks."

Horace dropped the corpse and stepped forward, inches from Marzele. "And you think you're not complicit in all of it? You think you're better than us? It didn't seem that way in Hammertree. You seemed full of revenge then."

"That was wrong," Marzele said. "Even after what the people in that town did all those years ago—even after what they did to my mother—it was wrong of us. That was not of Solendaron."

"I have news for you, Marzele. Solendaron is not here. Never was. A fairy tale and nothing more." Horace brought the blade up between them and licked the blood from it. "Power comes from within us, not from above. Power comes from me." Horace spat the blood at Marzele.

Marzele took a step back. He let out an anguished groan that turned into a scream as he lifted his axe. The smile grew on Horace's face as he brought his blade up much quicker than Marzele expected and struck the axe out of Marzele's grip.

A light flashed as Marzele's now-empty hands ignited. Horace's eyes went wide with shock. "How are you able to do that? We're blocked from using our abilities here. It's impossible!"

"I suffered for weeks on Terminus Rock, blocked from accessing the light of Solendaron because of the minerals they filled that place with. It seems I've overpowered them now. Perhaps Solendaron has not forsaken me after all. Perhaps it was only *I* who abandoned *Him*."

Marzele thrusted his glowing hands at Horace and melted the flesh from his old companion's face.

WHEN HIS MOTHER'S VISION WENT DARK, DENNY WOKE UP to find Lang and Taron standing over him. They were winded and furious. Taron reached for him first, and he knew it was pointless to resist. She pulled him up by his collar and punched him in the face. Denny would have slammed back to the ground, but she kept her hold on him and gave him another punch. This one knocked a tooth from his gums. He turned and spat it out, only to be greeted by Lang's boot approaching his face. It connected with his temple, sending sparks across his vision, but he remained conscious. Another blow came down on him, this one hitting his ear on the opposite side. His ears began to ring as if he still had that hood over his head.

"Hey!" He recognized Palignon's voice through the ringing. "Let go of the boy."

Taron complied, and Denny collapsed to the ground. "You know, boss," she said, "we're getting real sick of you and your commands. This far out of Aepistelle, nobody would doubt us if we said you were torn apart by a bear or attacked by some local savages."

"I'm your commanding officer," Palignon said. "How dare you speak to me that way?"

"We figured it out," Lang said. "Can't believe you told the prisoner before you told your own troops. Your daughter is a freak just like this kid, isn't she?"

Denny heard the zing of Palignon's sword being unsheathed. His vision came back to him, and he looked up to see the overconfident grins on Lang's and Taron's faces. They stepped away from Denny and began to approach Palignon. There was no way the lieutenant could take down two of his own highly trained soldiers. Palignon knew it as well as Denny did, but he stood his ground anyway. They each took another step toward him and away from Denny.

That was when the boy remembered his own weapon.

He jumped to his feet, swaying from the pain of his head wounds. He pulled out his kalis and slashed at Lang's back. The man screamed in pain and shock while Taron rushed at Palignon.

Denny used his shortness to his advantage, blocking blows from Lang and striking at the man's legs. Palignon clashed with Taron, showing off the skills he'd gained in his many years of training but rarely got to use against his enemies. As Taron swung her sword wildly at Palignon and missed, he slammed his boot into her kneecap, sending her backward into her partner. Lang was caught unawares and stumbled toward Denny, allowing the boy to stick his blade straight through the man's belly.

Taron landed on top of her dying coconspirator. She screamed in anger and jumped back to her feet before Denny and Palignon could take advantage of her position. She ran into the trees despite her injured knee. Denny realized what direction she was headed.

"Arnem!" he yelled.

Palignon understood. "I'll protect him. Go do what you came here for. Go find your parents."

Denny's face trembled as he fought back tears. He couldn't bring himself to say out loud what he knew inside: his parents were both dead.

There was no saving them.

There was only revenge.

Denny nodded, turned, and ran alongside the tracks toward the massacre at the prison village.

# Chapter Thirty-Eight

## ARNEM | DENNY

Arnem awoke to a kick in the gut. When he opened his eyes, he looked up to see a bloodied Private Alice Taron scowling down at him.

"Get. Up," Taron growled.

Arnem moved his arms, only to realize his ropes had already been cut. He wriggled his hands from what remained of them and pushed himself to his feet.

"Where is Denny?" he asked. The boy's ropes lay on the ground, but Denny was nowhere to be seen. Had they changed their minds about bringing the prisoners in alive? Was that Denny's blood on her?

"He's gone. You can't save him now."

"No!" Tears streamed down Arnem's face. "You couldn't have...you didn't..."

"What is it with your kind? You and Palignon both, giving up your lives for these little brats, trying to protect them from themselves. They're freaks of nature. Mistakes. They deserve nothing but death. They pollute this world."

"No," Arnem said. "They're better than us. They're

unique. They're gifts, maybe from some god or another, maybe from the planet itself. But they are not mistakes."

"Your sword," she said as she tossed it to him. He caught it with his good hand and held it away from him as if he was repulsed by it. "Get it out. I don't want to take you down when you're unarmed. I used to idolize you and your companions—Richard, Jestan, Maachel. Now I know you were all a bunch of traitors, but when I was a kid, you were my heroes. You've let me down, so that will make me feel better about killing you."

"No," Arnem said. "I won't fight you."

Taron flicked her wrist, sending the tip of her sword across Arnem's neck. Arnem felt blood drip down, though the cut wasn't too deep. "Fight me, coward," Taron said.

"The only coward here is you, Private Taron."

Arnem looked over her shoulder at Palignon. Taron turned to face the newcomer.

"I'll kill you first, then," she said. Taron charged at Palignon.

"Where's Denny?" Arnem called out over the clash of steel.

"Finding his parents," Palignon replied. "Go. I'll finish this."

Arnem nodded. He ran with his sword to the next clearing, untied one of the horses, mounted it, and sped off along the tracks.

DENNY'S INSTINCTS TOLD HIM TO DROP AT THE SOUND OF an approaching horse, but his adrenaline wouldn't allow it. He continued his run along the track as the rider neared.

"You're all right, Denny!" Arnem called out. "Thank the gods."

Denny came to a halt and turned to face his friend. At the sight of the older man, his tears began to flow.

"They're gone," Denny managed. "Killed by Marzele and his friends."

"I'm so sorry, Denny. If that's true, we'll save whoever is left. There are many poor souls there who need our help. And maybe—just maybe—your vision was not correct and your parents are okay."

"They're dead, Arnem. I was there in her head when it happened. But you're right—whoever else is alive there needs help. I have nothing to lose now, so I'm going to them... alone."

"I'm not leaving you again, Denny." Arnem reached for him, ready to pull Denny up onto the horse with him.

Denny took a step back. "No, Arnem. You have Selah at home. You have the girls to think about. They're your family."

"Yes, but you're my family, too. You're my son, Denny. Maybe not by blood or even by law, but according to the gods or the fates or whatever calls the real shots in this world, you are my family."

"No..." A vision flashed through Denny's mind, wide awake and conscious as he was—Arnem burning, dying. "No! Turn around, Arnem! Run before it's too late!"

Arnem dismounted his horse. "Please, son. Calm down. I'm here for you."

"You don't understand, Arnem—"

Movement behind Arnem caught his eye. Someone emerged from the trees on the other side of the train tracks. Had it been a few months earlier, the moonlight would have reflected off his bald head, but now his scalp was covered in hair.

"You!" Denny screamed.

"Listen to me, child," Marzele said as he approached Arnem and Denny. "What happened back there, it wasn't—"

"You killed them!" Denny yelled. He shook in anger. Heat rose through his body, and his vision filled with a red glow. "You murdered my parents! You killed them!"

Arnem stepped toward Denny, reaching for the boy's shoulder. "Calm down, Denny. I understand that you're upset about what happened, but for your own sake, you need to calm down."

"No," Denny said. The heat inside him was now fully ablaze. "No! Noooooooooo!!!!"

The ground shook. Flashes of light radiated from all of the trees at once. The leaves that littered the ground around them burst into flame, consuming fallen branches and twigs and weeds. The horse's hide lit up, sending the creature running off into the forest, which was now fully aflame. A different glow came from Marzele's hands, one Denny had seen before back in Emyhrsen many months ago.

"Take a deep breath," Arnem pleaded. Denny turned to him, still screaming. Smoke escaped from Arnem's cloak. "Please, Denny, calm down! You must—"

Arnem's calmness turned to a pained cry as flames lapped at his skin from inside his clothing. He stepped back and dropped to the ground.

"Denny, you must stop this!" Marzele called.

Denny wanted to stop it. He wanted to control his anger and despair. He wanted to feel like the world had not abandoned him, taken everything from him. But he couldn't.

Marzele ran toward Arnem to help him, though Arnem was now fully aflame. Denny noticed that the glow from Marzele's hands had spread to the rest of the man's body, somehow protecting him from the fire that consumed everything else around them.

And still Arnem burned. "Please, Denny," the smoldering man cried out between screams of pain. "Stop this, please." More screams as flames melted away his skin. "I love you, son."

And then silence as the fire burned away any life that remained in him.

Arnem the Loyal was no more.

Denny fell to the ground—there was no more clean air to breathe—and the world plunged into darkness.

# Chapter Thirty-Nine
## GEMMA

When Gemma's eyes opened, she didn't find Syntha aiming a sword or machete at her face in a twisted but playful way, as she had in previous days. Instead she found the young woman slouched at the foot of the bed in tears.

Gemma sat up. "What happened? Is Kosar hurt?"

"No, but he was spotted on his ship by someone on a small fishing vessel this morning."

"That's great! I need to get dressed so I can greet him when he arrives." Gemma studied her friend. "What's the problem, then?"

Instead of answering, Syntha shook her head erratically and burst into tears again. Gemma kicked off her covers and walked on her knees to the foot of the bed, where she embraced Syntha.

"It's something to do with Ysidro, isn't it?"

"Yes. I fear the worst. When the fishermen greeted Kosar and his crew across the waves and inquired about Ysidro,

Kosar told them he would not be returning to the Southern Reaches."

"What could have happened to Ysidro?"

"I fear King Davin had him executed."

"But why?"

"Word of our activities may have gotten out. Perhaps Davin received bad intelligence that pointed to Ysidro even though he had nothing to do with our little operation. There's more, though, Gemma."

"What is it?"

"Kosar's ship was flanked by two Aepistelle military vessels."

"An escort? Maybe they wanted to ensure his safety if something really did happen to Ysidro."

"Damn it, Gemma, why are you so naive?" Syntha asked, but her face conveyed panic, not hatred, so Gemma forgave the young woman for her words. "Kosar's ship no longer flies the flag of the Southern Reaches. His family's crest was nowhere to be seen. Davin's house sigil adorned his ship instead."

"And why hasn't he arrived yet?" Gemma asked as she looked out the windows that faced the harbor below.

"The ships turned into Harpoon Bay a few miles north of here. The Aepistelle naval base is there."

Gemma's heart sank. "You have me frightened now. Still, we shouldn't jump to conclusions before we know the truth. Let's be ready for Kosar's arrival and find out what happened from him. He's been gone only a few days, but I've missed him."

Syntha stepped back. Her cheeks were pink from wiping away tears. Her lips trembled as if she were afraid to speak.

"What is it?" Gemma asked. "Don't tell me there's more."

"There is something you should know about Kosar.

During our last trip to Capital City, when he met you for the first time, he had a reason to be there."

"He was writing about Davin's return," Gemma said.

"Yes, that was his cover story. But officially, he was there for a private meeting with King Davin."

"He actually met with the king? What about?"

Syntha's eyes dropped to the floor in shame. "He would not tell me. He would not allow me to attend with him as his personal guard either."

"He was hiding something from you, then."

"Kosar is my cousin, my dearest friend," Syntha said. "But that doesn't mean we always see eye to eye or that he is always honest with me. There's a side to him you haven't seen."

"Maybe I have," Gemma said. "During dinners with his family, he seemed to become a different person. I lost count of how many meals ended with someone walking out in anger, and he was the instigator every time. It confused me. He's such a different person away from his father and brother. He's inquisitive, caring, driven to bring truth to the kingdom. Yet he is petty and quick to anger with Ysidro and Joseph."

"It's always been that way," Syntha said. "I stopped dining with the family years ago because I could not stomach that side of him. Even though he is a bastard, Uncle Joseph has always treated him as a legitimate son worthy of his position in the family, but Kosar does return that love and respect. There is something dark in him, Gemma."

"I...I know." Gemma reached out to wipe away a tear that slid down Syntha's cheek. Tears of her own formed in the corners of her eyes. "I've known all along that there was something dark under the surface, but I didn't want to admit it. I didn't want to believe that I could fall for another man just like Walker. I wanted him to be someone else."

Syntha turned away from Gemma and opened the

doors to the balcony. The morning breeze carried with it the fresh scent of the ocean, reminding Gemma of her parents. Perhaps the wisest decision she'd made had been to hold off on asking them to join her in the Southern Reaches.

From the doorway to the balcony, Syntha turned back to Gemma. "Isn't that always the way of things? Evil men using their privilege and charm to get a hold on us?"

Gemma's brow furrowed. "So that's it? We've decided he is evil?"

"I think we're about to find out," Syntha said. She pointed toward road that passed along the coast and up the hill on which the palace perched. "Look."

Gemma followed her out into the cool air and peered over the railing. Kosar was speeding along on his horse, flanked by a group of soldiers. Gemma's eyes met Syntha's, and no words needed to be said. Gemma turned and ran to her dressing room. She pulled on the same pair of slacks, shirt, and cloak she'd worn the previous day. She grabbed her machete and fixed its sheathe to her belt. She caught her reflection in the mirror and realized her tussled hair would have to stay that way.

Syntha opened the door to the hallway and looked in both directions. "It's clear." She waved Gemma out.

Gemma immediately turned right toward the main stairs but stopped when Syntha grabbed her shoulder.

"Wrong way, Gemma. You must head out the back toward the stable."

"I'm not leaving you to protect the governor alone. That's what you're planning, isn't it?"

"Am I that predictable?"

"More like loyal to your family, to the uncle who gave you a great life in this palace."

Syntha nodded. "Very well. Let us ensure Uncle Joseph is safe from Kosar."

"Uncle Joseph, I fear the worst for…"

Syntha trailed off as she stepped through the doorway of the dining hall. Gemma followed and saw Governor Herron picking at the contents of his breakfast plate, a green grape speared on his fork. A stern-faced man sat in the seat normally occupied by Ysidro. His uniform was adorned with Aepistelle military regalia.

"What is this, my dear uncle?" Syntha asked.

Joseph looked up, a sudden warmth returning to his eyes. He let his fork clatter down onto the plate. "Forgive me for not rising," he said, gesturing at his wheelchair and smiling softly at his oft-repeated joke. "This is Colonel Roundtree, just in from Capital City." The guest gave them an annoyed glance, then did a double take when he recognized Gemma from the wanted posters. He pushed his chair back from the table, then hesitated as Joseph continued, "It seems that King Davin believes the Southern Reaches is part of a larger plot among the regions of Aepistelle to engage in treasonous acts."

The colonel rose, a napkin falling from his lap. "That's right. As of this moment, the Aepistelle military will have a permanent presence in each of the regional governors' palaces. Perhaps if His Majesty is convinced there are no illegal activities happening, he will lift this order. For now, though, I shall enjoy supping at this table and being a part of any conversations that occur here."

"That's not all King Davin has done," said a voice behind Gemma.

She turned and watched Kosar approach from the foyer.

Soldiers flanked him on either side, and three followed behind. Gemma noted the hardened expression on his face, something she hadn't seen since the first time they'd met on the roof of the University Press's office in Capital City when she didn't yet trust him. Gemma and Syntha stepped aside to let the newcomers pass. As he entered the room, Kosar nodded to Syntha, who glared at him. He turned to Gemma and made to kiss her, but she dropped her head and turned away. He pulled back before his lips met her temple.

"What is happening, my son?" Joseph asked. He reached for the wheels on his chair and moved back from the table, as if this would allow him to escape in a more timely fashion if necessary.

"I see you've started breakfast without me," Kosar said, moving to his usual chair. He reached over to his father's plate and plucked a strip of bacon from it.

"Where is Ysidro?" Syntha called across the room.

"I'll get to that. Please"—he gestured to Syntha, Gemma, and the colonel—"sit and let me speak."

Gemma and Syntha remained where they stood, but the colonel returned to his chair and took another bite of the Herron family's food. Kosar tore off a crispy section of the bacon and dropped the rest onto his father's plate. "Very well, then. As you may have noticed, my dear brother has not returned to the castle yet. The wagon should be making its way up the hill now. The servants will carry his corpse in when it arrives."

"Corpse?" Governor Herron asked. "What do you mean?"

"Well, Ysidro is in a fine casket provided by the generous King Davin himself, long may he reign."

"Ysidro is..." The governor's sentence morphed into a sob.

Kosar reached over and patted Joseph's stub where his knee had once been. "Dead? I'm afraid so."

Syntha lunged toward the table. The soldiers behind them reached for their swords, but Gemma rushed forward and grabbed Syntha's arm to stop her. "What did you do to him?" Syntha cried out.

"Oh, he did it to himself. King Davin identified traitors within his governors' households, and he couldn't allow them to go unpunished. Ysidro and the other eldest children of the governors are all dead, may they rest in peace. Who am I to argue with our fine king?" Kosar shot Syntha a look of challenge, or perhaps he was warning her to keep quiet about their activities in the barn.

"And may we address the other issue here?" Colonel Roundtree asked. He pointed to Gemma. "She's a wanted criminal, harbored here by your father, it seems."

"Ah, yes, Miss Calvertson." Kosar winked at Gemma, and it took everything in her not to rush at him and slice his eyes out with her machete. "King Davin is aware of her presence here. The rest of her friends are being rounded up and imprisoned across the kingdom, but His Majesty decreed that Gemma is to remain here under my care for the time being until he is ready to deal with her."

Governor Herron's sobs turned into loud cries. Tears poured down his face as he mourned the loss of his true son.

"Dear gods, old man," Kosar said as he rose from his chair. "So much for my appetite. Gemma, let us speak in your room. Guards, keep an eye on my cousin and father in the meantime. Make sure they don't try to make a run for it. Not that my father would get far on one leg, but you know what I mean."

He crossed the room and grabbed Gemma by the elbow. She reached for her machete, but Kosar squeezed her arm, and she relented.

They made it up the stairs without a word. Once they

were inside her room, Kosar pulled her around to face him. Their lips were only inches apart, but Gemma felt repulsed by the idea of ever kissing him again.

"So this is who you've become?" Gemma asked. She shook her arm out of his grip and took a step back.

"I am who I've always been, Gemma. A bastard. A survivor. Someone who makes things happen for himself."

"By letting your own brother be executed when he was innocent?"

"What was I supposed to do, Gemma? Take the fall myself?"

"Ysidro had nothing to do with our activities, Kosar."

"He was a waste of air. Not passionate about anything in this world except inheriting his father's wealth. He wasn't leadership material. He wouldn't have been good for the people of the Southern Reaches when it was his time to take over for our father. He was weak and stupid."

"But you let him take the fall for us!"

"Those little escapades of ours are in the past, Gemma. An hour from now, that barn will be nothing but ashes blowing over the fields. We had a good run while it lasted, but there's no need for all that anymore."

"What are you saying?" Gemma asked.

"My father—my real father—has brought me into the fold. I can change things from within now, Gemma. I can—"

"Your real father? And who is that?"

Kosar's smile scared her. "King Davin himself. Just as I always suspected, I've outranked Ysidro this whole time. Our entire lives, he thought he was better than me, but that was only because my so-called father, Joseph Herron, was hiding who I truly was." He took a step toward Gemma and made to stroke her arm, but she took another step back, bumping into the footboard of her bed. "I am your prince now, my love. I am royalty. You'll never want for anything again. You'll never have to worry about hiding your identity. I'll clear your reputation with King Davin. Your family will be safe."

"Get away from me," Gemma said. "You're not who I thought you were. I know I can be a terrible judge of character, but you are my biggest mistake yet."

"Ouch," Kosar said. "Very well, if that's how you feel, I'll leave you alone for now. But give it some time, and you'll see that this is best for everyone. I'll send for you this evening, but first I have some old friends to see."

Kosar turned and slammed the door as he left.

*Old friends to see?* Gemma thought. *The barn—Alyssa and the others. He means to kill them himself.*

She listened as Kosar's footsteps receded along the hall and down the first flight of stairs. Then she opened her door and caught the sound of two pairs of heavy boots making their way up—soldiers, sent by Kosar to make sure she didn't escape. Gemma turned left and made her way down the servants' staircase at the back of the palace. At the bottom, she snuck out a service door, across the yard, and into the stable, where her horse awaited her.

She looked around. Kosar's mare was not there. *He plans to ride out to the barn with the soldiers and show off his new station as prince*, she thought.

Gemma saddled up her horse and led him out of the stable. She mounted and turned the horse toward the road that descended the hill, but then another thought entered her mind.

*Syntha.*

Gemma brought the horse around and rushed toward a low gate instead. The horse leapt over it and landed in the courtyard gardens where she'd strolled with Ysidro after one of the abruptly ended meals before the brothers' fateful trip up north. She followed the cobblestone path toward the outer doors to the dining hall. Syntha stood over her uncle, who was still in hysterics over the loss of his son. The colonel and the soldiers had left them alone. Gemma's shadow fell through the window and onto Syntha, who turned with a start. Syntha kissed her uncle on his forehead, then ran out the back door.

"He's headed to the barn," Gemma said.

Syntha climbed onto the horse behind her. "We must avoid the main road. The other soldiers have arrived, and they're with him now."

"We're trapped, then?" Gemma asked as they approached the stable.

Syntha jumped off and hastily readied her own horse. "Follow me." She mounted, burst out of the stall, and raced past Gemma. She sped to the edge of the hill. From where Gemma watched in confusion, it appeared that Syntha was about to ride her horse off the edge of a cliff.

"Syntha!" she screamed, but her friend responded with a whoop of excitement. Gemma rode to the ledge and found a steep path down the side of the hill; Syntha was already halfway down.

Gemma took a deep breath and urged her horse to follow.

# Chapter Forty

## GEMMA

Two of Syntha's security detail emerged from the cornfield they'd been situated in as Gemma and Syntha approached. They smiled at their boss, but their positivity quickly faded as they saw the distress on the faces of the two women.

"Get everyone out!" Syntha shouted as they approached. The guards stared in confusion. "Now!"

They turned and ran toward the barn, only to be left in the dust kicked up as Gemma and Syntha sped past on their horses.

"Should we close the gates?" one of the guards called back.

Gemma turned and yelled, "There's no use! Davin's military is on its way." Beyond the fences that outlined the farm, she spotted a cloud of dust from the approaching riders, who were hot on their trail.

Alyssa stepped out of the barn to see what the commotion was about. She flashed her warm smile at Gemma before realizing there was something wrong. Regret fell over Gemma. Here was a young woman around her age with similar interests and a bright personality. She was someone Gemma could see herself becoming close friends with. She hadn't had many close friends back home in Capital City; she'd thrown herself into her studies at the university while most of her childhood companions had gone off and married. During the short time Gemma had spent with Alyssa and the other journalists, she had finally felt like she belonged in a group of likeminded people. And now it seemed it was all over for them.

"Get the others!" Gemma shouted. "We need to leave!"

"But we're just about done printing today's edition," Alyssa said in confusion. "Byrna and Clarnen are readying the wagon for delivery to our distribution partners and—"

"There will be no more distributions, Lyss. It's done." Gemma and Syntha reached the barn and jumped off their horses in sync, as if they'd trained together for years. Theirs was another friendship that had become special to Gemma in such a short time, and it too seemed likely to unravel because of Kosar's actions.

Gemma waved for Alyssa to follow them into the barn. The two security guards came in just behind them, panting from their sprint through the fields.

"Everyone listen up," Syntha called out. "My dear cousin has decided to switch sides. He's on his way here now with a cadre of King Davin's soldiers. This is a moment we've always feared—we knew it could happen, just not quite like this. Initiate termination protocol."

Byrna and Clarnen looked at each other and shrugged. Lorne dropped his glass of water, and it shattered at his feet. Zinnie sat surrounded by books she'd been researching, tears streaming down her face.

"This is really the end?" Zinnie asked.

Syntha ignored them. She ran to a closet in one corner of the barn and rolled out a barrel. She kicked off the stopper on one side, and a stream of liquid flowed out. "Do your duties!" she yelled at the stunned onlookers.

Everyone snapped out of their stupor at that. The reporters grabbed stacks of papers and armfuls of scrolls and piled them together. Lorne rushed to the closet and rolled another barrel out and across the barn, toward the wagon the crew had just loaded up with freshly printed newspapers. Clarnen jogged over and helped him lift the barrel onto the wagon. They fumbled together to get the cap off and then soaked the papers. Clarnen reached for a lantern hanging off a nearby post and lobbed it at the stack. The wagon and the papers went up in flames. Byrna did the same to the stacks the women had made on the large round table, and all their hard work turned to cinders.

Outside, the approaching horses sounded like thunder. One of the soldiers blew a tune on a brass horn to announce their arrival. Inside, the security crew opened a wooden crate and pulled out large canvas bags containing a cache of swords. They handed them out to the reporters and led everyone to the back door.

Syntha was the first one out the door. She checked that the coast was clear and ushered everyone out. Gemma was the last in the barn, and just before she left, she turned and saw a soldier kick open the front door. Kosar stepped in and locked eyes with her through the flames.

"They're escaping through the rear!" Kosar shouted to his soldiers without taking his eyes off Gemma.

Through the smoke, Gemma saw the young man she'd fallen in love with so easily over these last couple of weeks. He was handsome. Smart. A great fighter. Passionate about so many of the same things as Gemma. And yet there was a whole other side of him that was hideous. It had shown itself to her too late. Gemma shook her head in disappointment and closed the back door behind her.

Syntha grabbed her sleeve and pulled her along, and they followed the others through the back of the farm. The crew hadn't kept up the illusion of cultivating crops on this side—weeds and cornstalks and other plants had been left to grow wild. The ground was uneven, which made for slow going. The others hadn't gotten too far ahead.

Gemma heard a snapping sound and felt a sudden rush of air as something sailed inches from her head. Clarnen fell to the ground with an arrow lodged in the back of his neck.

More bowstrings snapped. More arrows flew. Horses approached, soldiers yelling out as if they were enjoying the hunt.

Lorne turned and lifted the sword he'd been handed. He waved for Gemma and Syntha to pass him.

Gemma stopped and pulled out her machete. Syntha did the same with her sword. The first horseman sped toward them and slashed down at Syntha. Their swords clashed, and he lost his balance. He fell off the horse, rolled, and jumped to his feet. Lorne ran at him and engaged him in combat. The next rider halted at his own accord and dismounted. He smiled at the prospect of fighting two women. Gemma and Syntha turned to each other, and Gemma rolled her eyes. Syntha winked and ran at the soldier. She had a good four inches on the man and many more years of training. His sword hand was severed and lying in the dirt within seconds.

A third soldier rode up behind Gemma and swung at her as he passed. Her machete met his blade, slid off, and sliced his ankle. He cried out in pain and anger as he brought his horse around for another pass. He lifted his sword as he sped at her, but a stone hit the back of his head. In his shock, he lost balance and fell from the horse. A woman screamed and rushed toward him.

"Alyssa!" Gemma yelled. "You need to run. Go!"

The soldier rose to his feet, dazed but furious. Alyssa ignored Gemma. She dropped the next stone she was about to throw and shifted the sword into her dominant hand.

"You're a traitor to your people," Alyssa said to the soldier. "Nothing but a cold-blooded murderer." She slashed at him, but she was not trained. It was a sloppy attempt, and the soldier easily knocked the weapon from her hand.

"Should have stuck with the rocks, little girl," he said.

Alyssa dropped down and attempted to grab a handful of dirt to throw at him. He made to cut her down, but Gemma rushed forward and sliced through his sword hand. Quincy's reworking of her blade had been very effective—the machete cut clean through the bone as the soldier cried out in pain. Alyssa threw the dirt into his eyes, picked up her fallen sword, and thrust it into his throat.

"Look out!" Syntha called, but it was too late. An arrow pierced Alyssa's chest.

"Lyss, no!" Gemma cried. She lunged toward the injured girl and caught her as she fell. "I'm so sorry. I'll get you somewhere safe, and we'll get this out of you."

"No," Alyssa said. "You need to keep going. Keep telling your story for all of us. Run, Gemma." Her eyes went from pained to hopeful to blank as the life passed from her. Gemma set her down gently in the dirt.

"Your story," Syntha said. "I forgot."

The woman turned and ran back toward the burning barn. Gemma raised her machete and ran after her. The flames had made their way through the ceiling and had started to spread along the roof. A rider sped toward Syntha, but she cut him down easily and pushed through the door. Gemma could see nothing but smoke and flames inside, but Syntha wasn't deterred. She disappeared into the barn, and the door swung shut behind her.

"Syntha, wait!" Gemma shouted. She didn't care about the manuscript. The story was within her. She could tell it again, write it down once more if this ordeal ever ended and she was allowed to go back to a peaceful life. What was in that barn was just a stack of papers.

*Let it burn*, she thought. *All of it.*

She reached for the door, her hands inches from the knob.

"Hold on, now, Gemma." She turned to find Kosar dismounting his horse. "You'll burn the flesh right off your hand if you touch that knob."

"Syntha is in there," Gemma said. She made for the door again, but Kosar leapt forward and tackled her to the ground. "That's your cousin! She needs help!"

"She has made her choice. Be happy someone is willing to die for you." He scrambled back to his feet and reached a hand out to Gemma. She swatted it away. "You should learn to enjoy wielding that kind of power over people, especially if you're to be my queen someday."

Gemma got to her feet on her own. "Queen? What are you talking about, Kosar?"

"My true father will forgive you. It won't be long now until he announces me as his heir. He's an old man. His days are numbered. I'll need a bride to sit alongside me on the dais of our kingdom's premiere palace."

Gemma turned toward the field where her companions were being slaughtered. "How can you think I'd marry you after the way you've turned your back on your family and friends? You brought this down on them."

"They're traitors, Gemma. They brought it down on

themselves. I would have been among them had I not played my cards right."

"So none of this was real to you? Exposing the crown for all its misdeeds? Standing up for the oppressed? The paper, the network of journalists? You used us all for your own ends."

"If I hadn't built something of value, I wouldn't have had leverage. Turned out I didn't really need it in the end, what with King Davin revealing that he's my true father. Not a total loss, though. I've made him proud with all of this."

A large crash sounded out as the roof collapsed. "Syntha!" Gemma yelled as she lunged for the door, but Kosar grabbed her by the hair and threw her to the ground once more.

"Damn it, Gemma, are you daft? Syntha is not walking out of there alive, and you won't either if you don't come with me. Do you know how many women would kill to be in your position right now?" He turned toward the back field, where the soldiers had the surviving journalists surrounded. "Where's Alyssa, anyway? She's always had a thing for me."

"Your soldiers killed her, you bastard," Gemma said as she leapt to her feet with her machete in her hand. She swung at him. Kosar sidestepped and unsheathed his own blade. He blocked Gemma's next blows with ease.

"You're no match for me," Kosar said.

"Because he's been trained by the best."

Gemma looked back to see Syntha emerging from the barn. She held the burlap bag that contained Gemma's manuscript. The bag was scorched on one side, as were Syntha's clothes. One cheek was blackened, as if she'd rubbed her face in a filthy hearth. Her eyes were red. Her blade was still sheathed.

Syntha tossed the sack aside and reached for the hilt of her sword, but Kosar didn't wait. He bared his teeth in a wicked smile and ran at her. The wall behind Syntha collapsed inward, sending burning shingles down over her. Between the debris and Kosar's advance, Syntha was doomed.

Gemma darted forward and swung her machete. It missed Kosar's scalp by millimeters, slicing off the ends of the hairs on the back of his head. He tripped and fell into Syntha, his blade just missing her. Gemma landed in the dirt, propelled by the momentum of her lunge, while Syntha collapsed under Kosar's weight as more debris from the deteriorating barn rained down on them.

Gemma watched them struggle under a pile of smoking wooden boards and shingles. There was no chance of the cousins using their blades in their position. Kosar landed punch after punch to Syntha's stunned face. Blood squirted from her nose. Gemma felt helpless as her friend was pummeled under the pile of burning debris.

And then she heard a sound.

A clicking. *Chittering*.

Gemma turned her head. Inches from her nose, crawling out from under the burning wreckage, was a hideous eight-legged creature nearly the size of her hand. Gemma shot back to her feet and reached for a fallen board. She set one end down in front of the arachnid like a ramp, and it clambered on.

"Kosar!" Gemma yelled.

Kosar stopped punching, his clenched fist dripping with Syntha's blood. He turned toward Gemma just as she catapulted the creature toward him. As it flew through the air, Kosar recognized it for what it was: a chitter-wench. It landed on his right cheek, and he screamed like a child. He jumped to his feet, but Syntha kicked his kneecap, sending him stumbling over the debris. Gemma lunged forward and swung the wooden board at Kosar, and it connected hard with the back of his head. He fell facedown in the dirt, the chitter-wench escaping into the rubble.

Gemma reached her hand out and Syntha took it. The injured woman struggled to her feet and pointed to the burlap sack. Gemma nodded and collected it. They mounted Kosar's horse and sped off.

The barn and everything it had stood for—truth and freedom, hope for a better future for the people of Aepistelle—burned to the ground behind them.

# Chapter Forty-One
## GEMMA

The morning sun broke through the clouds after their third night in the caverns. Syntha had suggested the hiding spot, having explored the caverns several times in her youth with Ysidro and Kosar. Gemma hadn't been sure it was a good idea to stay there if Kosar knew about the spot, but Syntha said he'd forgotten about it years ago.

Syntha winced as she ducked out of the narrow opening to join Gemma by the small fire where a rabbit was cooking on a spit.

"We really should get you back into town to see a doctor," Gemma said.

"Don't be ridiculous. It's just a small burn."

Syntha's injury hadn't seemed so bad during their confrontation with Kosar outside the burning barn, but once they'd made it to safety, she had collapsed in pain. They had no supplies whatsoever, only the clothes on their backs, their weapons, and the bag containing Gemma's manuscript. They had set Kosar's horse free once they'd arrived at the caverns so there would be one fewer mouth to feed.

"I can try asking for supplies at that farm up the hill," Gemma offered.

"We would only put the family in danger. They'd be accomplices if they didn't turn us in."

Gemma pulled the rabbit from the flame. It was quite well done, not unlike her friend after the barn incident.

"Anyway, it's my face I'm more worried about," Syntha quipped. "Ysidro was always the ugly one of the household, but after losing two teeth to Kosar the other day, I think I might be the new title holder. Should never have taught him hand-to-hand combat. My biggest regret."

Gemma's lips twitched on one side, but it couldn't possibly be classified as a smile. Syntha noticed. "You have nothing to be sorry for, Gemma. Nothing that happened was your fault."

"Alyssa...the others...they're all dead or locked away. I just wish I'd fought harder, gotten them out of there sooner. What if I had stopped Kosar from leaving the castle and you'd had a chance to escape and warn everyone before he could bring the soldiers down on them? I've grown too comfortable here, living in that palace, dining with the governor. And I can't stop thinking about where my other friends might be. Surely they haven't been as well off as I have since parting ways in Capital City."

She turned away from the fire. The caverns opened onto a small patch of land overlooking a steep cliff. Beyond that was the nation of Xaeltúve, its seemingly endless desert on the horizon.

"Gemma, I—"

Syntha's voice was drowned out by a thunderous rumble. She shot to her feet and Gemma followed. They pulled themselves up a steep incline to the top of the hill and took in the sight.

"Are you ready for a run?" Syntha asked.

Gemma shook her head. "This is the end of the line, I'm afraid. We can't escape this."

At least one hundred soldiers on horses made their way toward the cliff. A few wagons were scattered among them. Banners with King Davin's sigil were carried by some of the riders.

Syntha reached for her sword, but Gemma shot out a hand and rested it on Syntha's. "No more of that. As long as we don't fight, they'll bring us in alive. Kosar will have commanded it. We'll live to fight another day."

The soldiers arrived a few minutes later. Gemma and Syntha made a show of tossing their weapons to the ground so it was clear they had no intention of fighting. The first soldiers to arrive halted several feet from the pair and stood at attention as if awaiting orders from their commanders. Others moved aside to make way for the largest of the wagons. When it came to a stop, a footman opened the door. He called out, "His Royal Majesty, King Davin."

The king popped his head out and looked around at the assembled soldiers, then at Gemma. The smile that broke out on his face was identical to the one she'd seen when King Davin had arrived in Emyhrsen with Gemma's parents and Marzele as his hostages, the same smile Gemma and her friends had wiped away when they'd fought back and destroyed his ship. This time, however, there would be no fighting back. Not yet, anyway.

"Miss Gemma Calvertson," he said as he descended the steps from his wagon. "The apple of my dear son's eye. The constant pain in my royal behind."

He approached Gemma and Syntha as the soldiers looked

on. They reached for their weapons, ready to protect their king, but he motioned for them to stand down. They obeyed, though Gemma could see their reluctance. If she or Syntha made a move, the soldiers would pounce quickly.

"I've only just begun a fruitful relationship with dear Kosar. I'd hate to drive a wedge between us so soon by executing his lover. So what am I to do? I've promised a reward for your capture, plastered your face on posters across this great kingdom. Will I look weak if I spare your life? Or will mercy inspire support from my people?"

He stopped in front of Gemma and stared at her.

"Do...do you want me to answer that question?" Gemma asked.

Davin's eyebrows rose as he burst into a laugh.

"I guess I see why my son is fond of you. But no, I do not expect you to answer. I am merely thinking out loud, something you may see more of when you come home to Capital City with my son and me." He turned to Syntha. "And you, Kosar's longtime companion. On the one hand, you've kept him relatively safe all these years—a cousin and a close friend, a bodyguard and a training partner. On the other hand, you *were* part of the conspiracy against me. My soldiers have reported that all your little friends from that wretched farm were killed. Their guts are spread all over the fields behind the barn where you ran your little operation. I should probably let you join them in death, but instead I'd like to show you that I am a merciful man. You may gather your belongings and leave."

Syntha stared at him in shock.

"Go before I change my mind," Davin said.

Syntha looked at Gemma, who nodded. "It's okay. I'll see you again," she whispered.

Syntha reluctantly turned away, crawled into the cave, and

emerged with a cloak bundled under her arm. She took one last look at Gemma and then walked away through the mass of soldiers and wagons.

"Now," Davin said, "we have some more business to discuss. It seems your old friends have been getting into quite a bit of trouble all over my kingdom. You'll never believe what that naughty priest has been up to—murdering my former officers in cold blood, leading the genocide of an entire village."

"Marzele? He's a peaceful man. He wouldn't do such a thing."

"Oh, after I broke him on Terminus Rock, I wouldn't put anything past him. A desperate, faithless man will go to any extreme to sate the rage inside of him. And then there is the boy and Arnem Wynstone. I should use the past tense with Arnem, actually."

"What do you mean?" Gemma asked. She took a step back.

"Why don't I just show you?"

Davin turned around and signaled to the footman of a smaller carriage just behind his own. The footman opened the door, reached in, and pulled its occupant out into the sunlight. His hands were tied in front of him, and a large sack hung over his head and upper torso.

"Denny," Gemma said, but as the boy descended the steps and stood at full height, she realized he was shorter than her friend. "That's not...who is that?"

King Davin laughed, a disgusting and evil sound. He waved again, and the footman prodded the boy toward them.

"Remove it," Davin commanded, and the footman pulled the sack up to reveal a boy so pale Gemma could nearly see through his skin. Veins protruded from his head, his neck, his arms. He was as thin as Denny had been when Gemma had first met him, back when he'd been living on the streets. And this boy was hunched because of the weight on his back.

Gemma took a step to the side to get a better look. A dark purple blob protruded from the boy's spine, covering the space from just below his shoulders to the top of his buttocks. It was somewhat rounded, bubbling out in spots like a water-skin filled to bursting. The outer layer was translucent, a bladder that must have held a gallon of blood at least. The thing pulsed as if it were sharing breaths and heartbeats with the boy. Three thin tentacles stretched from its mass and pierced the boy's right side just below the ribs. The skin was scarred around the spots where his body had accepted this parasitic creature. Another tentacle stretched higher up, terminating inside the boy's right ear. He lifted his head slowly as if it pained him to do so. His eyes were cloudy and full of despair.

Davin chuckled. "This boy is how I've been able to learn about some of the things your friend Denny has been up to lately. He has quite a strong and unique ability, thanks to his connection with this creature I've procured for him, but I believe Denny possesses even more power than Chauncy here could ever dream of."

"Denny has visions he can't even control," Gemma said. "What's so powerful about that? Why does that scare you so much?"

"Oh, Gemma, there's still much you need to learn. His abilities have grown rapidly since your paths diverged, and I'm certain there is more to come for him. Not only that, but your friend is a danger. A killer, even."

"If Denny has killed anyone, it was in self-defense."

"Maybe, but I don't think Selah Wynstone and her daughters will see it that way when they find out what happened to their dear Arnem."

"Arnem? What do you mean?"

Davin's laugh was like needles to her heart. "See for yourself."

He reached up and tore the tentacle from the boy's ear. Blood sprayed across Gemma's face as Davin thrust the tentacle toward her. He grabbed Gemma's hair, pulled her in, and jammed the tentacle into her left ear.

Tiny fibers from the tip of the tentacle wriggled through Gemma's ear canal. Pain flashed behind her eyes. Her sinus cavities swelled up. Her breath caught in her throat, and she vomited at her feet.

"Sorry," Davin said, "I should have warned you that part would be a little uncomfortable."

A crimson film formed over Gemma's vision. She felt like she was falling unconscious, yet she was able to support her weight and stay standing.

"Go on," Davin urged the child. "Show her a little of what you've seen."

Scenes of Denny's and Arnem's journey flashed through Gemma's mind. She seemed to be inside Denny's head, watching his actions from his perspective. It was deeper than that, she realized, as she began to feel his anger and sorrow, the highs and the lows of Denny's last few weeks. Being locked away in a prisoner transport wagon. A severed head. Being ambushed in a tavern. A forest. A woman, presumably his mother, meeting her end. A fire. Arnem in flames.

Gemma's knees finally buckled, but Davin caught her and brought her back to standing. "Keep watching," he commanded. She couldn't see him, but she could sense his evil grin all the same.

The visions from Denny's perspective faded out, replaced by what appeared to be a tunnel of sorts, a cavern made of flesh and blood. There was a figure in its center—the boy,

Chauncy, but healthier, no monster strapped to his back. His smile was sad, tentative.

"He can't hear us here," the boy said, though his lips didn't move. "He wants these visions to make you afraid of this Denny, angry over the man's death. But there's more."

"What do you mean?" Gemma asked inside her mind, uncertain if her physical body was also speaking.

"Your friend Arnem is dead to the physical world, but I believe that can be reversed. He still lives, just in another plane of existence. I think there's a way to get to him. When I was locked up, I heard rumblings of such a thing from others before they were taken away. They all died in the fire that killed your friend, I think. Someone with great power, maybe Denny, might be able to reach Arnem and bring him back. It can't be me, though. I'm too weak from what Davin has done to me. I'm in so much pain, Gemma."

"I'm sorry. I'm so sorry for what's happened to you."

"I can feel that. Thank you. Please, I need you to end this for me. I can't go on like this. I can no longer live without this creature; it has invaded my heart, pumps my blood, works my lungs. Yet each day I lose another bit of myself, my consciousness, my free will. Please, help me end this."

"I will," Gemma said. "I promise."

She yanked the tentacle from her ear and severed her connection with the boy and his monstrous companion. Nausea overwhelmed her and she dropped to her knees.

"So, what do you think of my secret weapon?" Davin asked. "My people searched the farthest corners of the world to find that creature. I read of their existence in some of the ancient texts, but by all accounts it's been hundreds of years since one has graced these lands. However, I think your little friend Denny could do what this child can even without such a creature connected to him, and I can use this pair to track him down."

"You'll never find him," Gemma said.

She shot out her arm and grabbed her machete from where she'd dropped it. Her arm arced, and the blade came down on the creature on the boy's back, slicing it open. There was a sickly popping sound, and blood spewed out of both the boy and the creature. Its anchors under the boy's ribs tore from his flesh, and he collapsed to the ground.

"Thank you," he whispered with his last breath.

"No!" Davin darted forward. Gemma readied her machete again, but the soldiers moved in, knocked it from her hand, and locked her arms into a tight hold. She watched as Davin ignored the boy and cradled the creature instead. It deflated as it bled out until he was holding nothing but a sticky, fleshy film. Davin threw it aside and rose to his feet.

"Let go of her," he growled to the soldiers. They released Gemma and stepped back. Davin reached over and grabbed her chin, pulling her gaze away from the boy's corpse. "We're going to need to tame you if you're to come back to Capital City with us, Miss Calvertson."

Gemma took a step back and slipped down the slope to the area where the cooking fire still crackled. A trio of birds turned to her, then resumed pillaging the cooked rabbit in the rocks next to the fire. Gemma got back to her feet and walked to the cliffs overlooking Xaeltúve.

"Don't tell me you're thinking of jumping. Oh, the whims of the youth." Davin descended the slope as Gemma took another step toward the ledge. "Stop these dramatics and accept your fate. Your only options are to jump to an untimely death here or return to Capital City, where I will set you up with a position that's acceptable to us both. You can even send for your family. I'll make sure the old Calvertson town house is restored and ready for their return."

"How could you think I would join you? You demonize people like this boy, like Denny, drive them to death or imprison them. You hide Aepistelle's true history from our people. You are a monster."

"Now, Gemma, I'm not as bad as you make me out to be. All I've ever wanted is protect the people of this great kingdom. You know as well as I do how dangerous these powers can be if they're allowed to go unchecked. Maybe my methods have been extreme, I'll admit it, but my intentions are pure.

"Here's a proposition for you. If your passion lies in helping folks like Denny and the priest, then join my Royal Mystic Committee. I promise to implement new methods. No longer will we indiscriminately kill those with abilities. No longer will they be taken away in the middle of the night to one of our special prisons. We need to work with them to hone their abilities, to help them find control. If the program is successful, we'll make it permanent. Help us with this, and people like your friend Denny will be safe."

Gemma looked down from the edge of the cliff. Even if she were to survive the fall, she'd be too injured to run. What good would that do? How would it stop them from hunting her or Denny or Marzele? How would her parents ever be able to rejoin society?

"And what about Syntha? Will you let her go?"

"We already allowed her to walk away from here. As long as she doesn't cause trouble, we will ignore past her misdeeds."

"I don't trust you," Gemma said. "I don't believe you'll stick to your word. But it seems there is no other option. I'm tired of running and hiding. After everything I've been through, nothing has changed. Things have only gotten worse. Too many people have gotten hurt. So yes, I will come with you and do what I can to make a change that way."

Davin smiled. "Come, then." He held out his hand to her.

Gemma took one final look at the valley beyond. She wanted to see hope in it. Freedom. But all she saw was more death, more pain, more sorrow. Her friends were out there somewhere, hurt and alone and afraid. Gemma might be their only hope of finding peace.

And so she took King Davin's hand and followed him up the hill to his army and the future that awaited her.

# Epilogue
## FOUR MONTHS LATER

The farm seven miles outside the capital of the Southern Reaches had been confiscated by the crown. The seizure of the land, which formally belonged to a trust owned by a chain of shell corporations, had not been contested by anyone. Though the government now owned it on paper, nobody came to clear away the wreckage from the fire that had consumed it.

At least, not for the first four months. When the winter storms—which in the Southern Reaches consisted of only moderate rain and wind—enveloped the farmlands, a small procession of wagons made its way down the weed-strewn road. The drivers led their horses up to the pile of rubble that had once been a barn and proceeded to dig through the remains.

In the center of the mess was an oversize piece of machinery, the skeleton of which was still mostly intact, though any flammable bits had long since deteriorated. The group methodically disassembled the structure and placed the pieces in a series of wooden crates on the wagons. Once the foreman was satisfied they'd collected what they needed, they drove the wagons to the nearest train station.

They loaded the crates onto a conscripted boxcar. The foreman slid the doors closed and clamped a lock in place. He stepped back, taking in the sign painted on the door: PROPERTY OF THE ROYAL MYSTIC COMMITTEE.

"Lieutenant Palignon, we're ready to board and embark on our northerly journey," the train's conductor called out.

The foreman—Palignon—nodded and stepped onto the train.

Four days later, the train arrived at Pinedrop Station in the north of Aepistelle. A single wagon awaited Palignon and the cargo; they would need to take multiple trips to transport all of the crates to their final destination.

"How was the journey?" the wagon's driver asked as they rode through the town of Pinedrop with the first load.

"It was uneventful," Palignon said. "That's exactly what we need right now: peace and quiet."

"You'll like this place, then," the driver—Syntha—said. "A farm at the edge of civilization. Used to belong to Richard the Elusive."

It was another three months before they managed to procure the parts needed to get the printing press up and running again. By then, several drums had been prepared with the opening chapters of Gemma Calvertson's manuscript. The truth about King Davin and his atrocities had yet to reach its audience, but Syntha and Palignon were committed to making it happen, one page at a time.

Syntha looked at Palignon from the opposite end of the press. He nodded to confirm that the first roll of paper was loaded and ready to go. She smiled at him.

"Time to get this thing running."

GEMMA CALVERTSON'S STORY WILL CONCLUDE IN *THE Realm Beyond*:

**Her last chance to save her kingdom will bring her to the brink of death.**

Three years after accepting King Davin's offer, Gemma has a successful career as an investigator of the supernatural with the Royal Mystic Committee. When she learns it may be possible to reunite with the dead in the Realm Beyond, she must set out on one more epic journey and gather strength from old friends. Does she have what it takes to rescue a departed companion from the clutches of death?

Back in Aepistelle, word of King Davin's nefarious history begins to leak out, leaving him scrambling to retain control. Can the remaining heroes overthrow the longtime ruler and bring peace and freedom back to the kingdom? The desperate madman will stop at nothing to stay in power, even if it means destroying his kingdom and crushing his own people in the process.

# Also by Ryan Hoyt

## EPIC FANTASY

### The Forest of Despair

A heroine's first adventure. A kingdom's last hope. The new female-led epic fantasy series The Pierced Shadow Archive begins here.

### The Witch of Ferathan

An alluring stranger. A trail of destruction. Will Ferathan survive her charm? *The Witch of Ferathan*, a Pierced Shadow Archive novella, is set seventy years before the events of *The Forest of Despair* and can be read as a standalone story.

### The Isle of Abandonment

She once saved a kingdom with her friends. Now she must do it alone. Gemma Calvertson's story continues months after the events of *The Forest of Despair* as she and her friends face their biggest challenges yet.

### The Realm Beyond

To help her friends and bring truth to the people of Aepistelle, she must join the ranks of her enemy King Davin and his Royal Mystic Committee. Gemma Calvertson's story ends here.

## HORROR AND DARK FICTION

### Raventree Hollow

Something evil is feeding off the sins of Raventree Hollow. Shirley Jackson's "The Possibility of Evil" meets Stephen King's *Needful Things* in *Raventree Hollow*, an American gothic horror tale set in the 1950s. A standalone story, it is the first book of the new *A Machete & Quill Horror* line.

### We Are Not Alone in the Dark

A high school bully, quarreling friends, and an abusive father are the least of Bryan's worries. When night comes, so do the visitors, and he can't fight back. Who will rescue Bryan if nobody believes him? A coming-of-age alien horror novel.

### Ditch of the Damned and Other Tales

A collection of five short stories by Ryan Hoyt.

### Senior Class: A Raventree Hollow Story

Pearl and Rosemary are the last of their kind. At 90 years old, death calls for them. Who will be the left standing? A short story chapbook set in the town of Raventree Hollow, this can be read as a standalone tale or enjoyed along with *Raventree Hollow*.

### Butterscotch: A Raventree Hollow Story

A family moves into an old home to find the previous owner has left behind a hutch with a candy dish. Aggressive neighbors, a trio of cats, and a hidden purple bag lead the family to seek out answers. "Butterscotch" is a short story chapbook set in the town of Raventree Hollow.

### Ditch of the Damned

While traveling with her family across the American frontier, Eudora is pulled off the wagon trail by a sensation deep within her bones. She ignores a warning sign and proceeds toward a hole in the earth in the middle of the wilderness. "Ditch of the Damned" is a short story set in 1847.

### The Hoarder's House

Erica's sister went missing in her own home. As Erica and her husband search for the lost woman, they find something luring in the depths of depravity.

### Freddy Goodman (Ain't No Good Man)

His coming-of-age story was *so* twenty years ago. So why do the words of that old witch still haunt him? A short story of contemporary fiction with elements of magical realism.

# Acknowledgments

Thank you for following Gemma (and me) on this journey through Aepistelle. Things got a little darker this time around, but I hope you are willing to stick with me and the characters that remain as we close out the series with the next novel.

I'm grateful for my beta readers who gave feedback to shape the final product you hold in your hands. Thanks David Howard and my daughter Natalie for braving an early draft of my manuscript. Thank you also to my wife Marsha and our other daughter Daisy for giving me time to work on the book in between everything else going on in our daily lives and encouraging me along the way.

The services of Alison Cherry (editor) and MiblArt (cover designer) rounded everything out and elevated this book to something worth printing and sharing. Thank you both. The original release of this book had cover art by Natalie Junqueira of Dawn Book Design.

To the people reading and sharing my books with friends and loved ones, it means the world to me. Thank you.